MARVEL Adventures

BLACK WIDOW® AND THE AVENGERS®

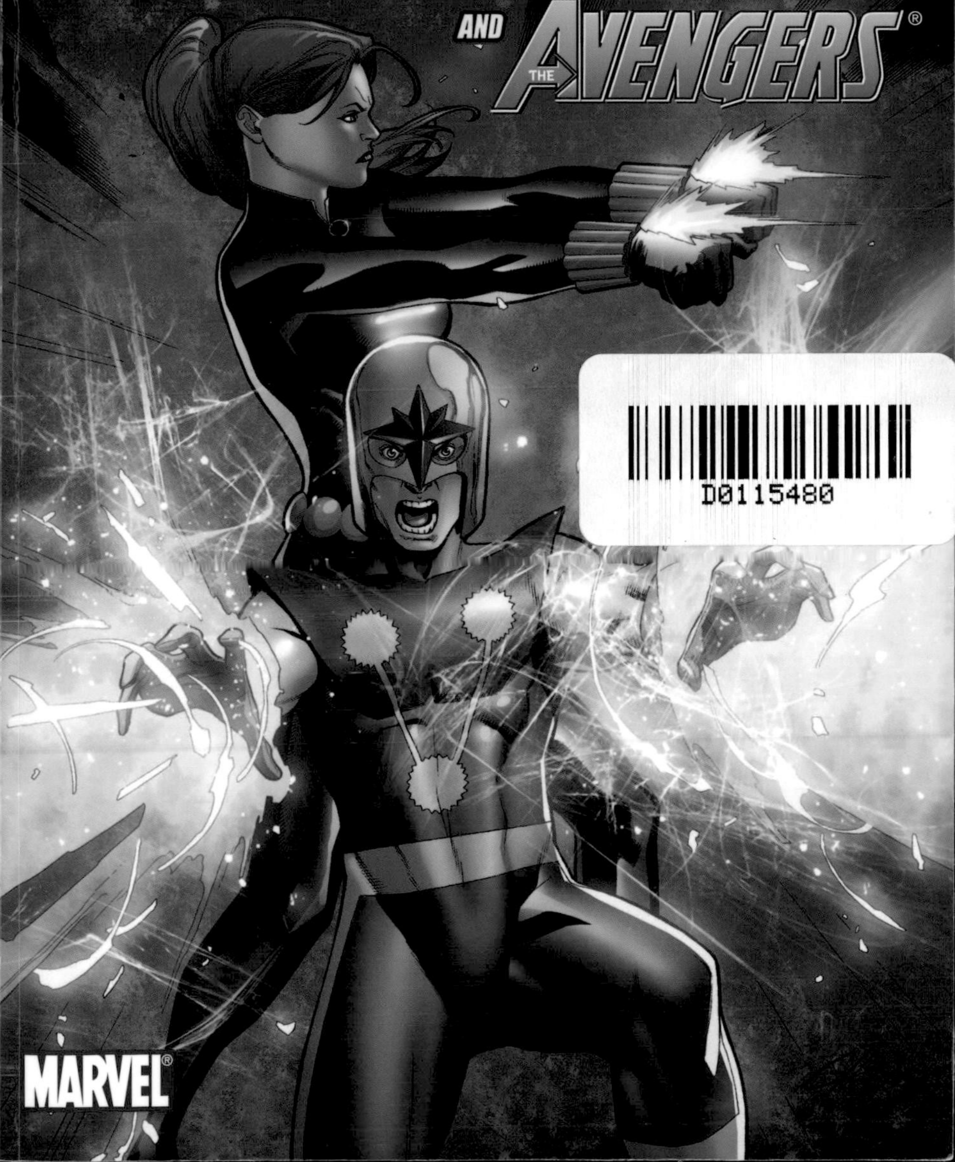

MARVEL®

Marvel Digests

Marvel Adventures Spider-Man
Vol. 1: The Sinister Six
ISBN # 0-7851-1739-3

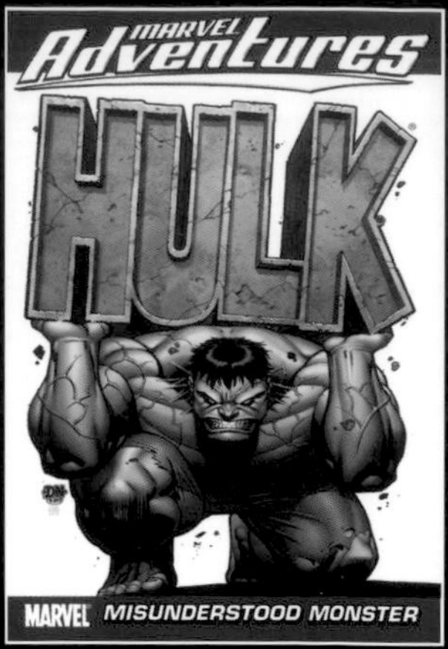

Marvel Adventures Hulk
Vol. 1: Misunderstood Monster
ISBN # 978-0-7851-2642-3

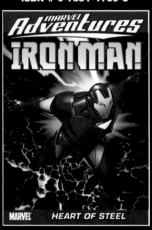

Marvel Adventures Iron Man
Vol. 1: Heart of Steel
ISBN # 978-0-7851-2644-7

Marvel Adventures the Avengers
Vol. 1: Heroes Assembled
ISBN # 0-7851-2306-7

Go To Marvel.Com For A Complete Listing Of Marvel Collected Editions!

MARVEL ADVENTURES BLACK WIDOW AND THE AVENGERS DIGEST. Contains material originally published in magazine form as MARVEL ADVENTURES SUPER HEROES #17-21. First printing 2010. ISBN# 978-0-7851-3324-7. Published by MARVEL WORLDWIDE, INC., a subsidiary of MARVEL ENTERTAINMENT, LLC. OFFICE OF PUBLICATION: 417 5th Avenue, New York, NY 10016. Copyright © 2009 and 2010 Marvel Characters, Inc. All rights reserved. $9.99 per copy in the U.S. (GST #R127032852); Canadian Agreement #40668537. All characters featured in this issue and the distinctive names and likenesses thereof, and all related indicia are trademarks of Marvel Characters, Inc. No similarity between any of the names, characters, persons, and/or institutions in this magazine with those of any living or dead person or institution is intended, and any such similarity which may exist is purely coincidental. **Printed in Canada.** ALAN FINE, EVP - Office of the President, Marvel Worldwide, Inc. and EVP & CMO Marvel Characters B.V.; DAN BUCKLEY, Chief Executive Officer and Publisher - Print, Animation & Digital Media; JIM SOKOLOWSKI, Chief Operating Officer; DAVID GABRIEL, SVP of Publishing Sales & Circulation; DAVID BOGART, SVP of Business Affairs & Talent Management; MICHAEL PASCIULLO, VP Merchandising & Communications; JIM O'KEEFE, VP of Operations & Logistics; DAN CARR, Executive Director of Publishing Technology; JUSTIN F. GABRIE, Director of Publishing & Editorial Operations; SUSAN CRESPI, Editorial Operations Manager; ALEX MORALES, Publishing Operations Manager; STAN LEE, Chairman Emeritus. For information regarding advertising in Marvel Comics or on Marvel.com, please contact Ron Stern, VP of Business Development, at rstern@marvel.com. For Marvel subscription inquiries, please call 800-217-9158. **Manufactured between 4/14/10 and 5/3/10 by WORLDCOLOR PRESS INC., ST. ROMUALD, QC, CANADA.**

10 9 8 7 6 5 4 3 2 1

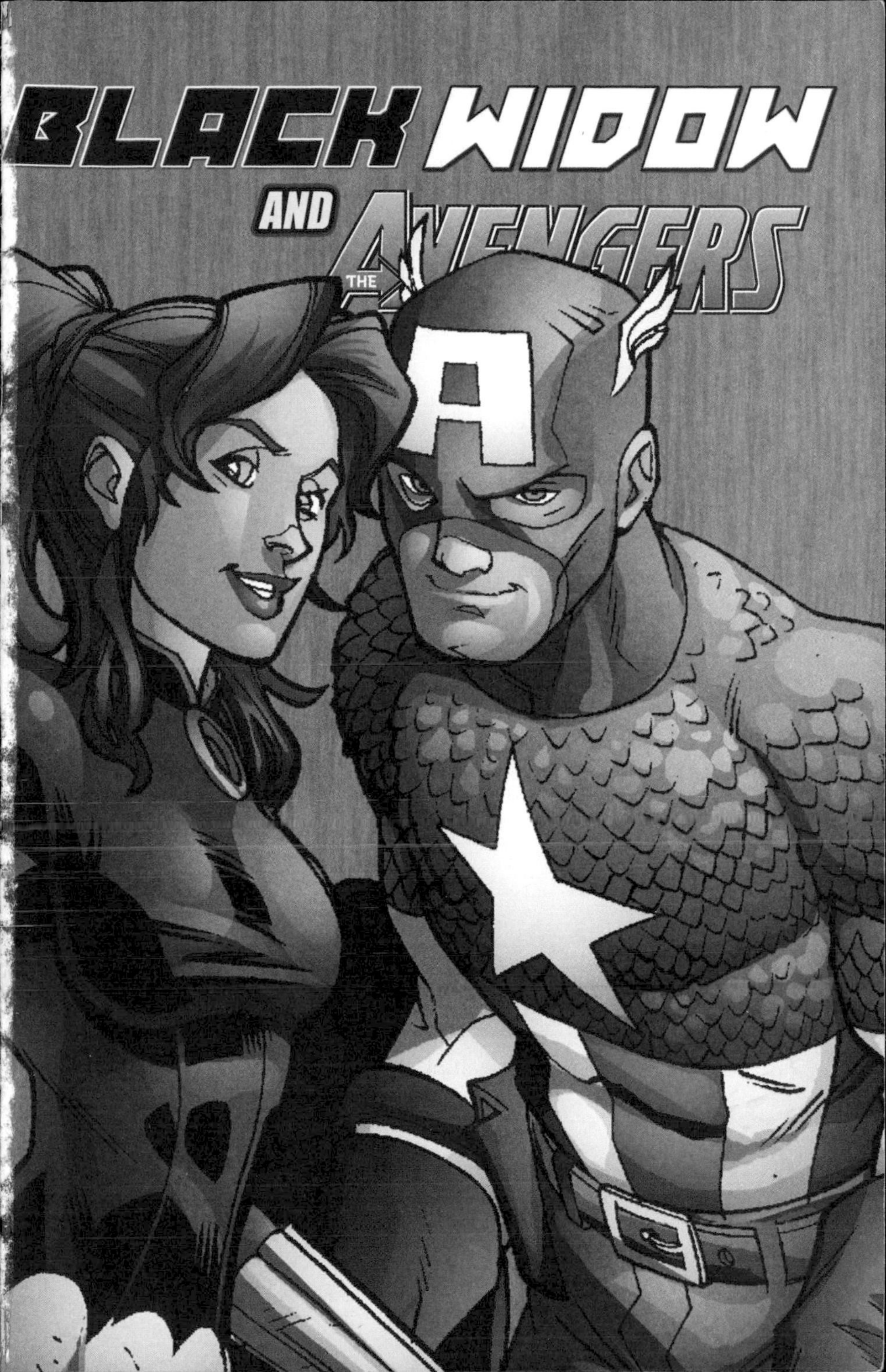
BLACK WIDOW
AND THE AVENGERS

BLACK WIDOW AND THE AVENGERS

Writer:
Paul Tobin
Artists:
Issues #17 & 18: *Ig Guara*
Issue #19: *Rob Di Salvo, Scott Koblish, Jacopo Camagni, Derec Donovan & Terry Pallot*
Issue #20: *Scott Koblish, Clayton Henry & Rob DiSalvo*
Issue #21: *Esdras Cristobal*
Colorists:
Sotocolor
Letterer:
Dave Sharpe
Cover Art:
Niko Henrichon, Chris Samnee & Clayton Henry with Chris Sotomayor and Wil Quintana
Assistant Editor:
Michael Horwitz
Editor:
Nathan Cosby

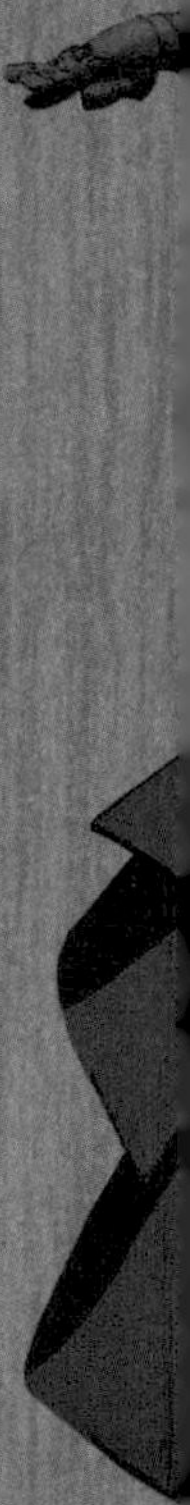

Collection Editor: *Cory Levine*
Assistant Editor: *Alex Starbuck*
Associate Editor: *John Denning*
Editors, Special Projects: *Jennifer Grünwald*
& Mark D. Beazley
Senior Editor, Special Projects: *Jeff Youngquist*
Senior Vice President of Sales: *David Gabriel*

Editor in Chief: *Joe Quesada*
Publisher: *Dan Buckley*
Executive Producer: *Alan Fine*

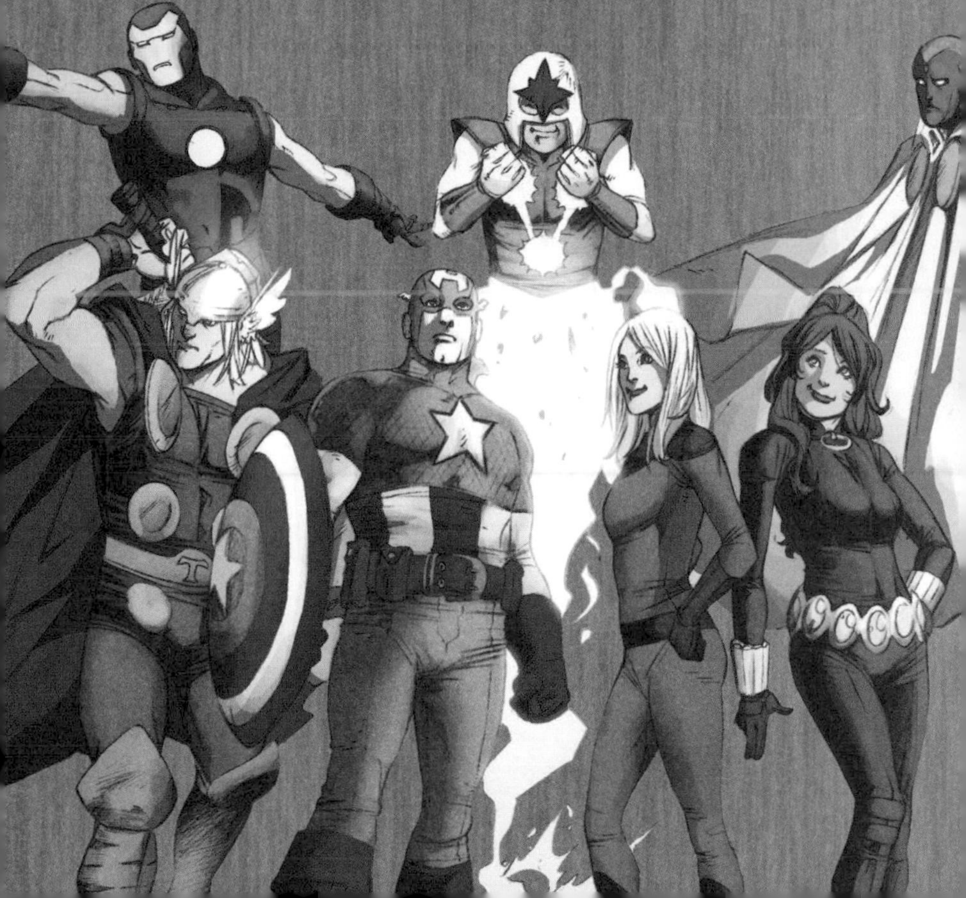

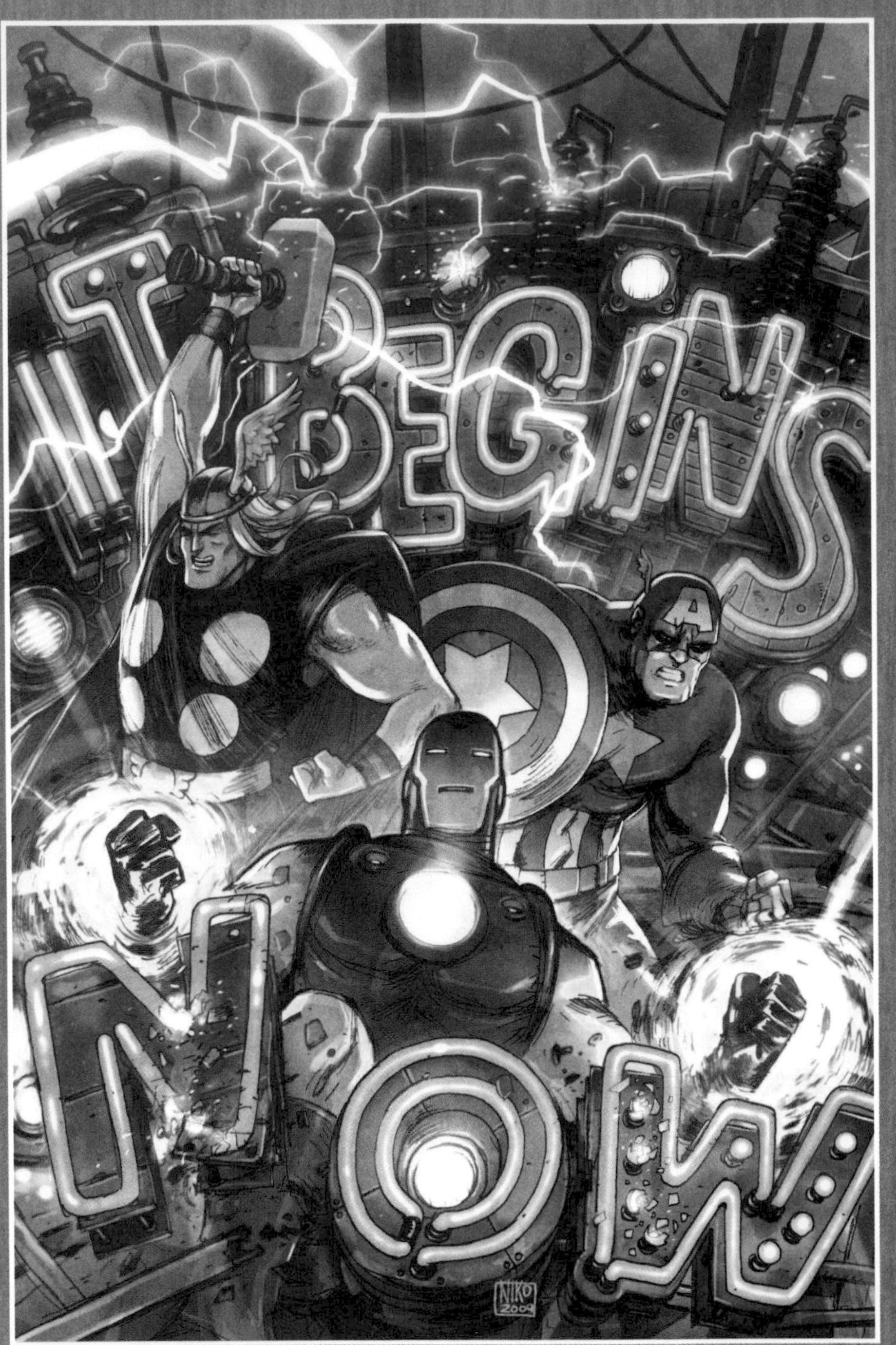
BEGINS
NOW
NIKO 2009

#17

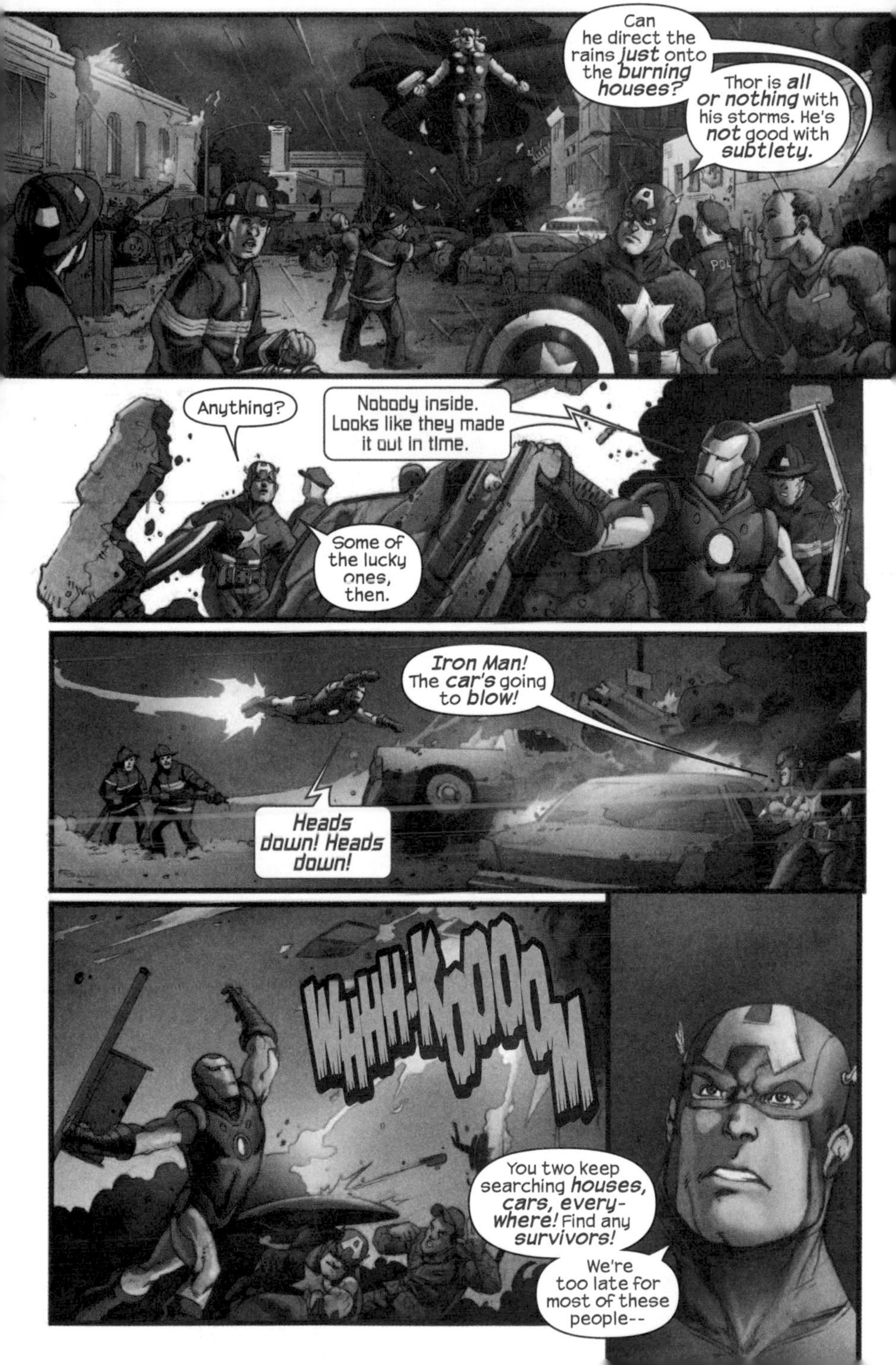

Can he direct the rains *just* onto the *burning houses?*
Thor is *all or nothing* with his storms. He's *not* good with *subtlety.*
Anything?
Nobody inside. Looks like they made it out in time.
Some of the lucky ones, then.
Iron Man! The *car's* going to *blow!*
Heads down! Heads down!
WHHH-KOOOOM
You two keep searching *houses, cars, every-where!* Find any *survivors!*
We're too late for most of these people--

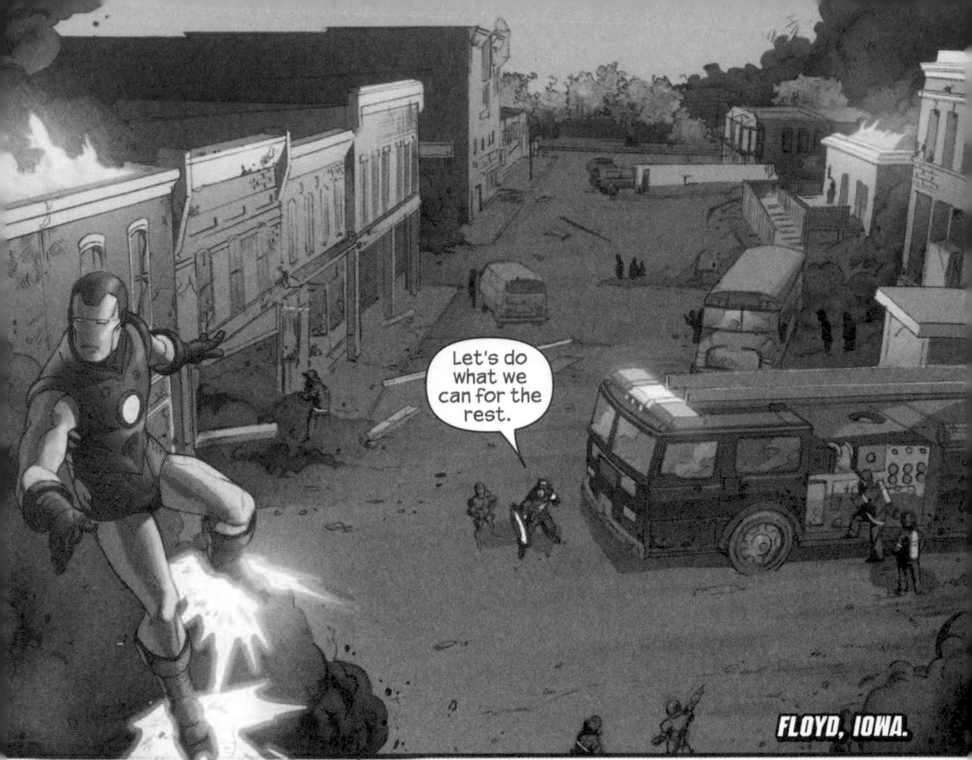
Let's do what we can for the rest.
FLOYD, IOWA.

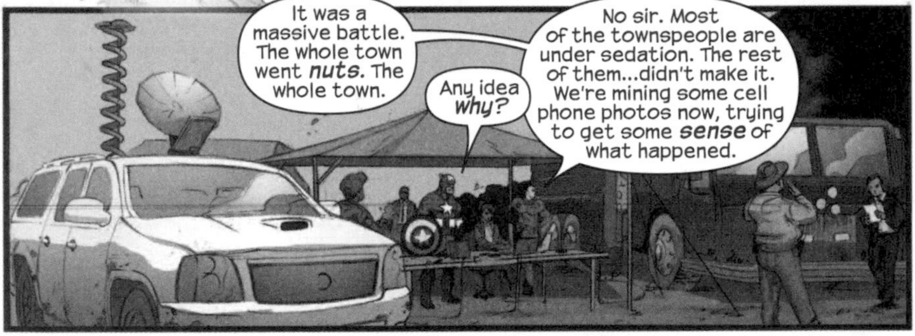
It was a massive battle. The whole town went *nuts.* The whole town.
Any idea *why?*
No sir. Most of the townspeople are under sedation. The rest of them...didn't make it. We're mining some cell phone photos now, trying to get some *sense* of what happened.

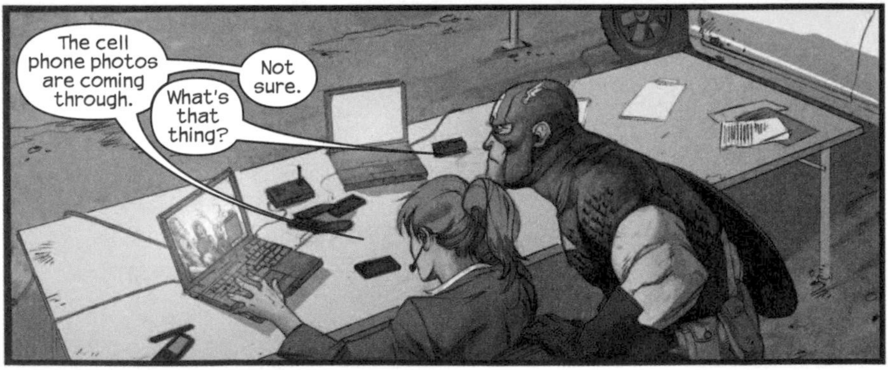
The cell phone photos are coming through.
What's that thing?
Not sure.

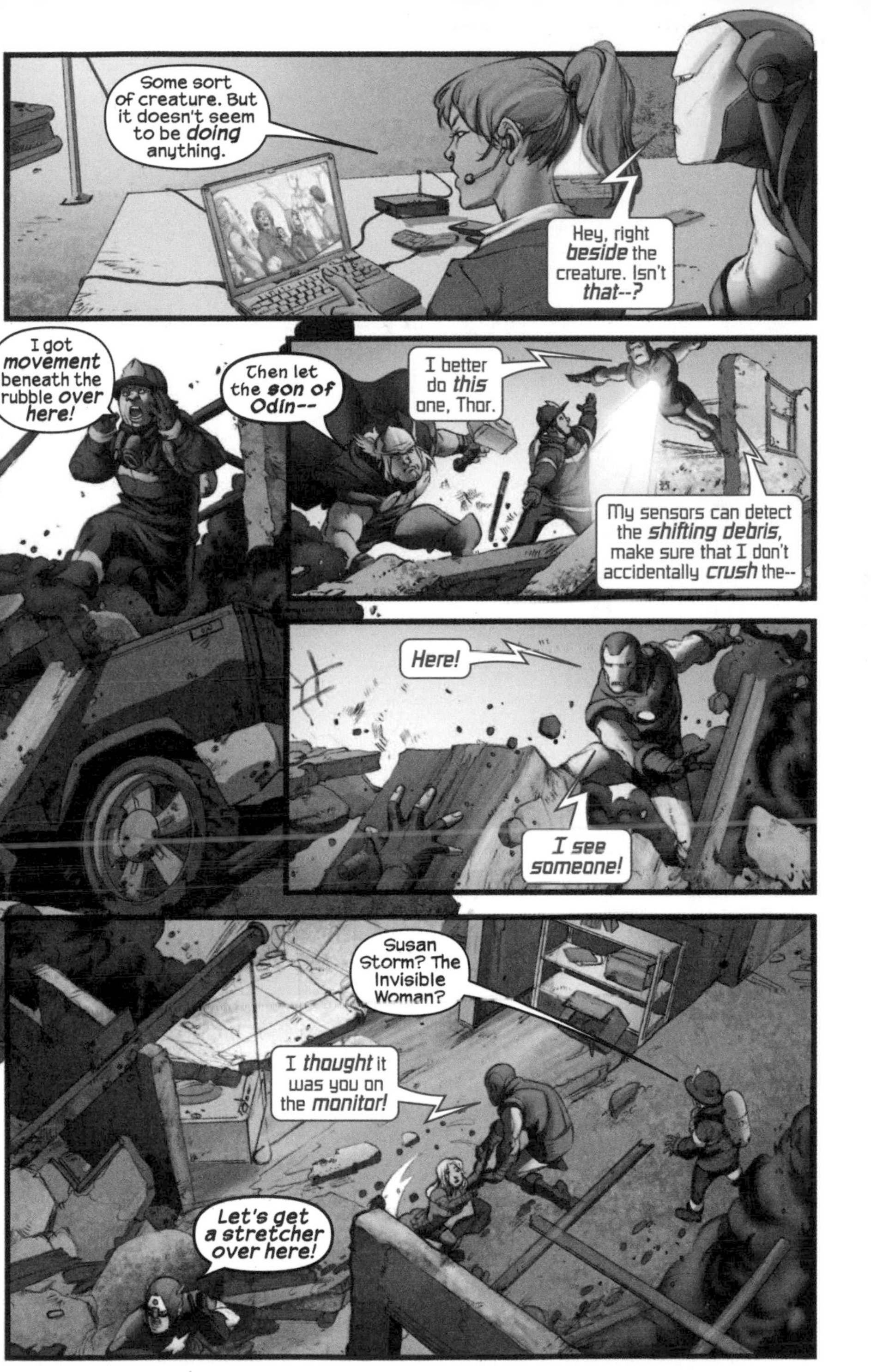
Some sort of creature. But it doesn't seem to be *doing* anything.
Hey, right *beside* the creature. Isn't *that*--?
I got *movement* beneath the rubble *over here!*
Then let the *son of Odin*--
I better do *this* one, Thor.
My sensors can detect the *shifting debris,* make sure that I don't accidentally *crush* the--
Here!
I see someone!
Susan Storm? The Invisible Woman?
I *thought* it was you on the *monitor!*
Let's get a stretcher over here!

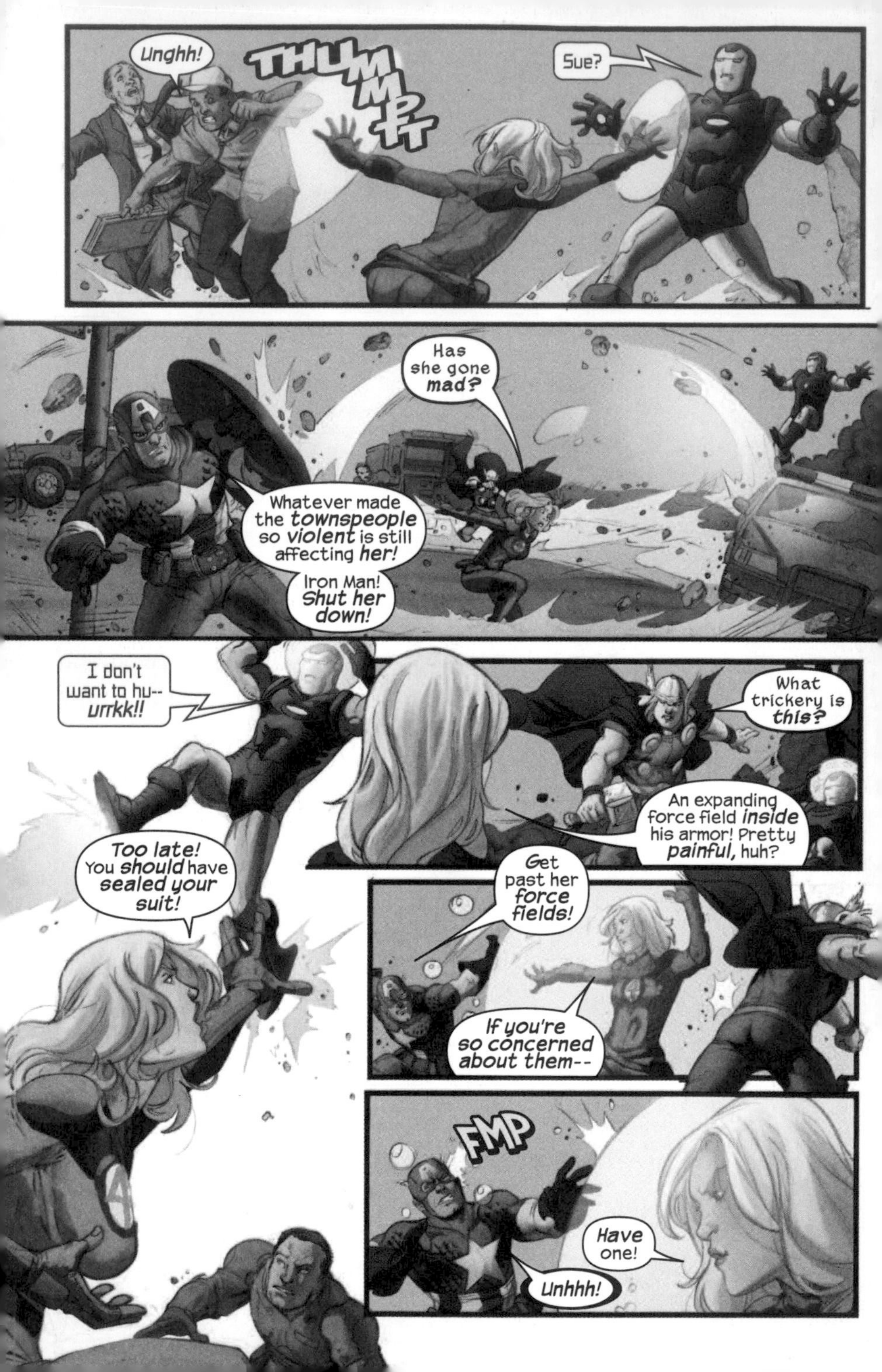
Unghh!
THUMMPTT
Sue?
Has she gone mad?
Whatever made the townspeople so violent is still affecting her!
Iron Man! Shut her down!
I don't want to hu-- urrkk!!
What trickery is this?
An expanding force field inside his armor! Pretty painful, huh?
Too late! You should have sealed your suit!
Get past her force fields!
If you're so concerned about them--
FMP
Have one!
Unhhh!

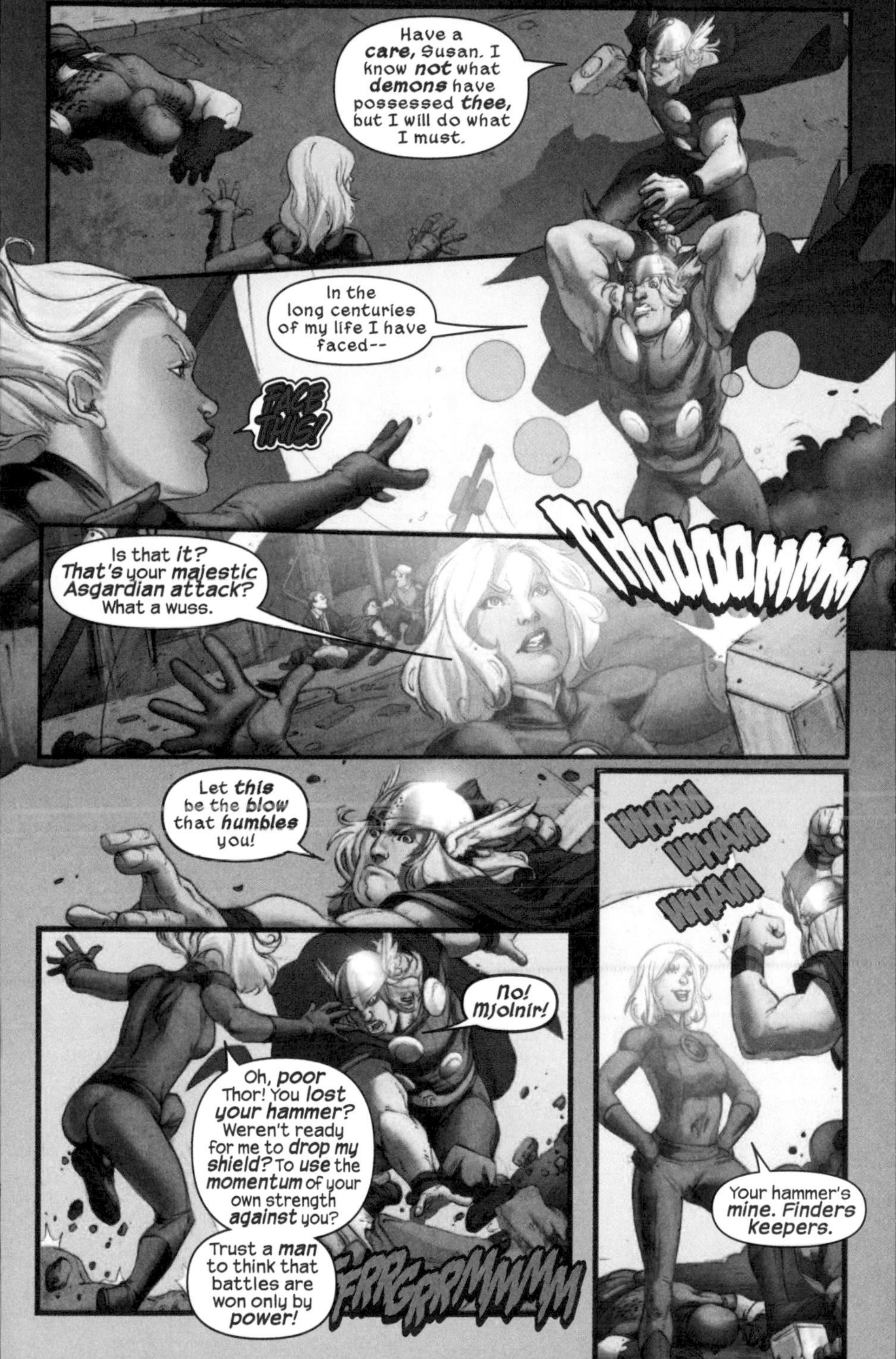
Have a care, Susan. I know not what demons have possessed thee, but I will do what I must.
In the long centuries of my life I have faced--
FACE THIS!
THOOOOMMM
Is that it? That's your majestic Asgardian attack? What a wuss.
Let this be the blow that humbles you!
WHAM
WHAM
WHAM
No! Mjolnir!
Oh, poor Thor! You lost your hammer? Weren't ready for me to drop my shield? To use the momentum of your own strength against you?
Trust a man to think that battles are won only by power!
FRRGRRMMMM
Your hammer's mine. Finders keepers.

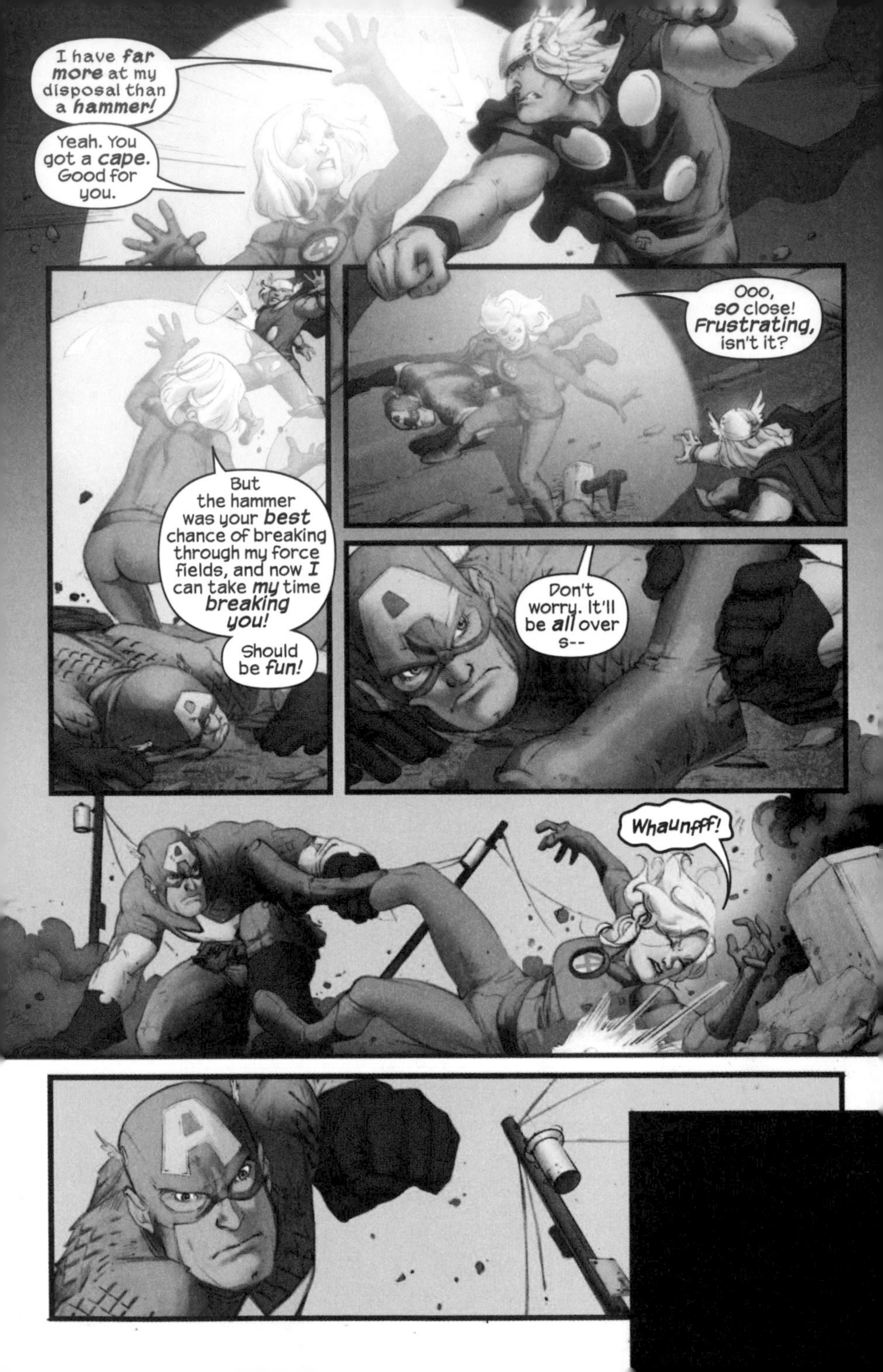
I have far more at my disposal than a hammer!
Yeah. You got a cape. Good for you.
But the hammer was your best chance of breaking through my force fields, and now I can take my time breaking you!
Should be fun!
Ooo, so close! Frustrating, isn't it?
Don't worry. It'll be all over s--
Whaunfff!

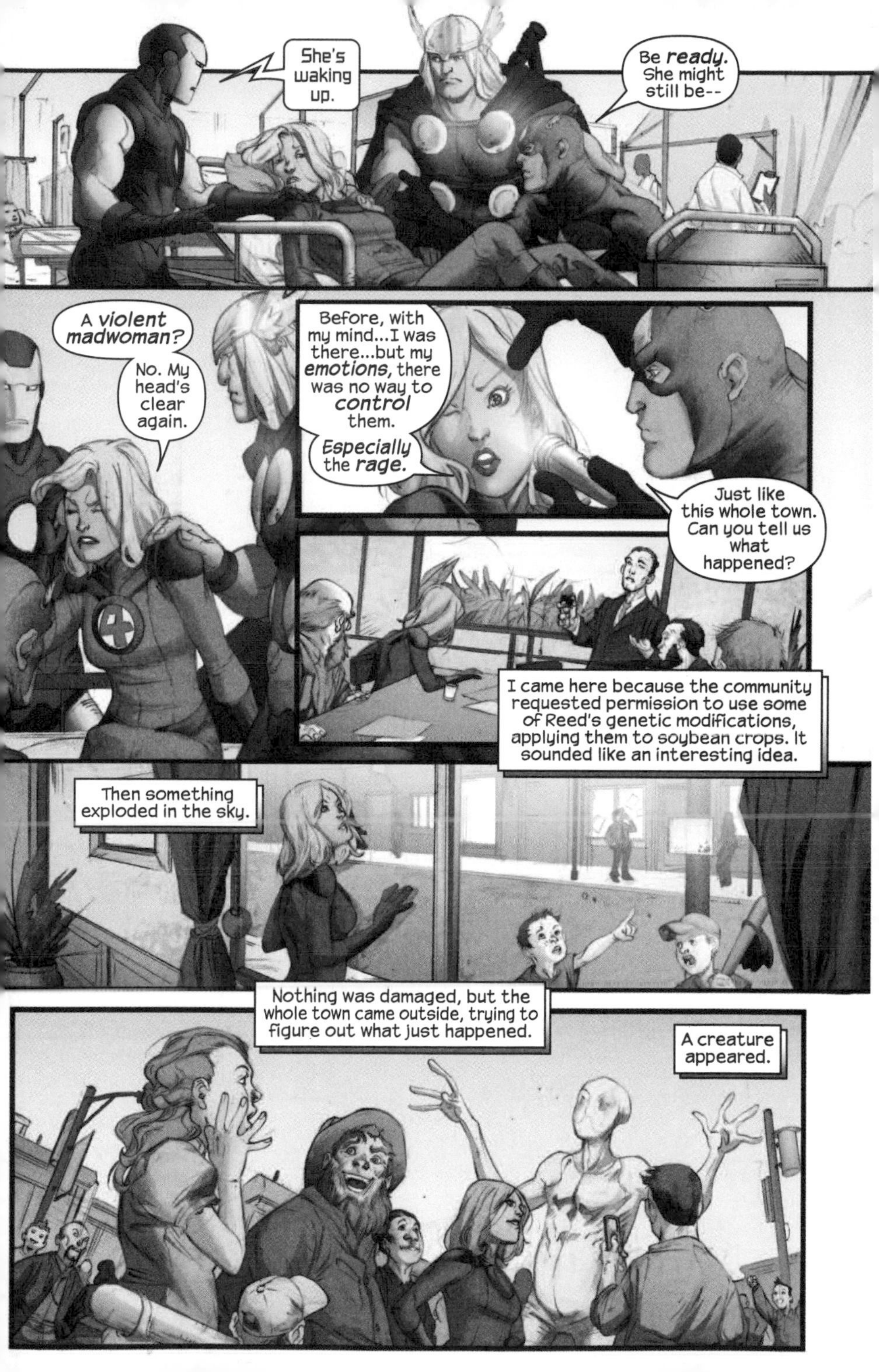
She's waking up.
Be *ready*. She might still be--
A *violent madwoman*?
No. My head's clear again.
Before, with my mind...I was there...but my *emotions*, there was no way to *control* them.
Especially the *rage*.
Just like this whole town. Can you tell us what happened?
I came here because the community requested permission to use some of Reed's genetic modifications, applying them to soybean crops. It sounded like an interesting idea.
Then something exploded in the sky.
Nothing was damaged, but the whole town came outside, trying to figure out what just happened.
A creature appeared.

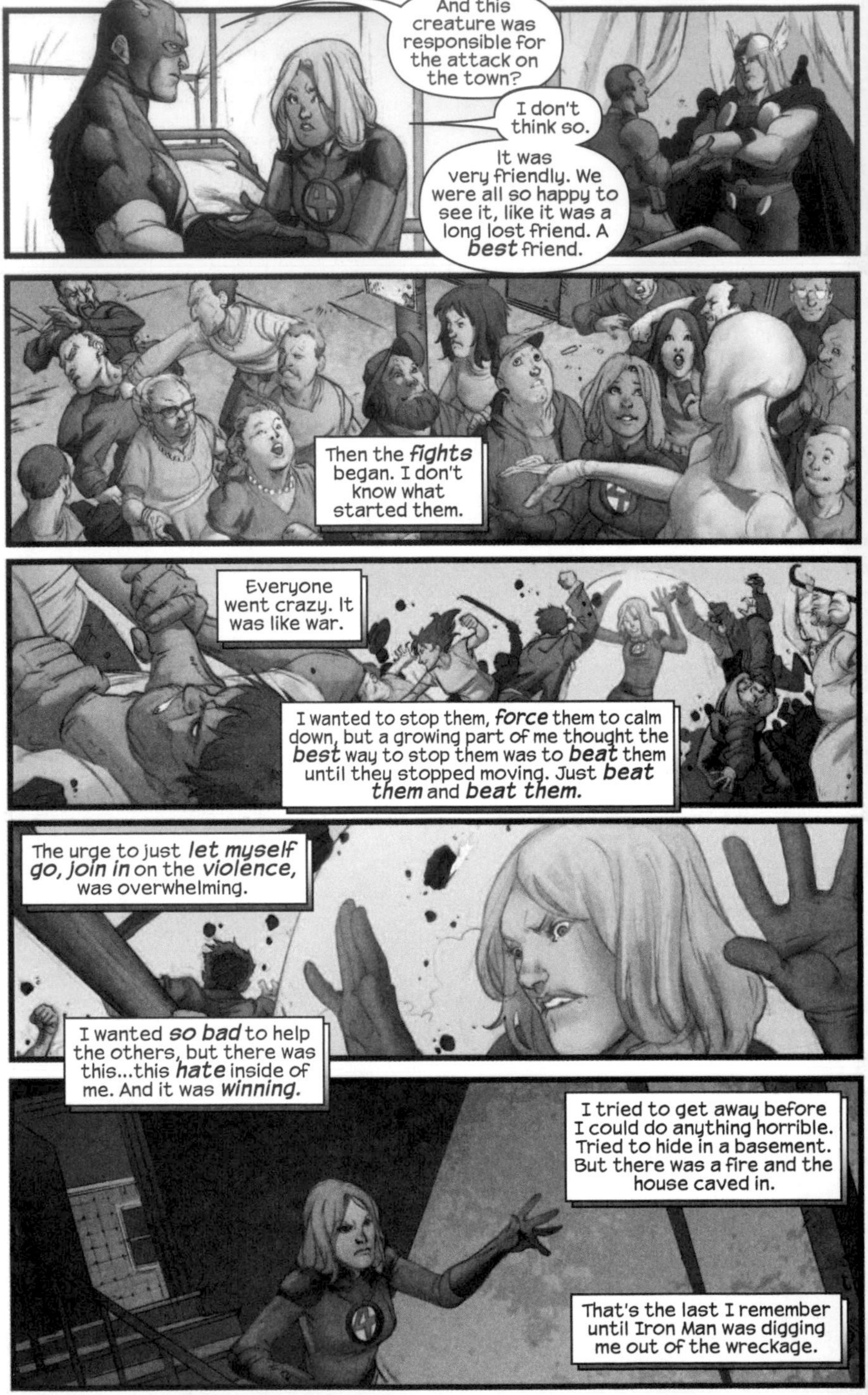

And this creature was responsible for the attack on the town?
I don't think so.
It was very friendly. We were all so happy to see it, like it was a long lost friend. A best friend.
Then the fights began. I don't know what started them.
Everyone went crazy. It was like war.
I wanted to stop them, force them to calm down, but a growing part of me thought the best way to stop them was to beat them until they stopped moving. Just beat them and beat them.
The urge to just let myself go, join in on the violence, was overwhelming.
I wanted so bad to help the others, but there was this...this hate inside of me. And it was winning.
I tried to get away before I could do anything horrible. Tried to hide in a basement. But there was a fire and the house caved in.
That's the last I remember until Iron Man was digging me out of the wreckage.

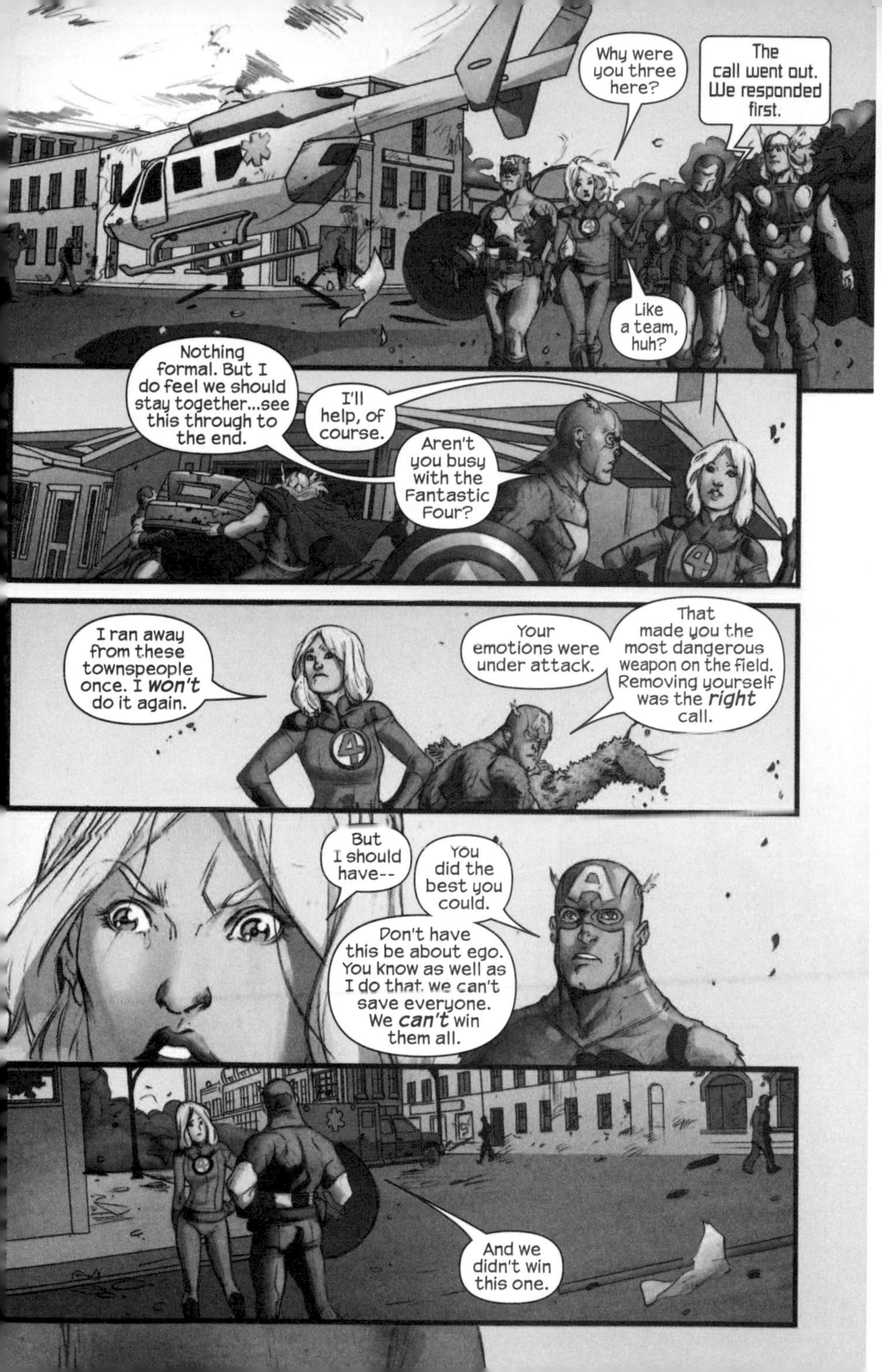
Why were you three here?
The call went out. We responded first.
Like a team, huh?
Nothing formal. But I do feel we should stay together...see this through to the end.
I'll help, of course.
Aren't you busy with the Fantastic Four?
I ran away from these townspeople once. I won't do it again.
Your emotions were under attack.
That made you the most dangerous weapon on the field. Removing yourself was the right call.
But I should have--
You did the best you could.
Don't have this be about ego. You know as well as I do that we can't save everyone. We can't win them all.
And we didn't win this one.

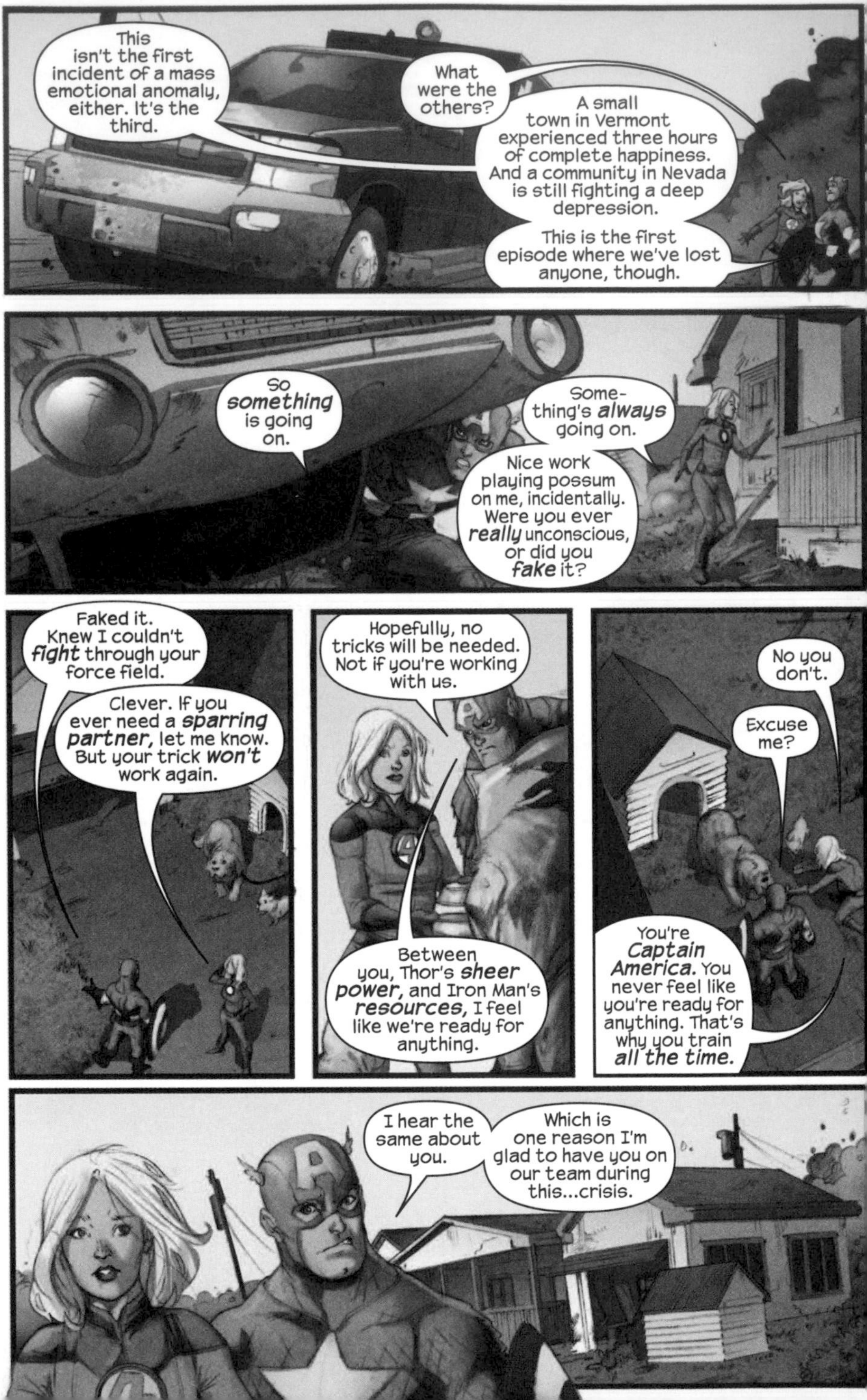
This isn't the first incident of a mass emotional anomaly, either. It's the third.
What were the others?
A small town in Vermont experienced three hours of complete happiness. And a community in Nevada is still fighting a deep depression.
This is the first episode where we've lost anyone, though.
So *something* is going on.
Some-thing's *always* going on.
Nice work playing possum on me, incidentally. Were you ever *really* unconscious, or did you *fake* it?
Faked it. Knew I couldn't *fight* through your force field.
Clever. If you ever need a *sparring partner,* let me know. But your trick *won't* work again.
Hopefully, no tricks will be needed. Not if you're working with us.
Between you, Thor's *sheer power,* and Iron Man's *resources,* I feel like we're ready for anything.
No you don't.
Excuse me?
You're *Captain America.* You never feel like you're ready for anything. That's why you train *all the time.*
I hear the same about you.
Which is one reason I'm glad to have you on our team during this...crisis.

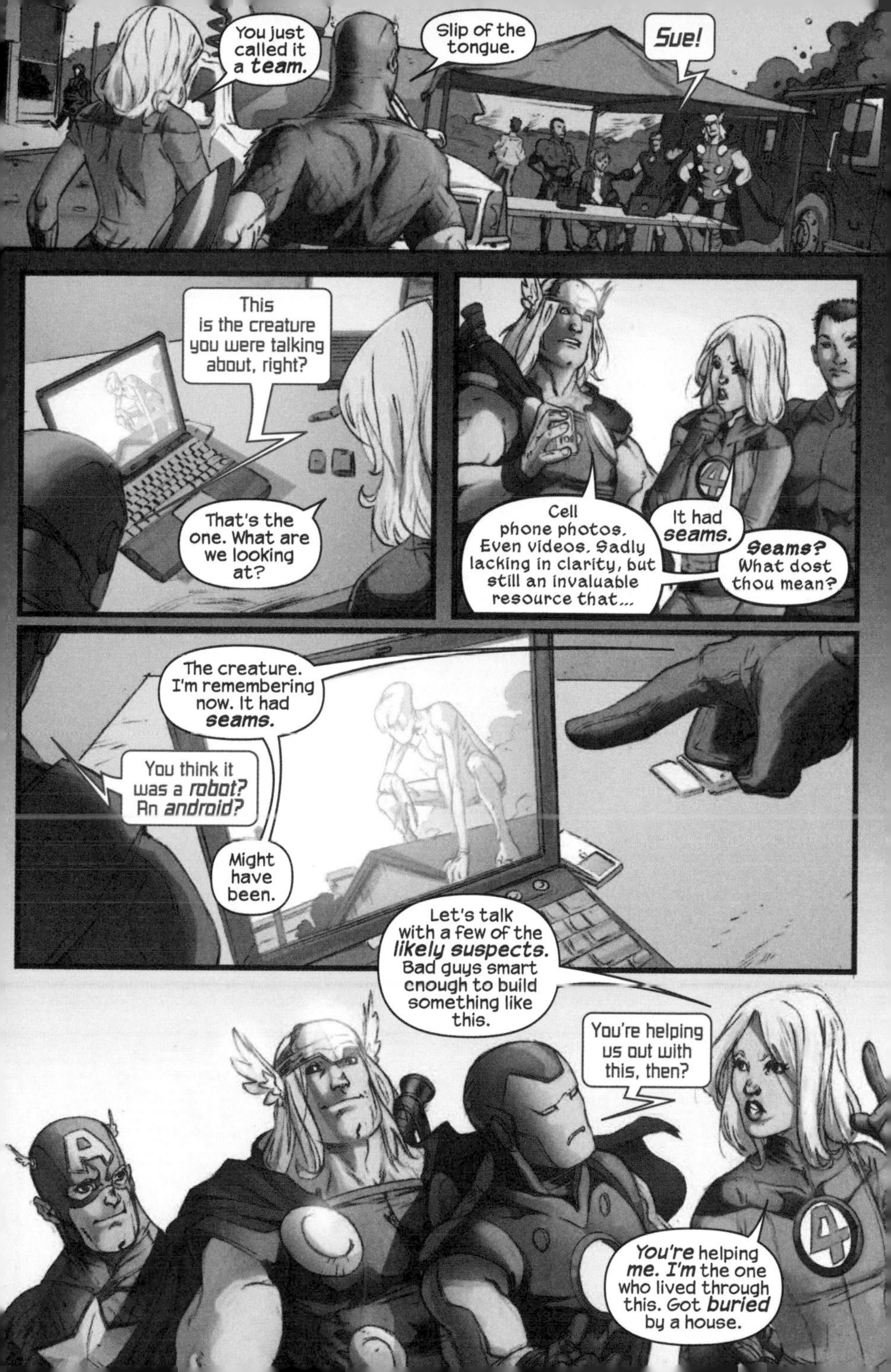

You just called it a team.
Slip of the tongue.
Sue!
This is the creature you were talking about, right?
That's the one. What are we looking at?
Cell phone photos. Even videos. Sadly lacking in clarity, but still an invaluable resource that...
It had seams.
Seams? What dost thou mean?
The creature. I'm remembering now. It had seams.
You think it was a robot? An android?
Might have been.
Let's talk with a few of the likely suspects. Bad guys smart enough to build something like this.
You're helping us out with this, then?
You're helping me. I'm the one who lived through this. Got buried by a house.

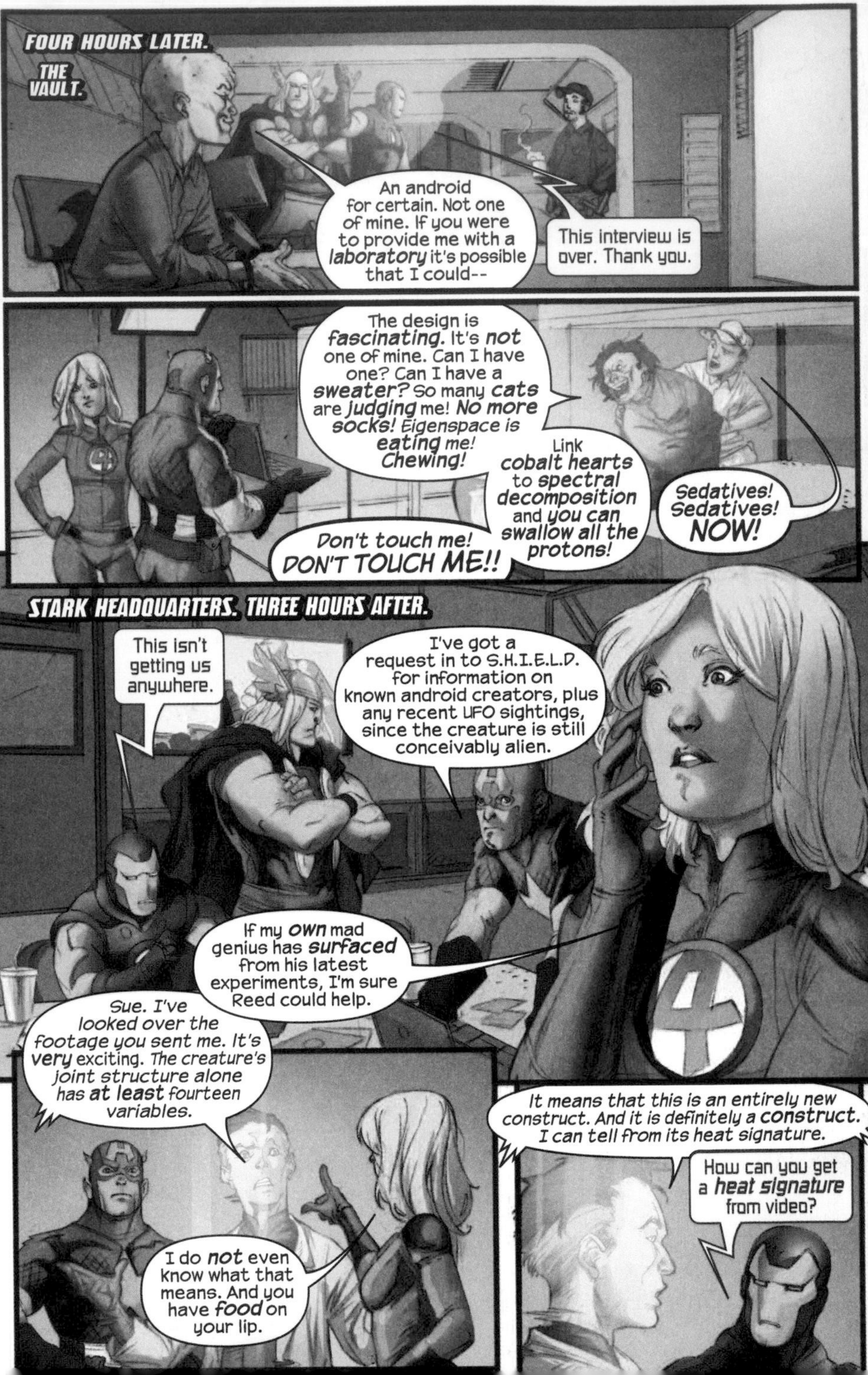
FOUR HOURS LATER.
THE VAULT.
An android for certain. Not one of mine. If you were to provide me with a laboratory it's possible that I could--
This interview is over. Thank you.
The design is fascinating. It's not one of mine. Can I have one? Can I have a sweater? So many cats are judging me! No more socks! Eigenspace is eating me! Chewing!
Link cobalt hearts to spectral decomposition and you can swallow all the protons!
Don't touch me! DON'T TOUCH ME!!
Sedatives! Sedatives! NOW!
STARK HEADQUARTERS. THREE HOURS AFTER.
This isn't getting us anywhere.
I've got a request in to S.H.I.E.L.D. for information on known android creators, plus any recent UFO sightings, since the creature is still conceivably alien.
If my own mad genius has surfaced from his latest experiments, I'm sure Reed could help.
Sue. I've looked over the footage you sent me. It's very exciting. The creature's joint structure alone has at least fourteen variables.
I do not even know what that means. And you have food on your lip.
It means that this is an entirely new construct. And it is definitely a construct. I can tell from its heat signature.
How can you get a heat signature from video?

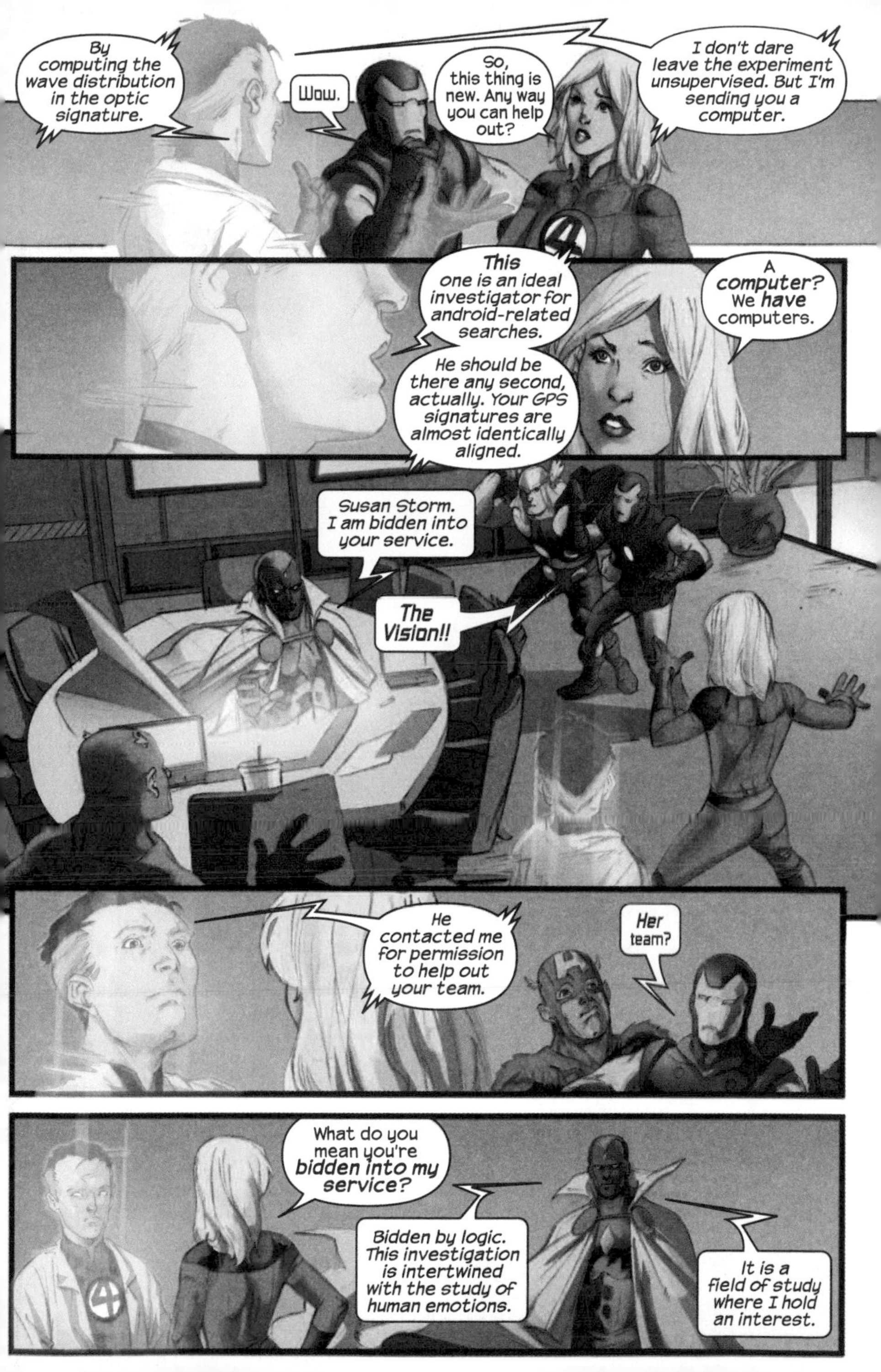
By computing the wave distribution in the optic signature.
Wow.
So, this thing is new. Any way you can help out?
I don't dare leave the experiment unsupervised. But I'm sending you a computer.
A computer? We have computers.
This one is an ideal investigator for android-related searches.
He should be there any second, actually. Your GPS signatures are almost identically aligned.
Susan Storm. I am bidden into your service.
The Vision!!
He contacted me for permission to help out your team.
Her team?
What do you mean you're bidden into my service?
Bidden by logic. This investigation is intertwined with the study of human emotions.
It is a field of study where I hold an interest.

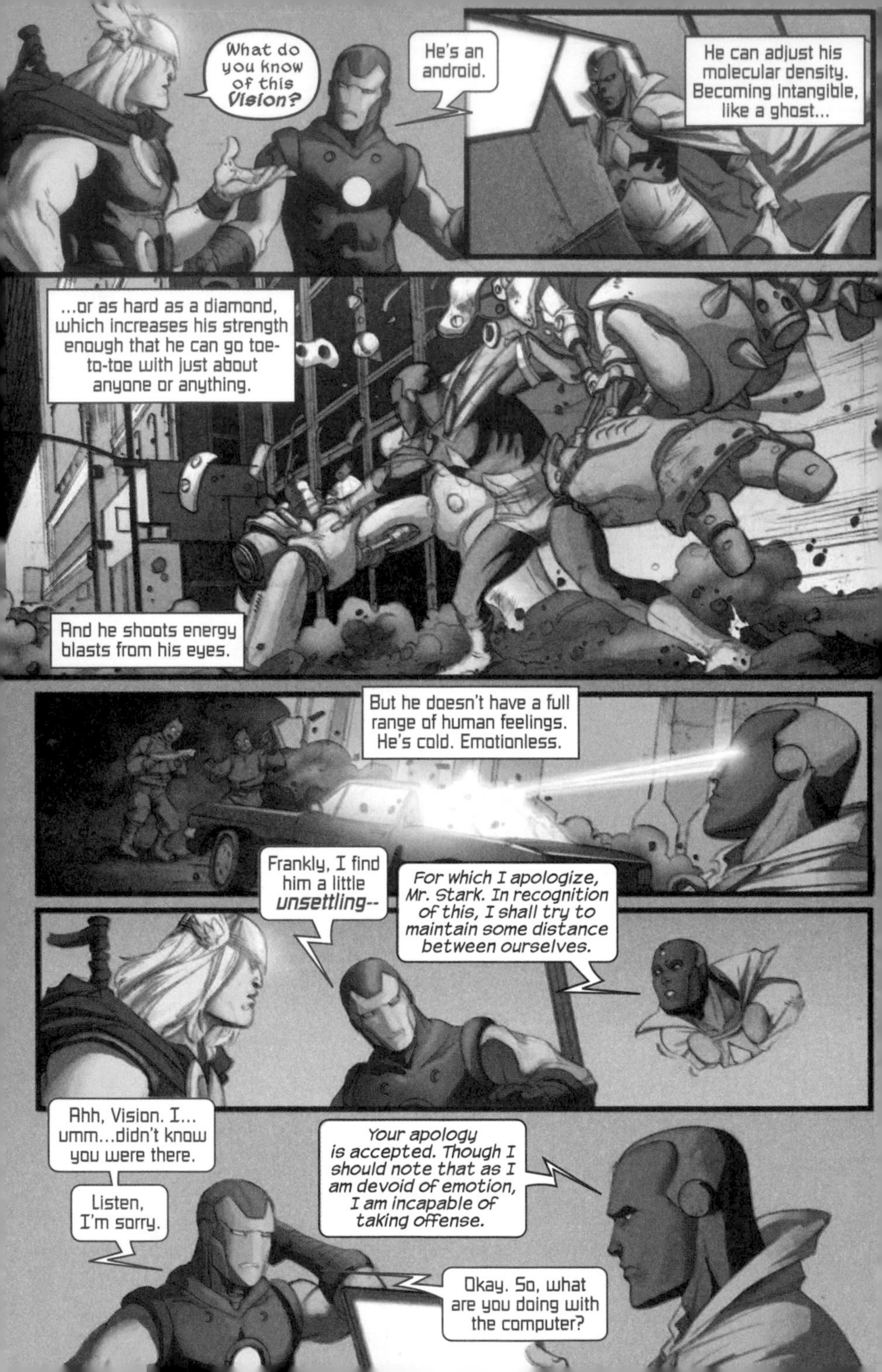
What do you know of this Vision?
He's an android.
He can adjust his molecular density. Becoming intangible, like a ghost...
...or as hard as a diamond, which increases his strength enough that he can go toe-to-toe with just about anyone or anything.
And he shoots energy blasts from his eyes.
But he doesn't have a full range of human feelings. He's cold. Emotionless.
Frankly, I find him a little unsettling--
For which I apologize, Mr. Stark. In recognition of this, I shall try to maintain some distance between ourselves.
Ahh, Vision. I... umm...didn't know you were there.
Listen, I'm sorry.
Your apology is accepted. Though I should note that as I am devoid of emotion, I am incapable of taking offense.
Okay. So, what are you doing with the computer?

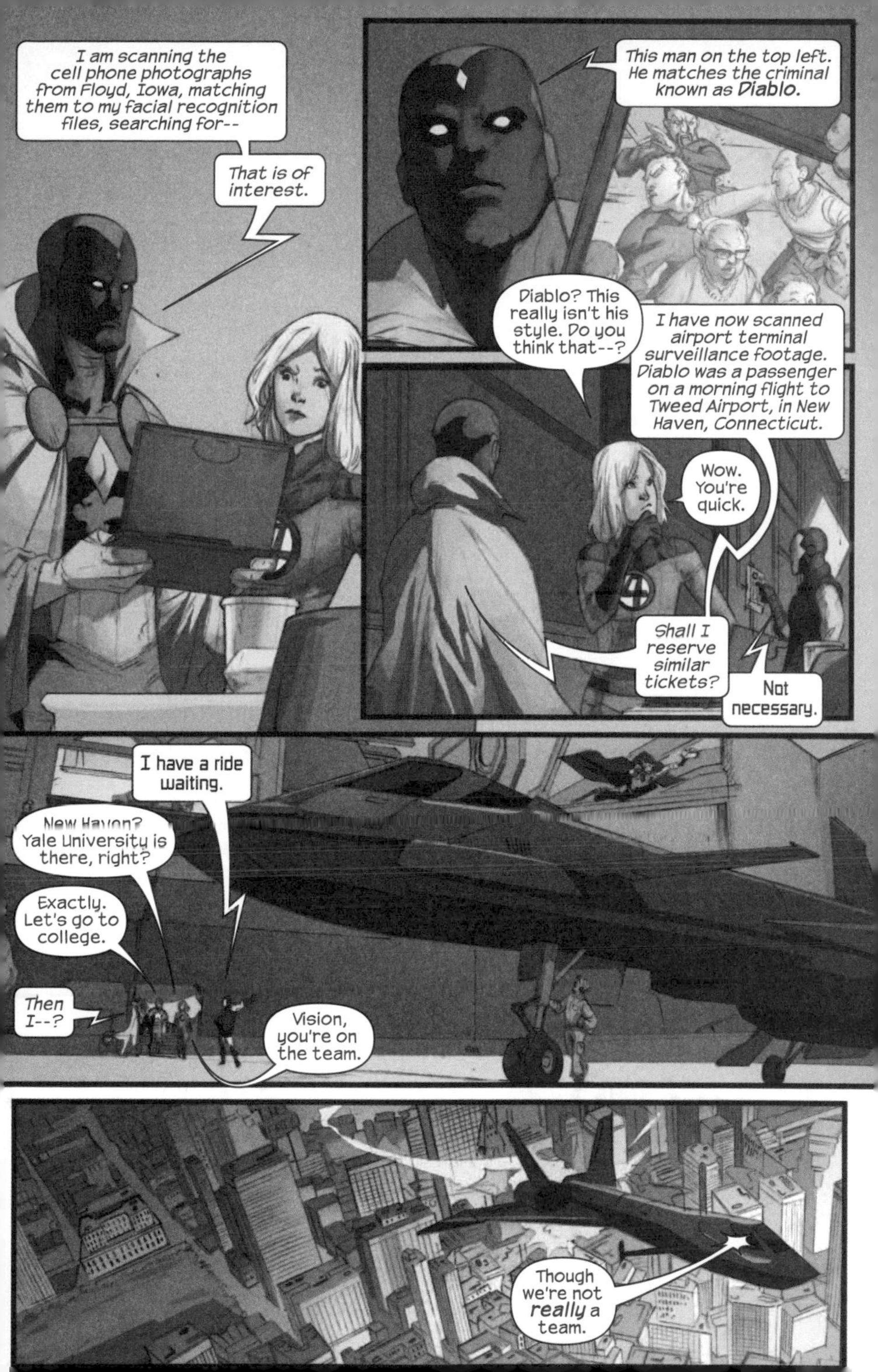

I am scanning the cell phone photographs from Floyd, Iowa, matching them to my facial recognition files, searching for--
That is of interest.
This man on the top left. He matches the criminal known as **Diablo.**
Diablo? This really isn't his style. Do you think that--?
I have now scanned airport terminal surveillance footage. Diablo was a passenger on a morning flight to Tweed Airport, in New Haven, Connecticut.
Wow. You're quick.
Shall I reserve similar tickets?
Not necessary.
I have a ride waiting.
New Haven? Yale University is there, right?
Exactly. Let's go to college.
Then I--?
Vision, you're on the team.
Though we're not *really* a team.

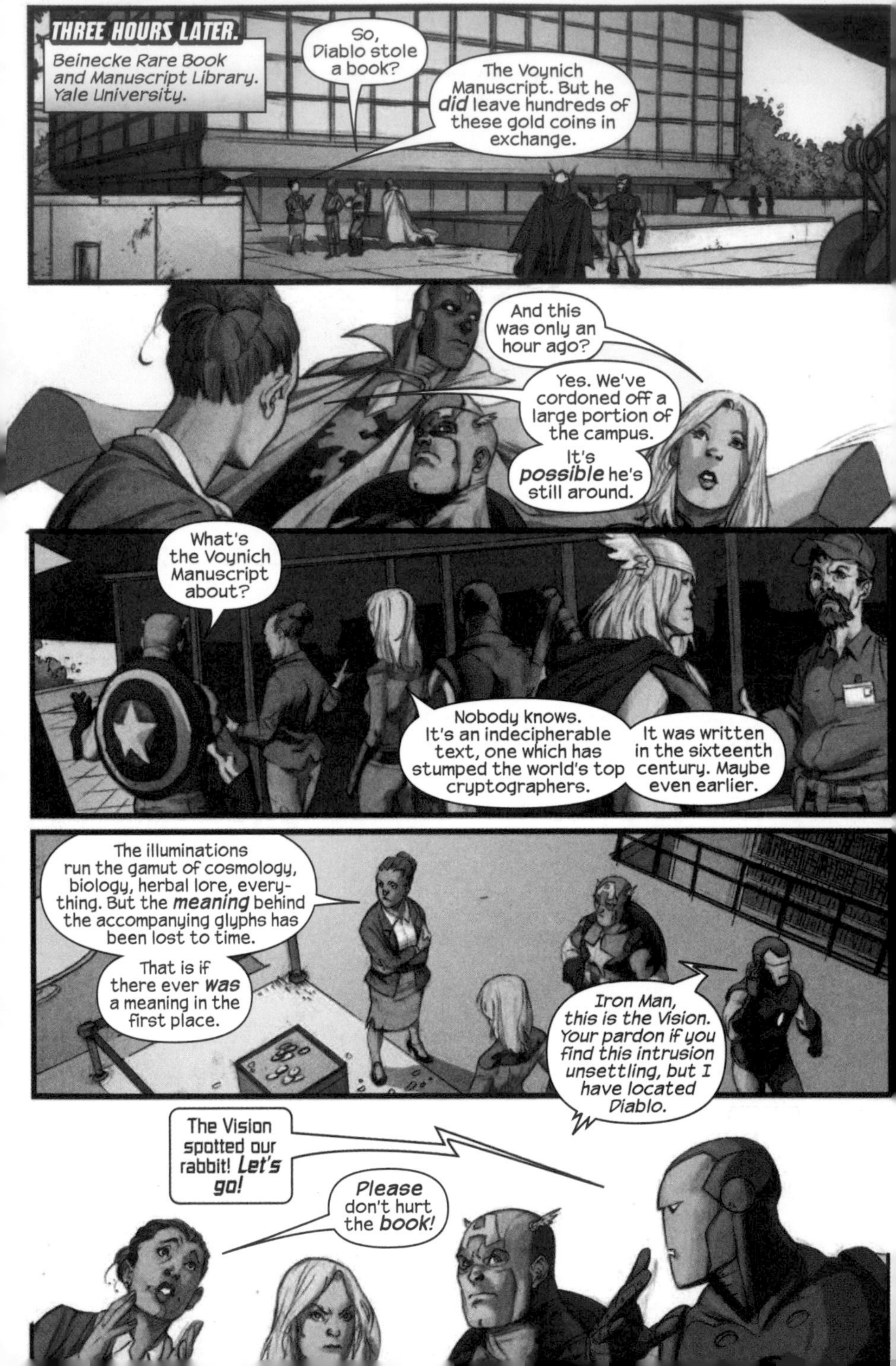
THREE HOURS LATER.
Beinecke Rare Book and Manuscript Library. Yale University.
So, Diablo stole a book?
The Voynich Manuscript. But he did leave hundreds of these gold coins in exchange.
And this was only an hour ago?
Yes. We've cordoned off a large portion of the campus.
It's possible he's still around.
What's the Voynich Manuscript about?
Nobody knows. It's an indecipherable text, one which has stumped the world's top cryptographers.
It was written in the sixteenth century. Maybe even earlier.
The illuminations run the gamut of cosmology, biology, herbal lore, everything. But the meaning behind the accompanying glyphs has been lost to time.
That is if there ever was a meaning in the first place.
Iron Man, this is the Vision. Your pardon if you find this intrusion unsettling, but I have located Diablo.
The Vision spotted our rabbit! Let's go!
Please don't hurt the book!

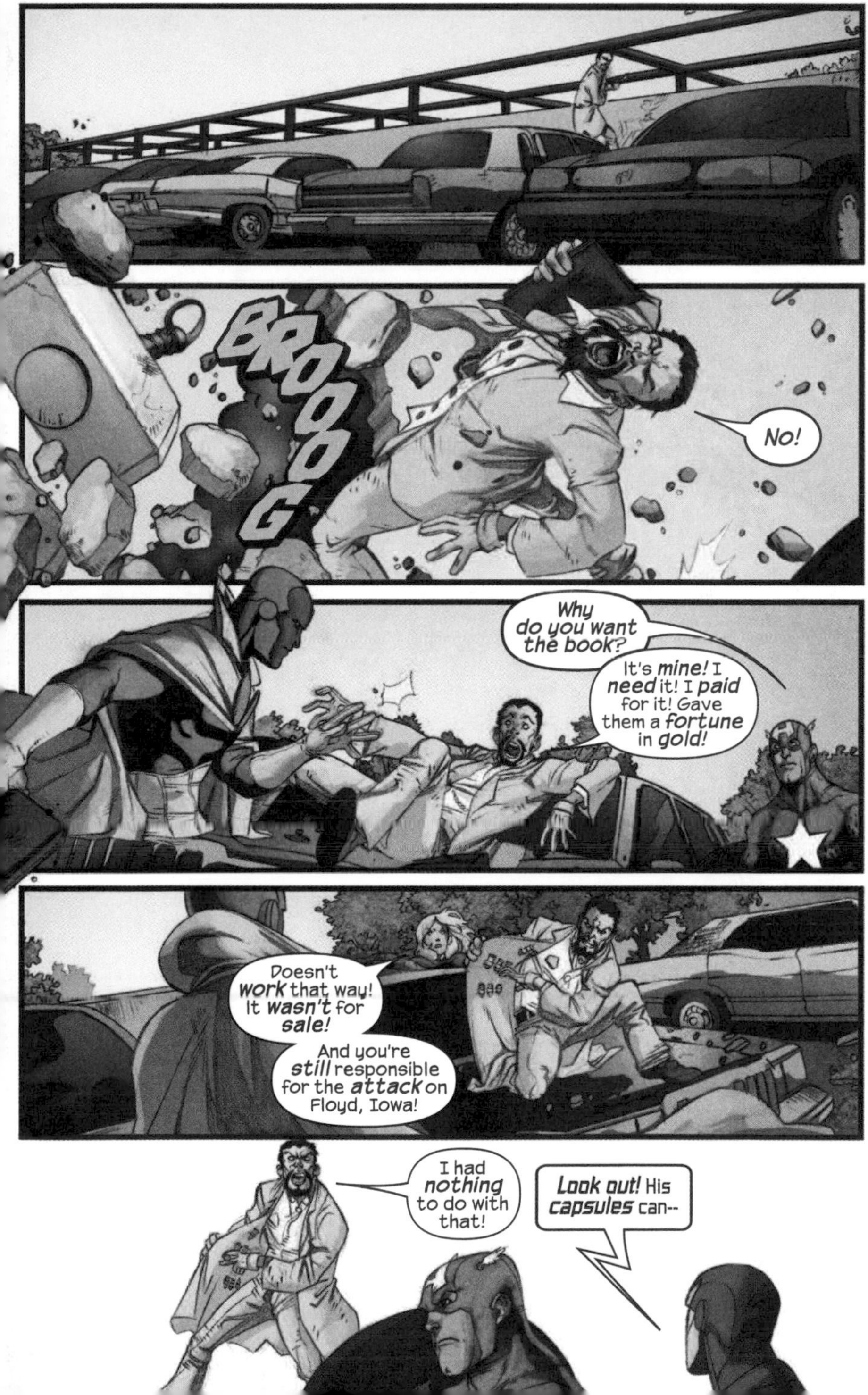
BROOOOG
No!
Why do you want the book?
It's mine! I need it! I paid for it! Gave them a fortune in gold!
Doesn't work that way! It wasn't for sale!
And you're still responsible for the attack on Floyd, Iowa!
I had nothing to do with that!
Look out! His capsules can--

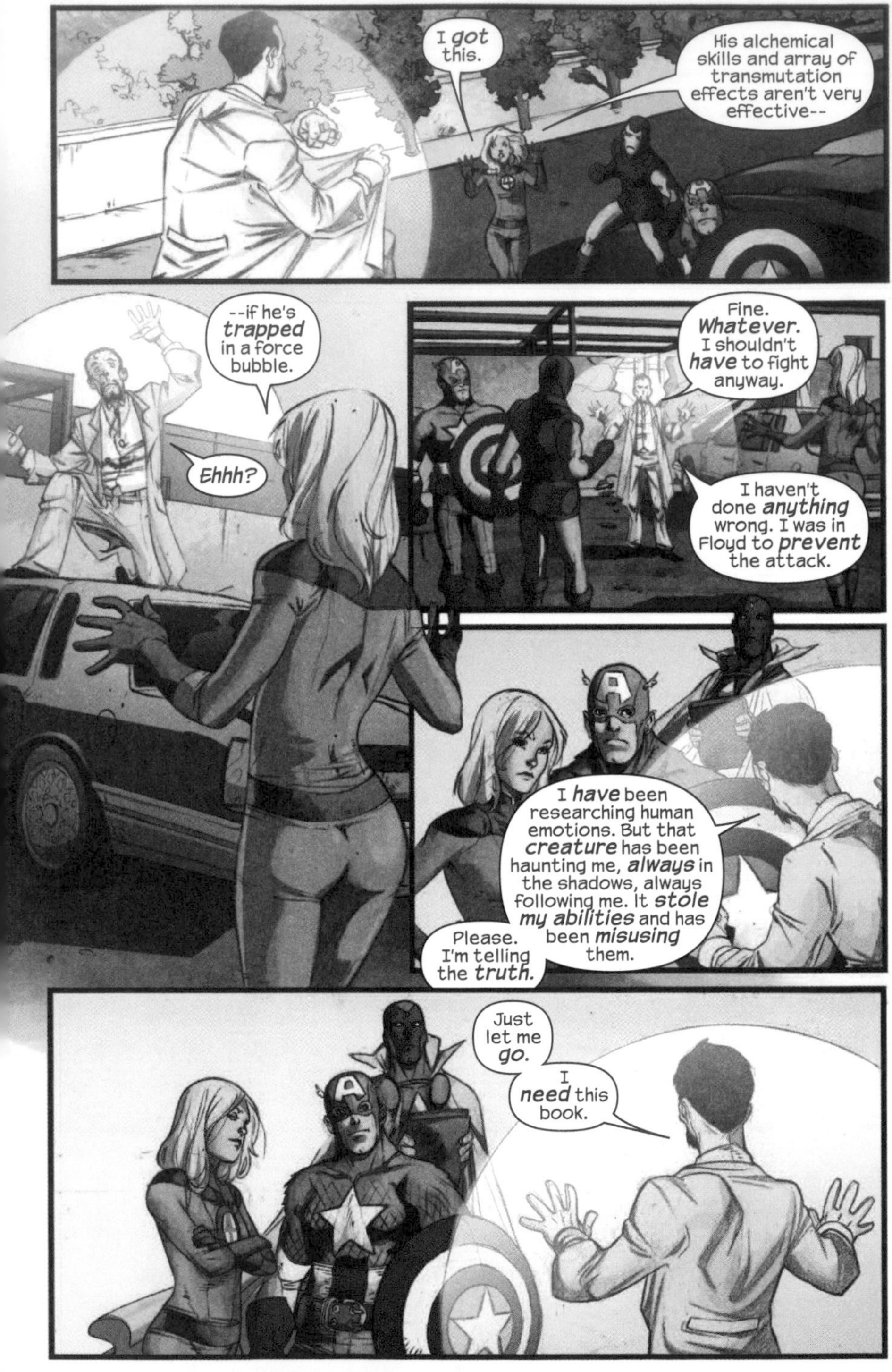
I got this.
His alchemical skills and array of transmutation effects aren't very effective--
--if he's trapped in a force bubble.
Ehhh?
Fine. Whatever. I shouldn't have to fight anyway.
I haven't done anything wrong. I was in Floyd to prevent the attack.
I have been researching human emotions. But that creature has been haunting me, always in the shadows, always following me. It stole my abilities and has been misusing them.
Please. I'm telling the truth.
Just let me go.
I need this book.

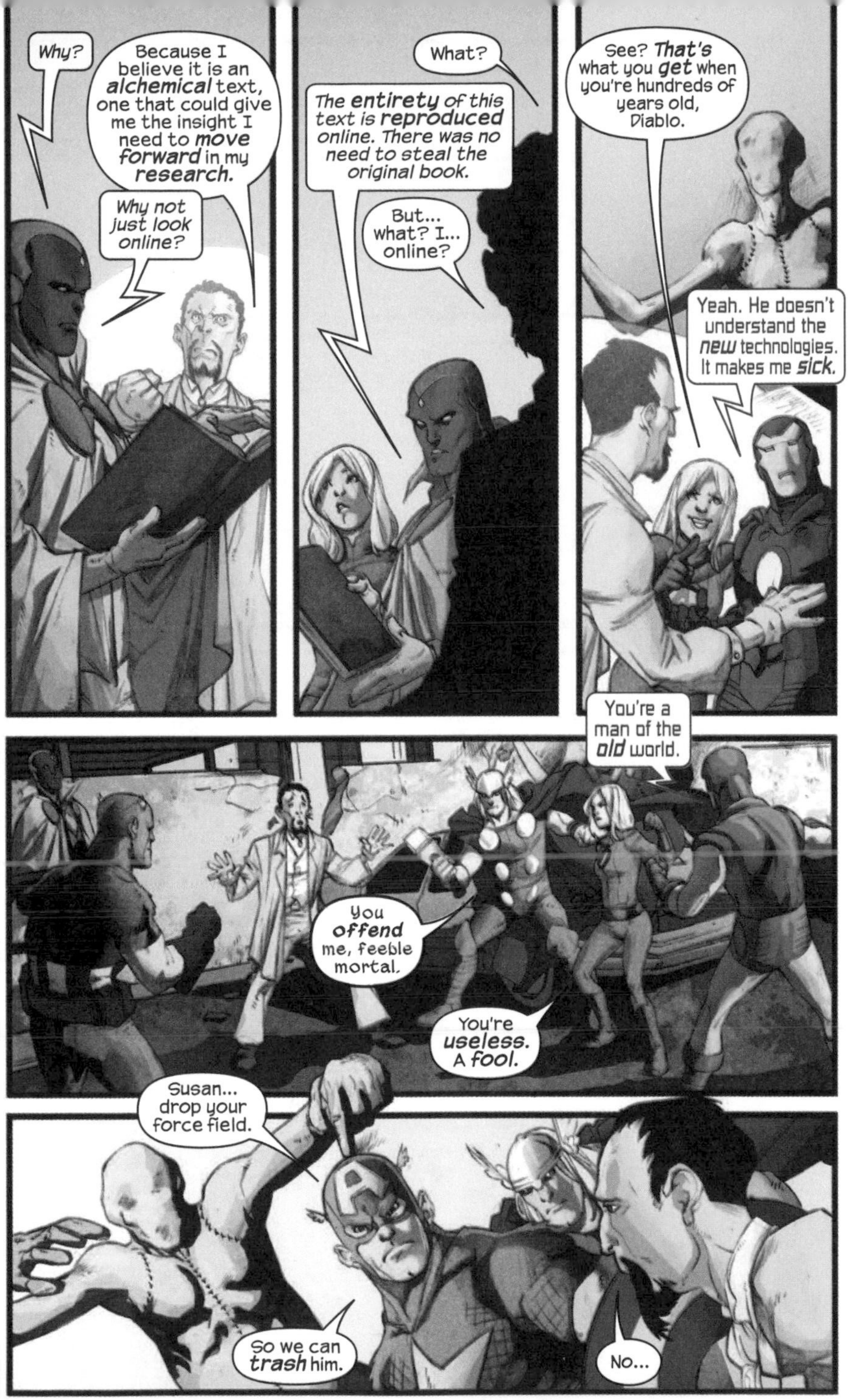
Why?
Because I believe it is an alchemical text, one that could give me the insight I need to move forward in my research.
Why not just look online?
What?
The entirety of this text is reproduced online. There was no need to steal the original book.
But... what? I... online?
See? That's what you get when you're hundreds of years old, Diablo.
Yeah. He doesn't understand the new technologies. It makes me sick.
You're a man of the old world.
You offend me, feeble mortal.
You're useless. A fool.
Susan... drop your force field.
So we can trash him.
No...

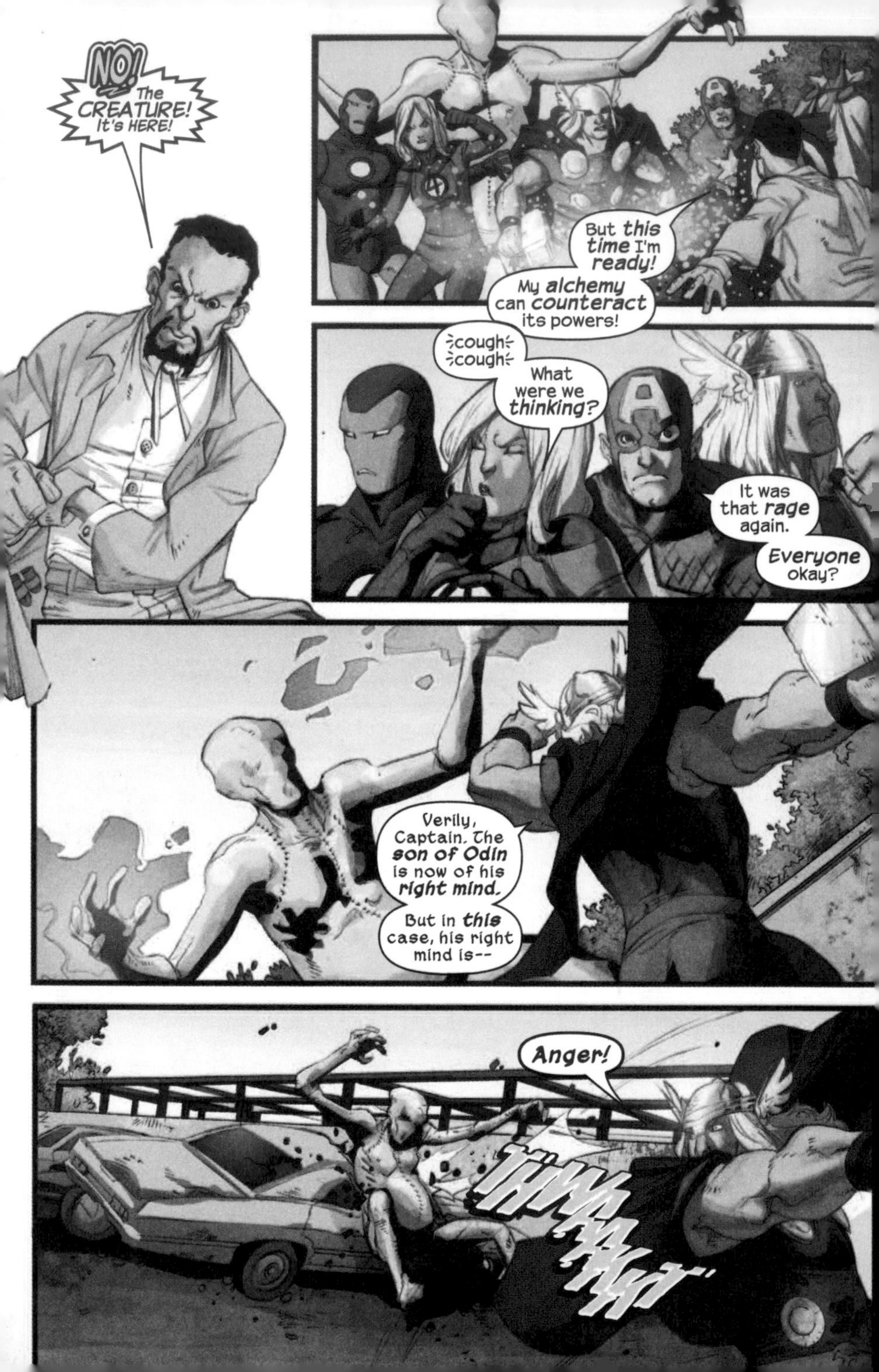
NO! The CREATURE! It's HERE!
But this time I'm ready!
My alchemy can counteract its powers!
cough cough
What were we thinking?
It was that rage again.
Everyone okay?
Verily, Captain. The son of Odin is now of his right mind.
But in this case, his right mind is--
Anger!
THWAKKT

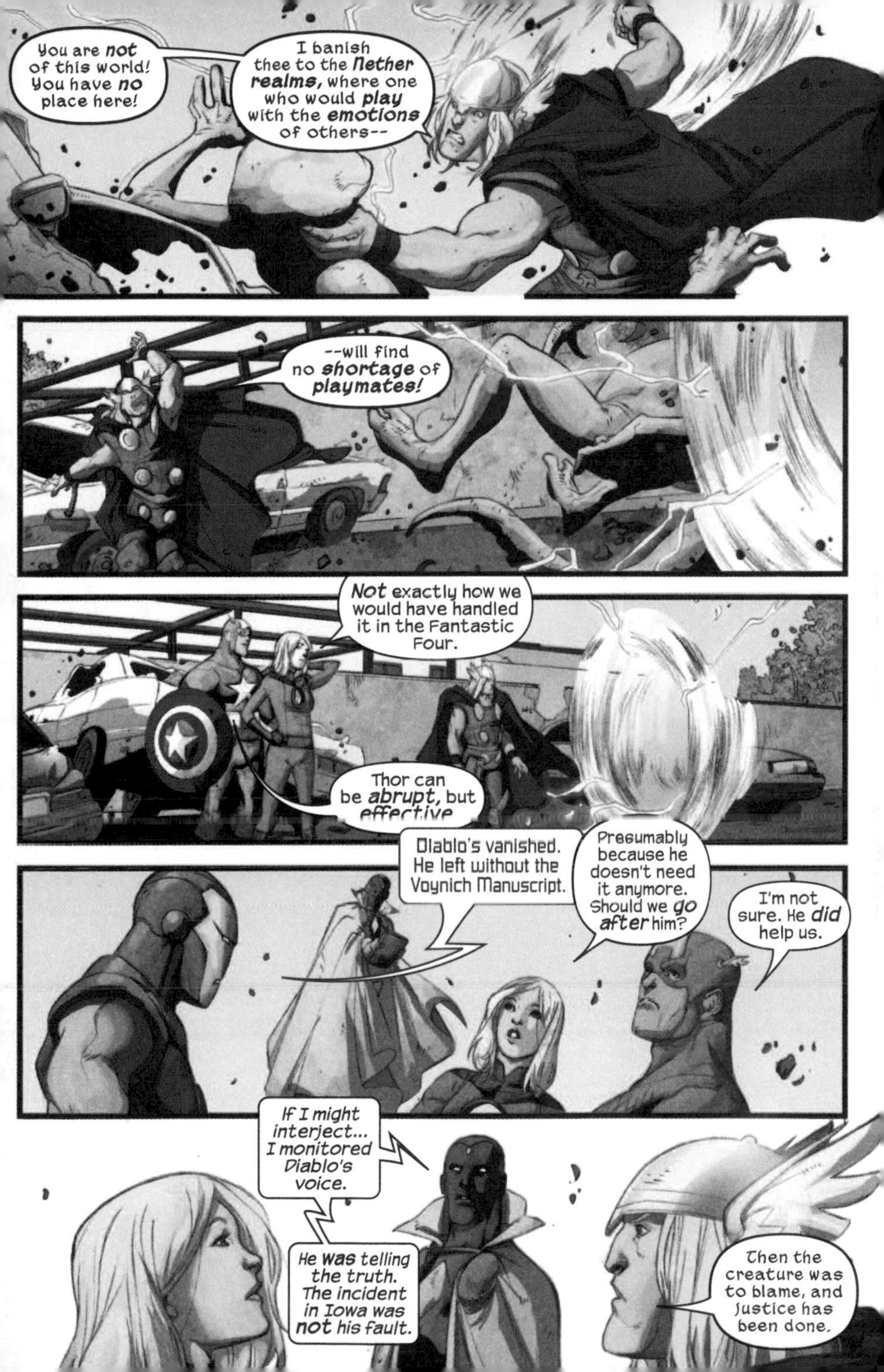
You are *not* of this world! You have *no* place here!
I banish thee to the *Nether realms,* where one who would *play* with the *emotions* of others--
--will find no *shortage* of *playmates!*
Not exactly how we would have handled it in the Fantastic Four.
Thor can be *abrupt,* but effective
Diablo's vanished. He left without the Voynich Manuscript.
Presumably because he doesn't need it anymore. Should we *go after* him?
I'm not sure. He *did* help us.
If I might interject... I monitored Diablo's voice.
He *was* telling the truth. The incident in Iowa was *not* his fault.
Then the creature was to blame, and justice has been done.

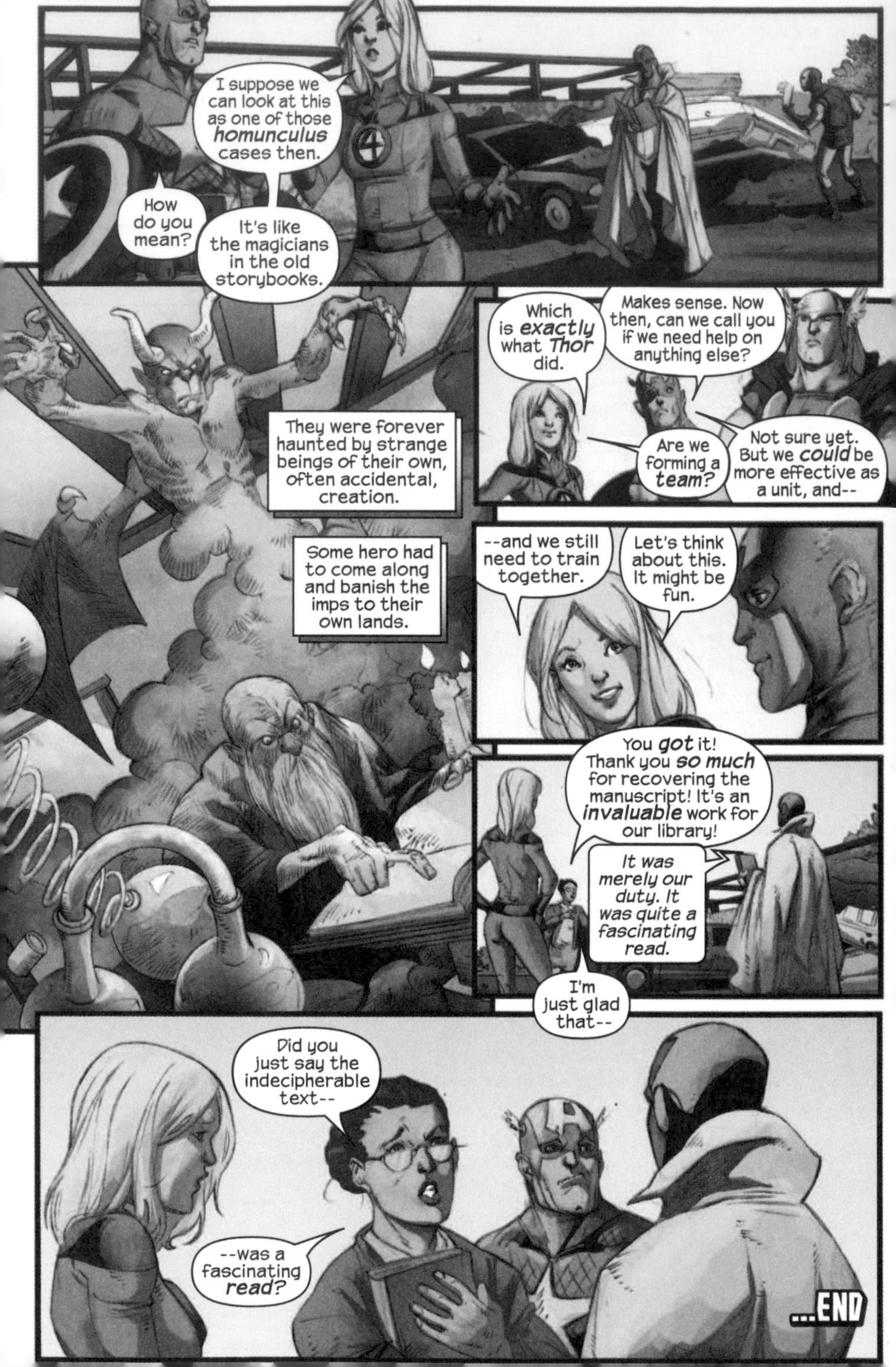

I suppose we can look at this as one of those *homunculus* cases then.
How do you mean?
It's like the magicians in the old storybooks.
They were forever haunted by strange beings of their own, often accidental, creation.
Some hero had to come along and banish the imps to their own lands.
Which is *exactly* what *Thor* did.
Makes sense. Now then, can we call you if we need help on anything else?
Are we forming a *team?*
Not sure yet. But we *could* be more effective as a unit, and--
--and we still need to train together.
Let's think about this. It might be fun.
You *got* it! Thank you *so much* for recovering the manuscript! It's an *invaluable* work for our library!
It was merely our duty. It was quite a fascinating read.
I'm just glad that--
Did you just say the indecipherable text--
--was a fascinating *read?*
...END

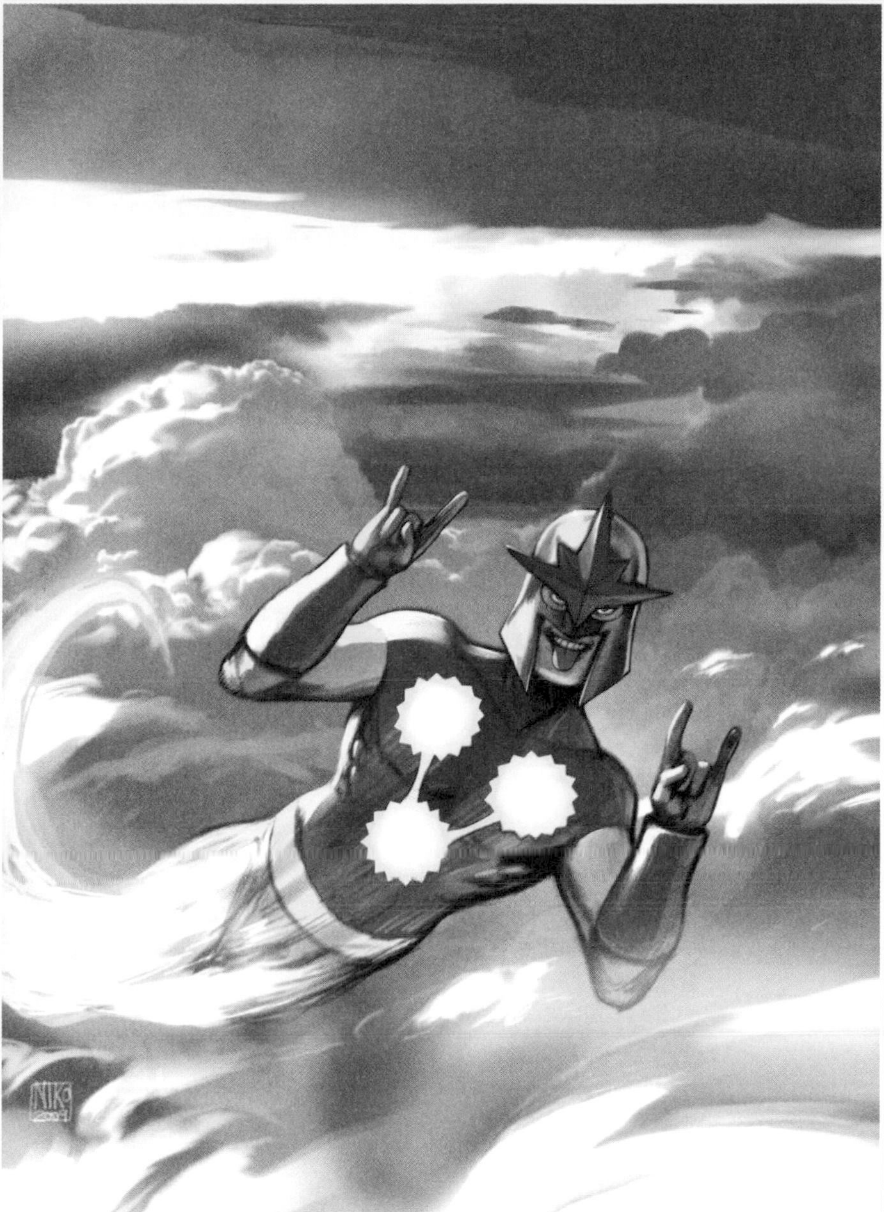
NIKO

#18

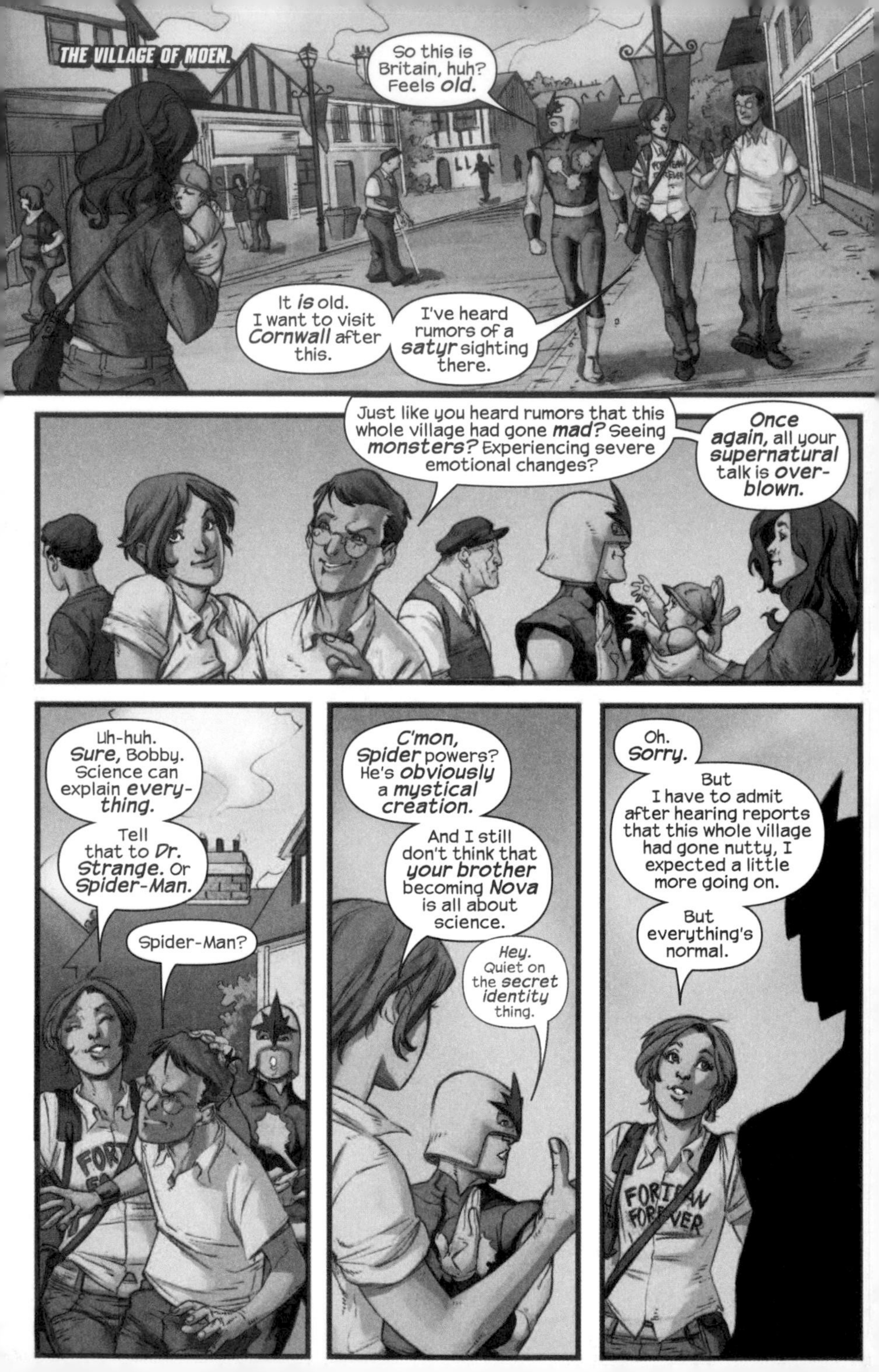
THE VILLAGE OF MOEN.
So this is Britain, huh? Feels old.
It is old. I want to visit Cornwall after this.
I've heard rumors of a satyr sighting there.
Just like you heard rumors that this whole village had gone mad? Seeing monsters? Experiencing severe emotional changes?
Once again, all your supernatural talk is over-blown.
Uh-huh. Sure, Bobby. Science can explain every-thing.
Tell that to Dr. Strange. Or Spider-Man.
Spider-Man?
C'mon, Spider powers? He's obviously a mystical creation.
And I still don't think that your brother becoming Nova is all about science.
Hey. Quiet on the secret identity thing.
Oh. Sorry.
But I have to admit after hearing reports that this whole village had gone nutty, I expected a little more going on.
But everything's normal.
FORTEAN FOREVER

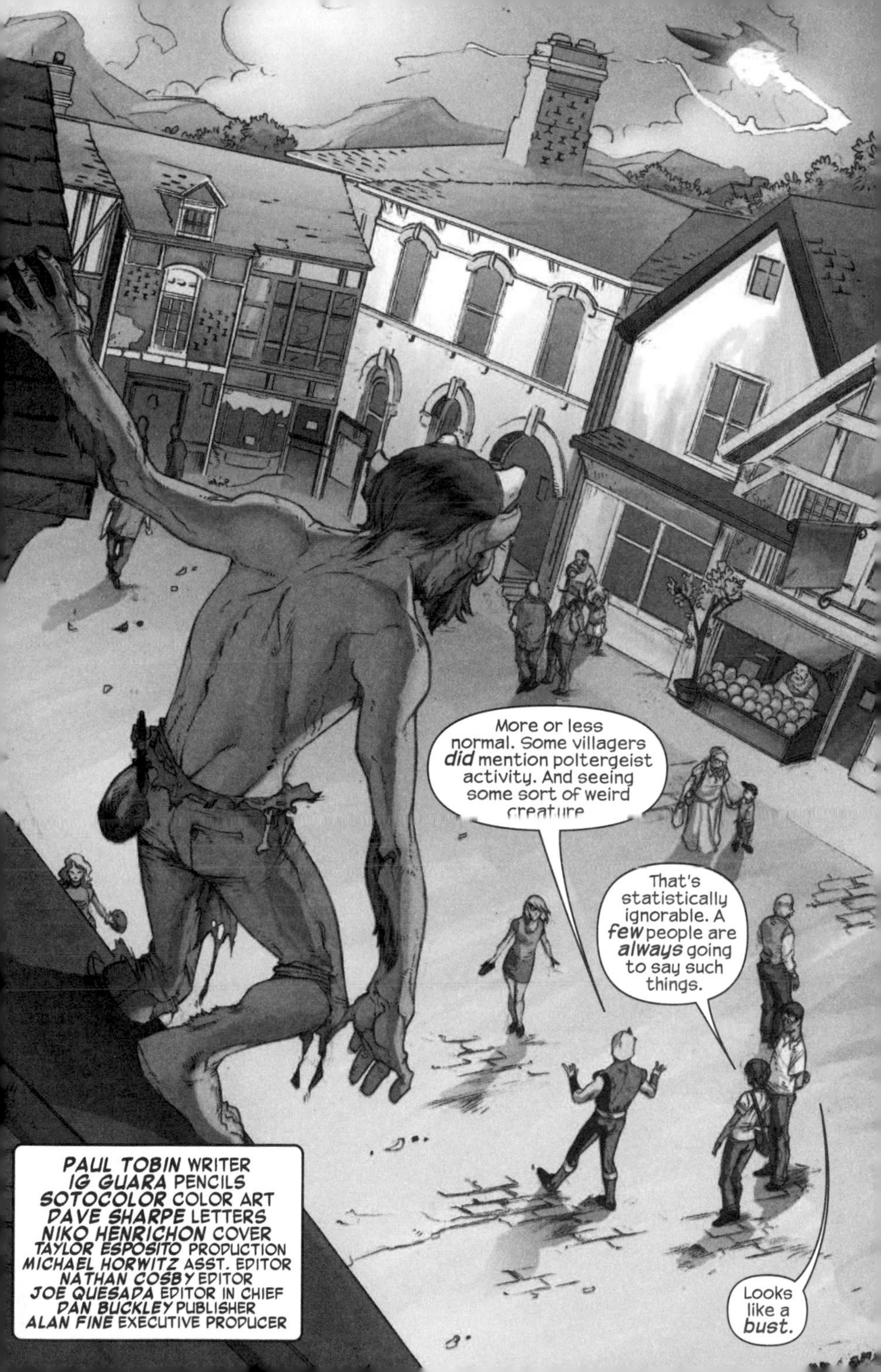
More or less normal. Some villagers did mention poltergeist activity. And seeing some sort of weird creature
That's statistically ignorable. A few people are always going to say such things.
Looks like a bust.
PAUL TOBIN WRITER
IG GUARA PENCILS
SOTOCOLOR COLOR ART
DAVE SHARPE LETTERS
NIKO HENRICHON COVER
TAYLOR ESPOSITO PRODUCTION
MICHAEL HORWITZ ASST. EDITOR
NATHAN COSBY EDITOR
JOE QUESADA EDITOR IN CHIEF
DAN BUCKLEY PUBLISHER
ALAN FINE EXECUTIVE PRODUCER

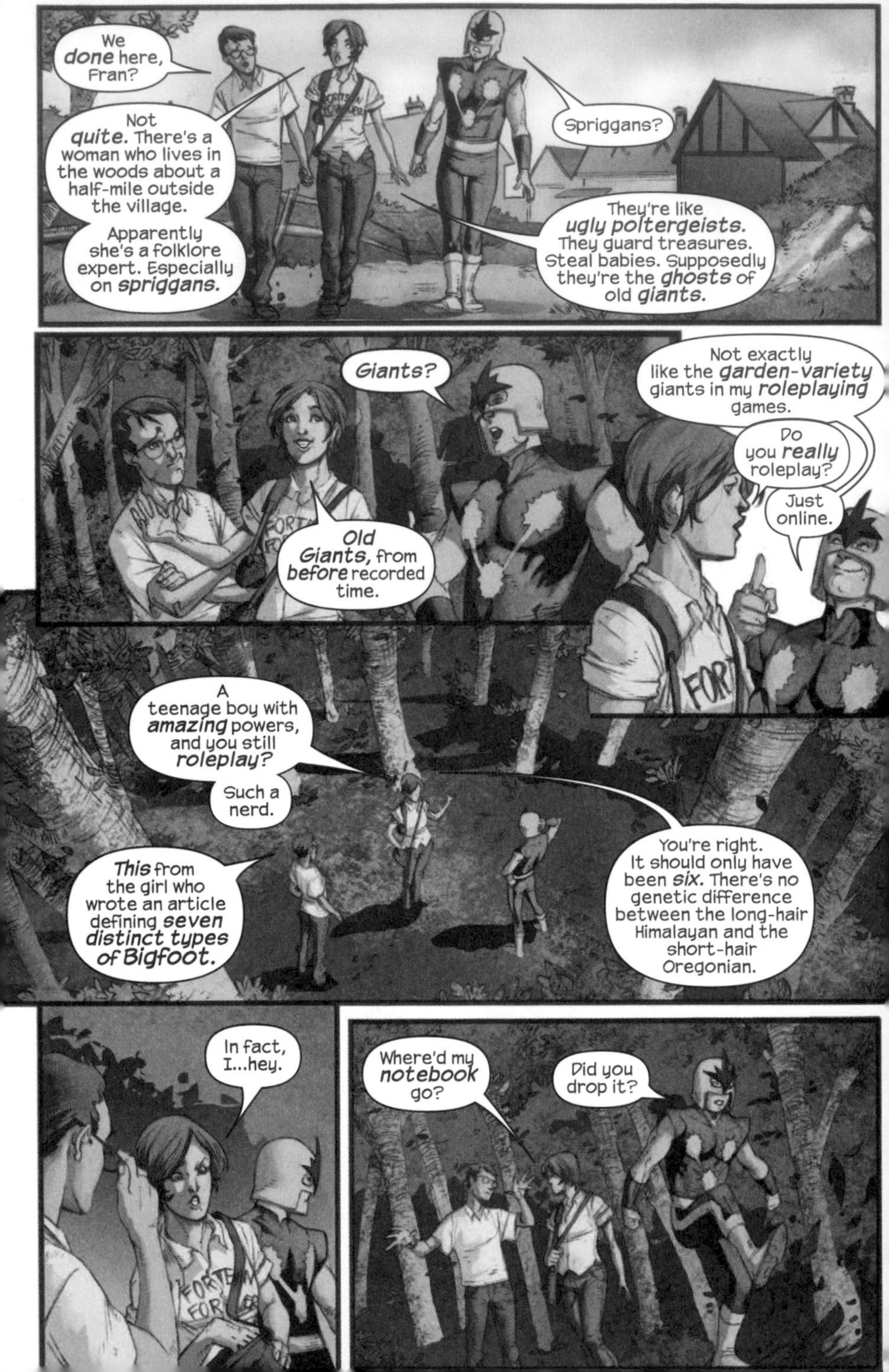
We done here, Fran?
Not quite. There's a woman who lives in the woods about a half-mile outside the village.
Apparently she's a folklore expert. Especially on spriggans.
Spriggans?
They're like ugly poltergeists. They guard treasures. Steal babies. Supposedly they're the ghosts of old giants.
Giants?
Old Giants, from before recorded time.
Not exactly like the garden-variety giants in my roleplaying games.
Do you really roleplay?
Just online.
A teenage boy with amazing powers, and you still roleplay?
Such a nerd.
This from the girl who wrote an article defining seven distinct types of Bigfoot.
You're right. It should only have been six. There's no genetic difference between the long-hair Himalayan and the short-hair Oregonian.
In fact, I...hey.
Where'd my notebook go?
Did you drop it?

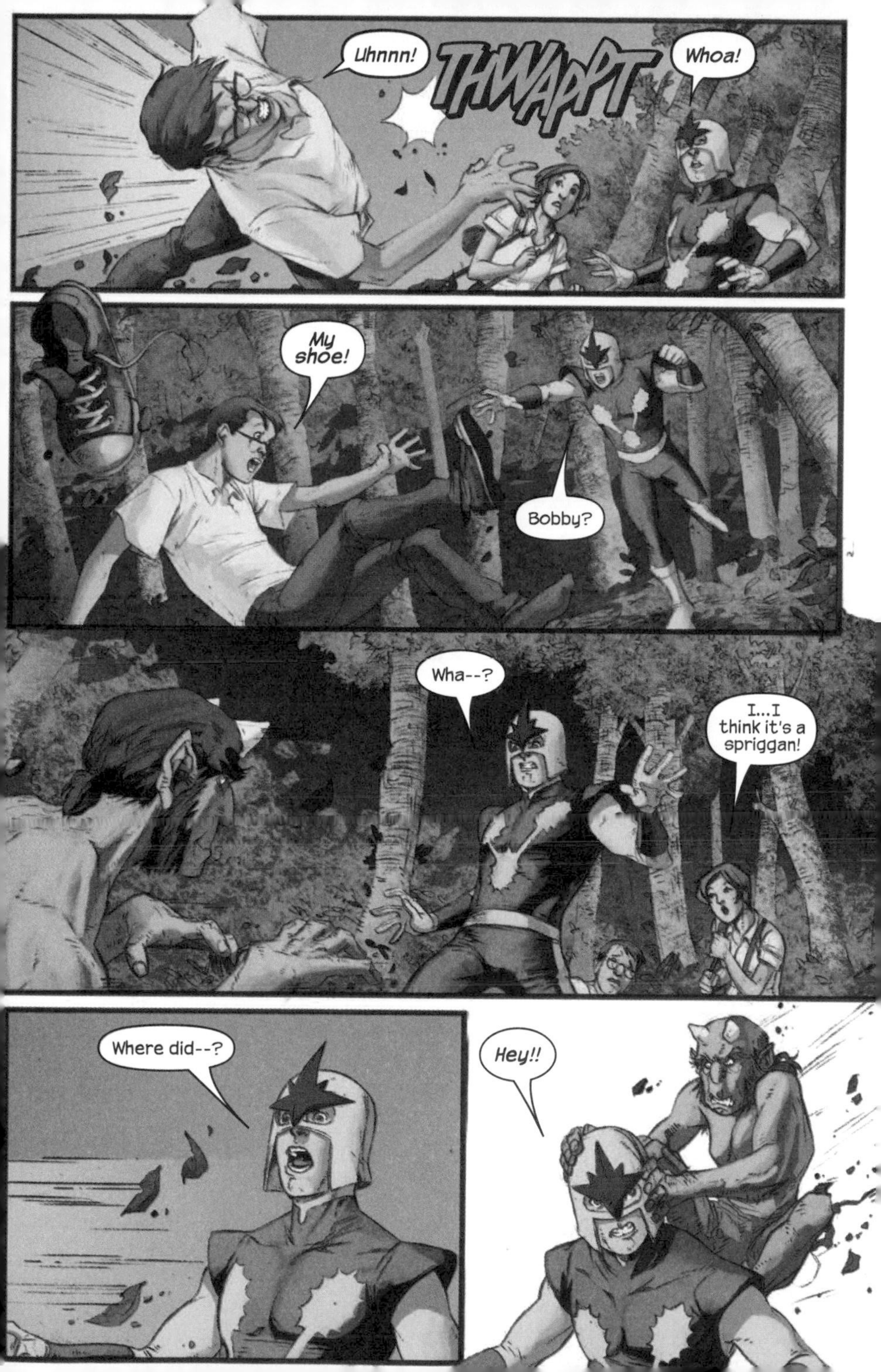
Uhnnn!
THWAPPT
Whoa!
My shoe!
Bobby?
Wha--?
I...I think it's a spriggan!
Where did--?
Hey!!

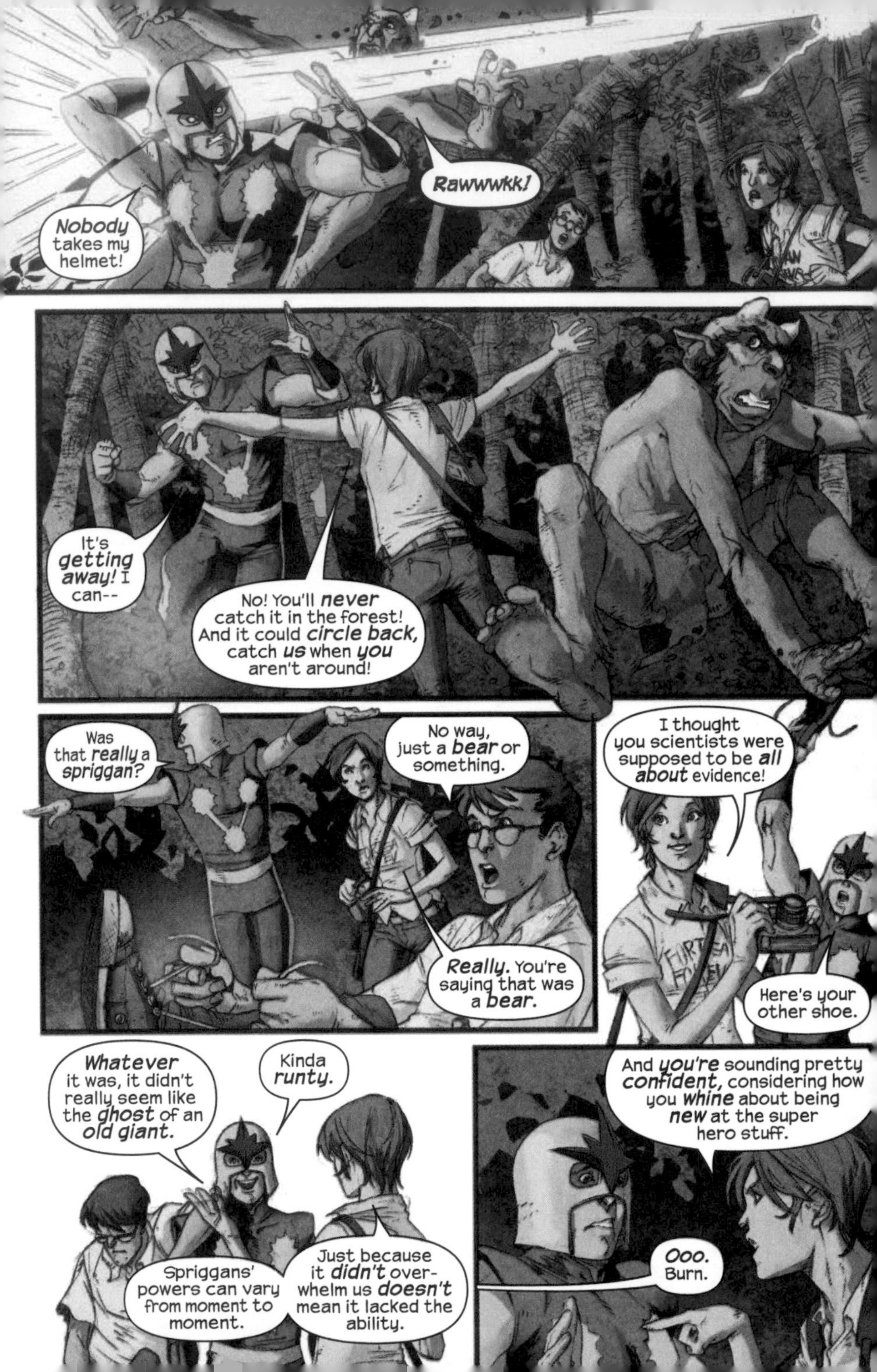

Nobody takes my helmet!
Rawwwkk!
It's getting away! I can--
No! You'll never catch it in the forest! And it could circle back, catch us when you aren't around!
Was that really a spriggan?
No way, just a bear or something.
Really. You're saying that was a bear.
I thought you scientists were supposed to be all about evidence!
Here's your other shoe.
Whatever it was, it didn't really seem like the ghost of an old giant.
Kinda runty.
Spriggans' powers can vary from moment to moment.
Just because it didn't over-whelm us doesn't mean it lacked the ability.
And you're sounding pretty confident, considering how you whine about being new at the super hero stuff.
Ooo. Burn.

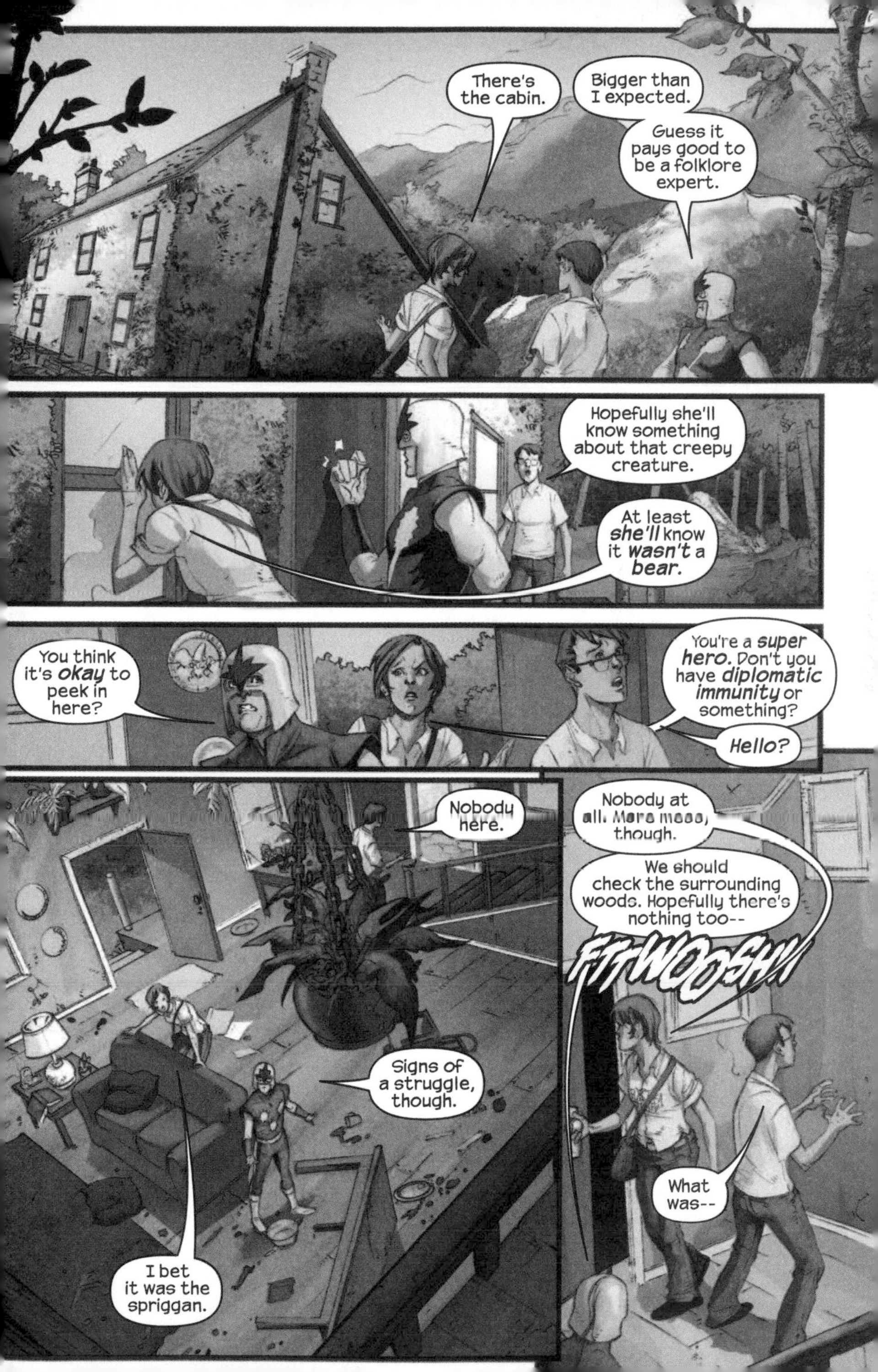
There's the cabin.
Bigger than I expected.
Guess it pays good to be a folklore expert.
Hopefully she'll know something about that creepy creature.
At least *she'll* know it *wasn't* a *bear.*
You think it's *okay* to peek in here?
You're a *super hero.* Don't you have *diplomatic immunity* or something?
Hello?
Nobody here.
Signs of a struggle, though.
I bet it was the spriggan.
Nobody at all. More mess, though.
We should check the surrounding woods. Hopefully there's nothing too--
FTTWOOSH!!
What was--

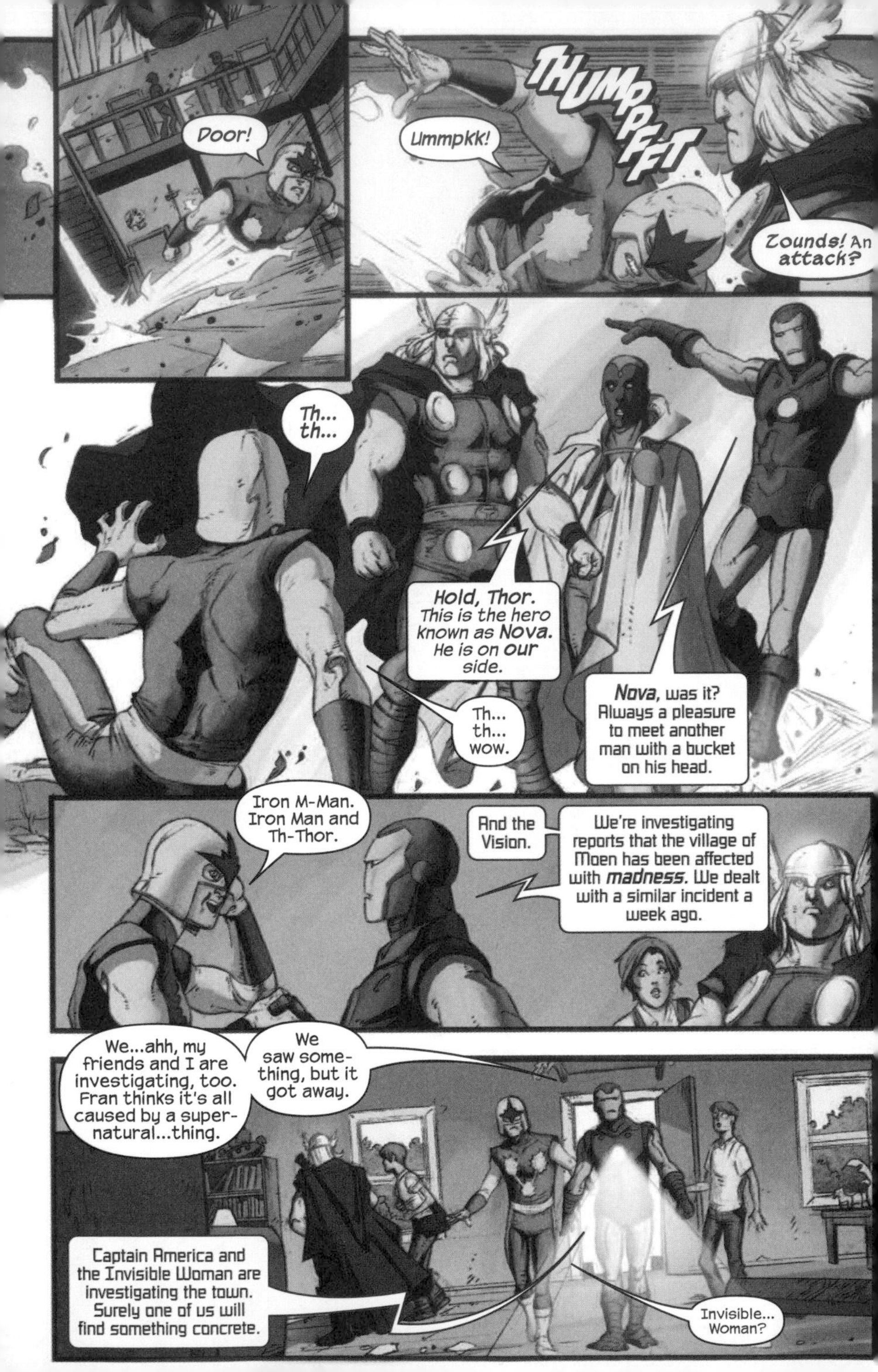

Door!
Ummpkk!
THUMPFFT
Zounds! An attack?
Th... th...
Hold, Thor. This is the hero known as Nova. He is on our side.
Th... th... wow.
Nova, was it? Always a pleasure to meet another man with a bucket on his head.
Iron M-Man. Iron Man and Th-Thor.
And the Vision.
We're investigating reports that the village of Moen has been affected with madness. We dealt with a similar incident a week ago.
We...ahh, my friends and I are investigating, too. Fran thinks it's all caused by a super-natural...thing.
We saw some-thing, but it got away.
Captain America and the Invisible Woman are investigating the town. Surely one of us will find something concrete.
Invisible... Woman?

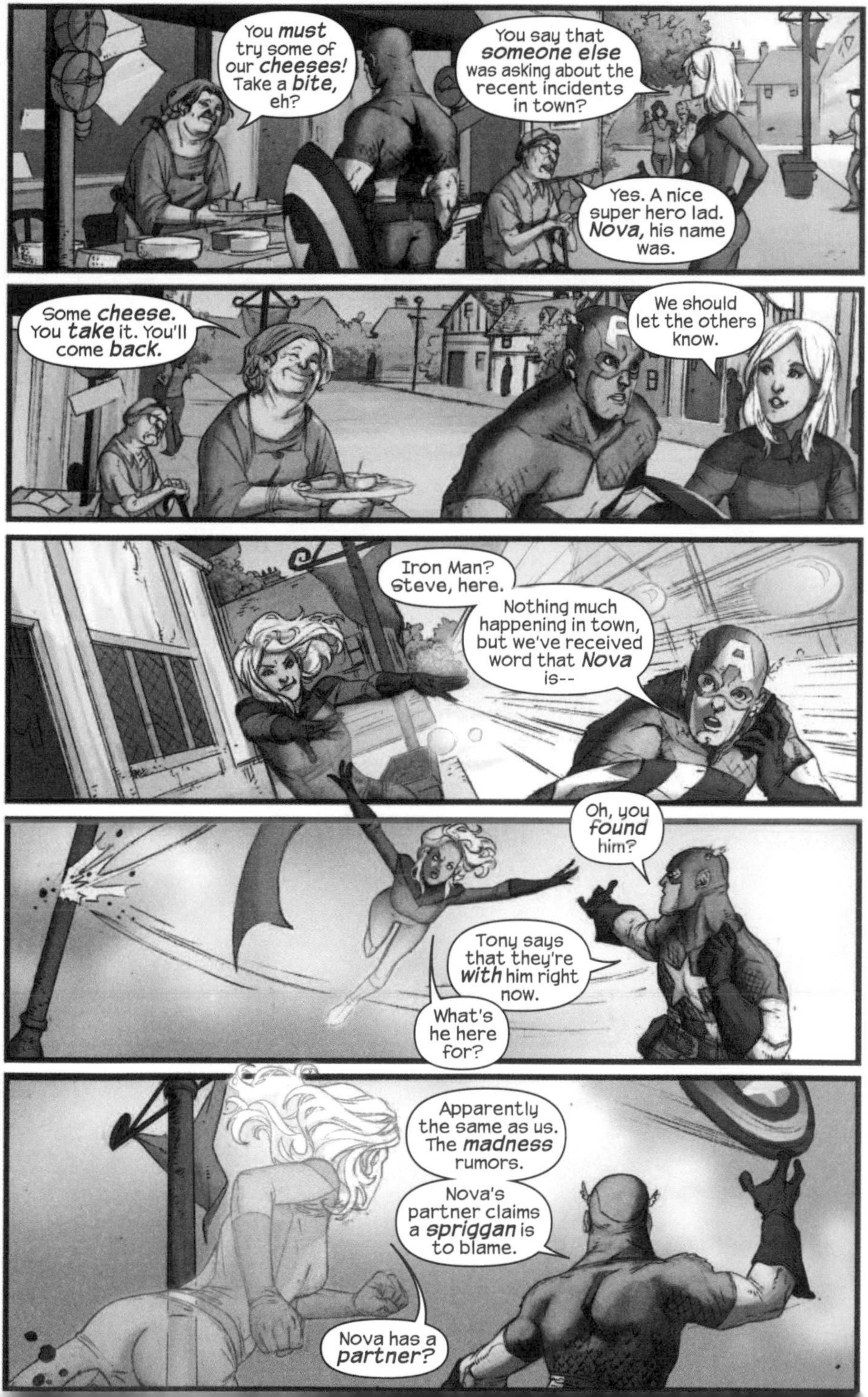
You *must* try some of our *cheeses!* Take a *bite,* eh?
You say that *someone else* was asking about the recent incidents in town?
Yes. A nice super hero lad. *Nova,* his name was.
Some *cheese.* You *take* it. You'll come *back.*
We should let the others know.
Iron Man? Steve, here.
Nothing much happening in town, but we've received word that *Nova* is--
Oh, you *found* him?
Tony says that they're *with* him right now.
What's he here for?
Apparently the same as us. The *madness* rumors.
Nova's partner claims a *spriggan* is to blame.
Nova has a *partner?*

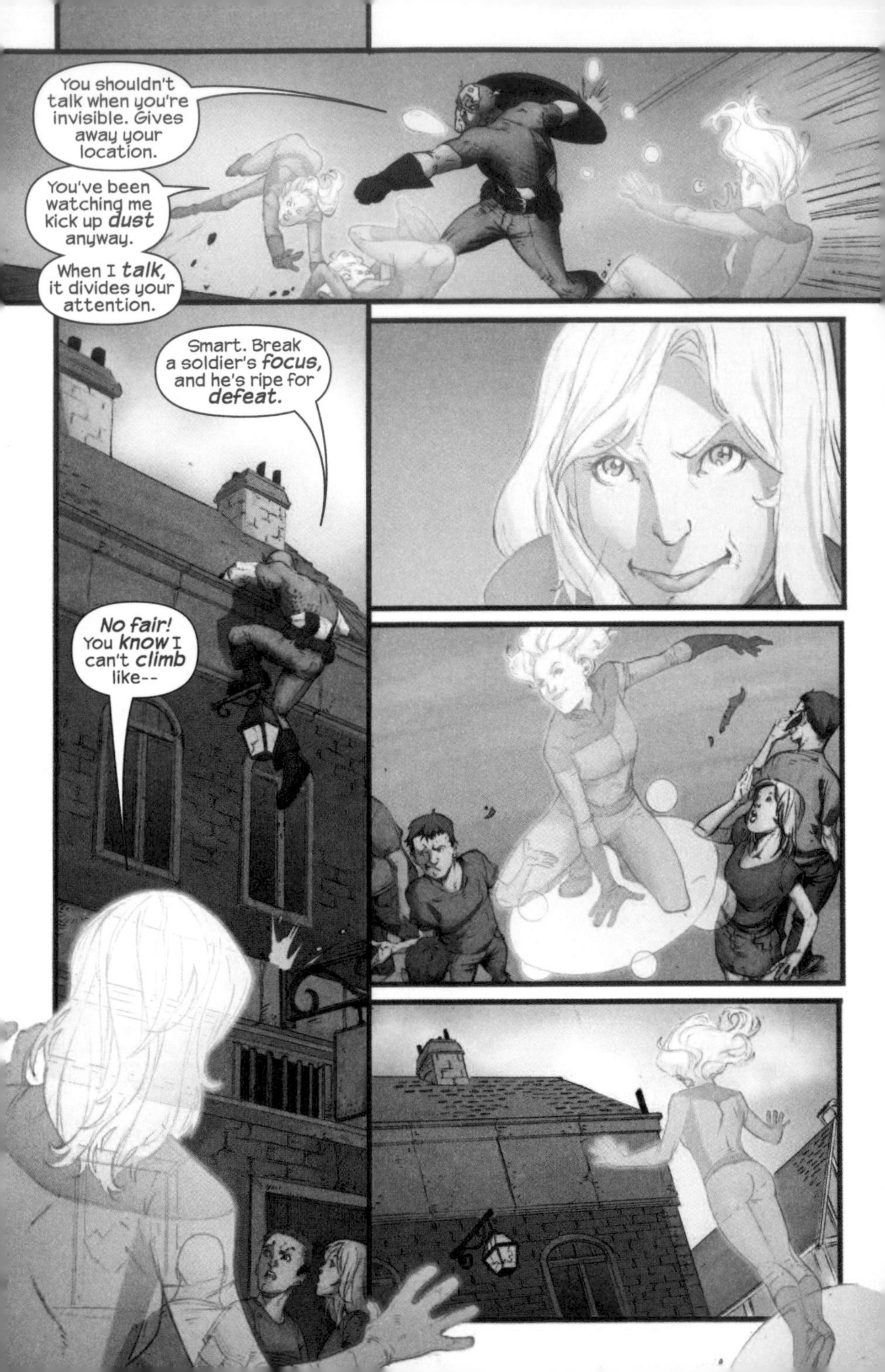
You shouldn't talk when you're invisible. Gives away your location.
You've been watching me kick up dust anyway.
When I talk, it divides your attention.
Smart. Break a soldier's focus, and he's ripe for defeat.
No fair! You know I can't climb like--

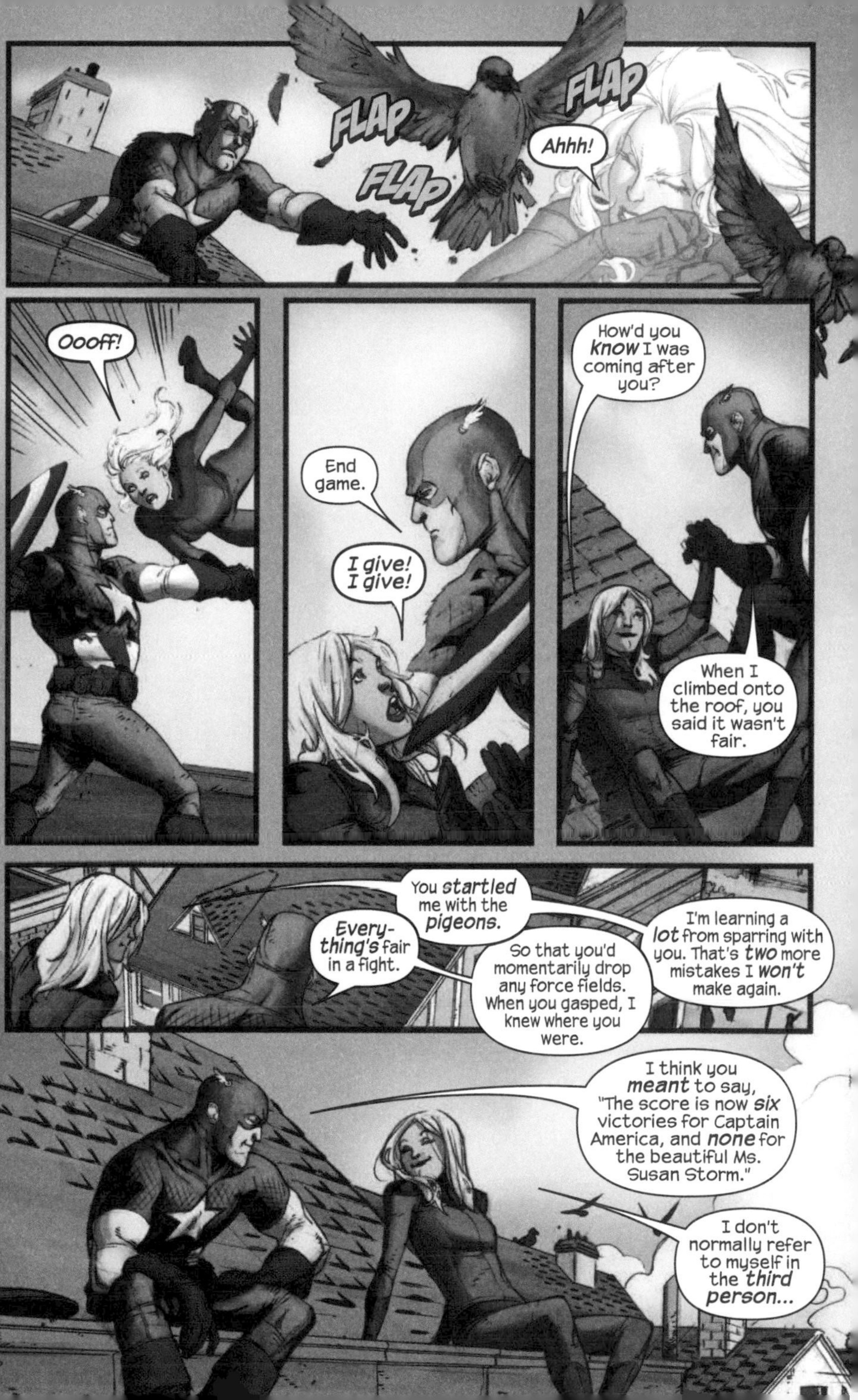
FLAP
FLAP
FLAP
Ahhh!
Oooff!
End game.
I give! I give!
How'd you know I was coming after you?
When I climbed onto the roof, you said it wasn't fair.
You startled me with the pigeons.
Every-thing's fair in a fight.
So that you'd momentarily drop any force fields. When you gasped, I knew where you were.
I'm learning a lot from sparring with you. That's two more mistakes I won't make again.
I think you meant to say, "The score is now six victories for Captain America, and none for the beautiful Ms. Susan Storm."
I don't normally refer to myself in the third person...

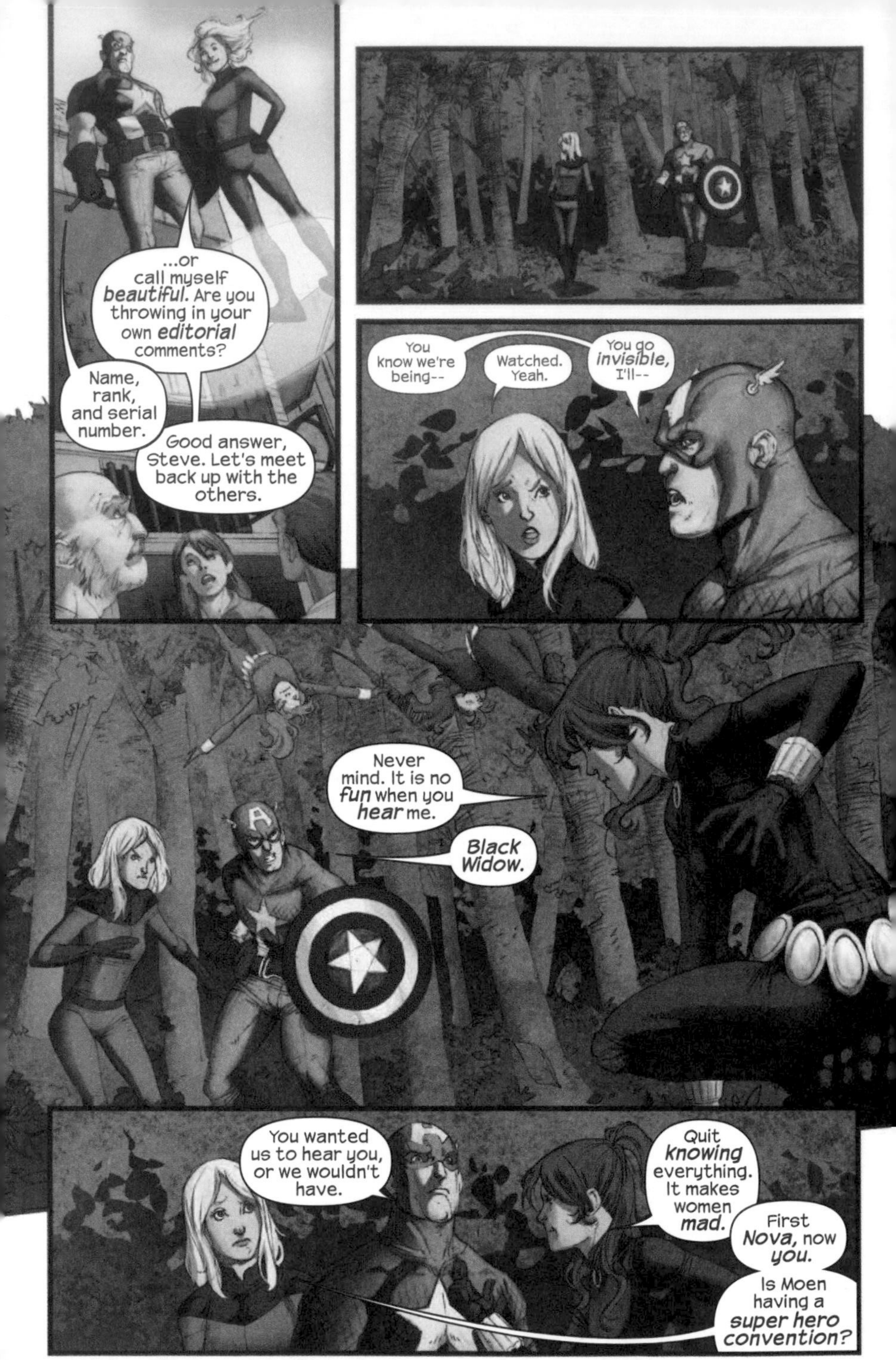
...or call myself beautiful. Are you throwing in your own editorial comments?
Name, rank, and serial number.
Good answer, Steve. Let's meet back up with the others.
You know we're being--
Watched. Yeah.
You go invisible, I'll--
Never mind. It is no fun when you hear me.
Black Widow.
You wanted us to hear you, or we wouldn't have.
Quit knowing everything. It makes women mad.
First Nova, now you.
Is Moen having a super hero convention?

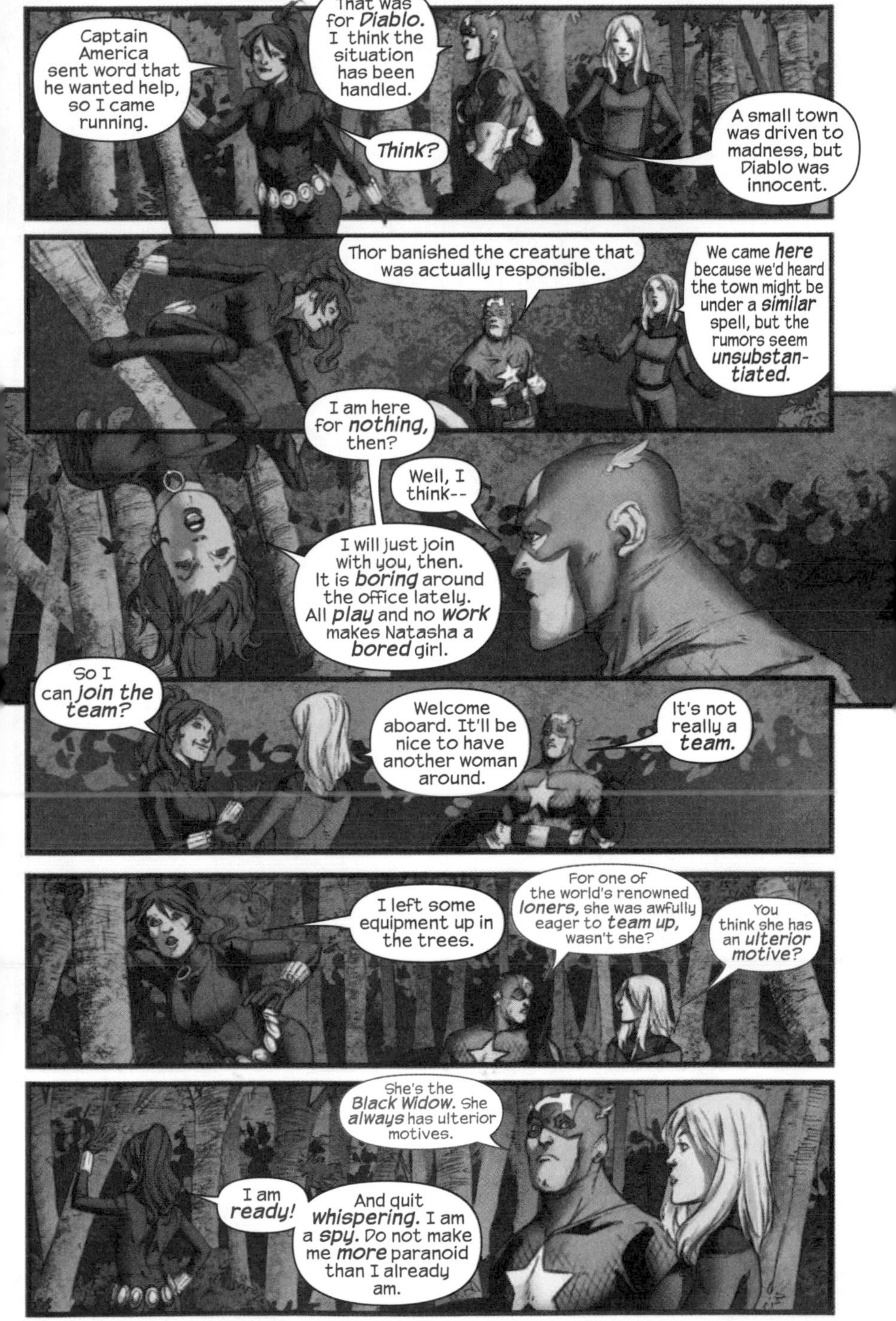

Captain America sent word that he wanted help, so I came running.
That was for Diablo. I think the situation has been handled.
Think?
A small town was driven to madness, but Diablo was innocent.
Thor banished the creature that was actually responsible.
We came here because we'd heard the town might be under a similar spell, but the rumors seem unsubstantiated.
I am here for nothing, then?
Well, I think--
I will just join with you, then. It is boring around the office lately. All play and no work makes Natasha a bored girl.
So I can join the team?
Welcome aboard. It'll be nice to have another woman around.
It's not really a team.
I left some equipment up in the trees.
For one of the world's renowned loners, she was awfully eager to team up, wasn't she?
You think she has an ulterior motive?
She's the Black Widow. She always has ulterior motives.
I am ready!
And quit whispering. I am a spy. Do not make me more paranoid than I already am.

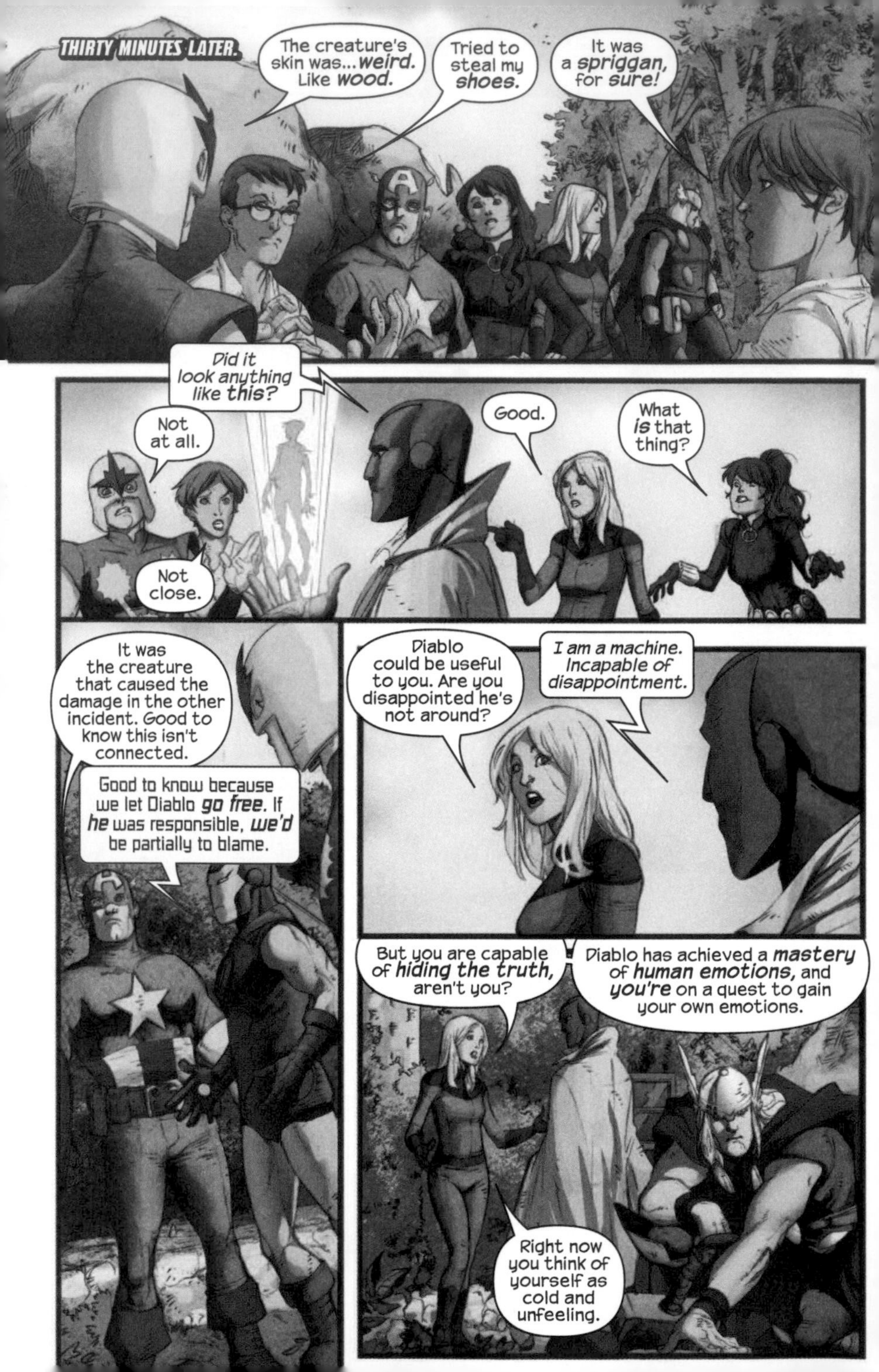
THIRTY MINUTES LATER.
The creature's skin was...weird. Like wood.
Tried to steal my shoes.
It was a spriggan, for sure!
Did it look anything like this?
Not at all.
Not close.
Good.
What is that thing?
It was the creature that caused the damage in the other incident. Good to know this isn't connected.
Good to know because we let Diablo go free. If he was responsible, we'd be partially to blame.
Diablo could be useful to you. Are you disappointed he's not around?
I am a machine. Incapable of disappointment.
But you are capable of hiding the truth, aren't you?
Diablo has achieved a mastery of human emotions, and you're on a quest to gain your own emotions.
Right now you think of yourself as cold and unfeeling.

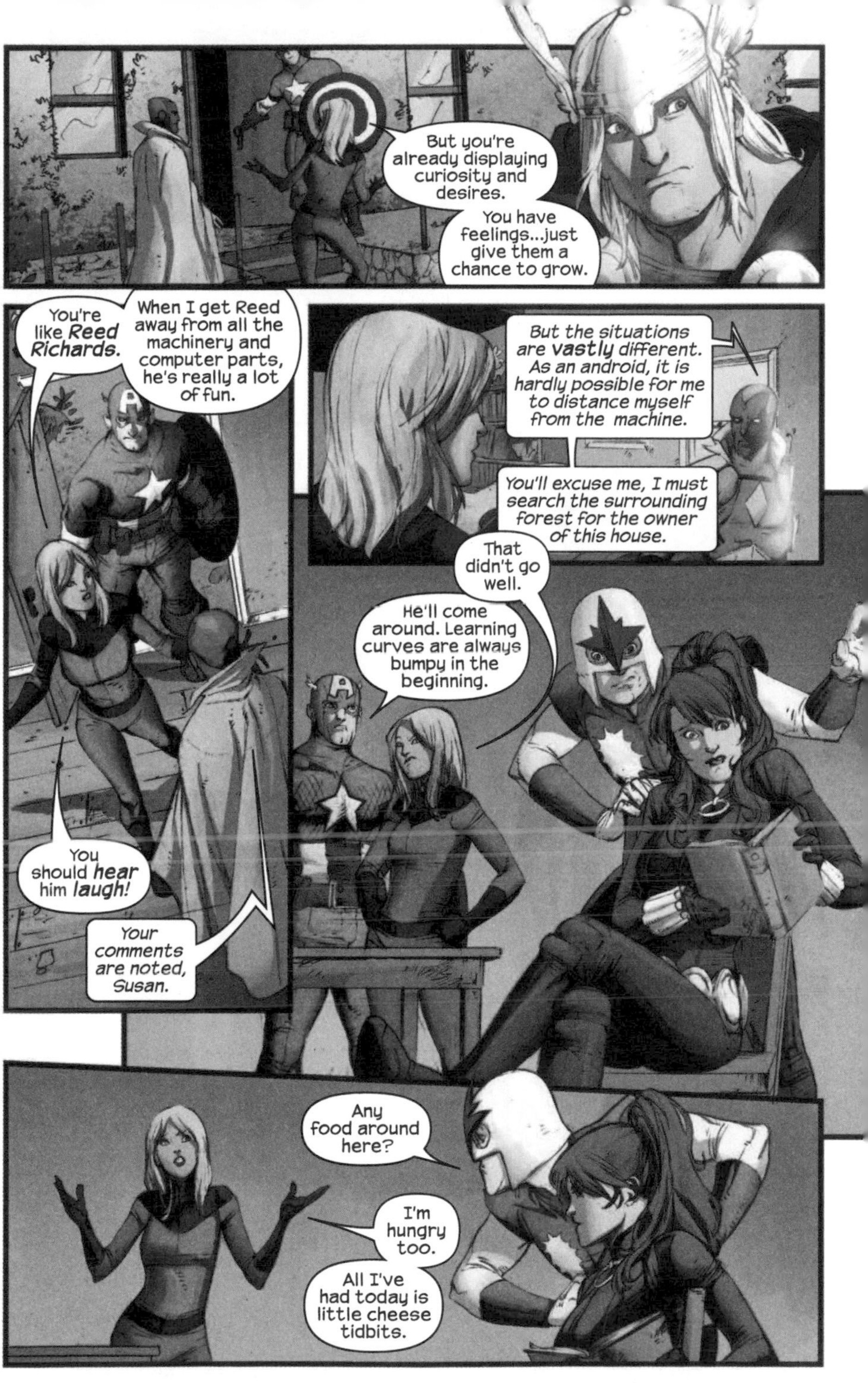

But you're already displaying curiosity and desires.
You have feelings...just give them a chance to grow.
You're like Reed Richards.
When I get Reed away from all the machinery and computer parts, he's really a lot of fun.
You should hear him laugh!
Your comments are noted, Susan.
But the situations are vastly different. As an android, it is hardly possible for me to distance myself from the machine.
You'll excuse me, I must search the surrounding forest for the owner of this house.
That didn't go well.
He'll come around. Learning curves are always bumpy in the beginning.
Any food around here?
I'm hungry too.
All I've had today is little cheese tidbits.

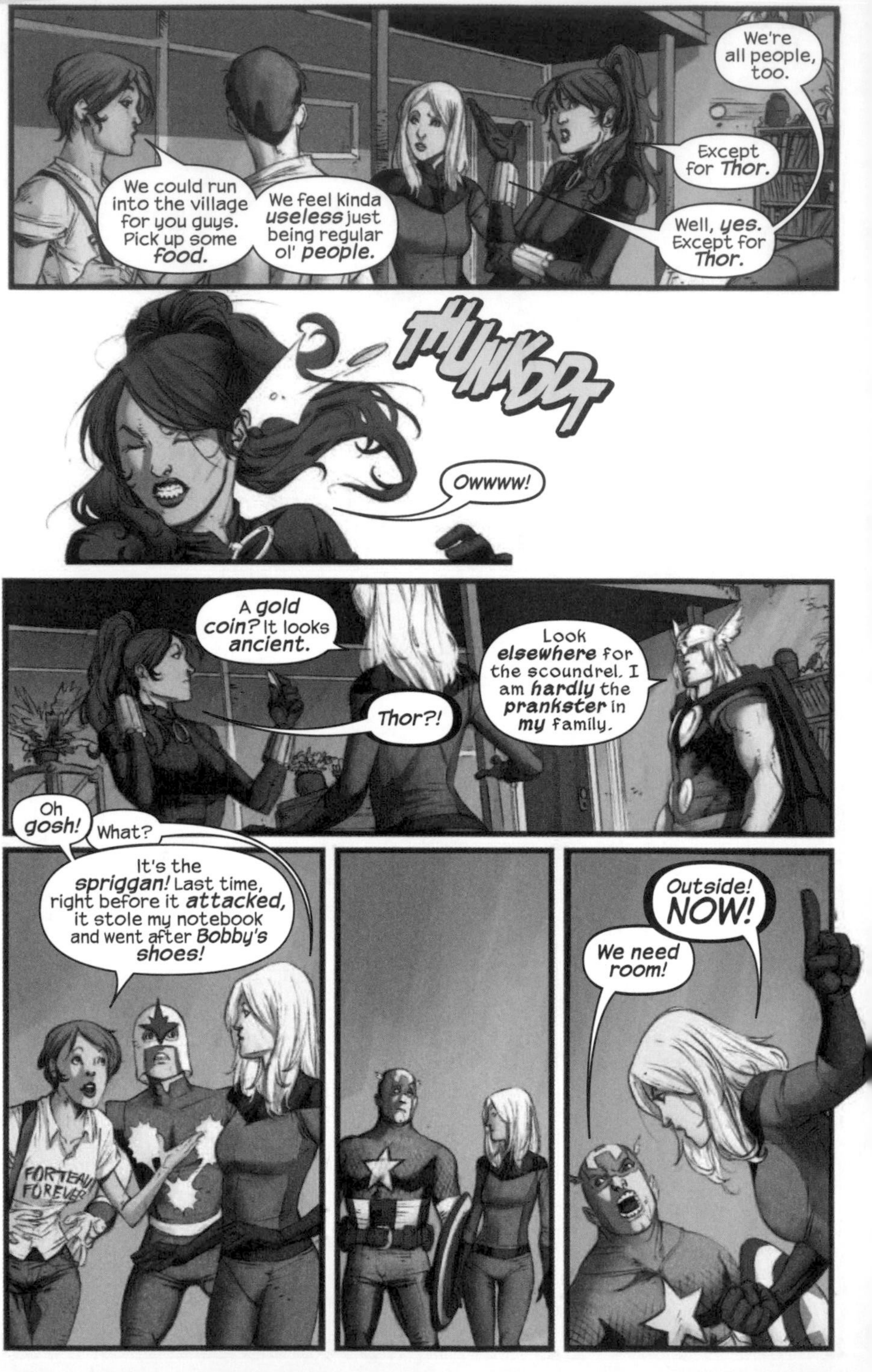

We could run into the village for you guys. Pick up some food.
We feel kinda useless just being regular ol' people.
We're all people, too.
Except for Thor.
Well, yes. Except for Thor.
THUNKDOT
Owwww!
A gold coin? It looks ancient.
Thor?!
Look elsewhere for the scoundrel. I am hardly the prankster in my family.
Oh gosh!
What?
It's the spriggan! Last time, right before it attacked, it stole my notebook and went after Bobby's shoes!
FORTEAN FOREVER
Outside! NOW!
We need room!

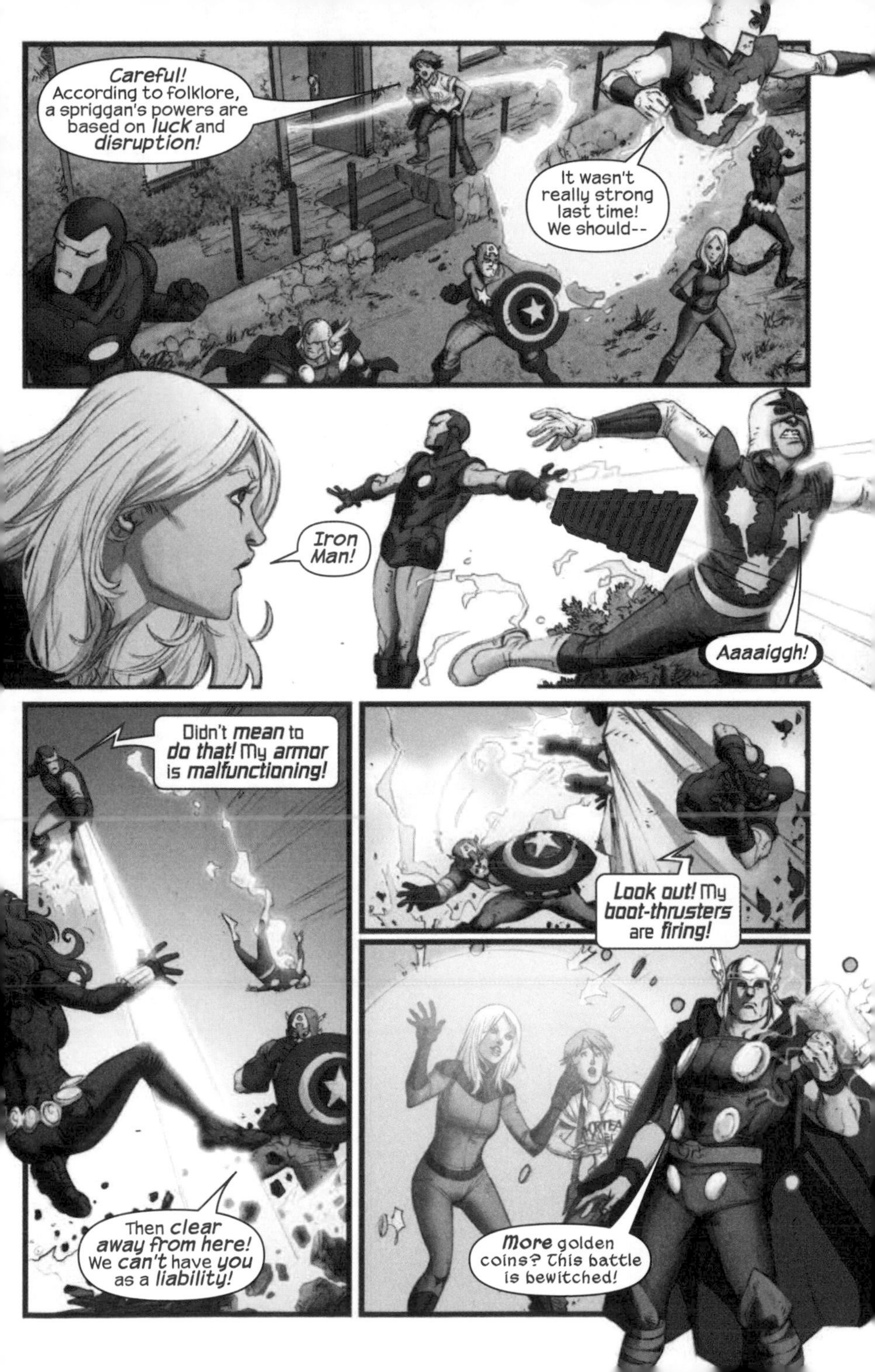

Careful! According to folklore, a spriggan's powers are based on luck and disruption!
It wasn't really strong last time! We should--
Iron Man!
Aaaaiggh!
Didn't mean to do that! My armor is malfunctioning!
Then clear away from here! We can't have you as a liability!
Look out! My boot-thrusters are firing!
More golden coins? This battle is bewitched!

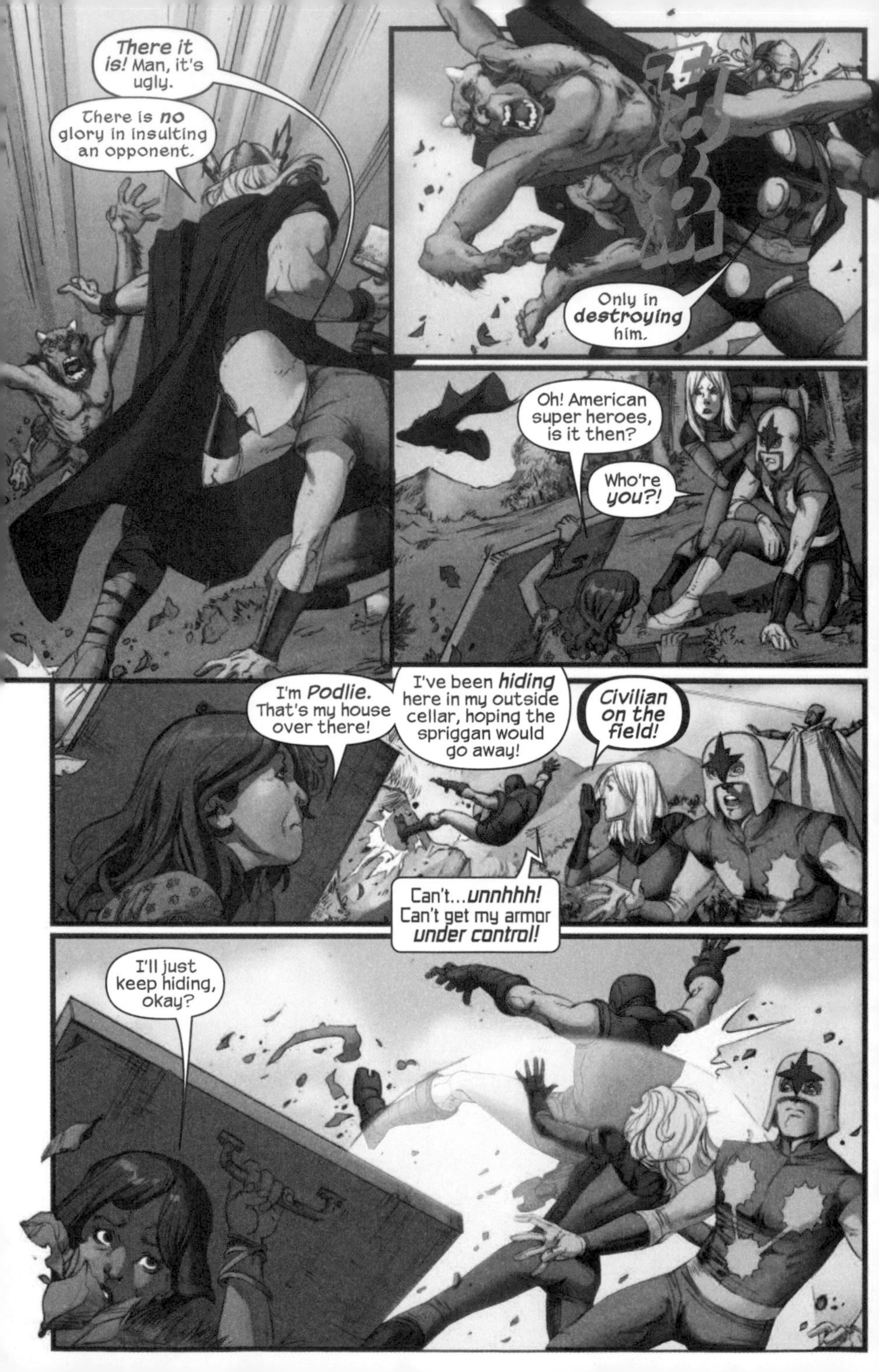
There it is! Man, it's ugly.
There is no glory in insulting an opponent.
Only in destroying him.
Oh! American super heroes, is it then?
Who're you?!
I'm Podlie. That's my house over there!
I've been hiding here in my outside cellar, hoping the spriggan would go away!
Civilian on the field!
Can't...unnhhh! Can't get my armor under control!
I'll just keep hiding, okay?

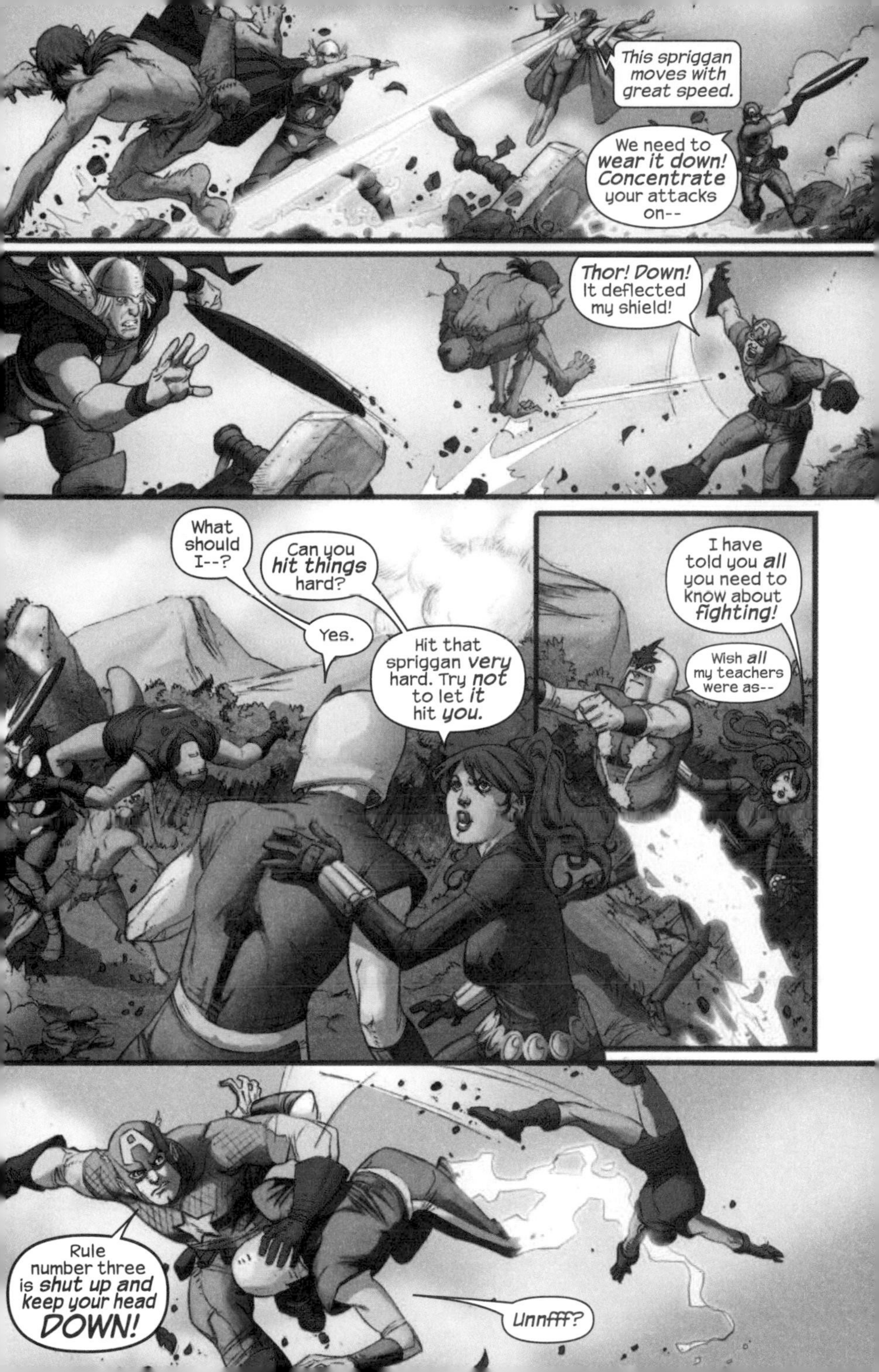
This spriggan moves with great speed.
We need to wear it down! Concentrate your attacks on--
Thor! Down! It deflected my shield!
What should I--?
Can you hit things hard?
Yes.
Hit that spriggan very hard. Try not to let it hit you.
I have told you all you need to know about fighting!
Wish all my teachers were as--
Rule number three is shut up and keep your head DOWN!
Unnfff?

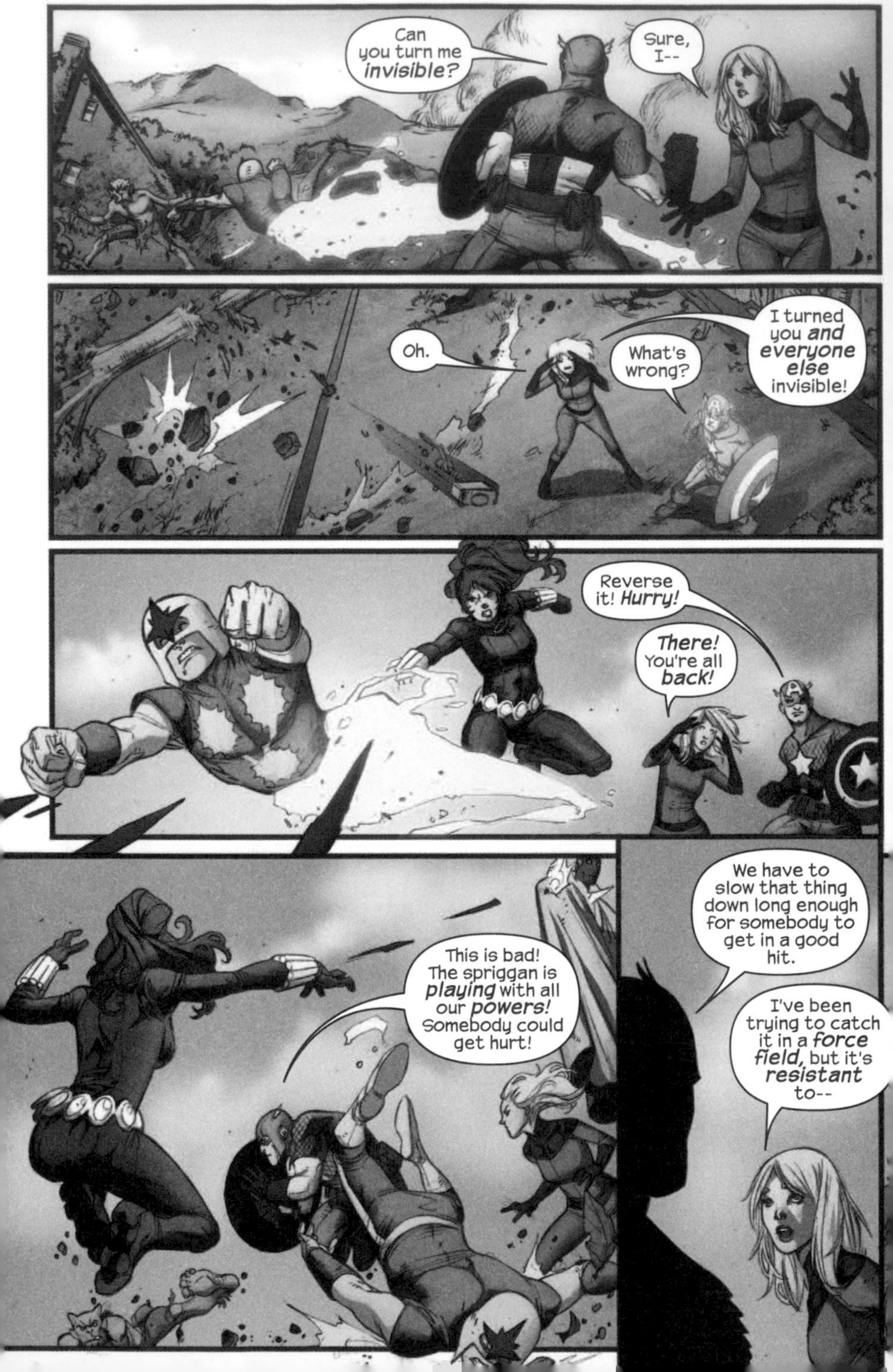
Can you turn me invisible?
Sure, I--
Oh.
What's wrong?
I turned you and everyone else invisible!
Reverse it! Hurry!
There! You're all back!
This is bad! The spriggan is playing with all our powers! Somebody could get hurt!
We have to slow that thing down long enough for somebody to get in a good hit.
I've been trying to catch it in a force field, but it's resistant to--

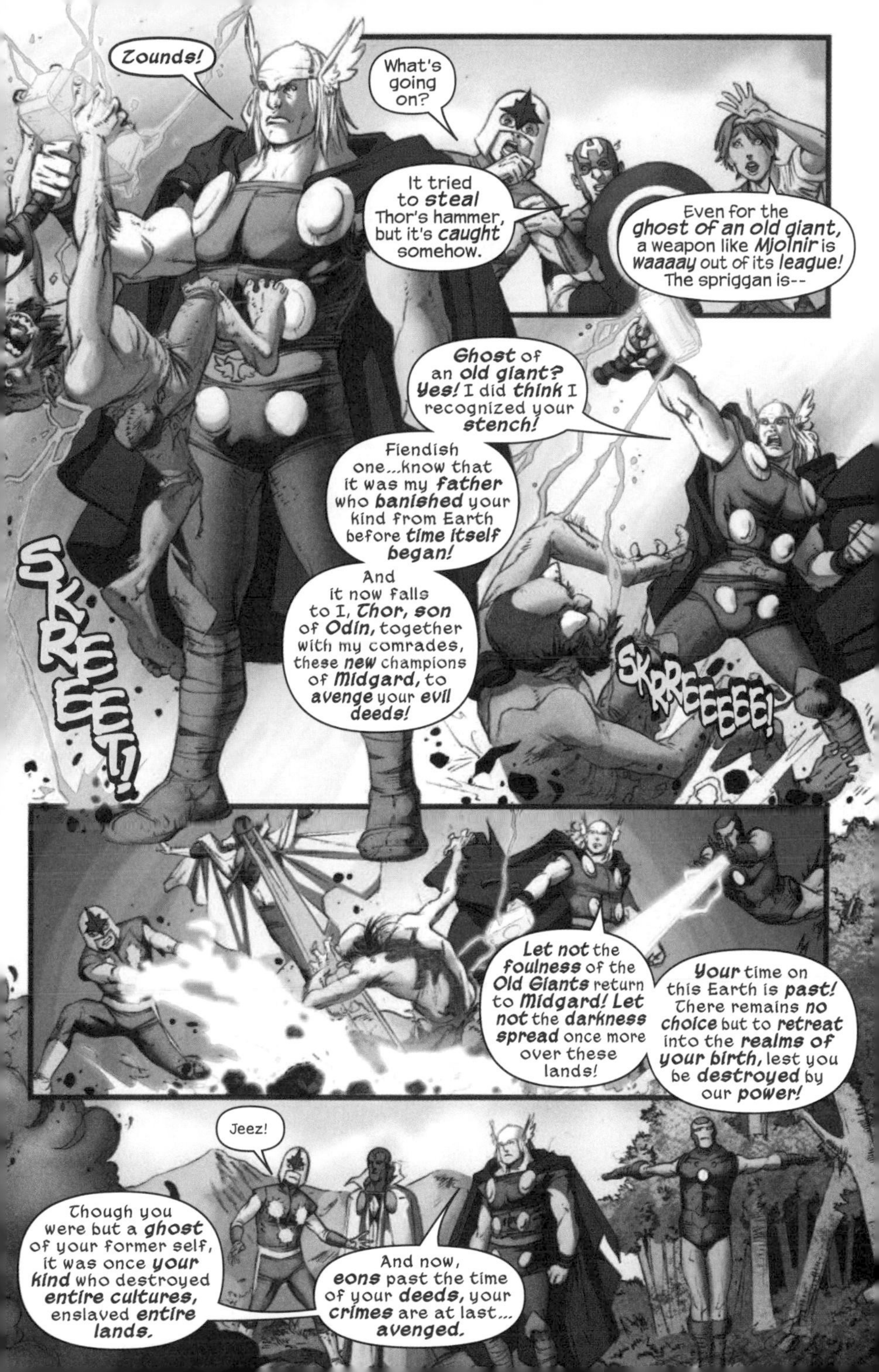
Zounds!
What's going on?
It tried to steal Thor's hammer, but it's caught somehow.
Even for the ghost of an old giant, a weapon like Mjolnir is waaaay out of its league! The spriggan is--
Ghost of an old giant? Yes! I did think I recognized your stench!
Fiendish one...know that it was my father who banished your kind from Earth before time itself began!
And it now falls to I, Thor, son of Odin, together with my comrades, these new champions of Midgard, to avenge your evil deeds!
SKREEEET!
SKRREEEEEE!
Let not the foulness of the Old Giants return to Midgard! Let not the darkness spread once more over these lands!
Your time on this Earth is past! There remains no choice but to retreat into the realms of your birth, lest you be destroyed by our power!
Jeez!
Though you were but a ghost of your former self, it was once your kind who destroyed entire cultures, enslaved entire lands.
And now, eons past the time of your deeds, your crimes are at last... avenged.

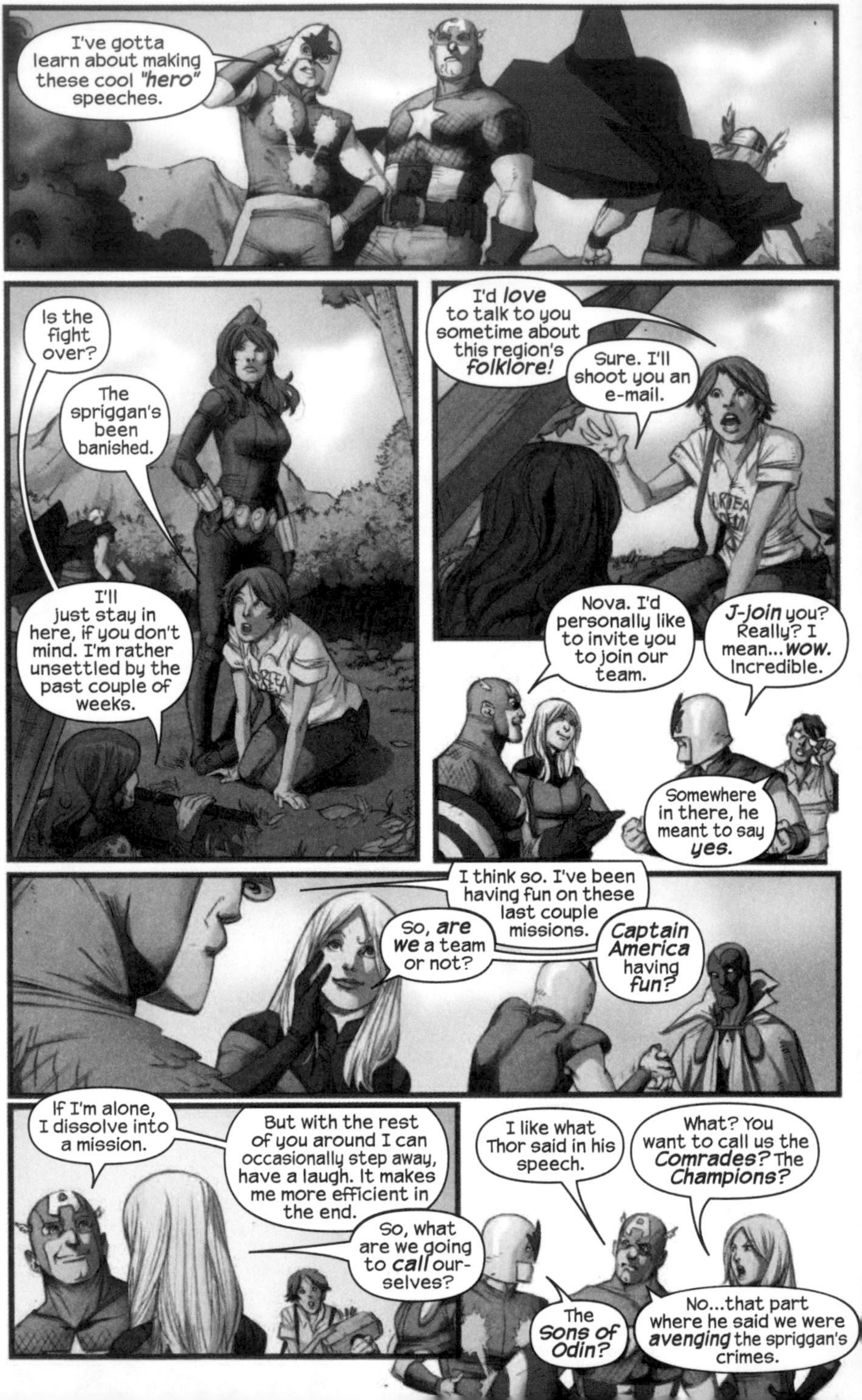
I've gotta learn about making these cool "hero" speeches.
Is the fight over?
The spriggan's been banished.
I'll just stay in here, if you don't mind. I'm rather unsettled by the past couple of weeks.
I'd love to talk to you sometime about this region's folklore!
Sure. I'll shoot you an e-mail.
Nova. I'd personally like to invite you to join our team.
J-join you? Really? I mean...WOW. Incredible.
Somewhere in there, he meant to say yes.
I think so. I've been having fun on these last couple missions.
So, are we a team or not?
Captain America having fun?
If I'm alone, I dissolve into a mission.
But with the rest of you around I can occasionally step away, have a laugh. It makes me more efficient in the end.
So, what are we going to call our-selves?
The Sons of Odin?
I like what Thor said in his speech.
What? You want to call us the Comrades? The Champions?
No...that part where he said we were avenging the spriggan's crimes.

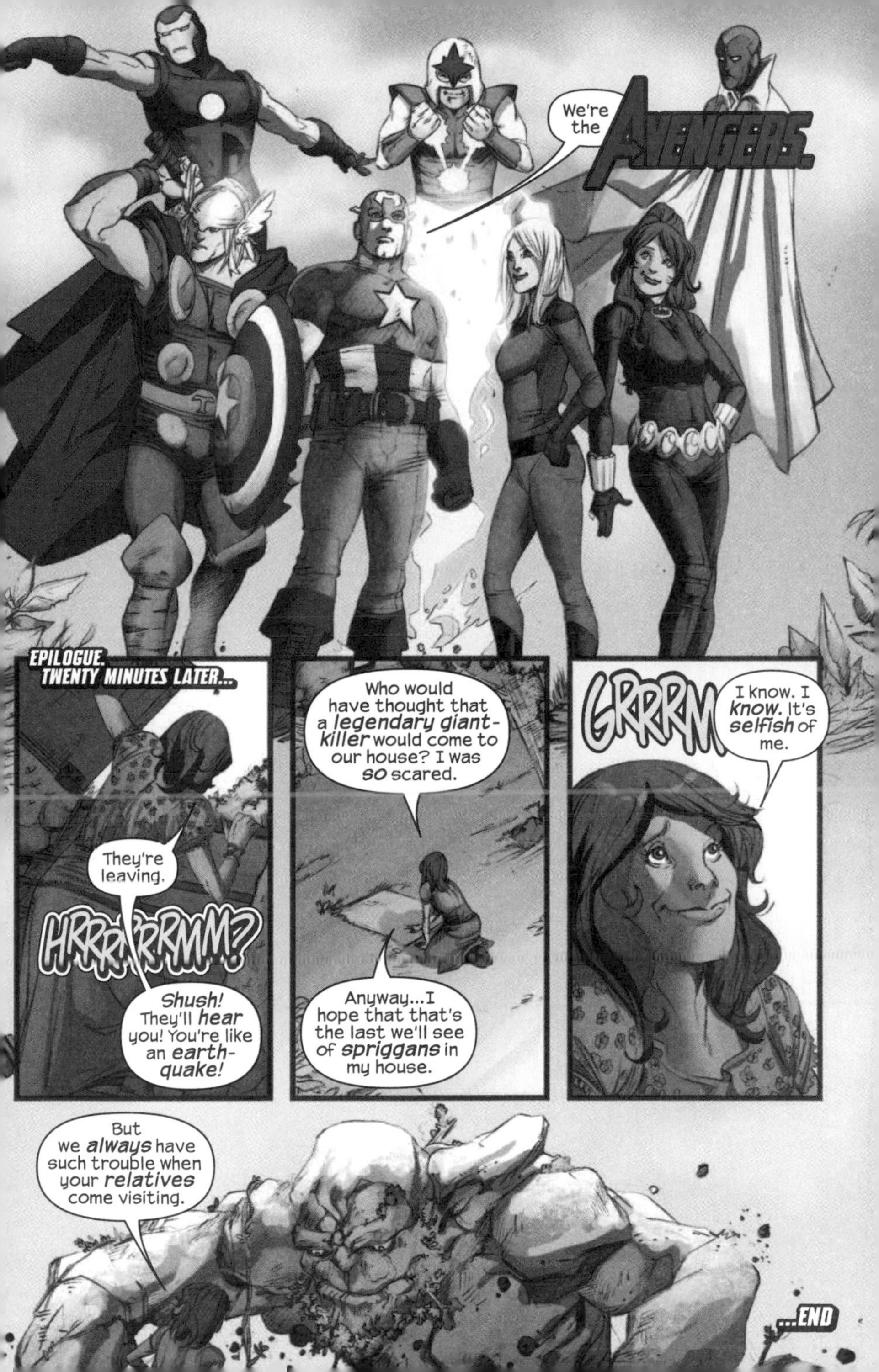

We're the AVENGERS.
EPILOGUE. TWENTY MINUTES LATER...
They're leaving.
HRRRRRRMM?
Shush! They'll hear you! You're like an earth-quake!
Who would have thought that a legendary giant-killer would come to our house? I was so scared.
Anyway...I hope that that's the last we'll see of spriggans in my house.
GRRRM
I know. I know. It's selfish of me.
But we always have such trouble when your relatives come visiting.
...END

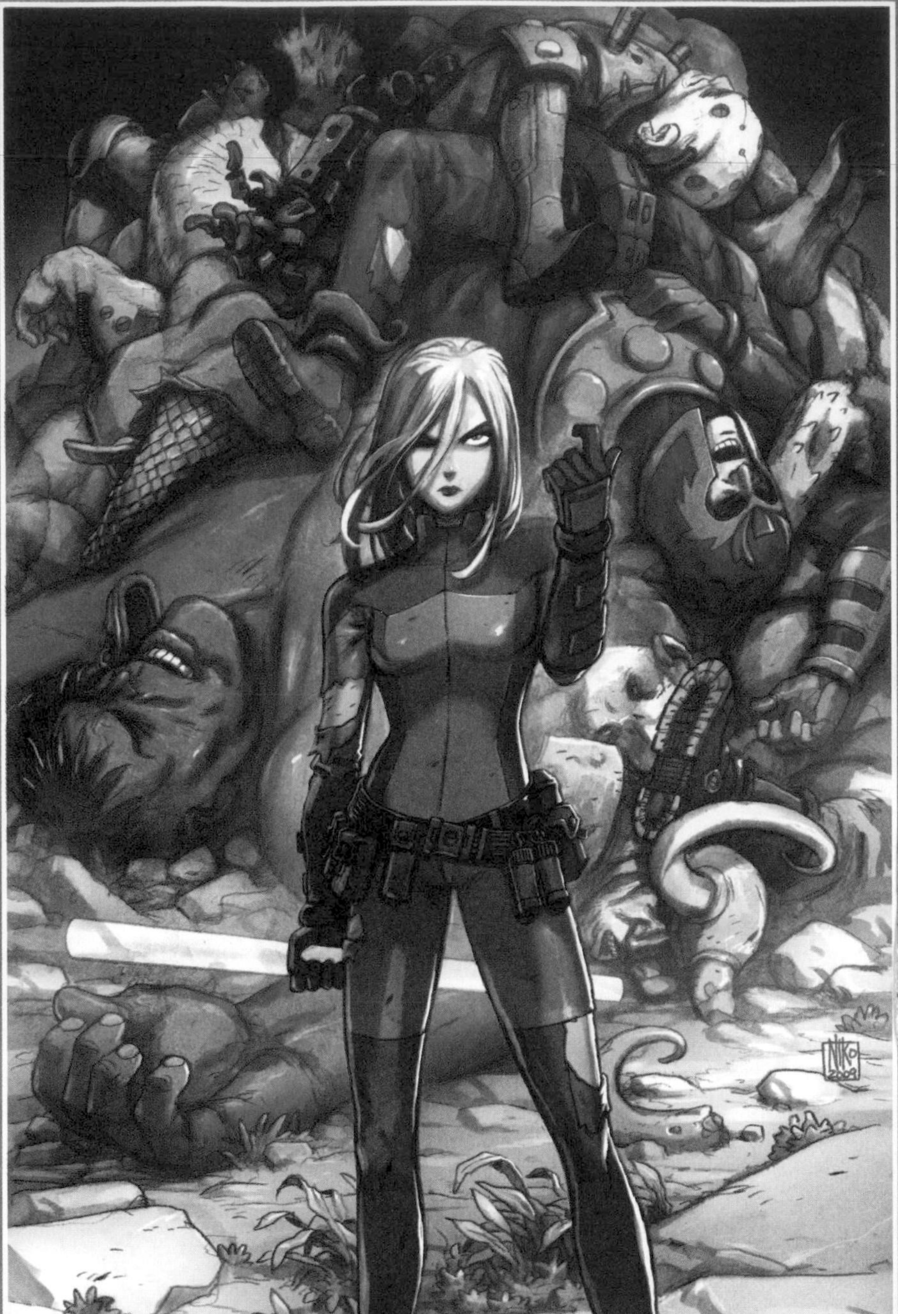
NIKO
2009

#19

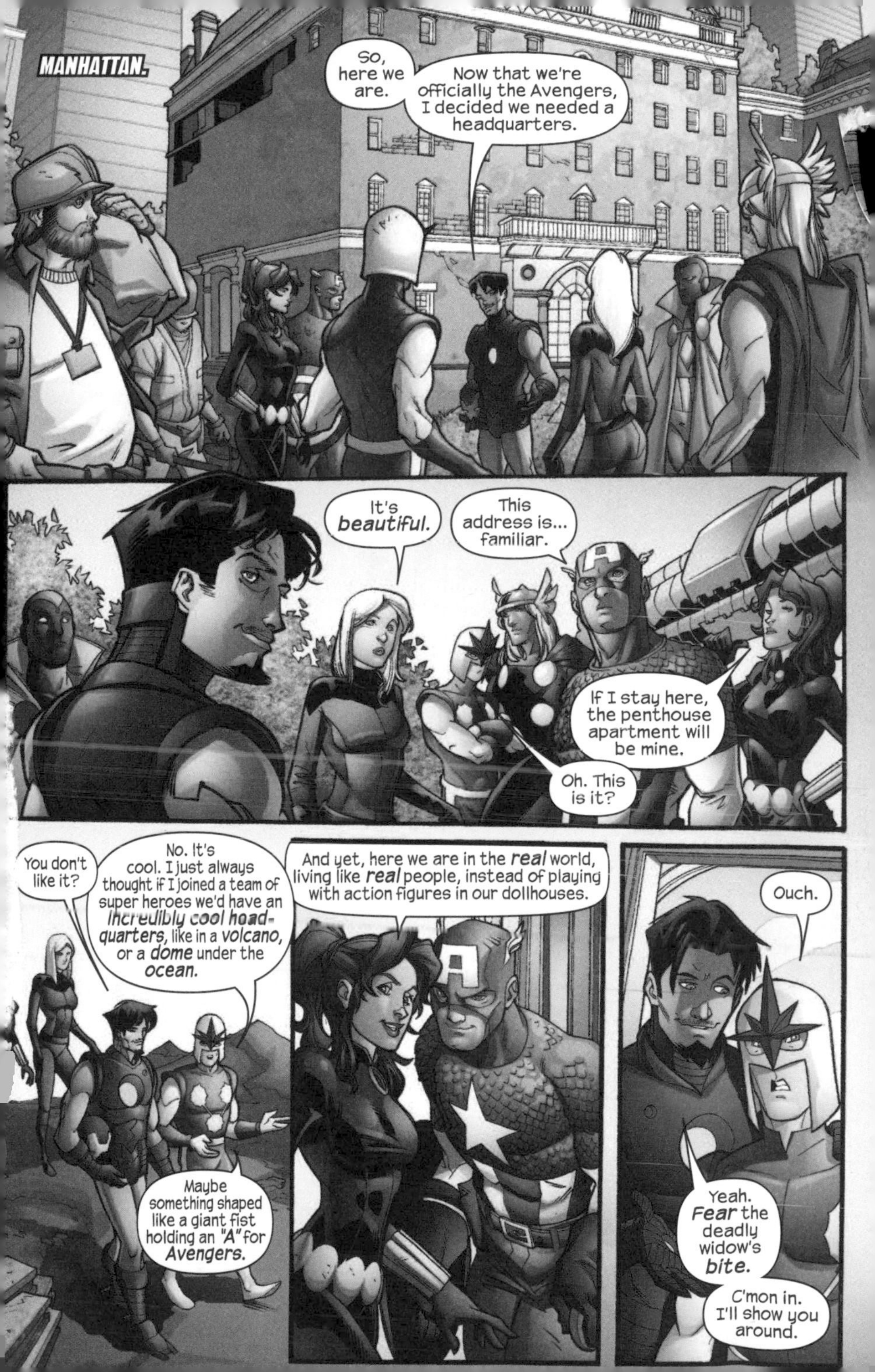

MANHATTAN.
So, here we are.
Now that we're officially the Avengers, I decided we needed a headquarters.
It's beautiful.
This address is... familiar.
If I stay here, the penthouse apartment will be mine.
Oh. This is it?
You don't like it?
No. It's cool. I just always thought if I joined a team of super heroes we'd have an incredibly cool headquarters, like in a volcano, or a dome under the ocean.
Maybe something shaped like a giant fist holding an "A" for Avengers.
And yet, here we are in the real world, living like real people, instead of playing with action figures in our dollhouses.
Ouch.
Yeah. Fear the deadly widow's bite.
C'mon in. I'll show you around.

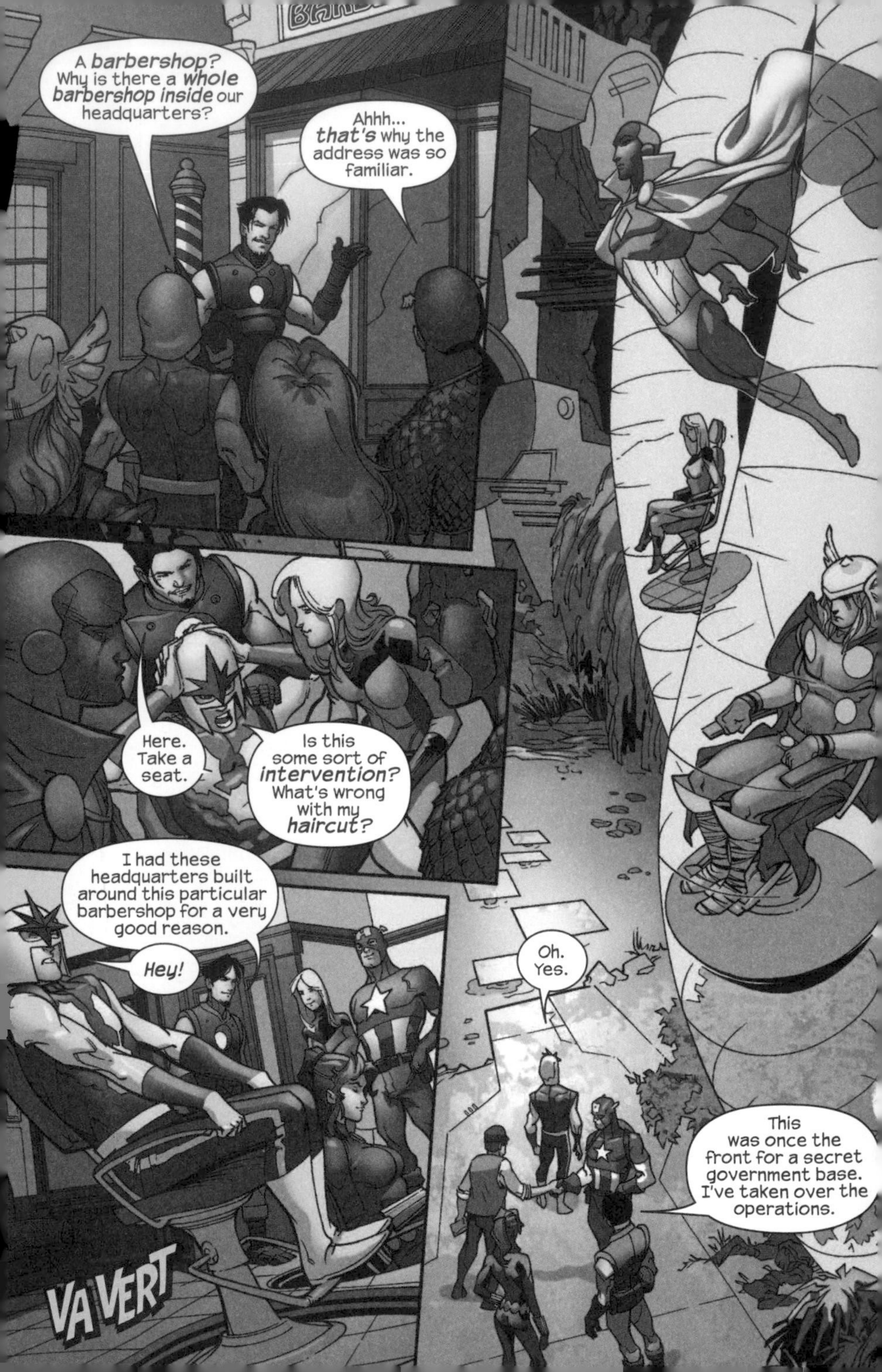

A barbershop? Why is there a whole barbershop inside our headquarters?
Ahhh... that's why the address was so familiar.
Here. Take a seat.
Is this some sort of intervention? What's wrong with my haircut?
I had these headquarters built around this particular barbershop for a very good reason.
Hey!
VA VERT
Oh. Yes.
This was once the front for a secret government base. I've taken over the operations.

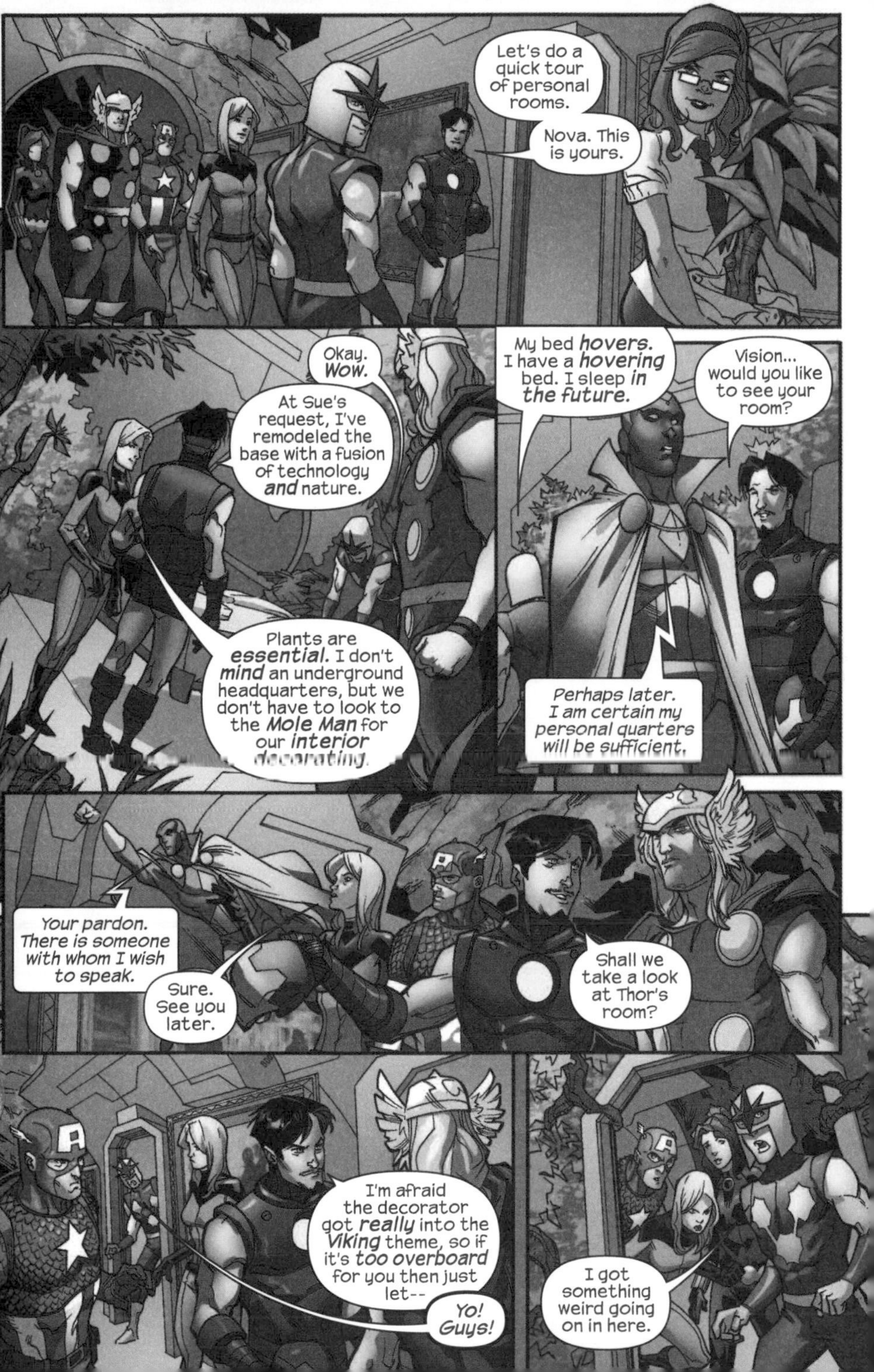
Let's do a quick tour of personal rooms.
Nova. This is yours.
Okay. **Wow.**
At Sue's request, I've remodeled the base with a fusion of technology ***and*** nature.
Plants are ***essential.*** I don't ***mind*** an underground headquarters, but we don't have to look to the ***Mole Man*** for our ***interior decorating***.
My bed ***hovers.*** I have a ***hovering*** bed. I sleep ***in the future.***
Vision... would you like to see your room?
Perhaps later. I am certain my personal quarters will be sufficient.
Your pardon. There is someone with whom I wish to speak.
Sure. See you later.
Shall we take a look at Thor's room?
I'm afraid the decorator got ***really*** into the ***Viking*** theme, so if it's ***too overboard*** for you then just let--
Yo! Guys!
I got something weird going on in here.

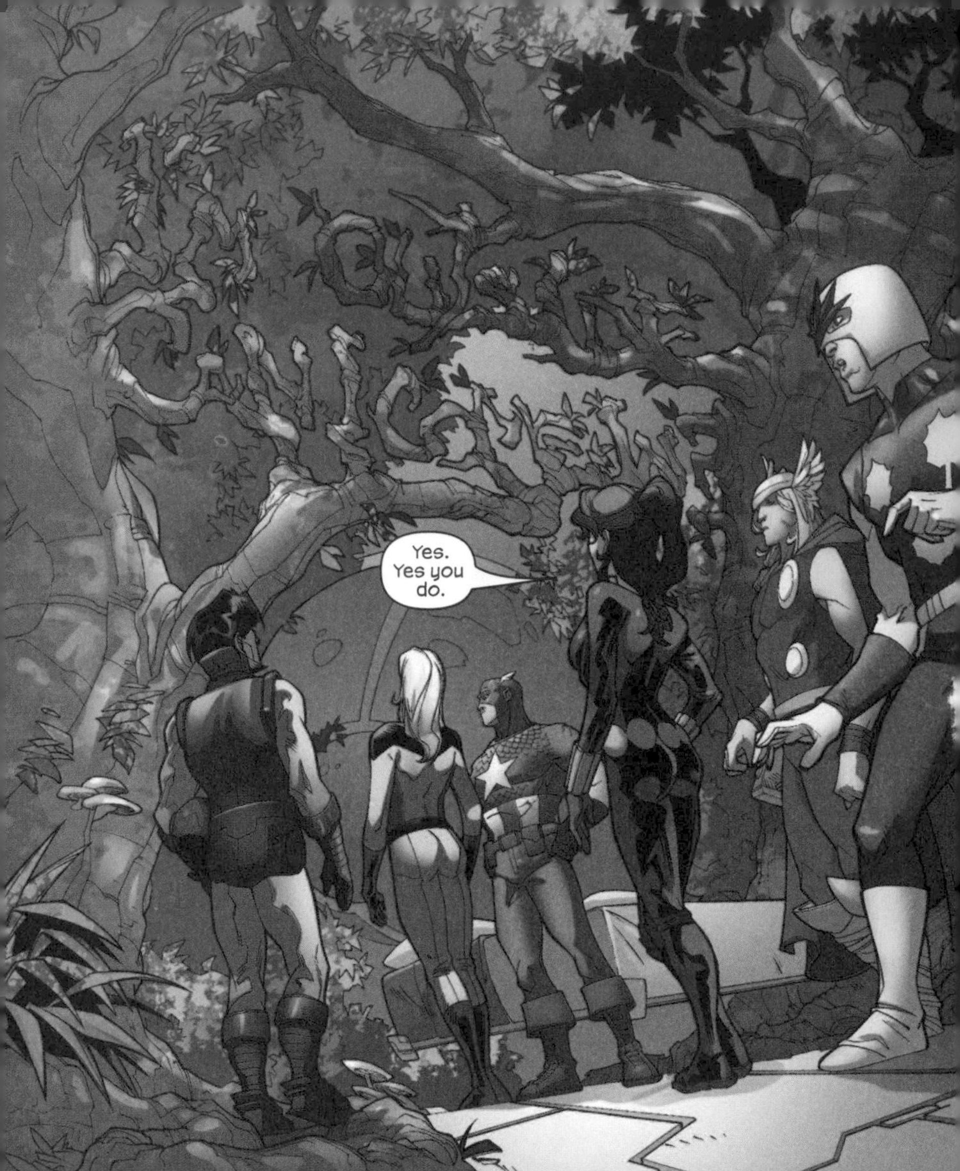
Yes. Yes you do.

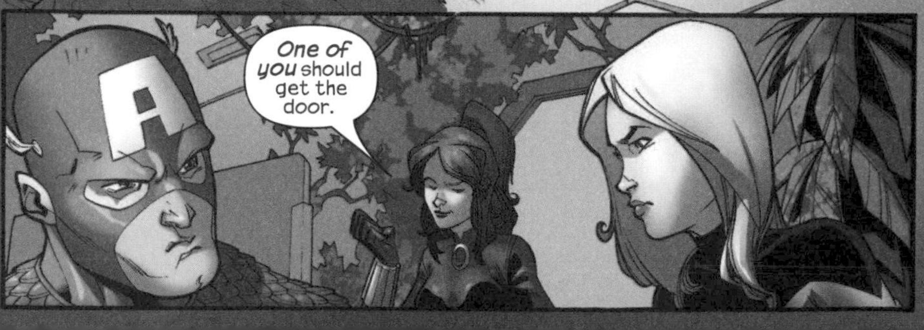
One of you should get the door.

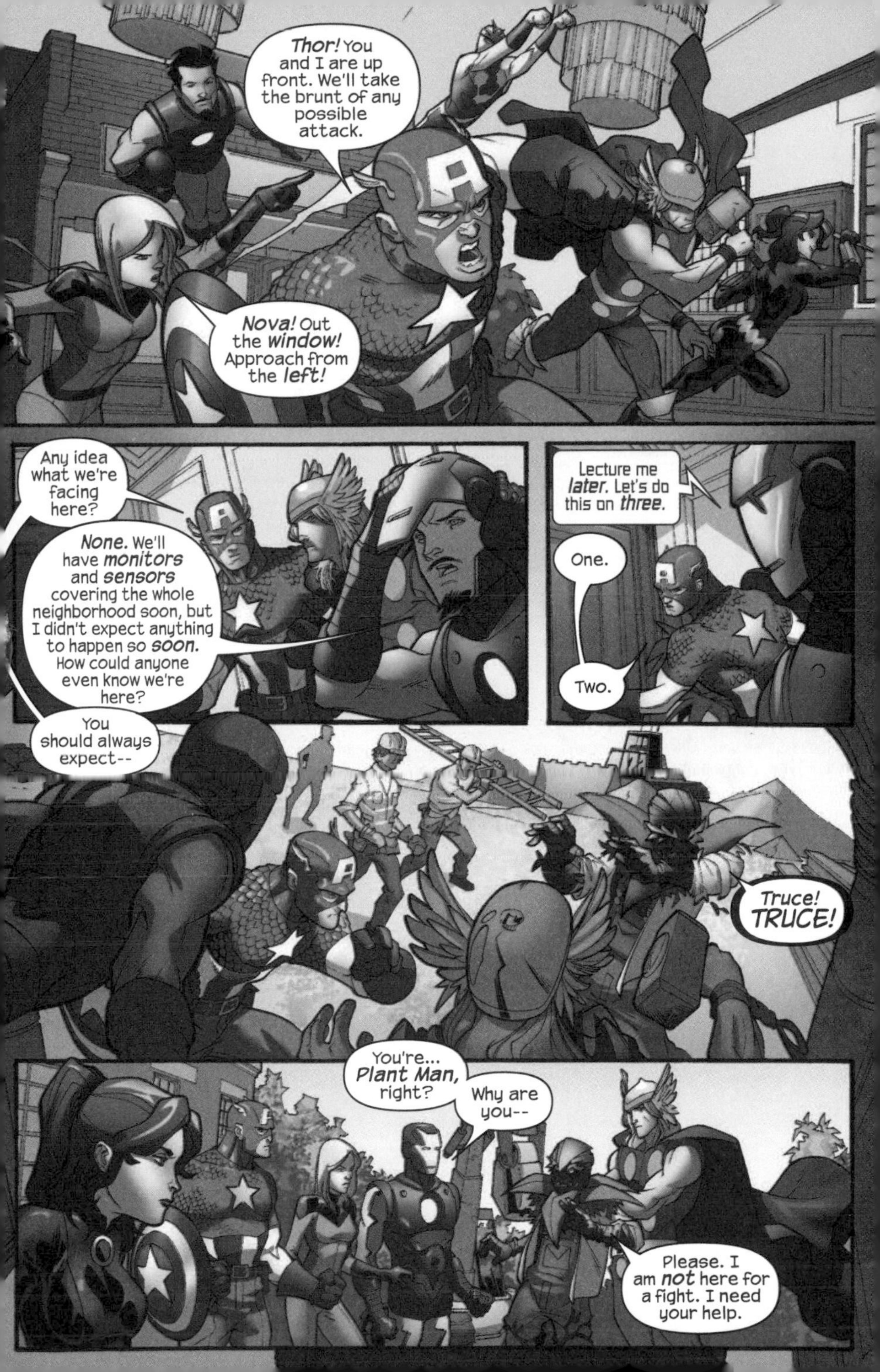
Thor! You and I are up front. We'll take the brunt of any possible attack.
Nova! Out the window! Approach from the left!
Any idea what we're facing here?
None. We'll have monitors and sensors covering the whole neighborhood soon, but I didn't expect anything to happen so soon. How could anyone even know we're here?
You should always expect--
Lecture me later. Let's do this on three.
One.
Two.
Truce! TRUCE!
You're... Plant Man, right?
Why are you--
Please. I am not here for a fight. I need your help.

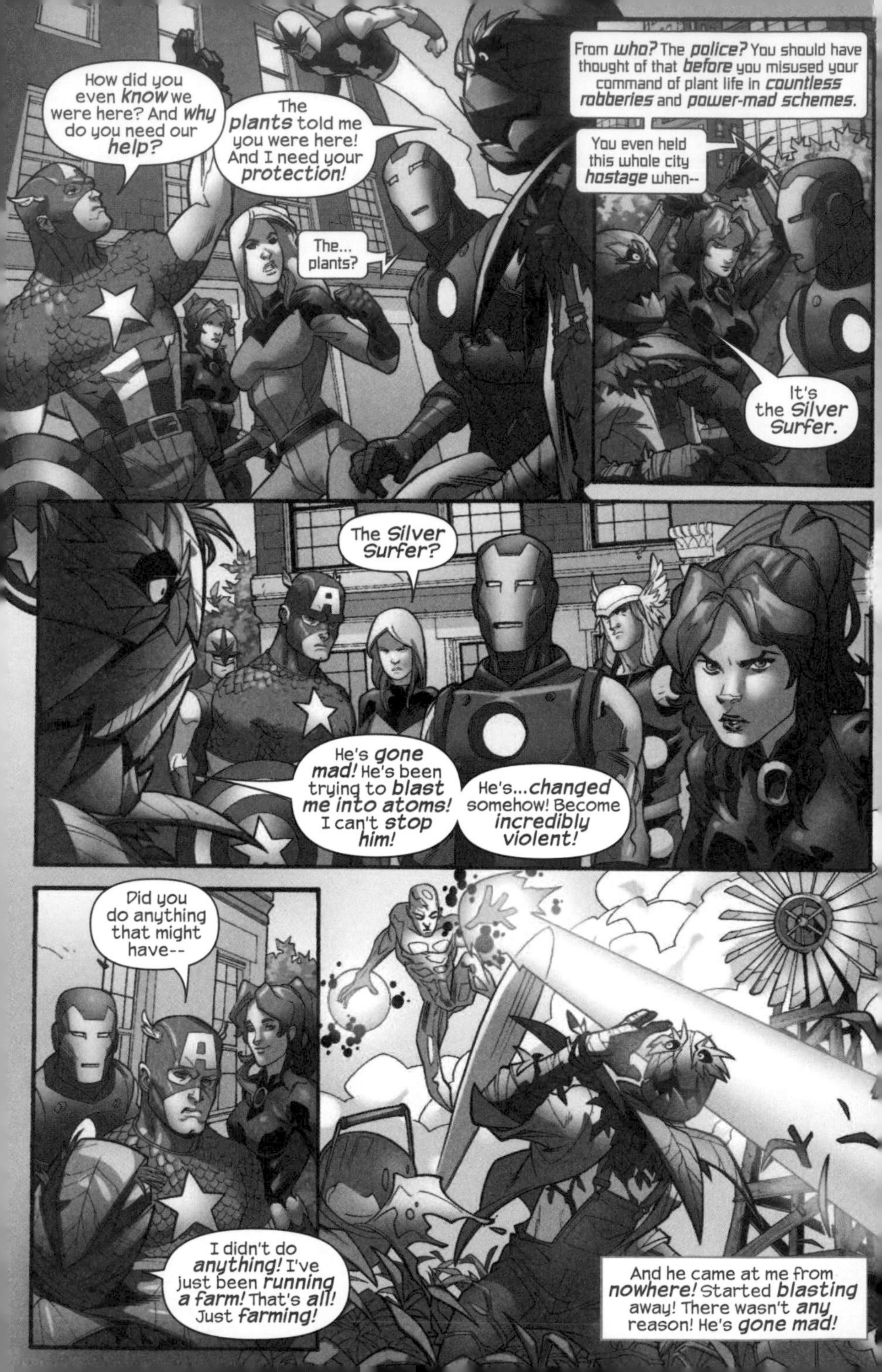

How did you even know we were here? And why do you need our help?
The plants told me you were here! And I need your protection!
The... plants?
From who? The police? You should have thought of that before you misused your command of plant life in countless robberies and power-mad schemes.
You even held this whole city hostage when--
It's the Silver Surfer.
The Silver Surfer?
He's gone mad! He's been trying to blast me into atoms! I can't stop him!
He's...changed somehow! Become incredibly violent!
Did you do anything that might have--
I didn't do anything! I've just been running a farm! That's all! Just farming!
And he came at me from nowhere! Started blasting away! There wasn't any reason! He's gone mad!

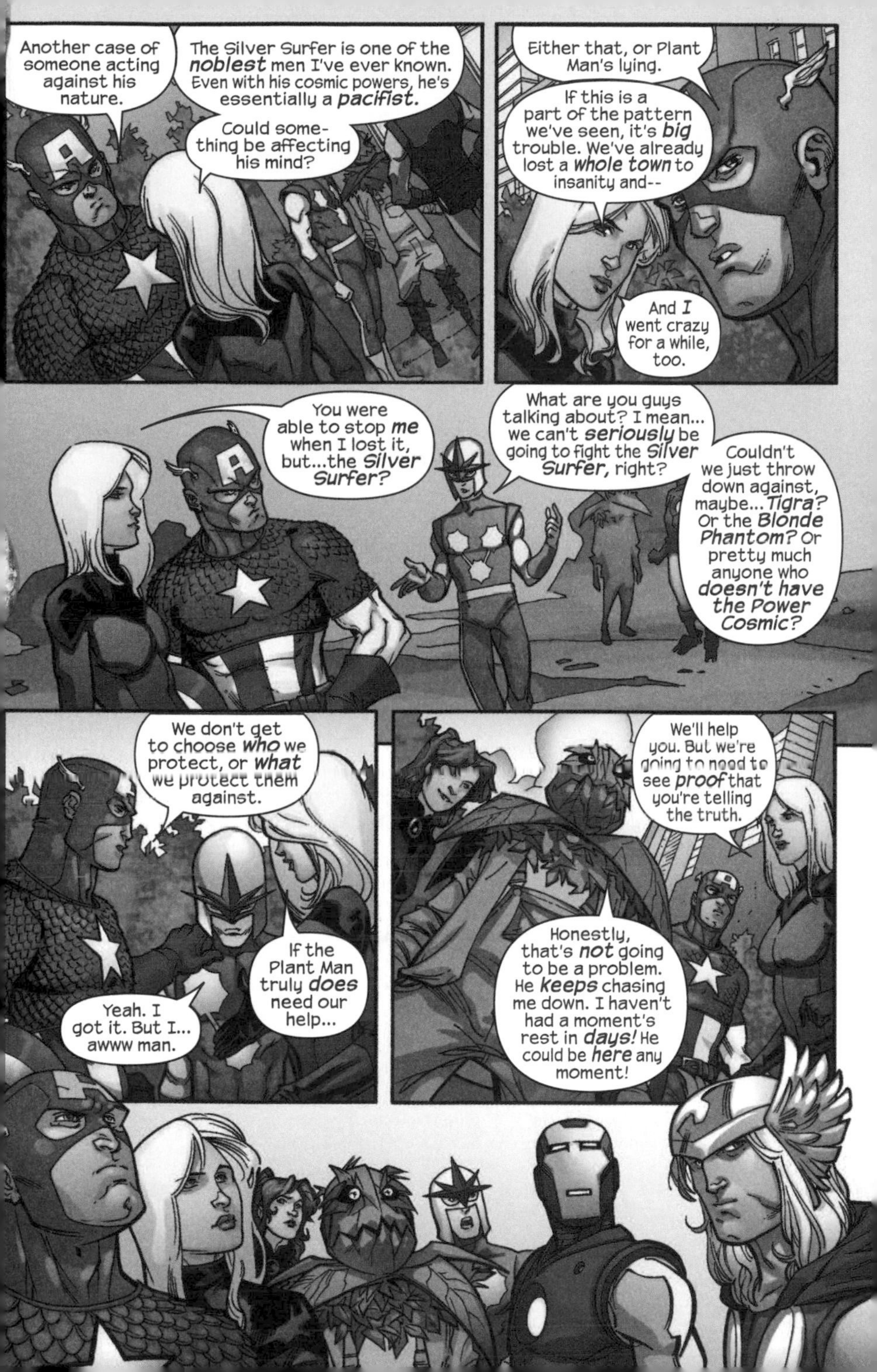
Another case of someone acting against his nature.
The Silver Surfer is one of the noblest men I've ever known. Even with his cosmic powers, he's essentially a pacifist.
Could something be affecting his mind?
Either that, or Plant Man's lying.
If this is a part of the pattern we've seen, it's big trouble. We've already lost a whole town to insanity and--
And I went crazy for a while, too.
You were able to stop me when I lost it, but...the Silver Surfer?
What are you guys talking about? I mean... we can't seriously be going to fight the Silver Surfer, right?
Couldn't we just throw down against, maybe...Tigra? Or the Blonde Phantom? Or pretty much anyone who doesn't have the Power Cosmic?
We don't get to choose who we protect, or what we protect them against.
If the Plant Man truly does need our help...
Yeah. I got it. But I... awww man.
We'll help you. But we're going to need to see proof that you're telling the truth.
Honestly, that's not going to be a problem. He keeps chasing me down. I haven't had a moment's rest in days! He could be here any moment!

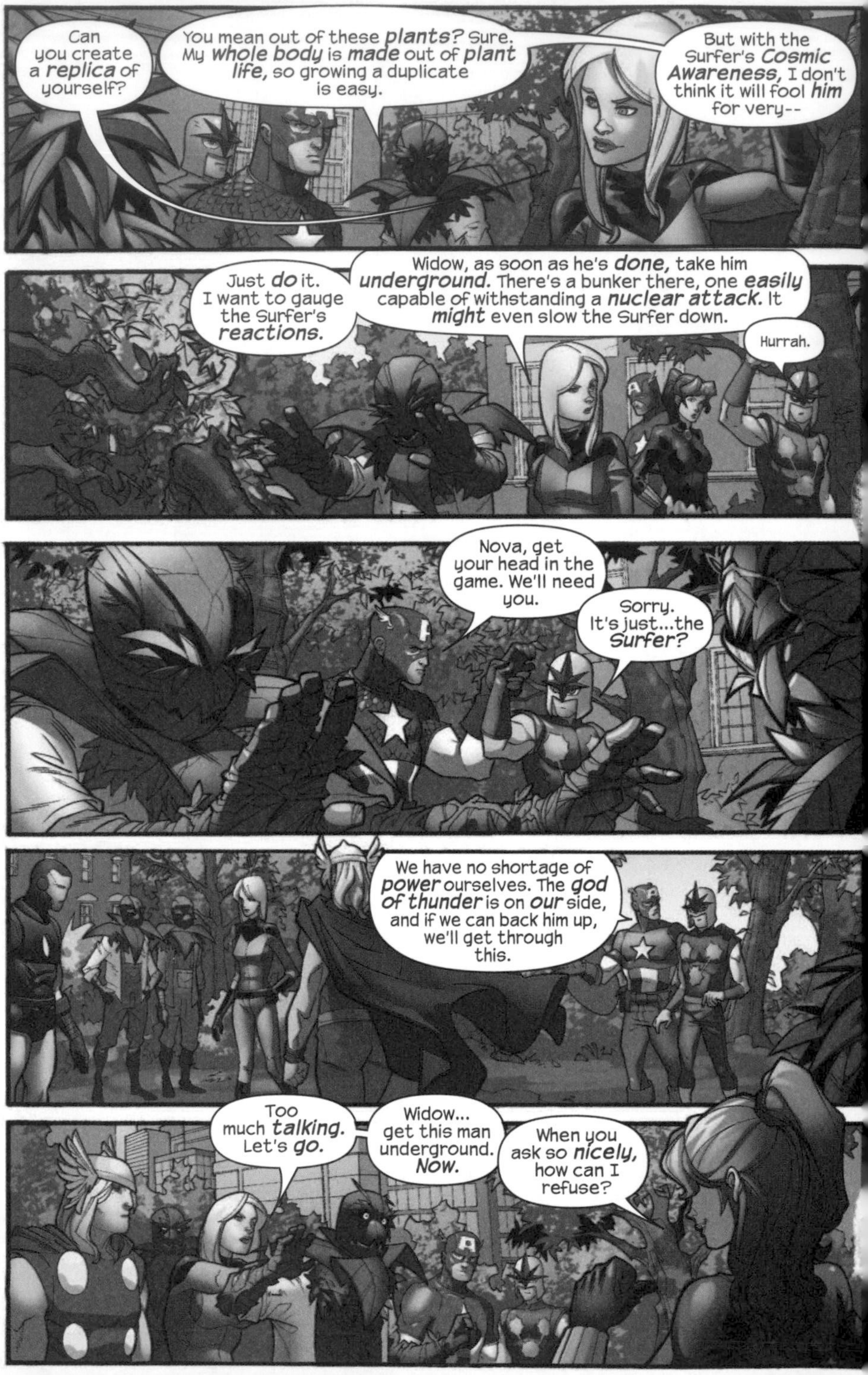
Can you create a replica of yourself?
You mean out of these plants? Sure. My whole body is made out of plant life, so growing a duplicate is easy.
But with the Surfer's Cosmic Awareness, I don't think it will fool him for very--
Just do it. I want to gauge the Surfer's reactions.
Widow, as soon as he's done, take him underground. There's a bunker there, one easily capable of withstanding a nuclear attack. It might even slow the Surfer down.
Hurrah.
Nova, get your head in the game. We'll need you.
Sorry. It's just...the Surfer?
We have no shortage of power ourselves. The god of thunder is on our side, and if we can back him up, we'll get through this.
Too much talking. Let's go.
Widow... get this man underground. Now.
When you ask so nicely, how can I refuse?

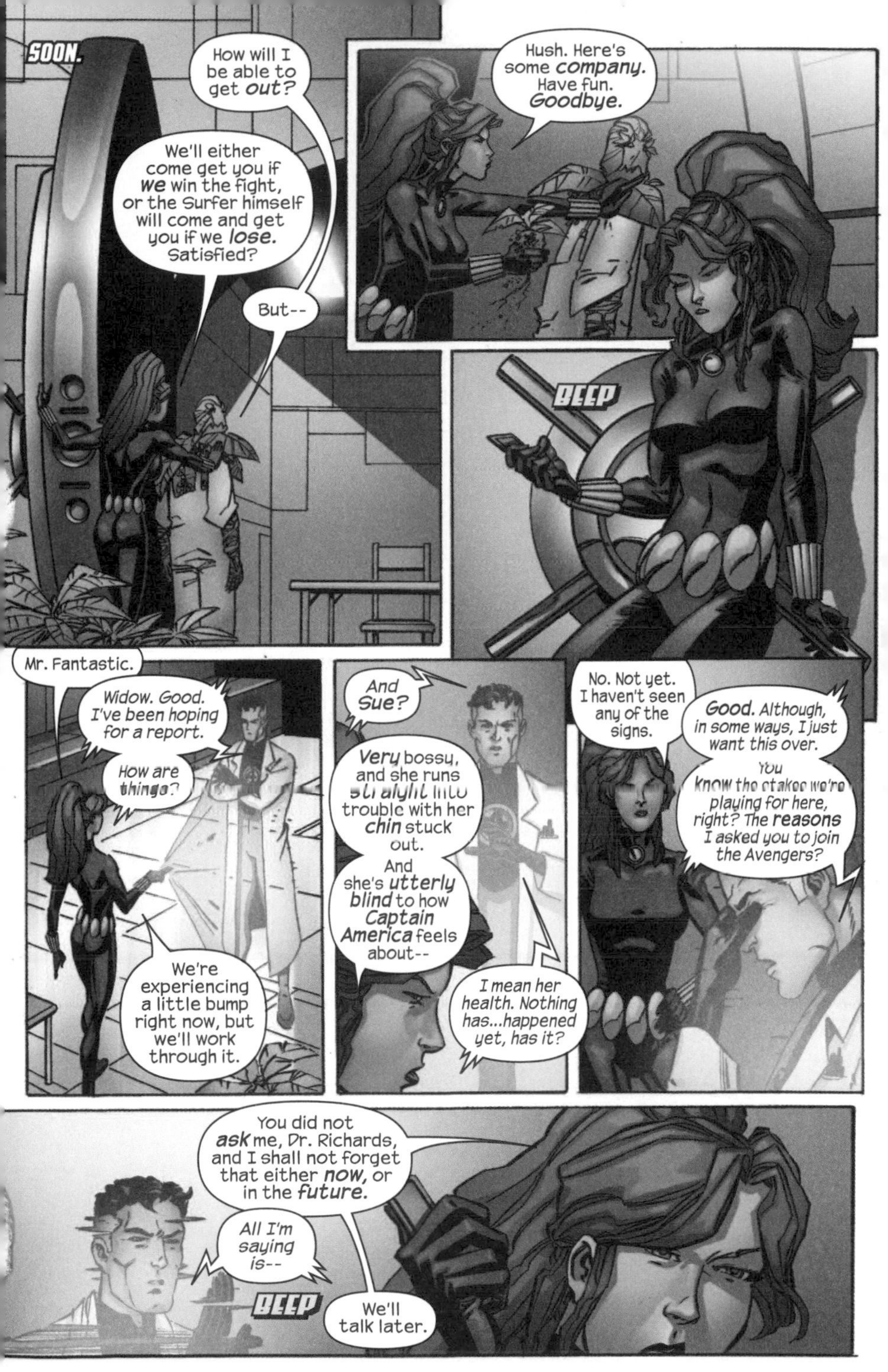
SOON.
How will I be able to get out?
We'll either come get you if we win the fight, or the Surfer himself will come and get you if we lose. Satisfied?
But--
Hush. Here's some company. Have fun. Goodbye.
BEEP
Mr. Fantastic.
Widow. Good. I've been hoping for a report.
How are things?
We're experiencing a little bump right now, but we'll work through it.
And Sue?
Very bossy, and she runs straight into trouble with her chin stuck out.
And she's utterly blind to how Captain America feels about--
I mean her health. Nothing has...happened yet, has it?
No. Not yet. I haven't seen any of the signs.
Good. Although, in some ways, I just want this over.
You know the stakes we're playing for here, right? The reasons I asked you to join the Avengers?
You did not ask me, Dr. Richards, and I shall not forget that either now, or in the future.
All I'm saying is--
BEEP
We'll talk later.

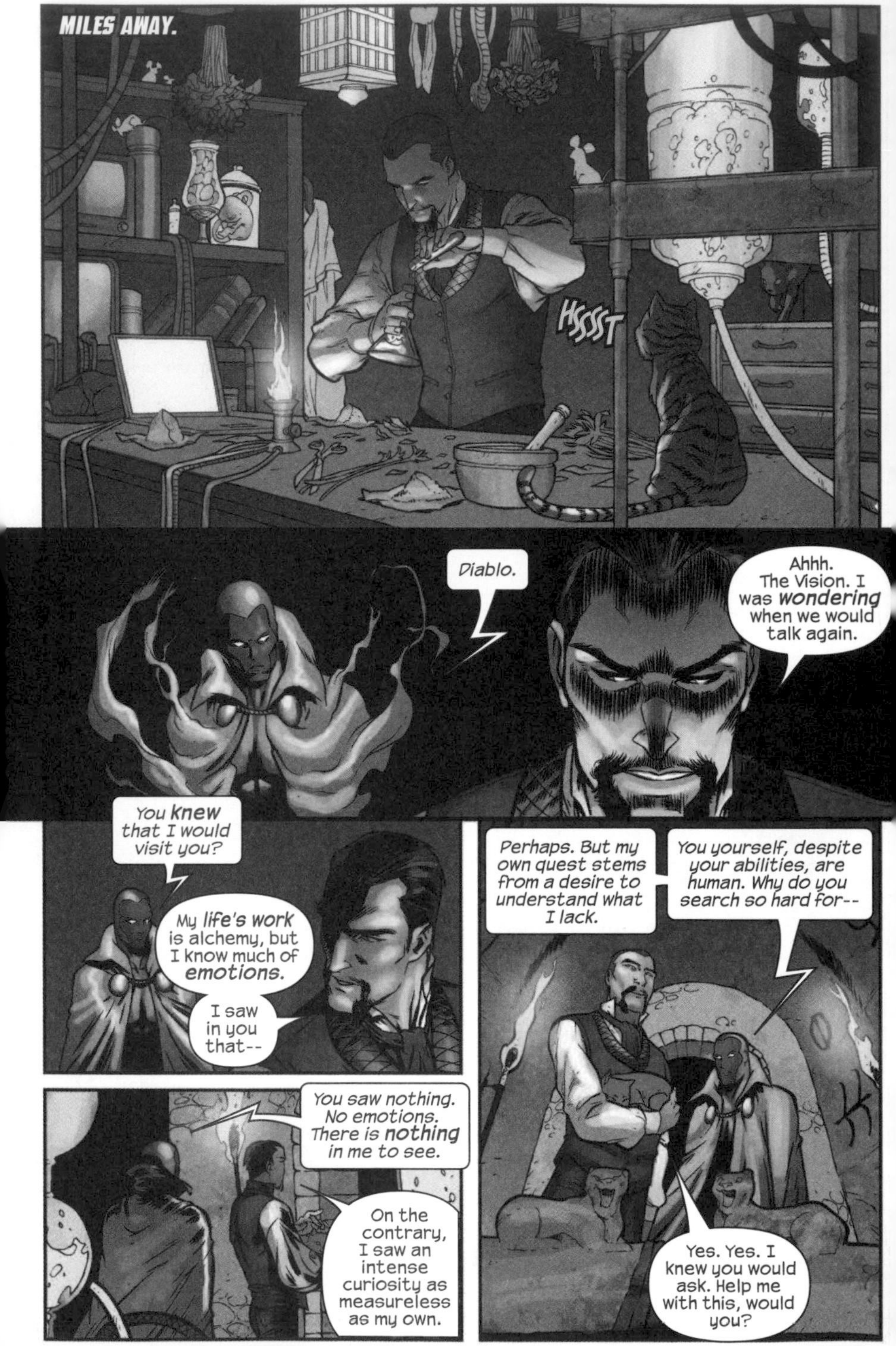
MILES AWAY.
HSSSST
Diablo.
Ahhh. The Vision. I was *wondering* when we would talk again.
You *knew* that I would visit you?
My *life's work* is alchemy, but I know much of *emotions*.
I saw in you that--
You saw nothing. No emotions. There is *nothing* in me to see.
On the contrary, I saw an intense curiosity as measureless as my own.
Perhaps. But my own quest stems from a desire to understand what I lack.
You yourself, despite your abilities, are human. Why do you search so hard for--
Yes. Yes. I knew you would ask. Help me with this, would you?

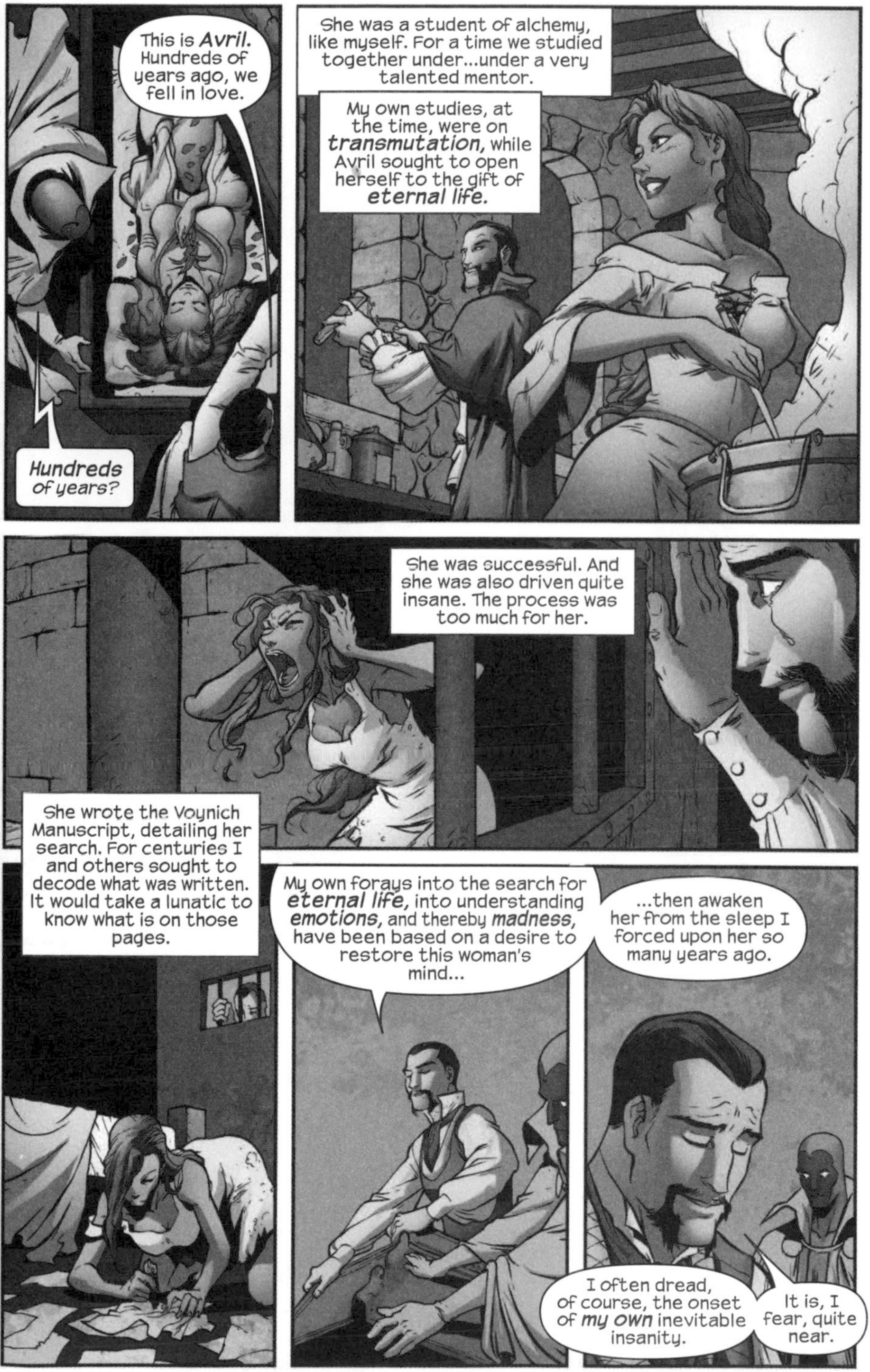

This is Avril. Hundreds of years ago, we fell in love.
Hundreds of years?
She was a student of alchemy, like myself. For a time we studied together under...under a very talented mentor.
My own studies, at the time, were on transmutation, while Avril sought to open herself to the gift of eternal life.
She was successful. And she was also driven quite insane. The process was too much for her.
She wrote the Voynich Manuscript, detailing her search. For centuries I and others sought to decode what was written. It would take a lunatic to know what is on those pages.
My own forays into the search for eternal life, into understanding emotions, and thereby madness, have been based on a desire to restore this woman's mind...
...then awaken her from the sleep I forced upon her so many years ago.
I often dread, of course, the onset of my own inevitable insanity.
It is, I fear, quite near.

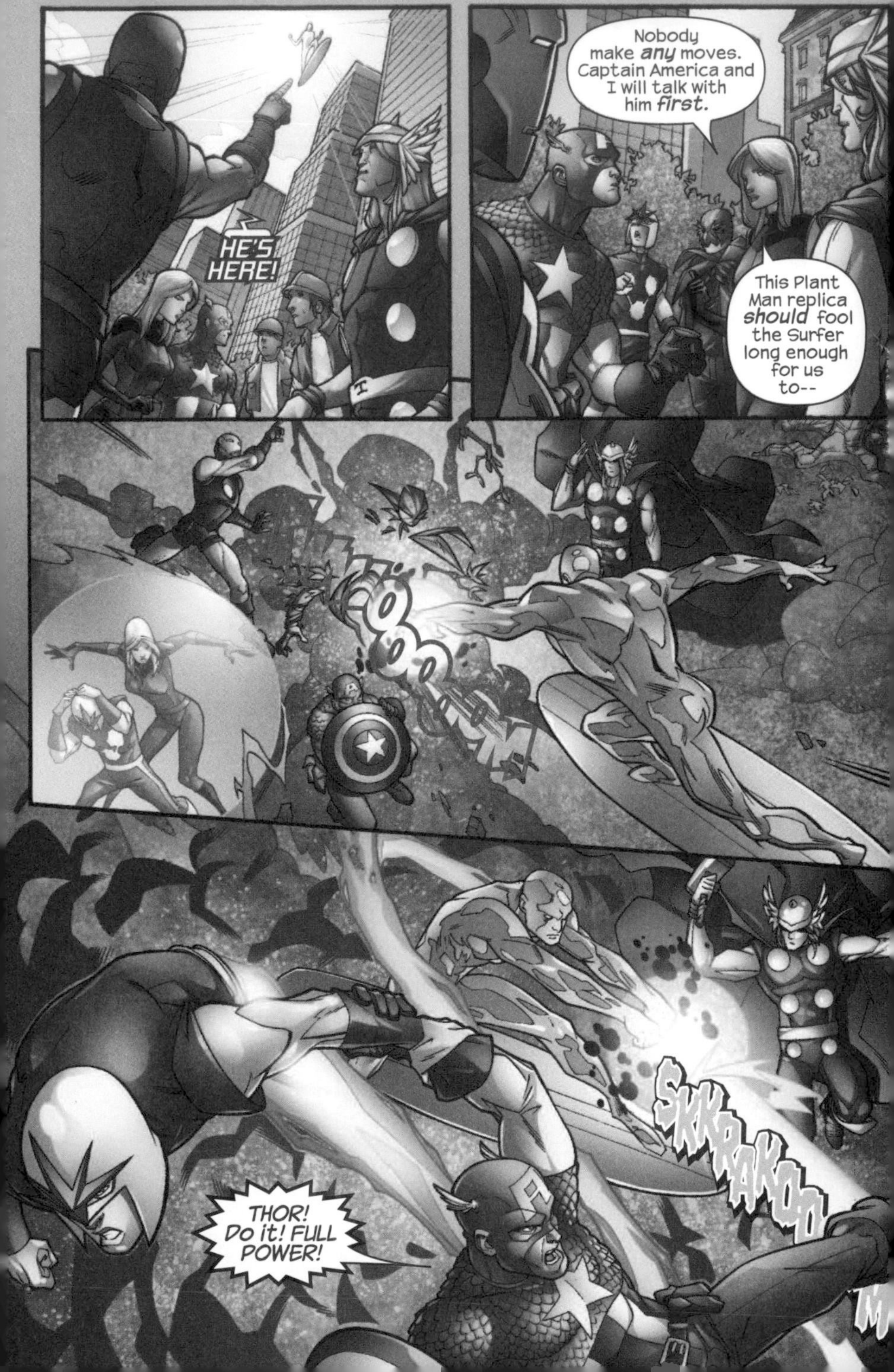
HE'S HERE!
Nobody make *any* moves. Captain America and I will talk with him *first.*
This Plant Man replica *should* fool the Surfer long enough for us to--
THOR! Do it! FULL POWER!
SKKRAKOOOM

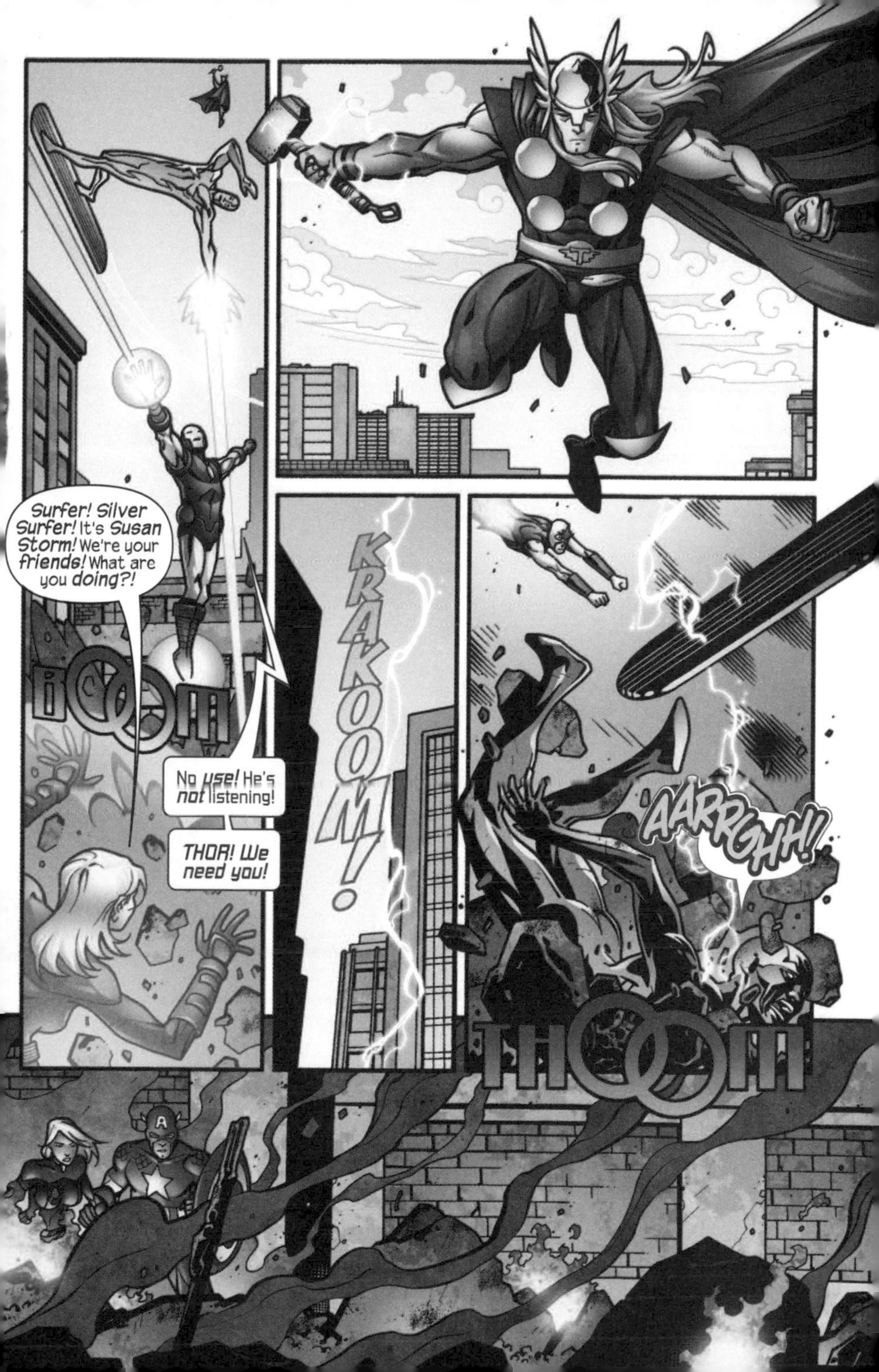
Surfer! Silver Surfer! It's Susan Storm! We're your friends! What are you doing?!
BOOM
No use! He's not listening!
THOR! We need you!
KRAKOOM!
AARRGHH!
THOOM

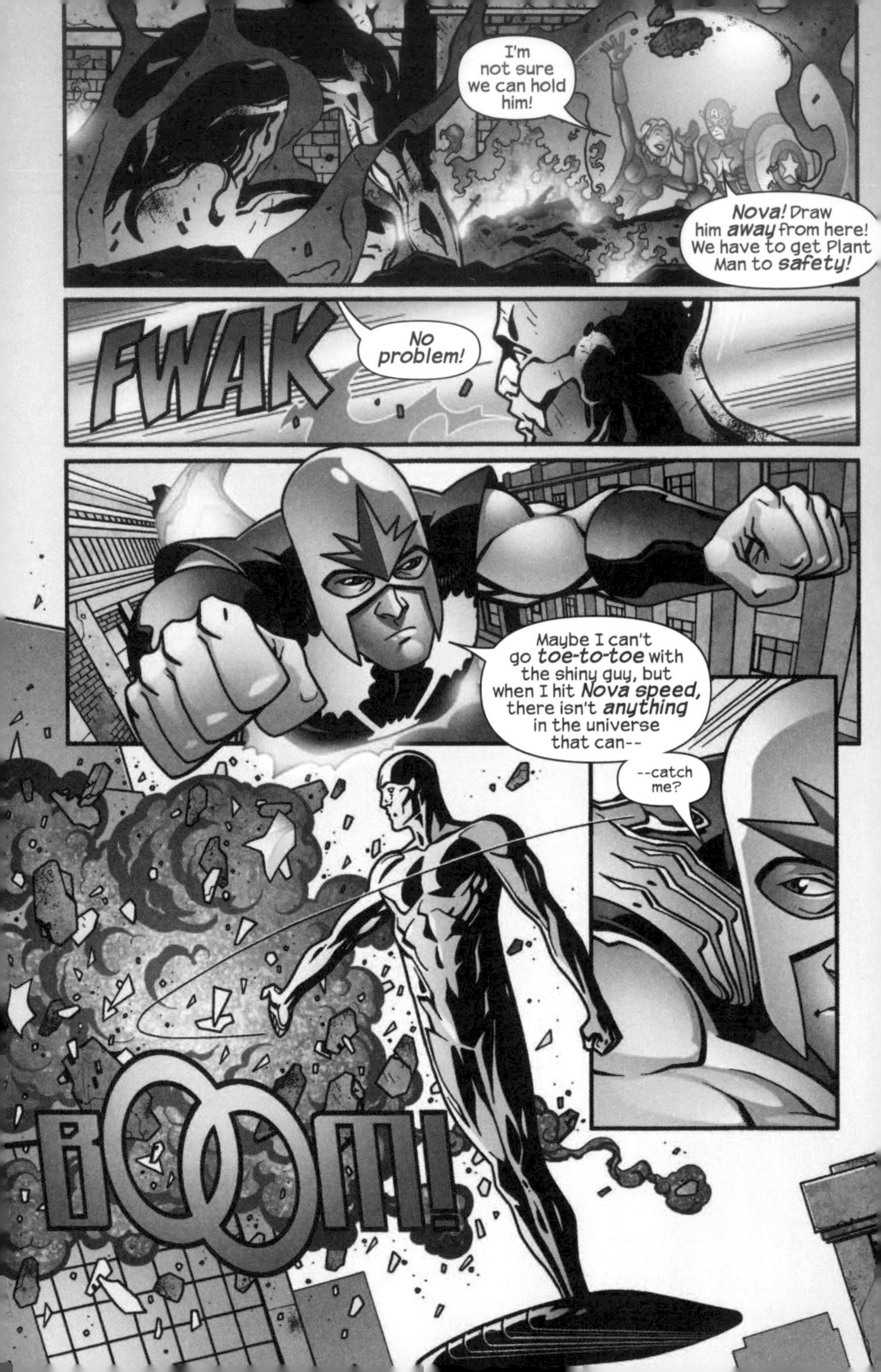
I'm not sure we can hold him!
Nova! Draw him away from here! We have to get Plant Man to safety!
FWAK
No problem!
Maybe I can't go toe-to-toe with the shiny guy, but when I hit Nova speed, there isn't anything in the universe that can--
--catch me?
BOOM!

MILES AWAY...

W-what's that?

You say that you've *read* the Voynich Manuscript?

Surely you mean that you've *studied* it? To say that you've *read* it would imply that--

I under-stand it, yes.

But, before it was *lost* to me, I studied the manuscript for *decades!* And now that it's been published online, I've been--

The secret was to consider each third letter as an individual code corresponding to the numerical sum of the two previous, and then to filter through mistakes, possibly decoys, in the writing, while the--

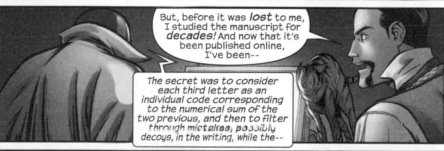

But if you've deciphered the manuscript, then no matter what it says, it will have clues to Avril's madness!

This is the starting point I've been searching for! A way to understand and, perhaps cure, her insanity!

If you like, I could simply upload a translation of the--

VEEp
VEEp
VEEp

What is that?

My communicator. It feels as though Iron Man is about to establish contact.

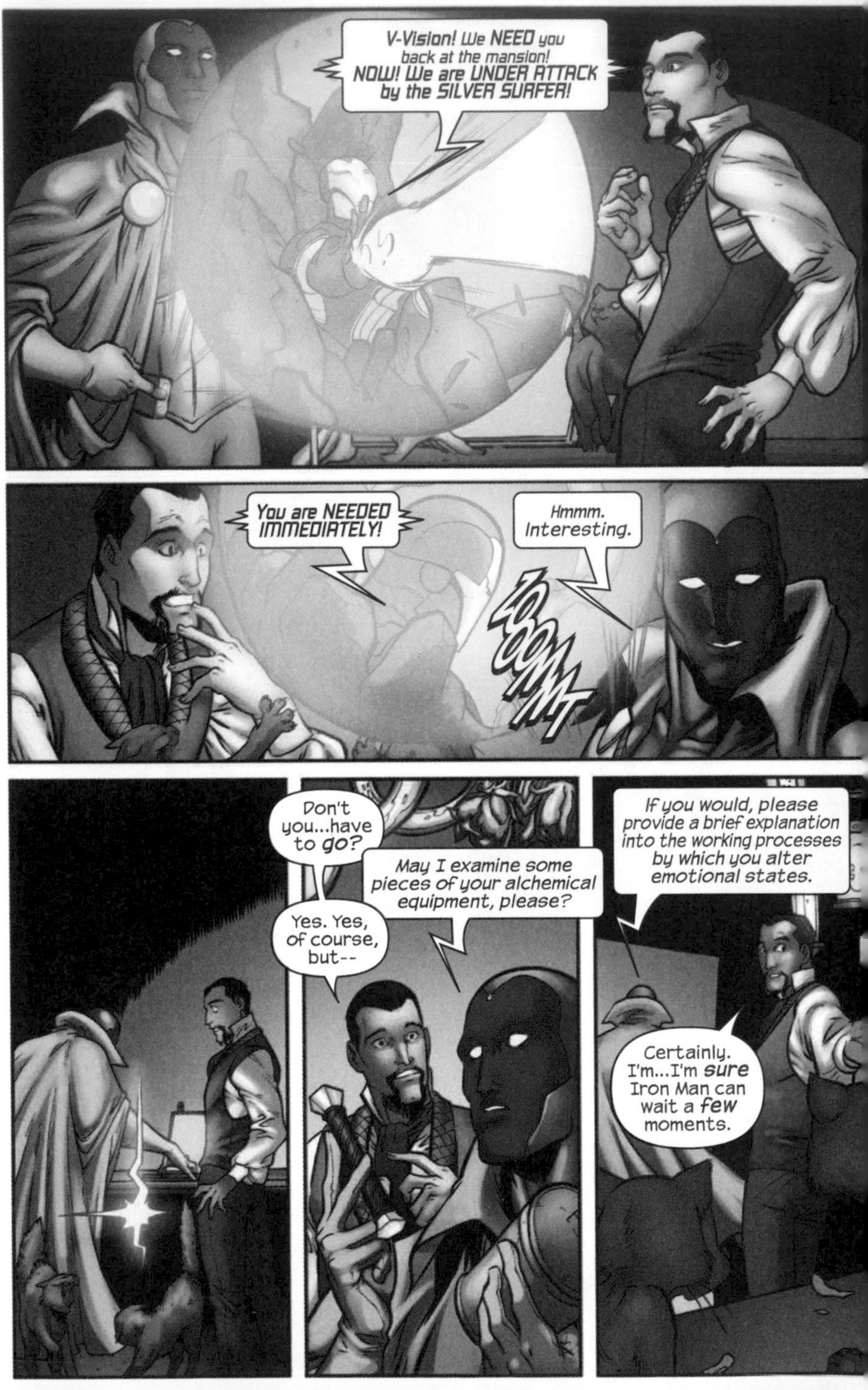

V-Vision! We NEED you back at the mansion! NOW! We are UNDER ATTACK by the SILVER SURFER!
You are NEEDED IMMEDIATELY!
Hmmm. Interesting.
ZOOOMT
Don't you...have to go?
May I examine some pieces of your alchemical equipment, please?
Yes. Yes, of course, but--
If you would, please provide a brief explanation into the working processes by which you alter emotional states.
Certainly. I'm...I'm sure Iron Man can wait a few moments.

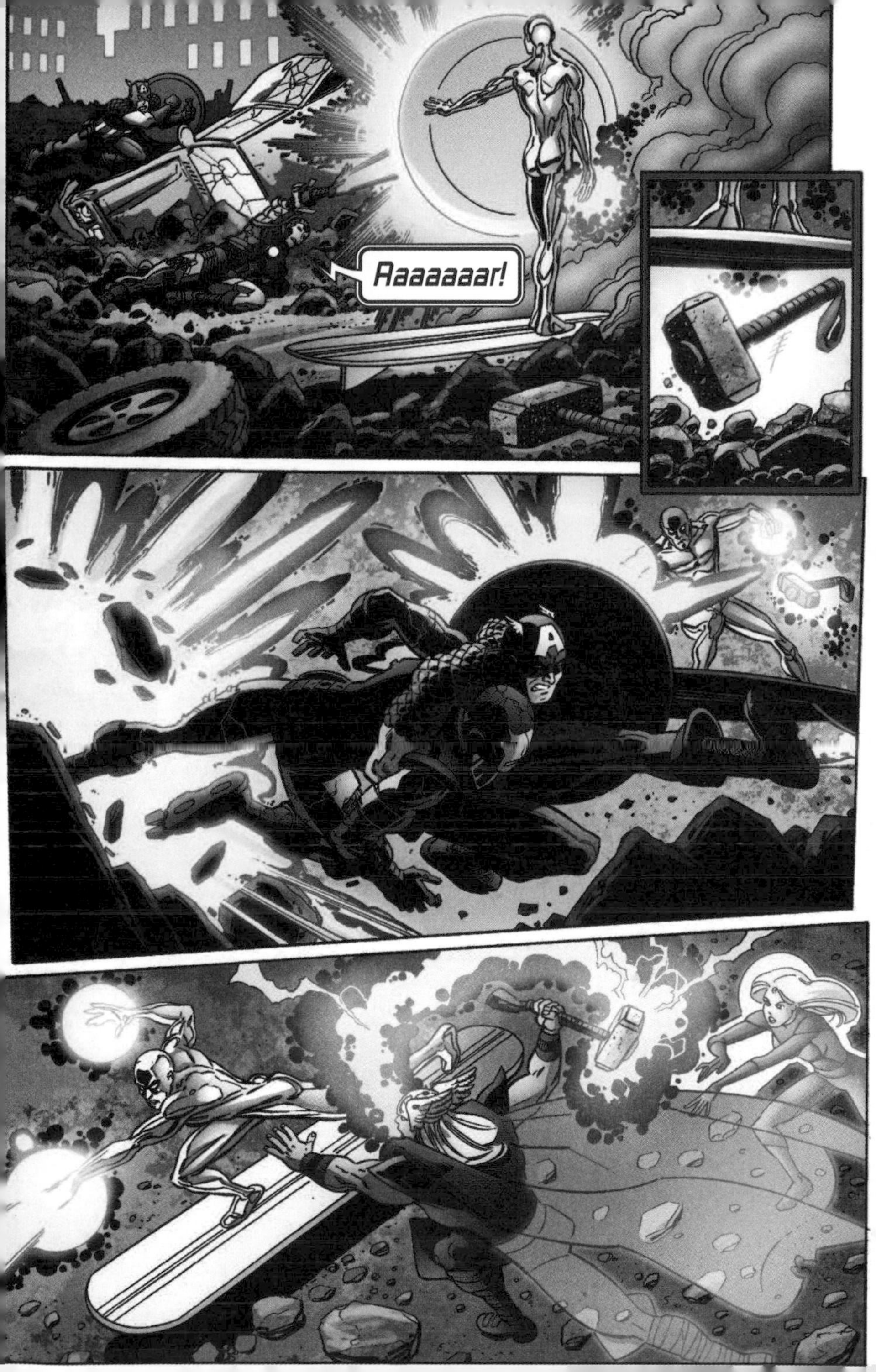
Raaaaaar!
WHOOM

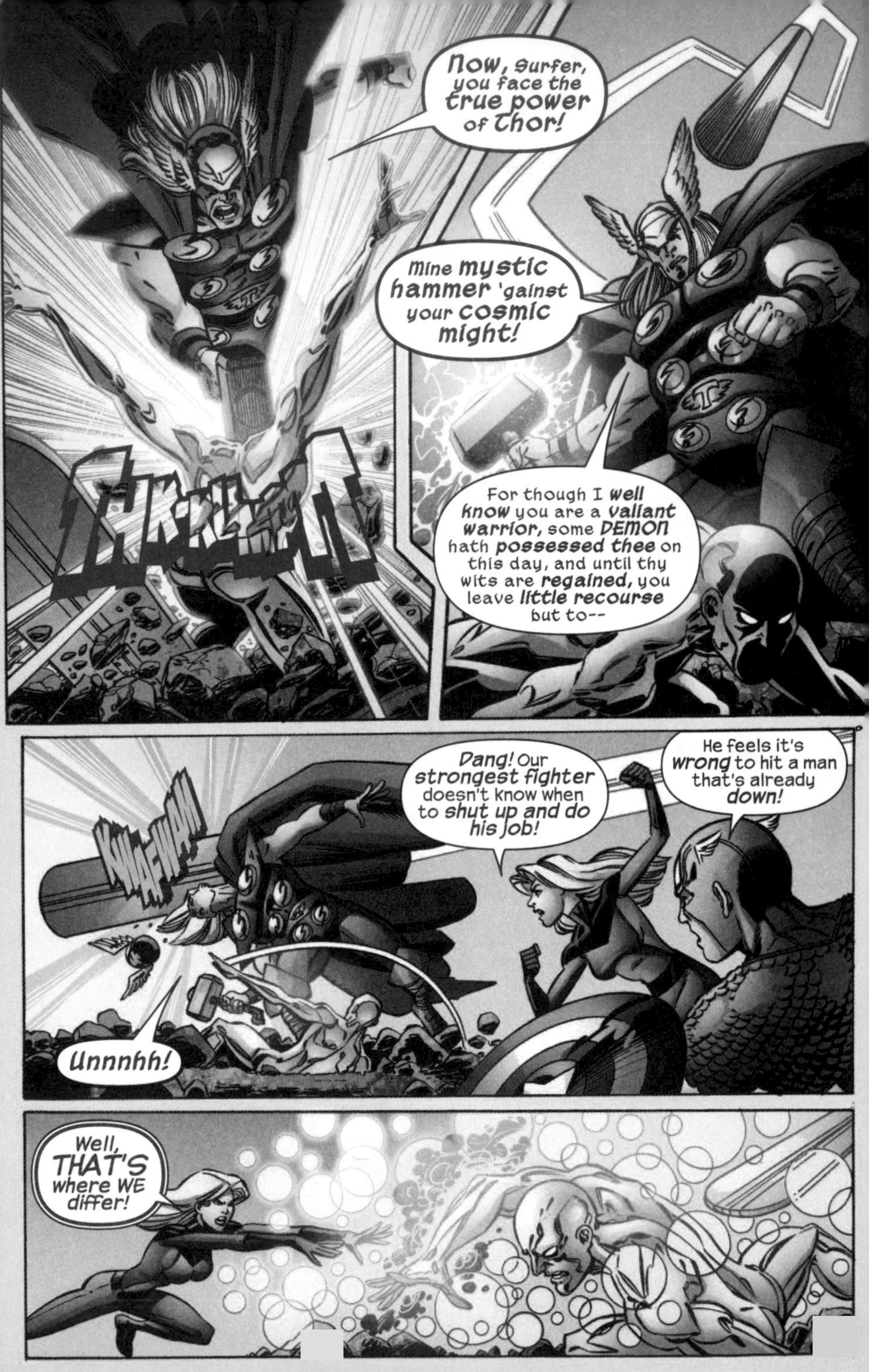

Now, Surfer, you face the true power of Thor!
Mine mystic hammer 'gainst your cosmic might!
For though I well know you are a valiant warrior, some DEMON hath possessed thee on this day, and until thy wits are regained, you leave little recourse but to--
KWAFWAM
Unnnhh!
Dang! Our strongest fighter doesn't know when to shut up and do his job!
He feels it's wrong to hit a man that's already down!
Well, THAT'S where WE differ!

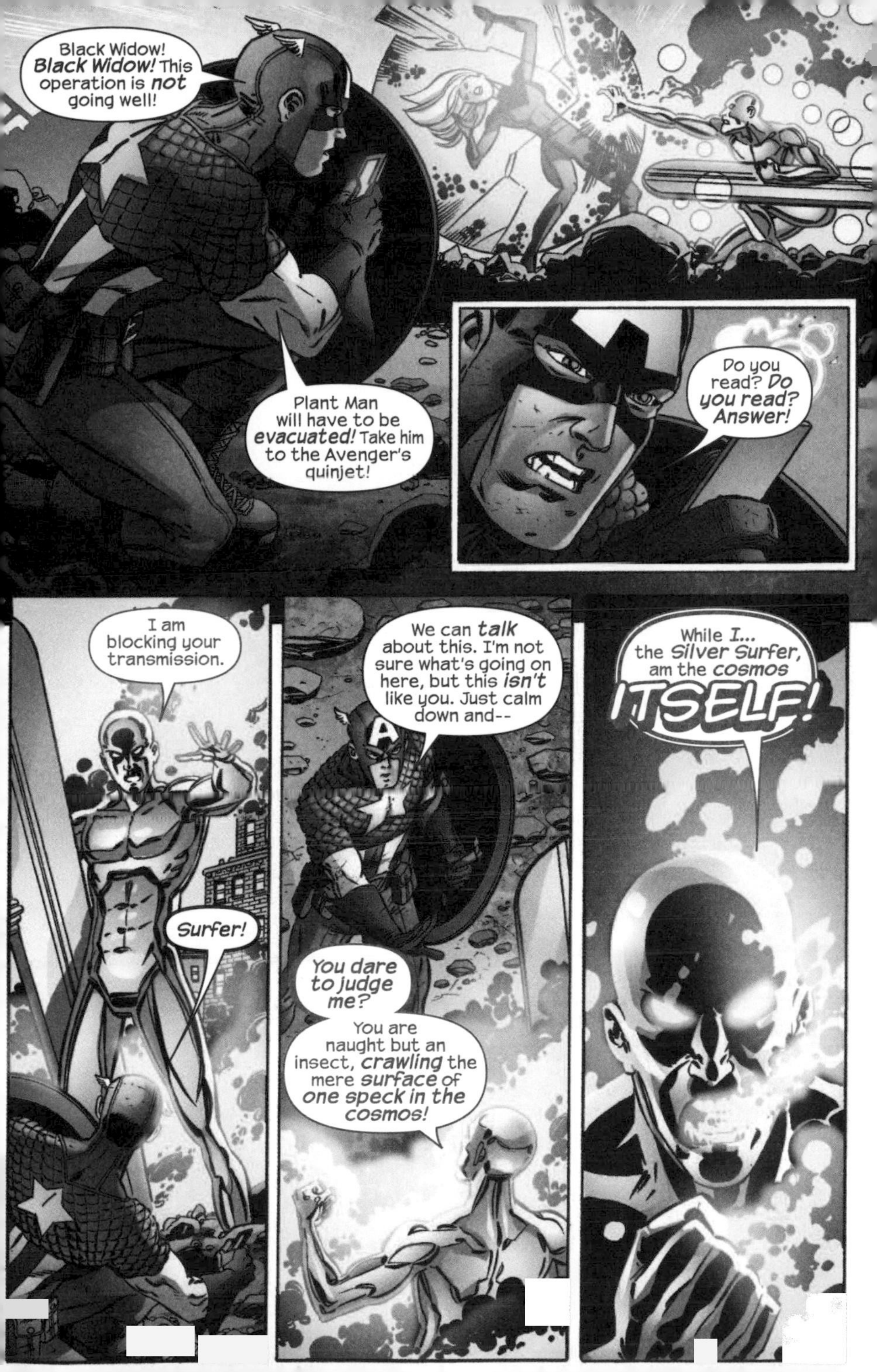
Black Widow! Black Widow! This operation is not going well!
Plant Man will have to be evacuated! Take him to the Avenger's quinjet!
Do you read? Do you read? Answer!
I am blocking your transmission.
Surfer!
We can talk about this. I'm not sure what's going on here, but this isn't like you. Just calm down and--
You dare to judge me?
You are naught but an insect, crawling the mere surface of one speck in the cosmos!
While I... the Silver Surfer, am the cosmos ITSELF!

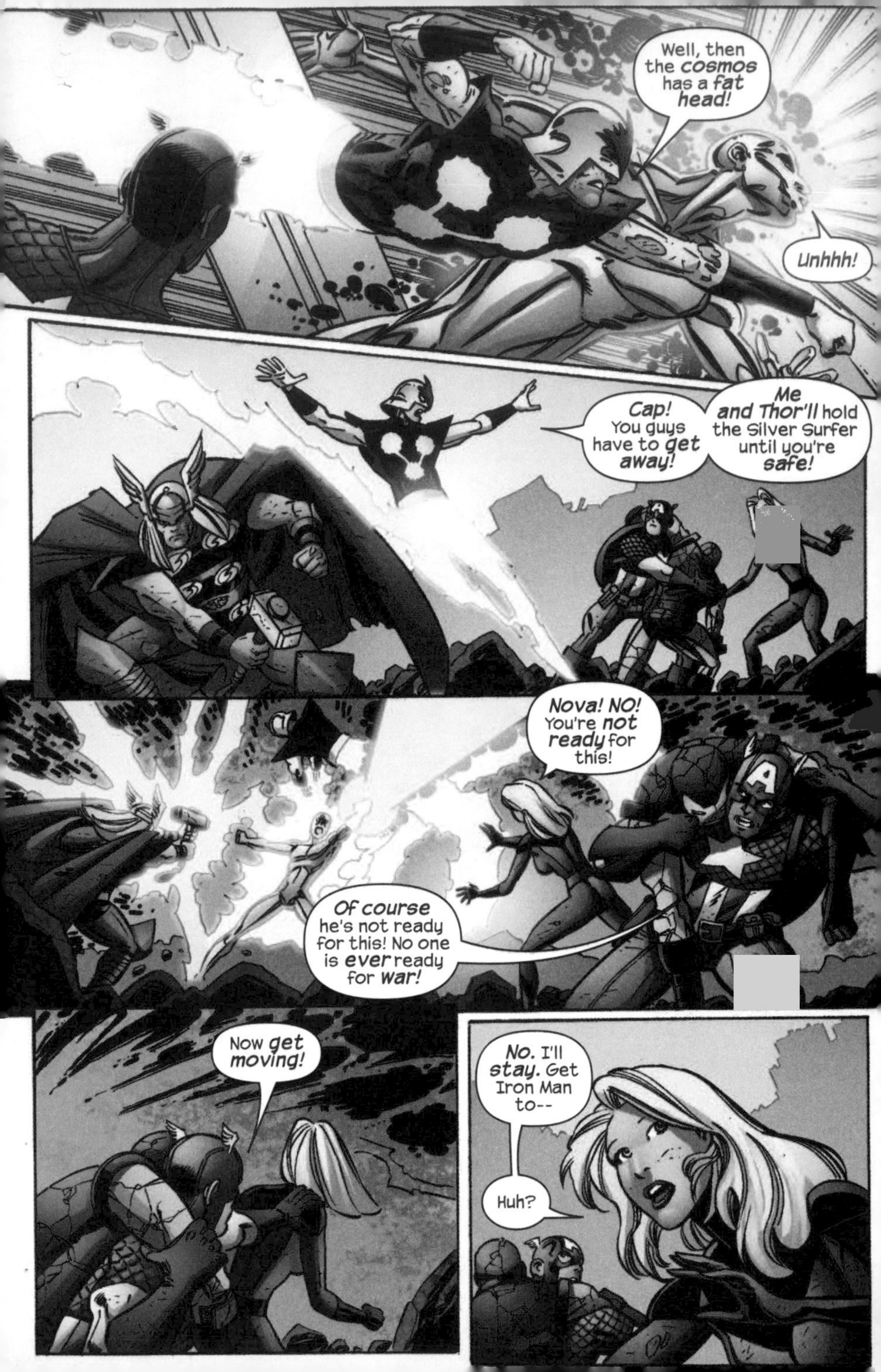
Well, then the cosmos has a fat head!
Unhhh!
Cap! You guys have to get away!
Me and Thor'll hold the Silver Surfer until you're safe!
Nova! NO! You're not ready for this!
Of course he's not ready for this! No one is ever ready for war!
Now get moving!
No. I'll stay. Get Iron Man to--
Huh?

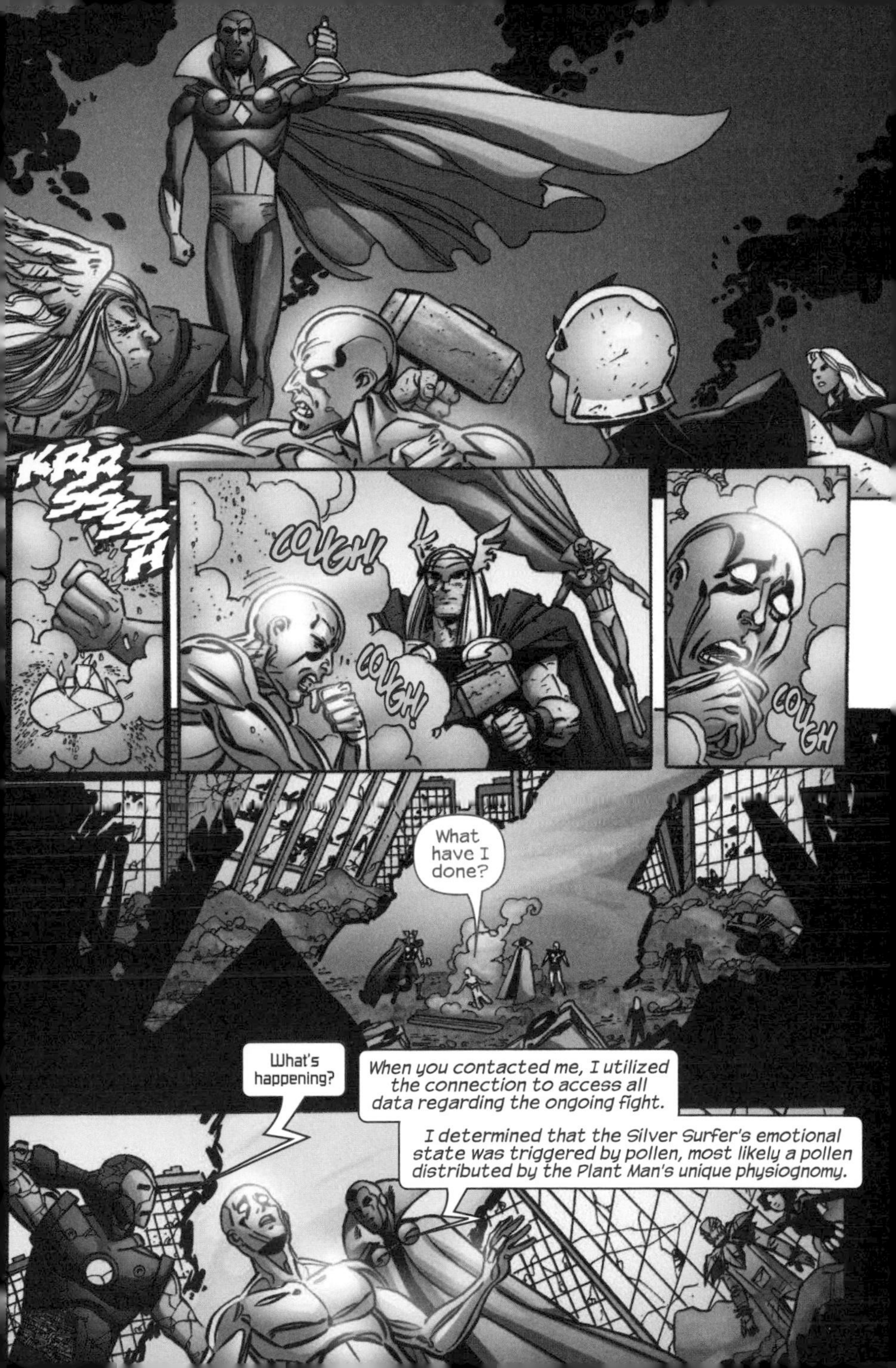
KRRSSSSSH
COUGH!
COUGH!
COUGH
What have I done?
What's happening?
When you contacted me, I utilized the connection to access all data regarding the ongoing fight.
I determined that the Silver Surfer's emotional state was triggered by pollen, most likely a pollen distributed by the Plant Man's unique physiognomy.

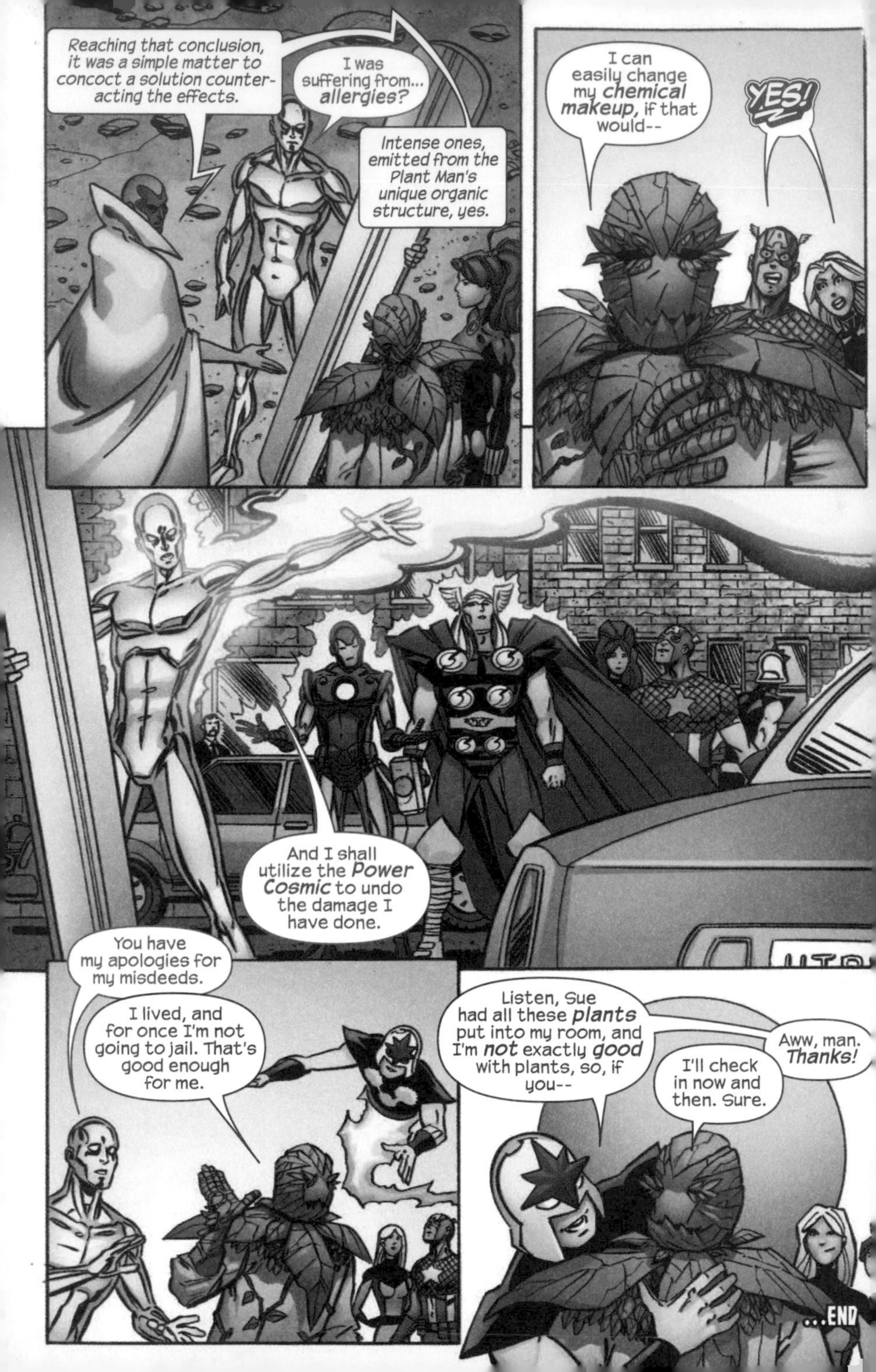

Reaching that conclusion, it was a simple matter to concoct a solution counter-acting the effects.
I was suffering from... *allergies?*
Intense ones, emitted from the Plant Man's unique organic structure, yes.
I can easily change my ***chemical makeup,*** if that would--
YES!
And I shall utilize the ***Power Cosmic*** to undo the damage I have done.
You have my apologies for my misdeeds.
I lived, and for once I'm not going to jail. That's good enough for me.
Listen, Sue had all these ***plants*** put into my room, and I'm ***not*** exactly ***good*** with plants, so, if you--
Aww, man. ***Thanks!***
I'll check in now and then. Sure.
...END

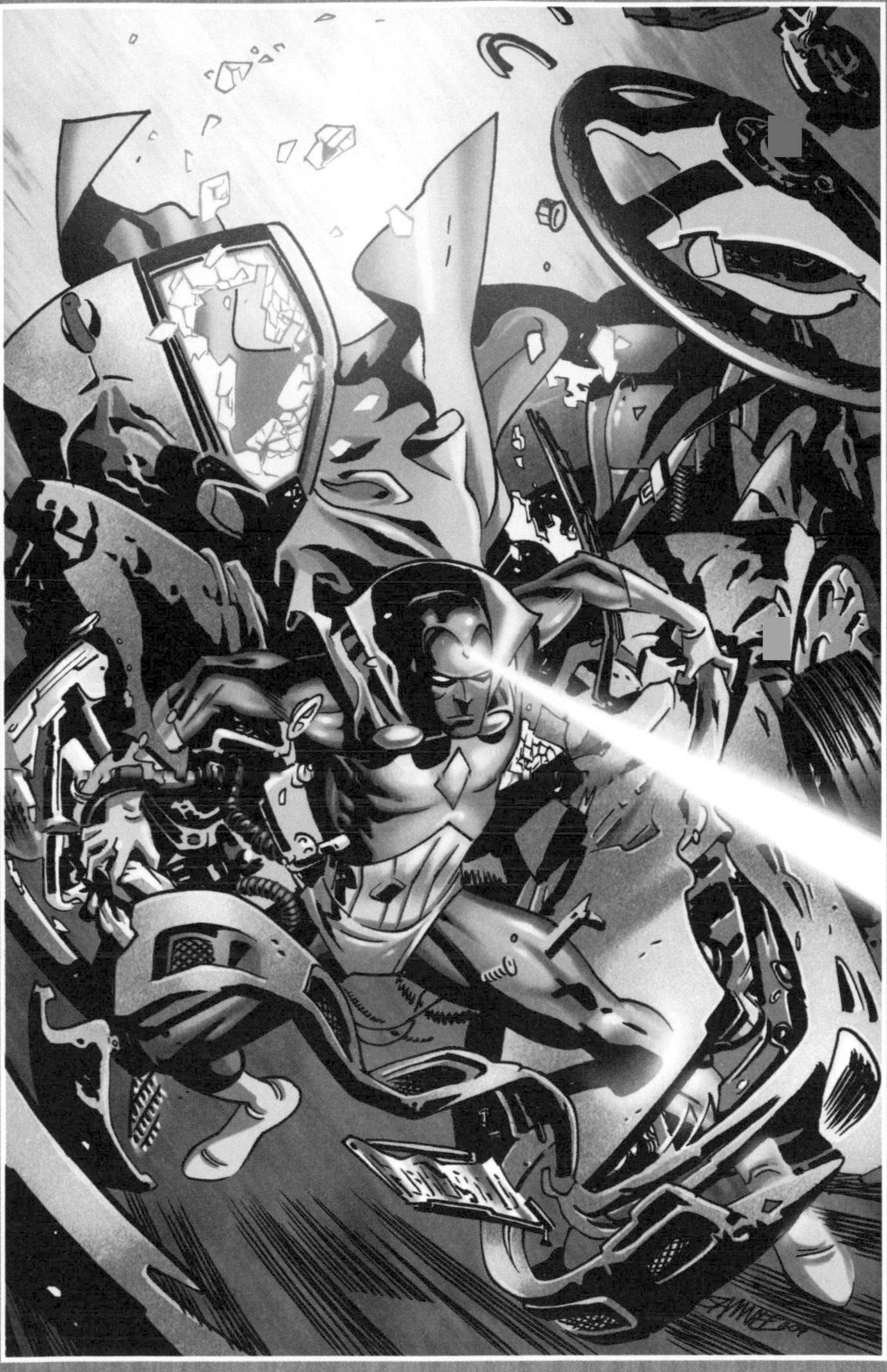

#20

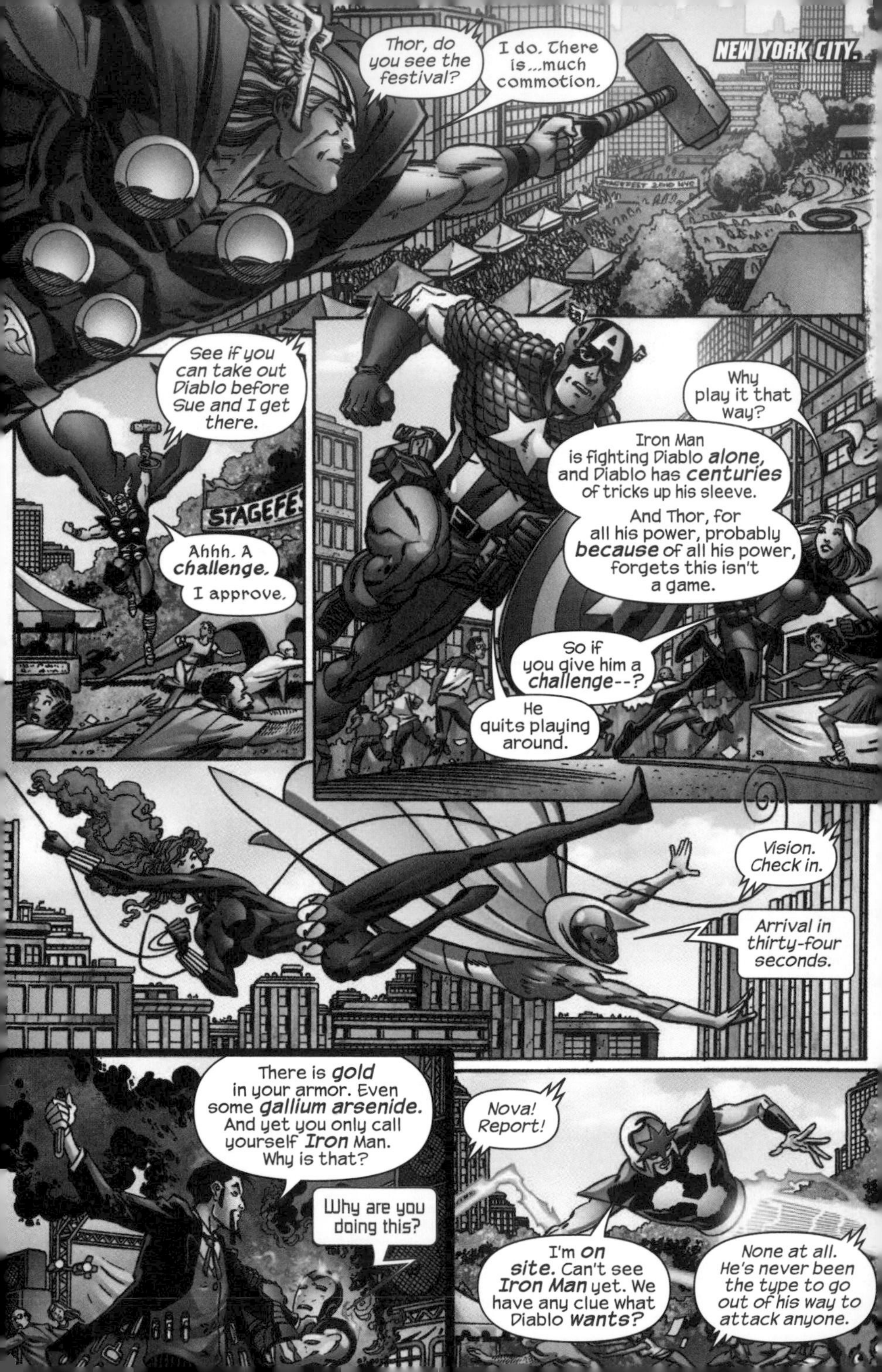
NEW YORK CITY.
Thor, do you see the festival?
I do. There is...much commotion.
STAGEFEST 2010 NYC
See if you can take out Diablo before Sue and I get there.
STAGEFES
Ahhh. A challenge. I approve.
Why play it that way?
Iron Man is fighting Diablo alone, and Diablo has centuries of tricks up his sleeve.
And Thor, for all his power, probably because of all his power, forgets this isn't a game.
So if you give him a challenge--?
He quits playing around.
Vision. Check in.
Arrival in thirty-four seconds.
There is gold in your armor. Even some gallium arsenide. And yet you only call yourself Iron Man. Why is that?
Why are you doing this?
Nova! Report!
I'm on site. Can't see Iron Man yet. We have any clue what Diablo wants?
None at all. He's never been the type to go out of his way to attack anyone.

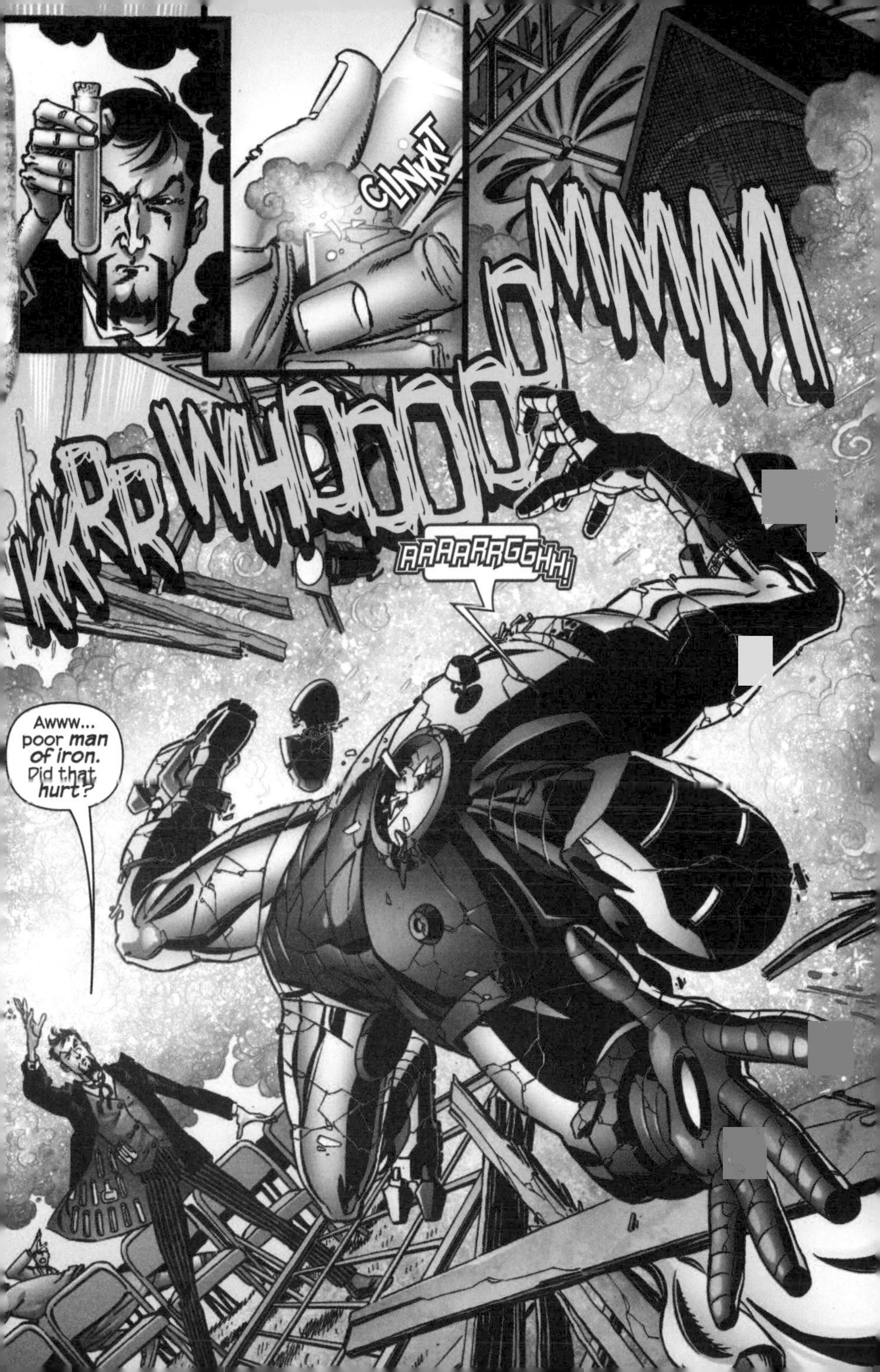
CLNKKT
KRRWHOOOOOOMMMM
AAAAARRGGHH!
Awww... poor man of iron. Did that hurt?

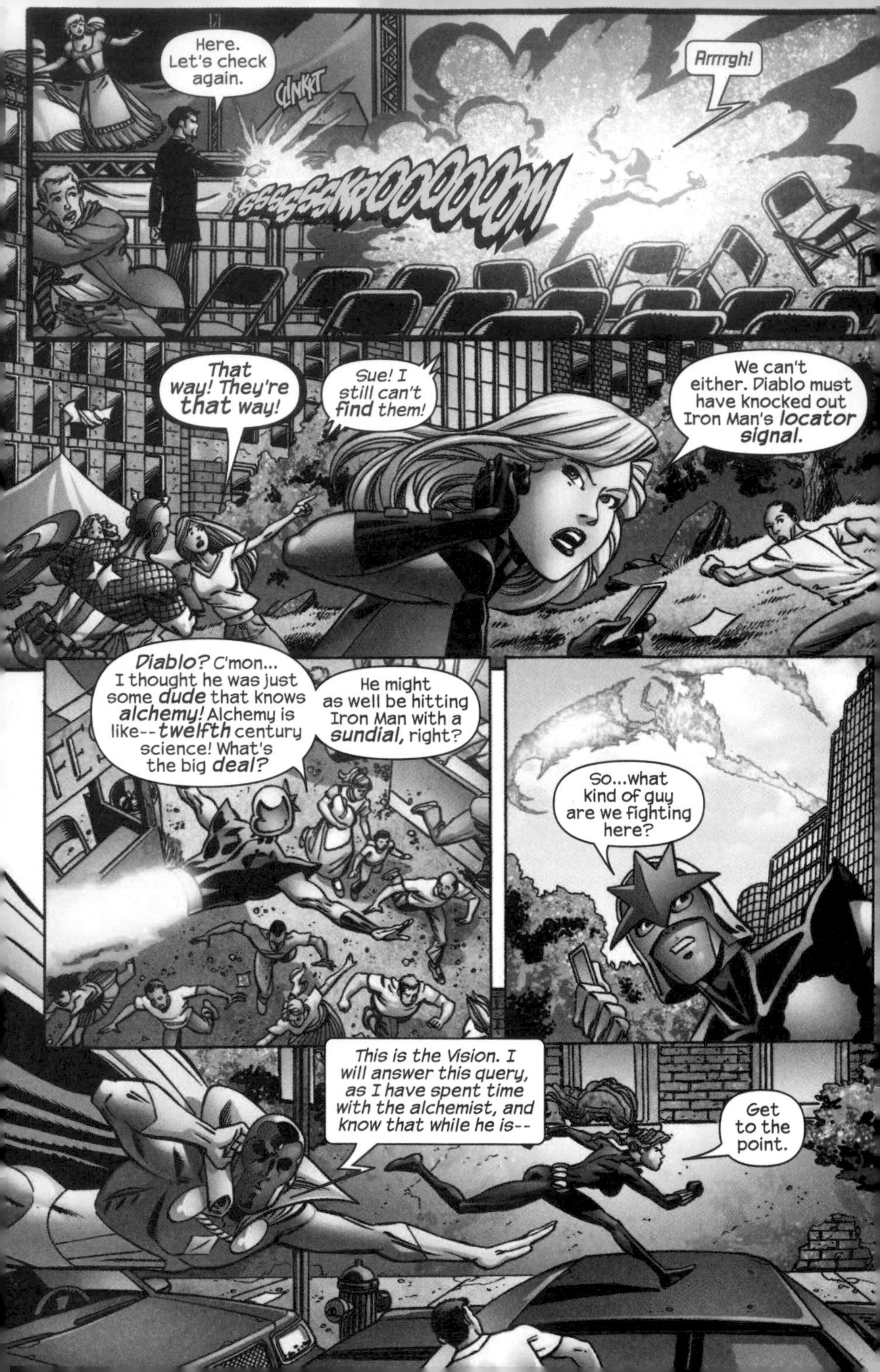
Here. Let's check again.
CLNKKT
SSSSSSKROOOOOOOM
Arrrrgh!
That way! They're that way!
Sue! I still can't find them!
We can't either. Diablo must have knocked out Iron Man's locator signal.
Diablo? C'mon... I thought he was just some dude that knows alchemy! Alchemy is like--twelfth century science! What's the big deal?
He might as well be hitting Iron Man with a sundial, right?
So...what kind of guy are we fighting here?
This is the Vision. I will answer this query, as I have spent time with the alchemist, and know that while he is--
Get to the point.

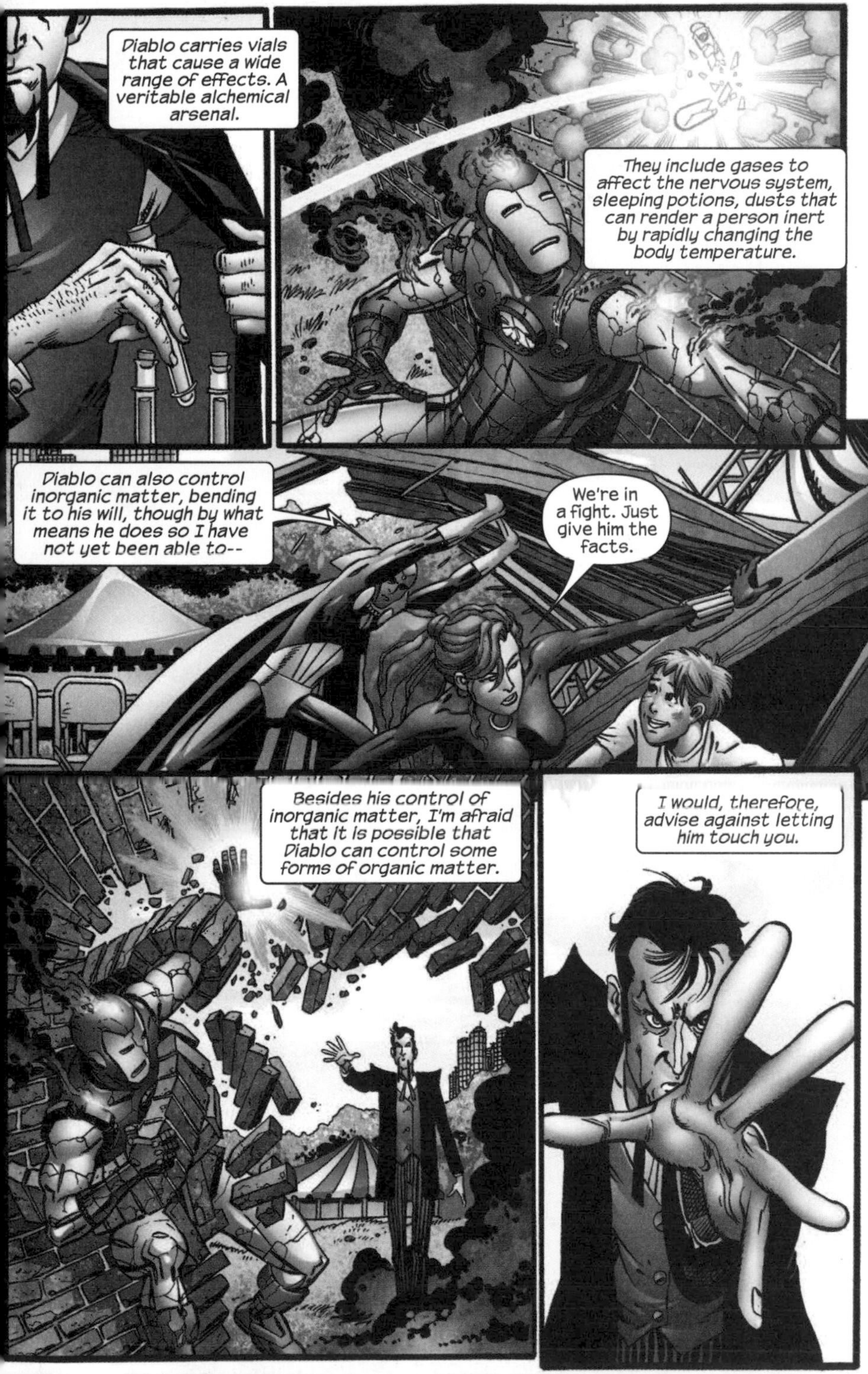
Diablo carries vials that cause a wide range of effects. A veritable alchemical arsenal.
They include gases to affect the nervous system, sleeping potions, dusts that can render a person inert by rapidly changing the body temperature.
Diablo can also control inorganic matter, bending it to his will, though by what means he does so I have not yet been able to--
We're in a fight. Just give him the facts.
Besides his control of inorganic matter, I'm afraid that it is possible that Diablo can control some forms of organic matter.
I would, therefore, advise against letting him touch you.

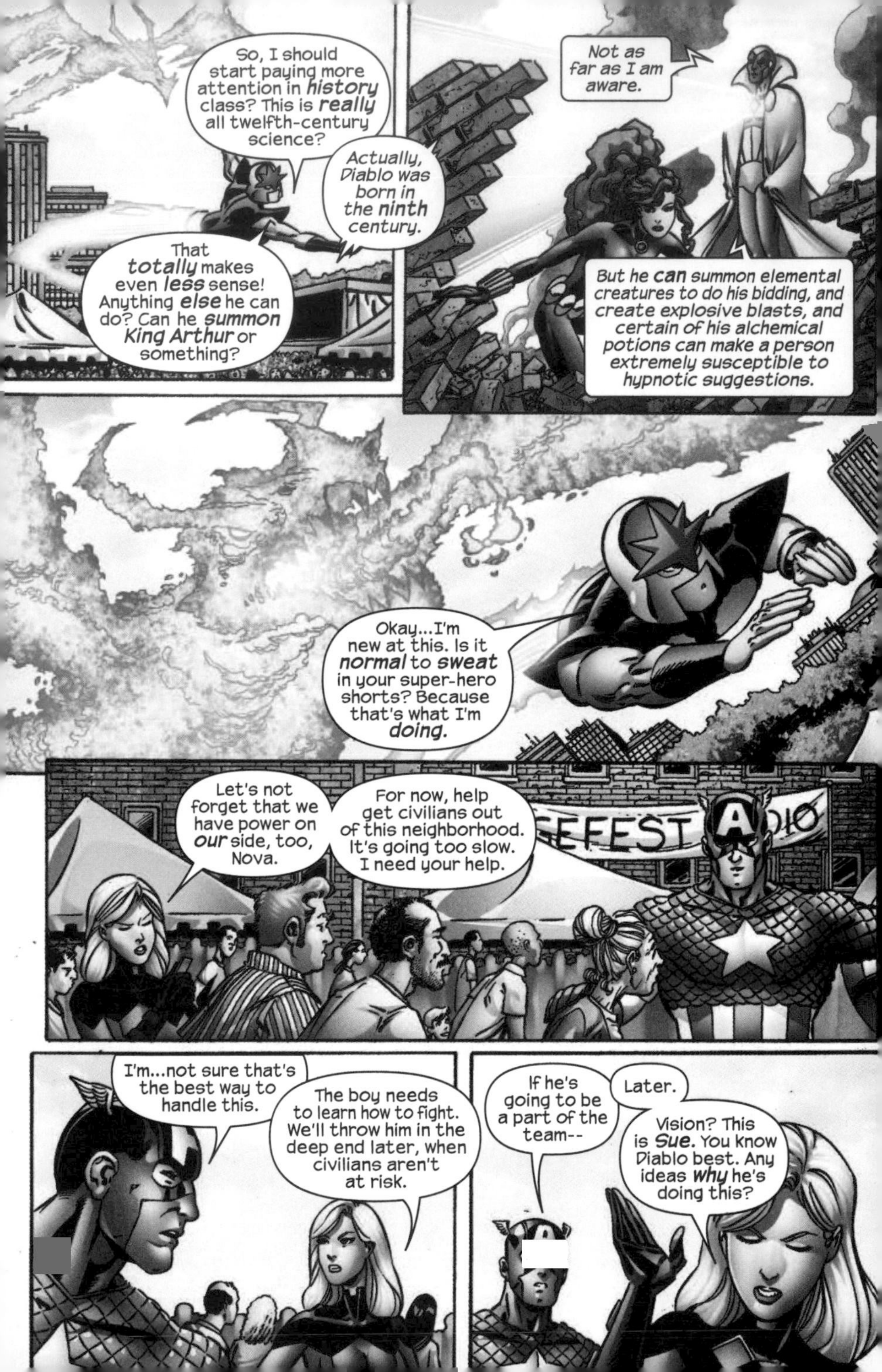

So, I should start paying more attention in history class? This is really all twelfth-century science?
Actually, Diablo was born in the ninth century.
That totally makes even less sense! Anything else he can do? Can he summon King Arthur or something?
Not as far as I am aware.
But he can summon elemental creatures to do his bidding, and create explosive blasts, and certain of his alchemical potions can make a person extremely susceptible to hypnotic suggestions.
Okay...I'm new at this. Is it normal to sweat in your super-hero shorts? Because that's what I'm doing.
Let's not forget that we have power on our side, too, Nova.
For now, help get civilians out of this neighborhood. It's going too slow. I need your help.
I'm...not sure that's the best way to handle this.
The boy needs to learn how to fight. We'll throw him in the deep end later, when civilians aren't at risk.
If he's going to be a part of the team--
Later.
Vision? This is Sue. You know Diablo best. Any ideas why he's doing this?

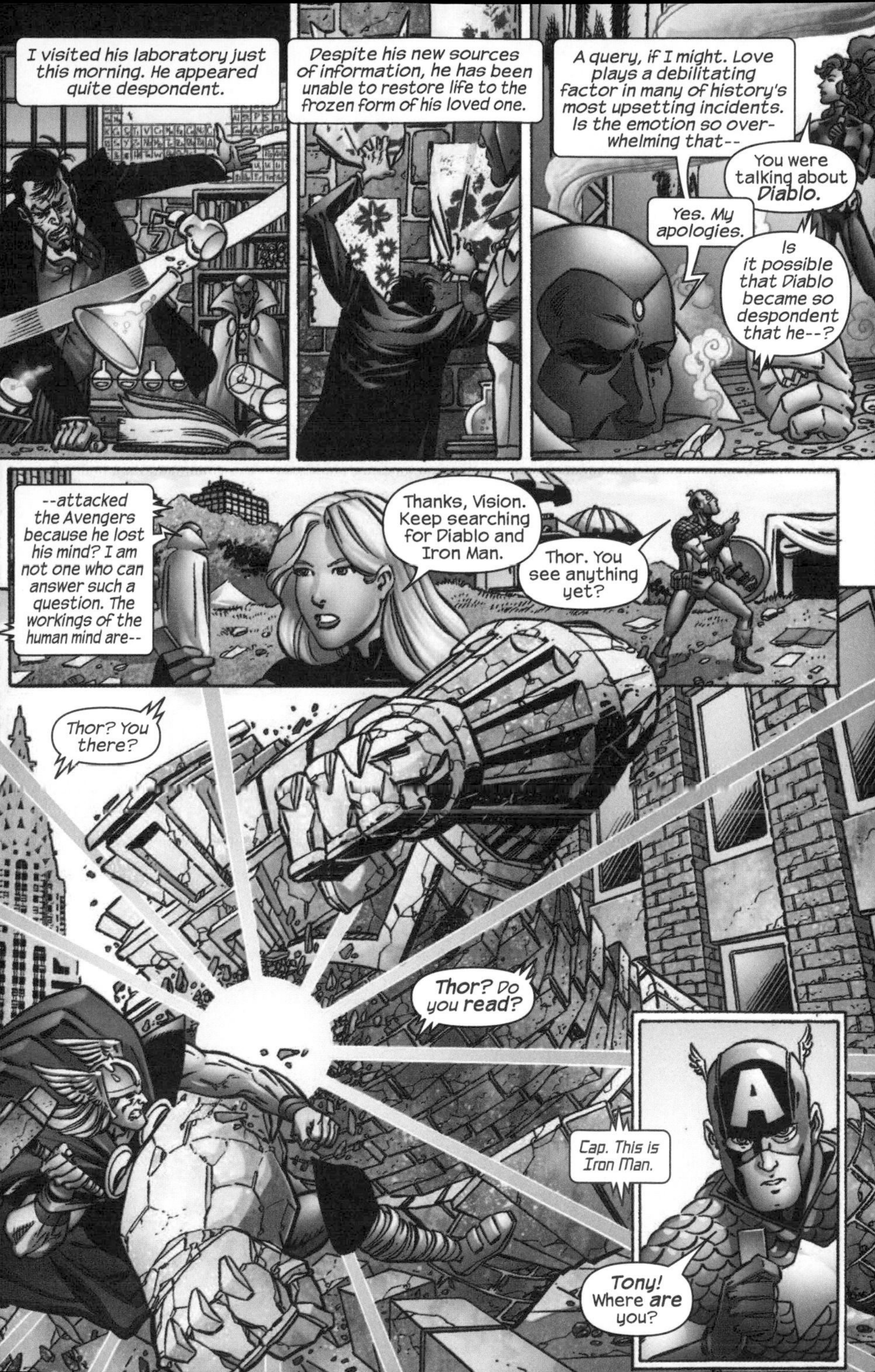
I visited his laboratory just this morning. He appeared quite despondent.
Despite his new sources of information, he has been unable to restore life to the frozen form of his loved one.
A query, if I might. Love plays a debilitating factor in many of history's most upsetting incidents. Is the emotion so over-whelming that--
You were talking about Diablo.
Yes. My apologies.
Is it possible that Diablo became so despondent that he--?
--attacked the Avengers because he lost his mind? I am not one who can answer such a question. The workings of the human mind are--
Thanks, Vision. Keep searching for Diablo and Iron Man.
Thor. You see anything yet?
Thor? You there?
Thor? Do you read?
Cap. This is Iron Man.
Tony! Where are you?

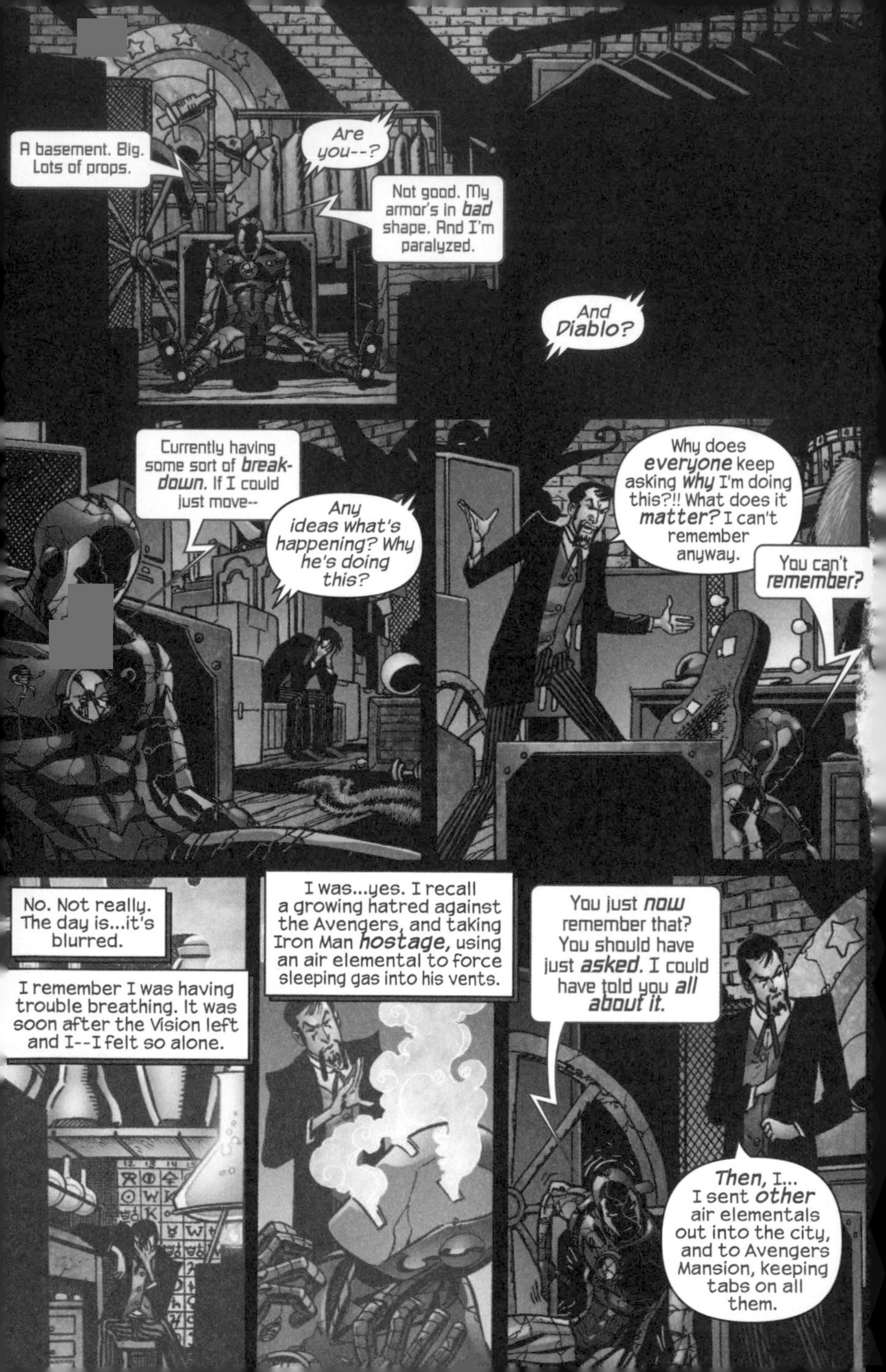
A basement. Big. Lots of props.
Are you--?
Not good. My armor's in *bad* shape. And I'm paralyzed.
And Diablo?
Currently having some sort of *break-down.* If I could just move--
Any ideas what's happening? Why he's doing this?
Why does *everyone* keep asking *why* I'm doing this?!! What does it *matter?* I can't remember anyway.
You can't *remember?*
No. Not really. The day is...it's blurred.
I remember I was having trouble breathing. It was soon after the Vision left and I--I felt so alone.
I was...yes. I recall a growing hatred against the Avengers, and taking Iron Man *hostage,* using an air elemental to force sleeping gas into his vents.
You just *now* remember that? You should have just *asked.* I could have told you *all about it.*
Then, I... I sent *other* air elementals out into the city, and to Avengers Mansion, keeping tabs on all them.

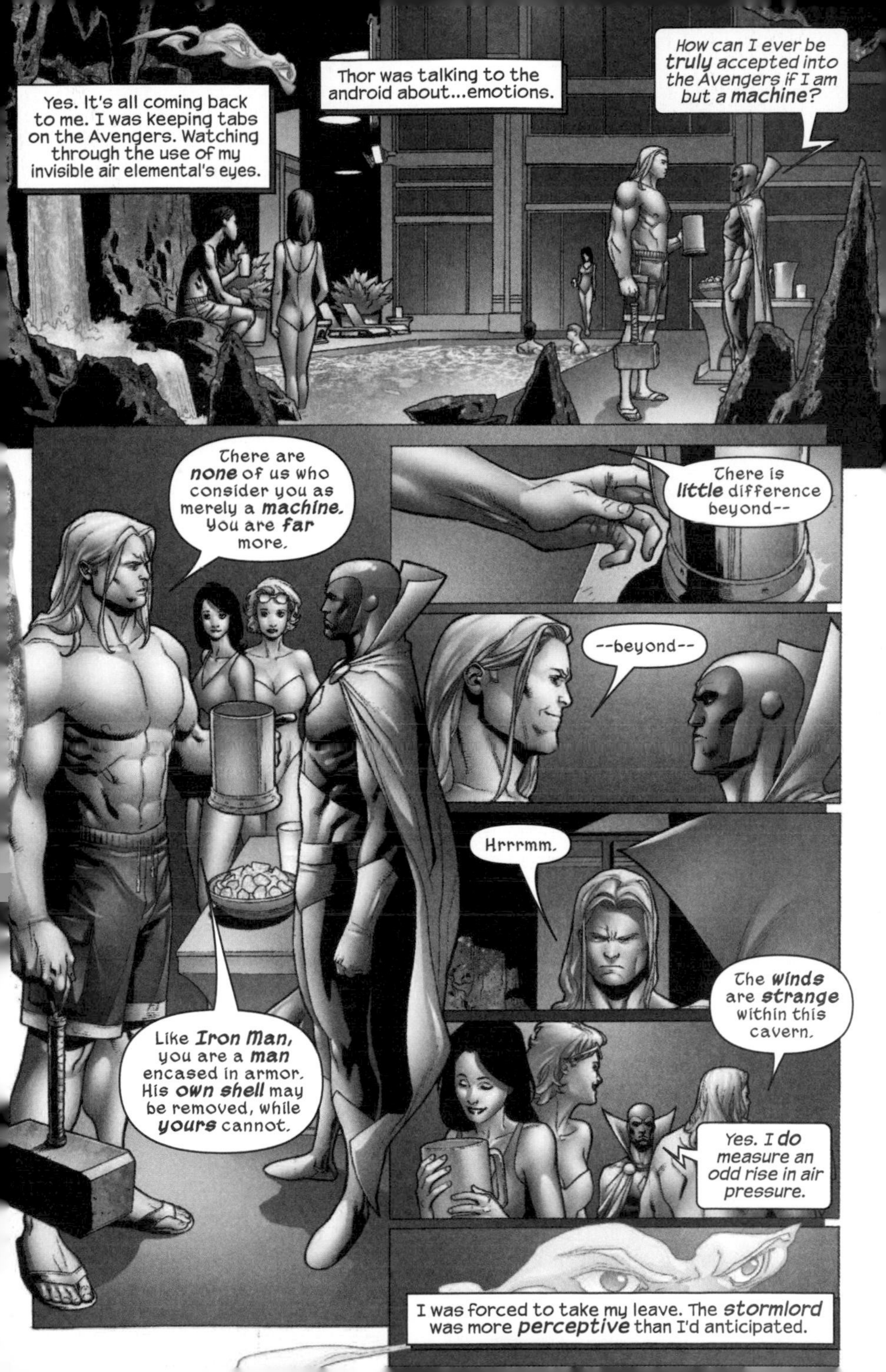
Yes. It's all coming back to me. I was keeping tabs on the Avengers. Watching through the use of my invisible air elemental's eyes.
Thor was talking to the android about...emotions.
How can I ever be truly accepted into the Avengers if I am but a machine?
There are none of us who consider you as merely a machine. You are far more.
Like Iron Man, you are a man encased in armor. His own shell may be removed, while yours cannot.
There is little difference beyond--
--beyond--
Hrrrmm.
The winds are strange within this cavern.
Yes. I do measure an odd rise in air pressure.
I was forced to take my leave. The stormlord was more perceptive than I'd anticipated.

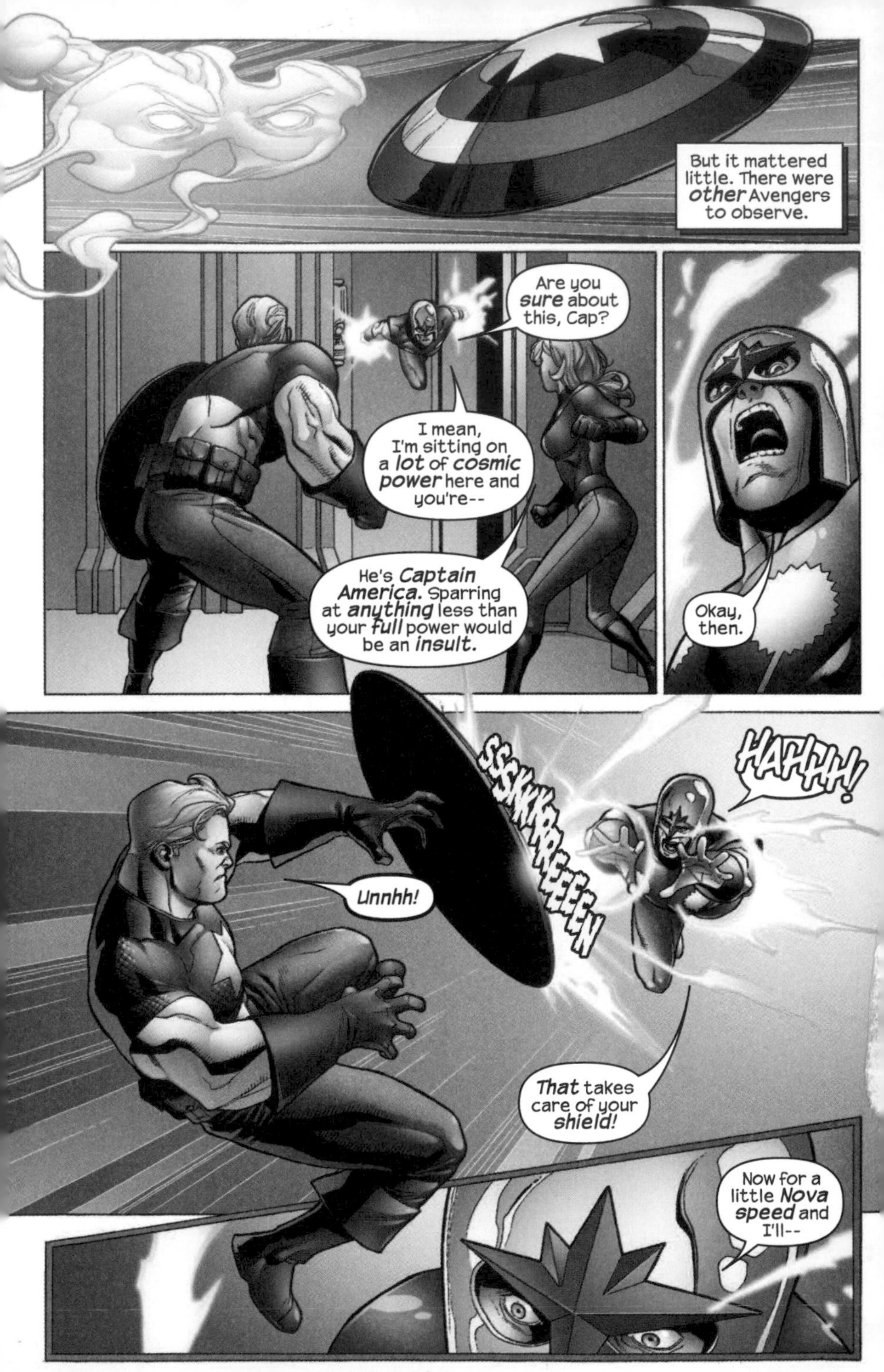
But it mattered little. There were *other* Avengers to observe.
Are you *sure* about this, Cap?
I mean, I'm sitting on a *lot* of *cosmic power* here and you're--
He's *Captain America.* Sparring at *anything* less than your *full* power would be an *insult.*
Okay, then.
SSKKRREEEEN
HAHHH!
Unnhh!
That takes care of your *shield!*
Now for a little *Nova speed* and I'll--

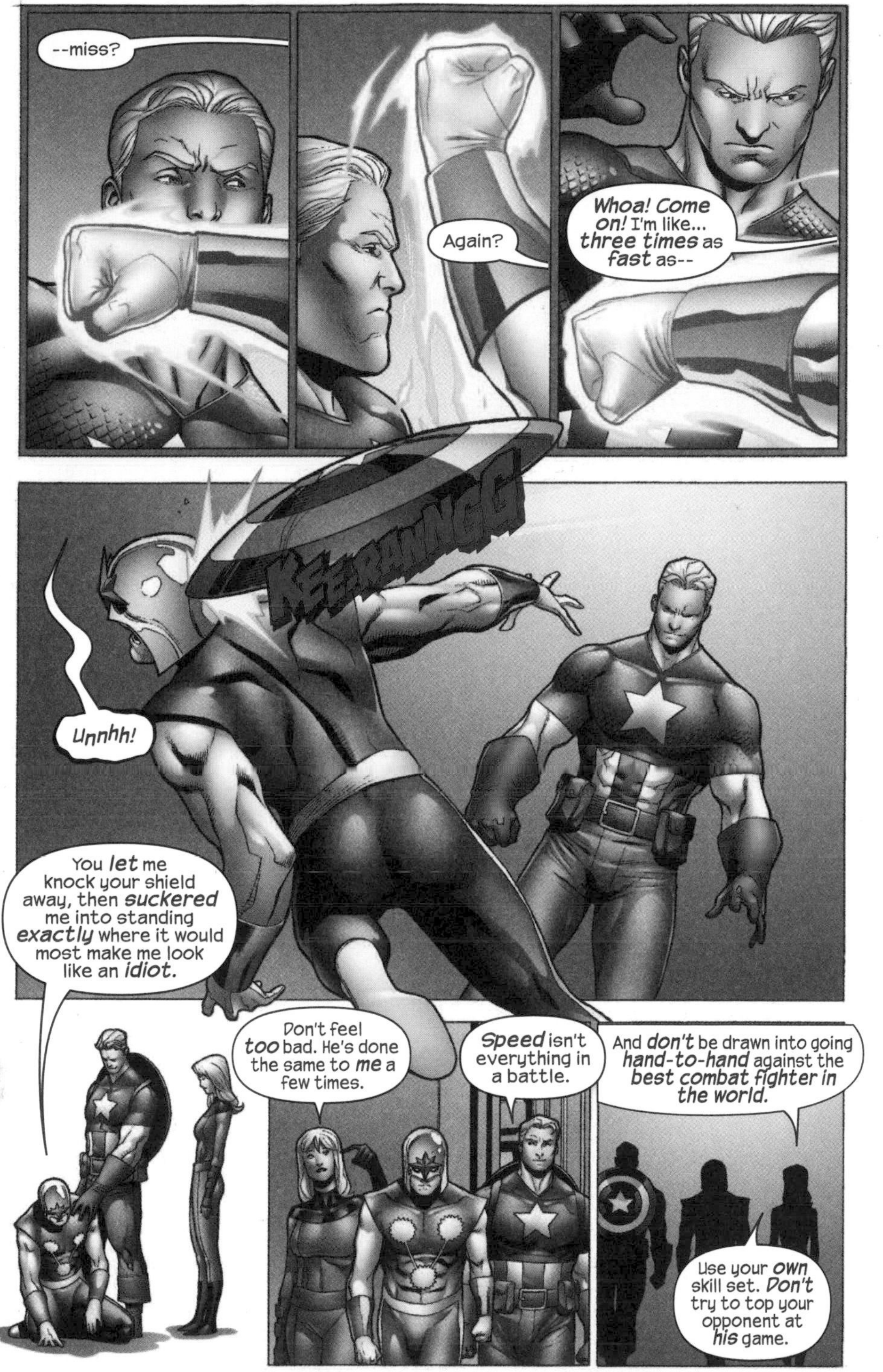
--miss?
Again?
Whoa! Come on! I'm like... three times as fast as--
KEERANNGG
Unnhh!
You let me knock your shield away, then suckered me into standing exactly where it would most make me look like an idiot.
Don't feel too bad. He's done the same to me a few times.
Speed isn't everything in a battle.
And don't be drawn into going hand-to-hand against the best combat fighter in the world.
Use your own skill set. Don't try to top your opponent at his game.

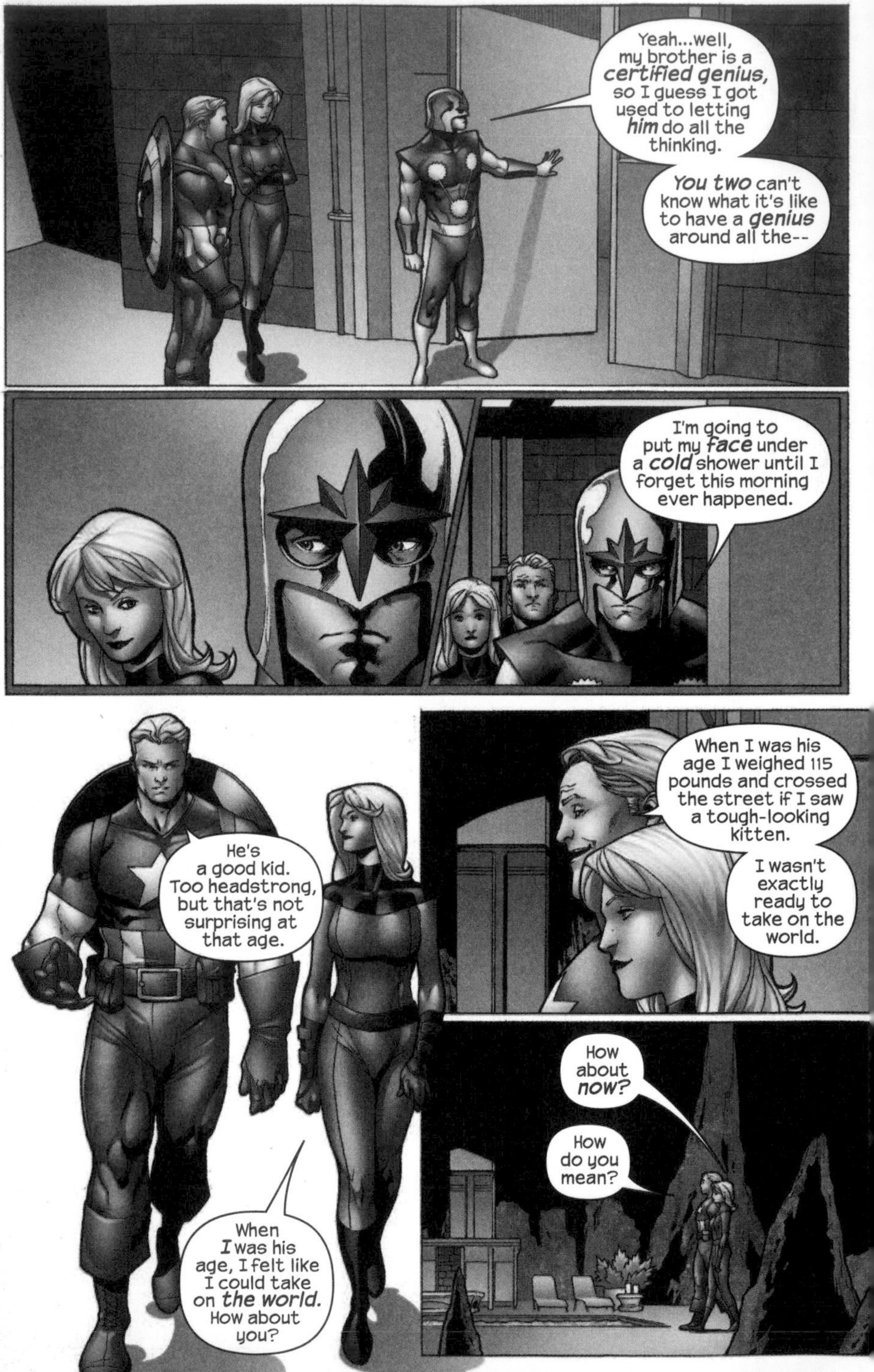
Yeah...well, my brother is a certified genius, so I guess I got used to letting him do all the thinking.
You two can't know what it's like to have a genius around all the--
I'm going to put my face under a cold shower until I forget this morning ever happened.
He's a good kid. Too headstrong, but that's not surprising at that age.
When I was his age, I felt like I could take on the world. How about you?
When I was his age I weighed 115 pounds and crossed the street if I saw a tough-looking kitten.
I wasn't exactly ready to take on the world.
How about now?
How do you mean?

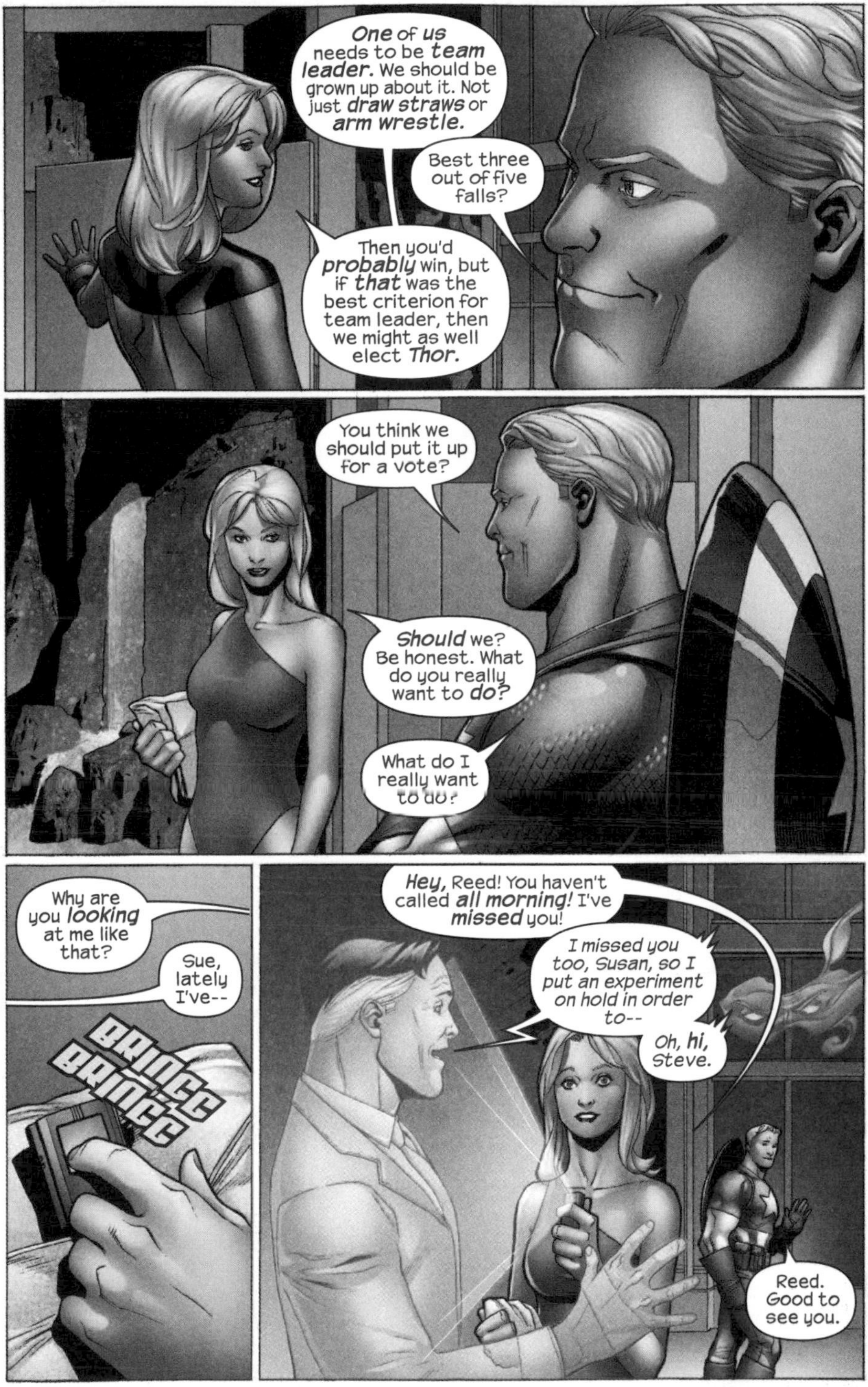
One of us needs to be team leader. We should be grown up about it. Not just draw straws or arm wrestle.
Best three out of five falls?
Then you'd probably win, but if that was the best criterion for team leader, then we might as well elect Thor.
You think we should put it up for a vote?
Should we? Be honest. What do you really want to do?
What do I really want to do?
Why are you looking at me like that?
Sue, lately I've--
BRINGG BRINGG
Hey, Reed! You haven't called all morning! I've missed you!
I missed you too, Susan, so I put an experiment on hold in order to--
Oh, hi, Steve.
Reed. Good to see you.

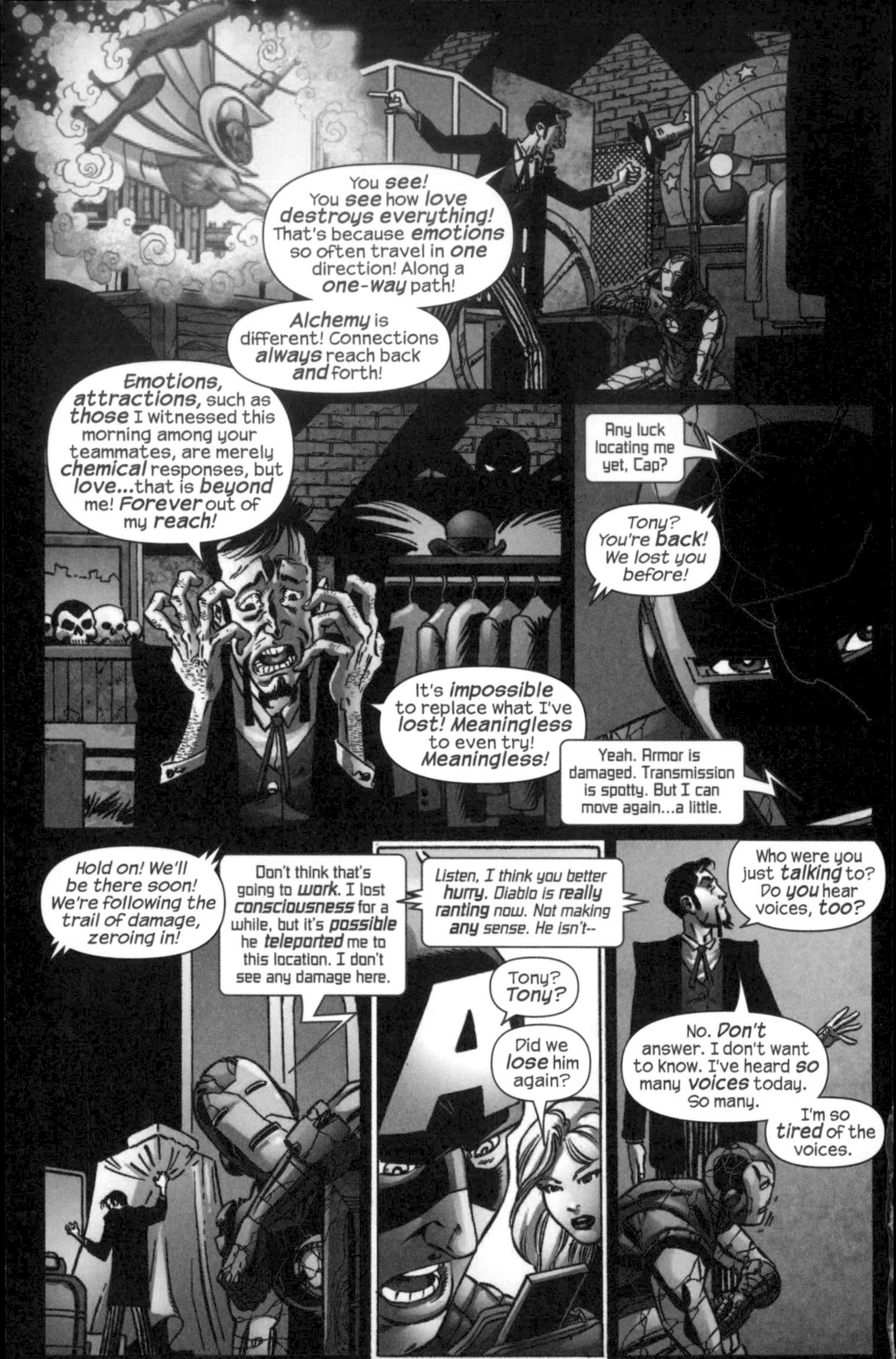
You see! You see how love destroys everything! That's because emotions so often travel in one direction! Along a one-way path!
Alchemy is different! Connections always reach back and forth!
Emotions, attractions, such as those I witnessed this morning among your teammates, are merely chemical responses, but love...that is beyond me! Forever out of my reach!
Any luck locating me yet, Cap?
Tony? You're back! We lost you before!
It's impossible to replace what I've lost! Meaningless to even try! Meaningless!
Yeah. Armor is damaged. Transmission is spotty. But I can move again...a little.
Hold on! We'll be there soon! We're following the trail of damage, zeroing in!
Don't think that's going to work. I lost consciousness for a while, but it's possible he teleported me to this location. I don't see any damage here.
Listen, I think you better hurry. Diablo is really ranting now. Not making any sense. He isn't--
Tony? Tony?
Did we lose him again?
Who were you just talking to? Do you hear voices, too?
No. Don't answer. I don't want to know. I've heard so many voices today. So many.
I'm so tired of the voices.

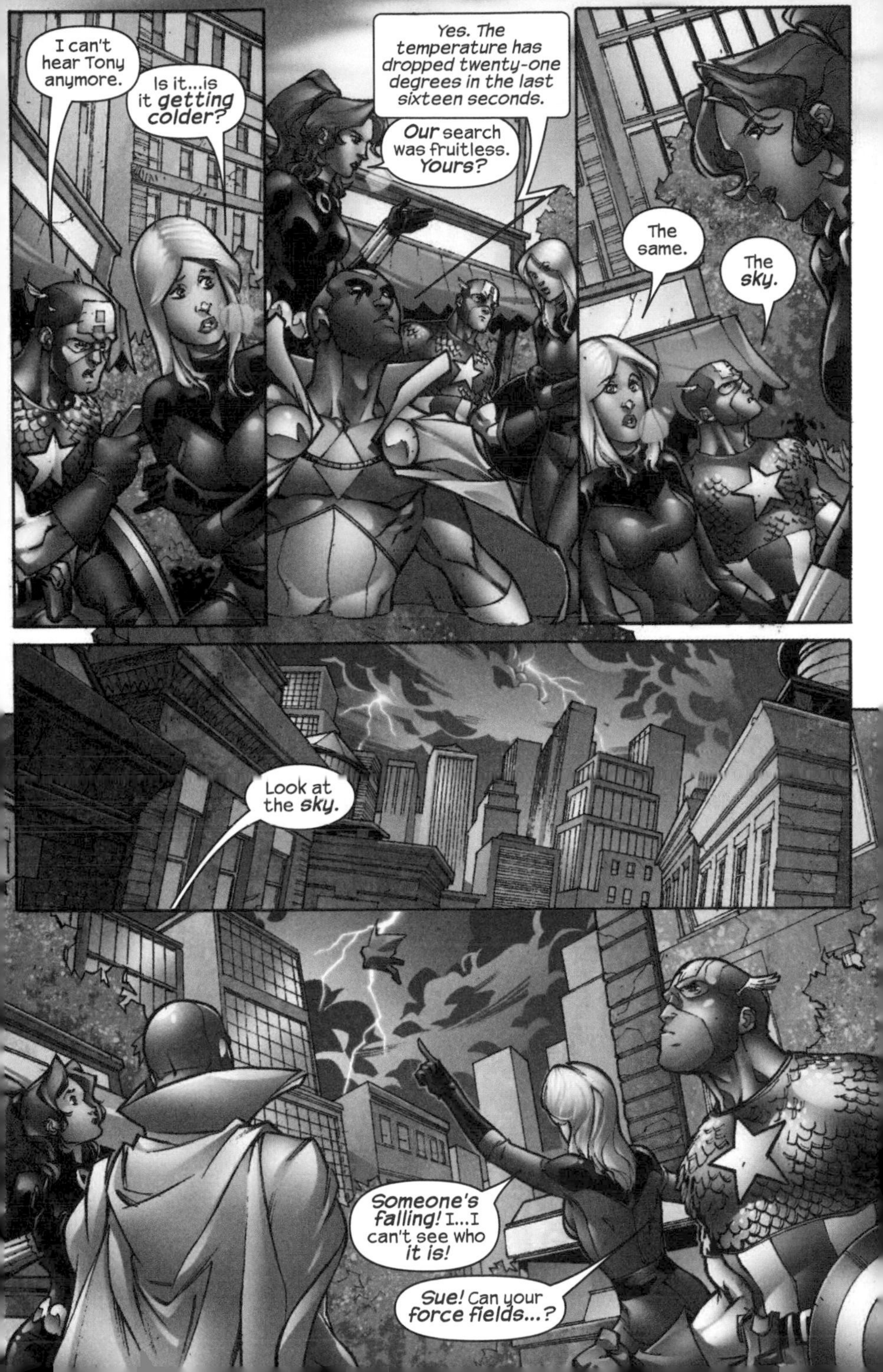

I can't hear Tony anymore.
Is it...is it *getting colder?*
Yes. The temperature has dropped twenty-one degrees in the last sixteen seconds.
Our search was fruitless. *Yours?*
The same.
The *sky.*
Look at the *sky.*
Someone's falling! I...I can't see who *it is!*
Sue! Can your *force fields...?*

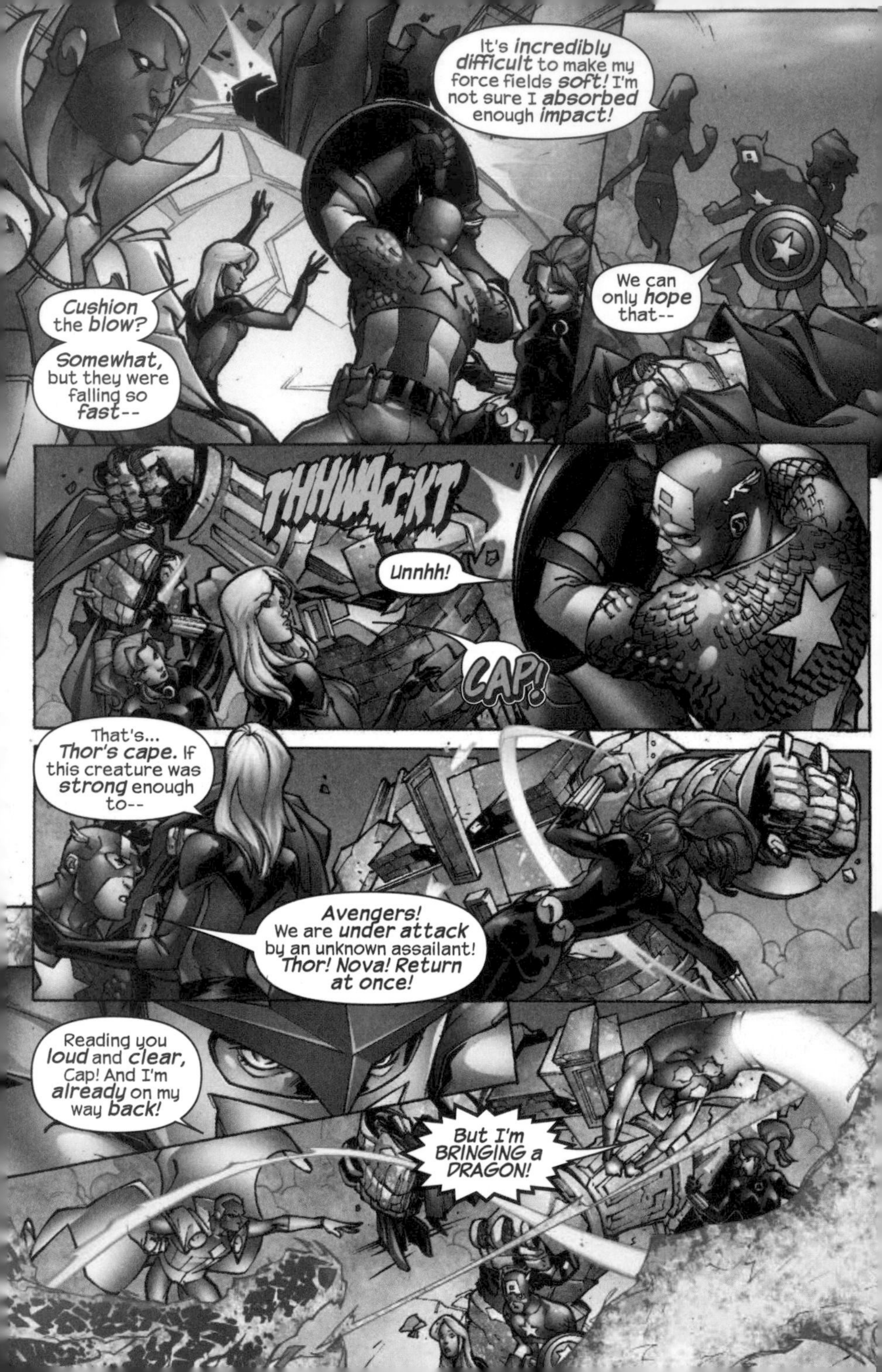

It's incredibly difficult to make my force fields soft! I'm not sure I absorbed enough impact!
Cushion the blow?
Somewhat, but they were falling so fast--
We can only hope that--
THHWACCKT
Unnhh!
CAP!
That's... Thor's cape. If this creature was strong enough to--
Avengers! We are under attack by an unknown assailant! Thor! Nova! Return at once!
Reading you loud and clear, Cap! And I'm already on my way back!
But I'm BRINGING a DRAGON!

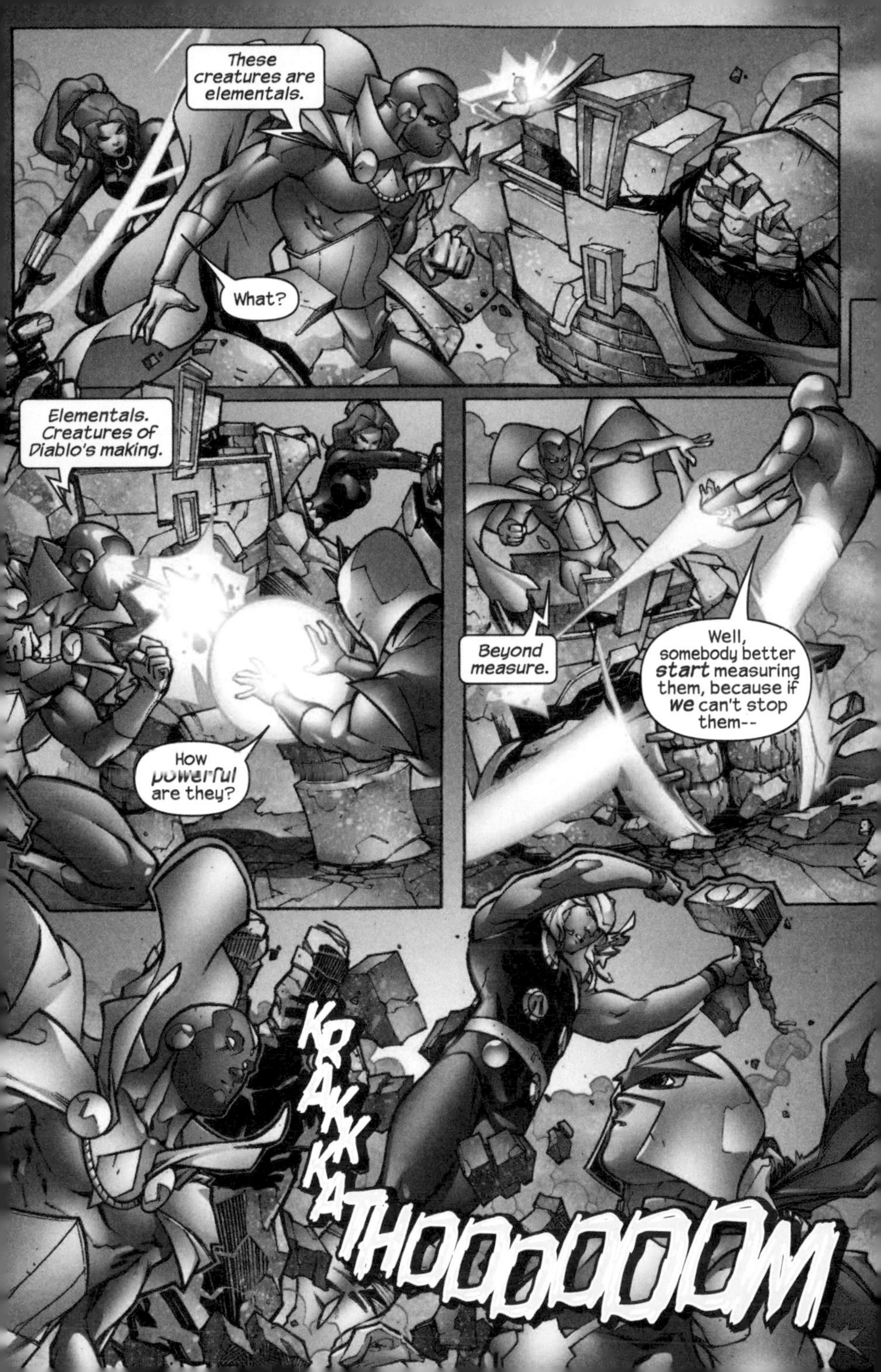

These creatures are elementals.
What?
Elementals. Creatures of Diablo's making.
How powerful are they?
Beyond measure.
Well, somebody better start measuring them, because if we can't stop them--
KRAKKA THOOOOOOOM

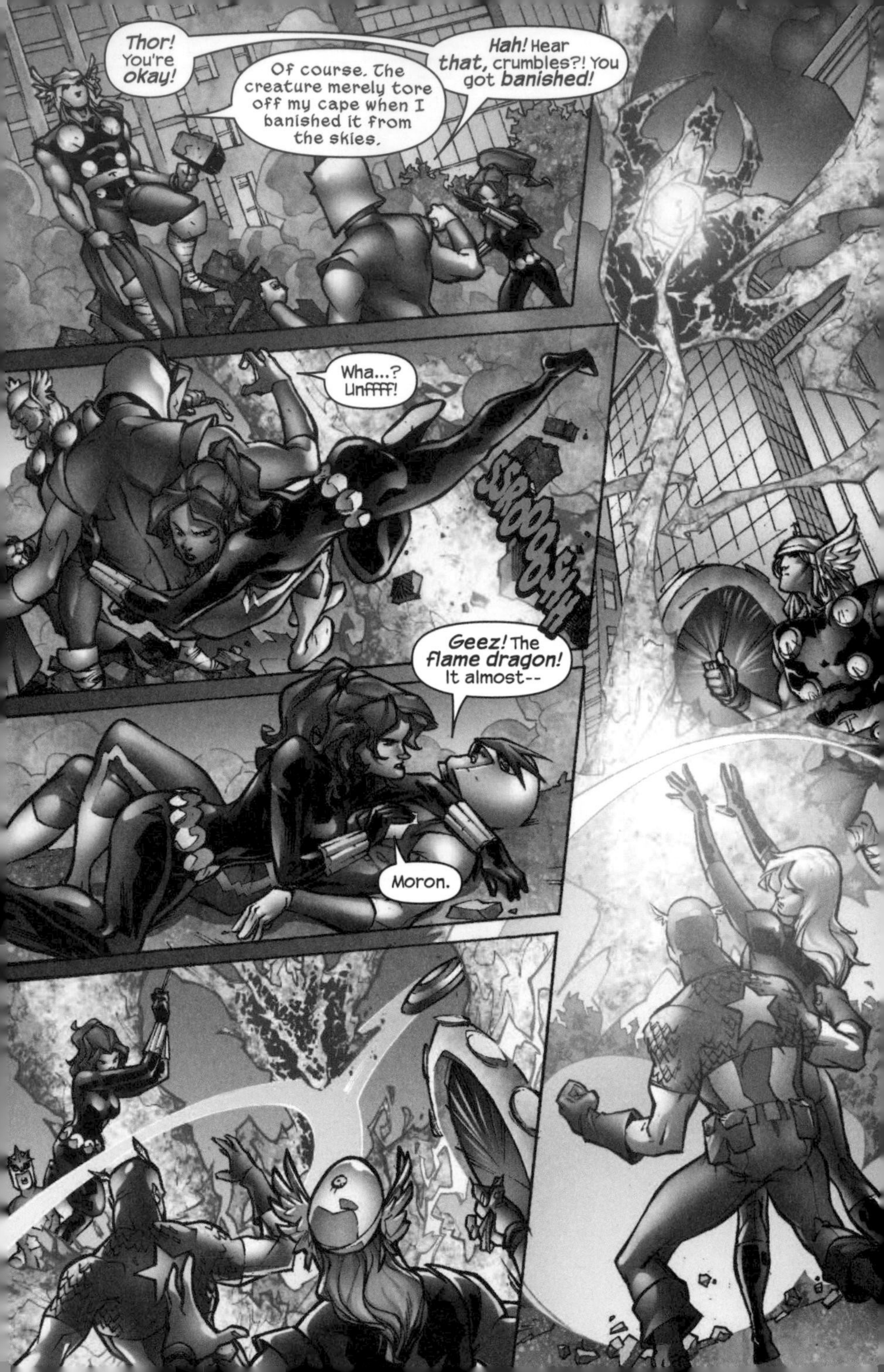

Thor! You're okay!
Of course. The creature merely tore off my cape when I banished it from the skies.
Hah! Hear that, crumbles?! You got banished!
Wha...? Unffff!
SSROOOSHH
Geez! The flame dragon! It almost--
Moron.

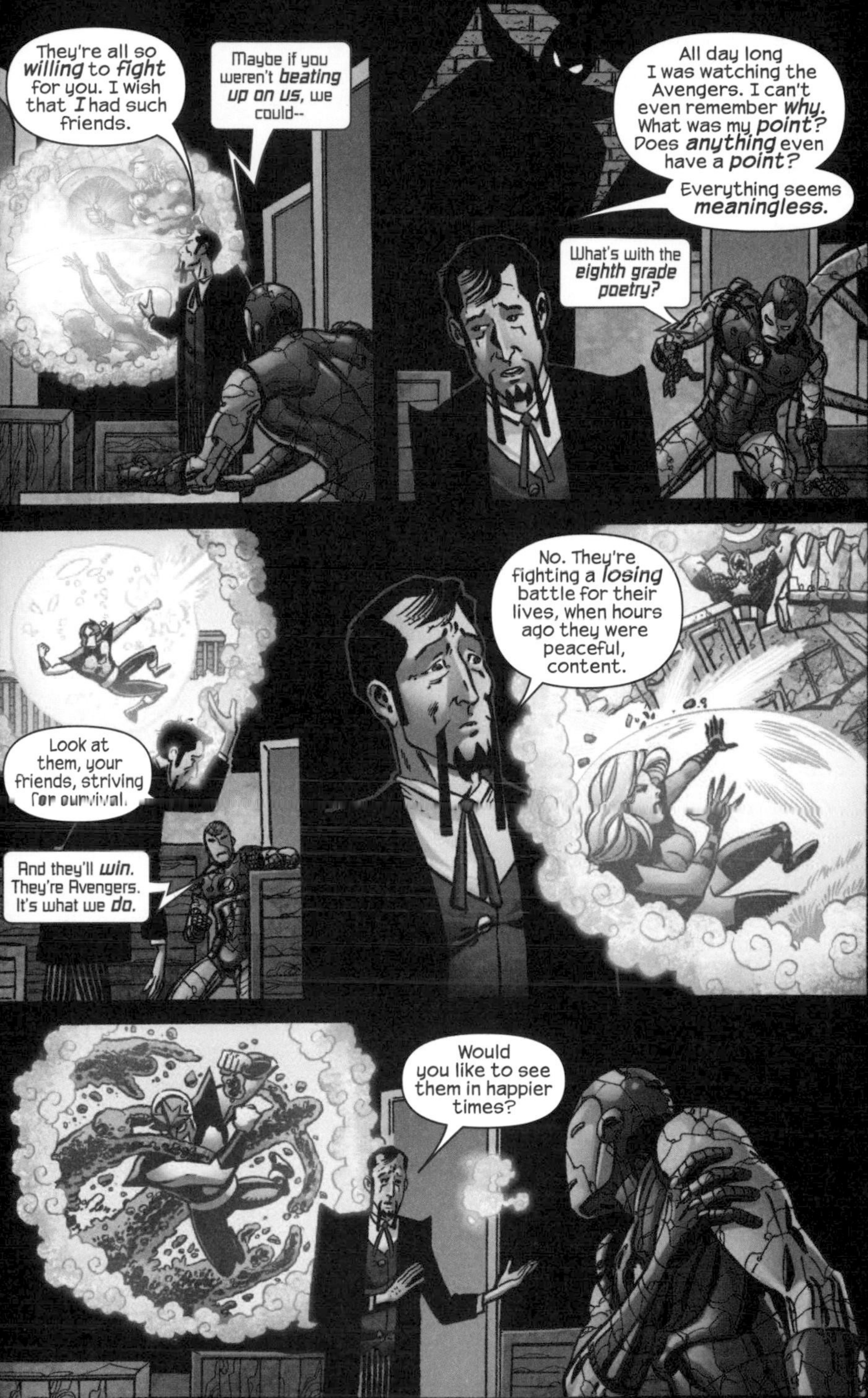

They're all so willing to fight for you. I wish that I had such friends.
Maybe if you weren't beating up on us, we could--
All day long I was watching the Avengers. I can't even remember why. What was my point? Does anything even have a point?
Everything seems meaningless.
What's with the eighth grade poetry?
Look at them, your friends, striving for survival.
And they'll win. They're Avengers. It's what we do.
No. They're fighting a losing battle for their lives, when hours ago they were peaceful, content.
Would you like to see them in happier times?

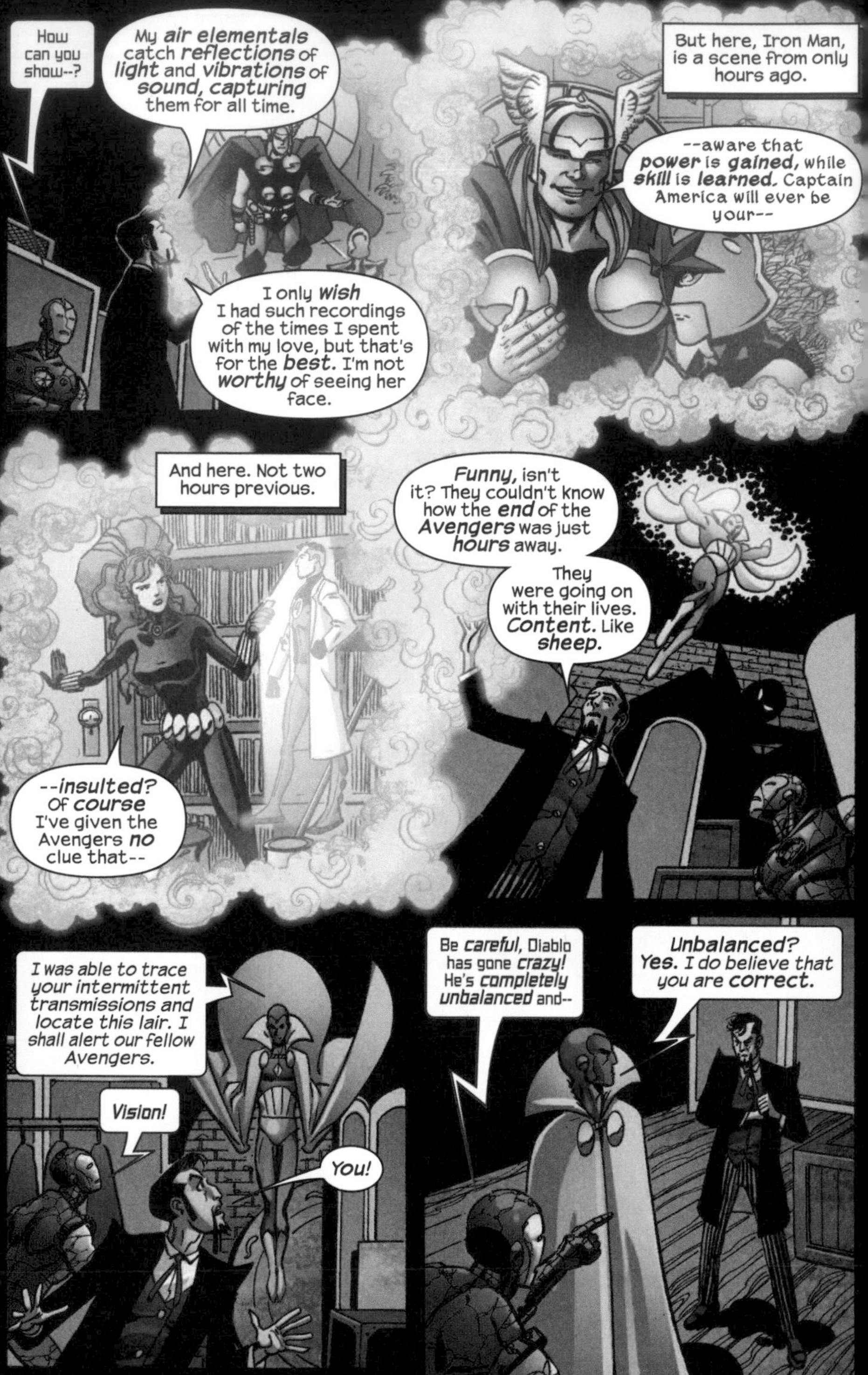
How can you show--?
My air elementals catch reflections of light and vibrations of sound, capturing them for all time.
But here, Iron Man, is a scene from only hours ago.
--aware that power is gained, while skill is learned. Captain America will ever be your--
I only wish I had such recordings of the times I spent with my love, but that's for the best. I'm not worthy of seeing her face.
And here. Not two hours previous.
--insulted? Of course I've given the Avengers no clue that--
Funny, isn't it? They couldn't know how the end of the Avengers was just hours away.
They were going on with their lives. Content. Like sheep.
I was able to trace your intermittent transmissions and locate this lair. I shall alert our fellow Avengers.
Vision!
You!
Be careful, Diablo has gone crazy! He's completely unbalanced and--
Unbalanced? Yes. I do believe that you are correct.

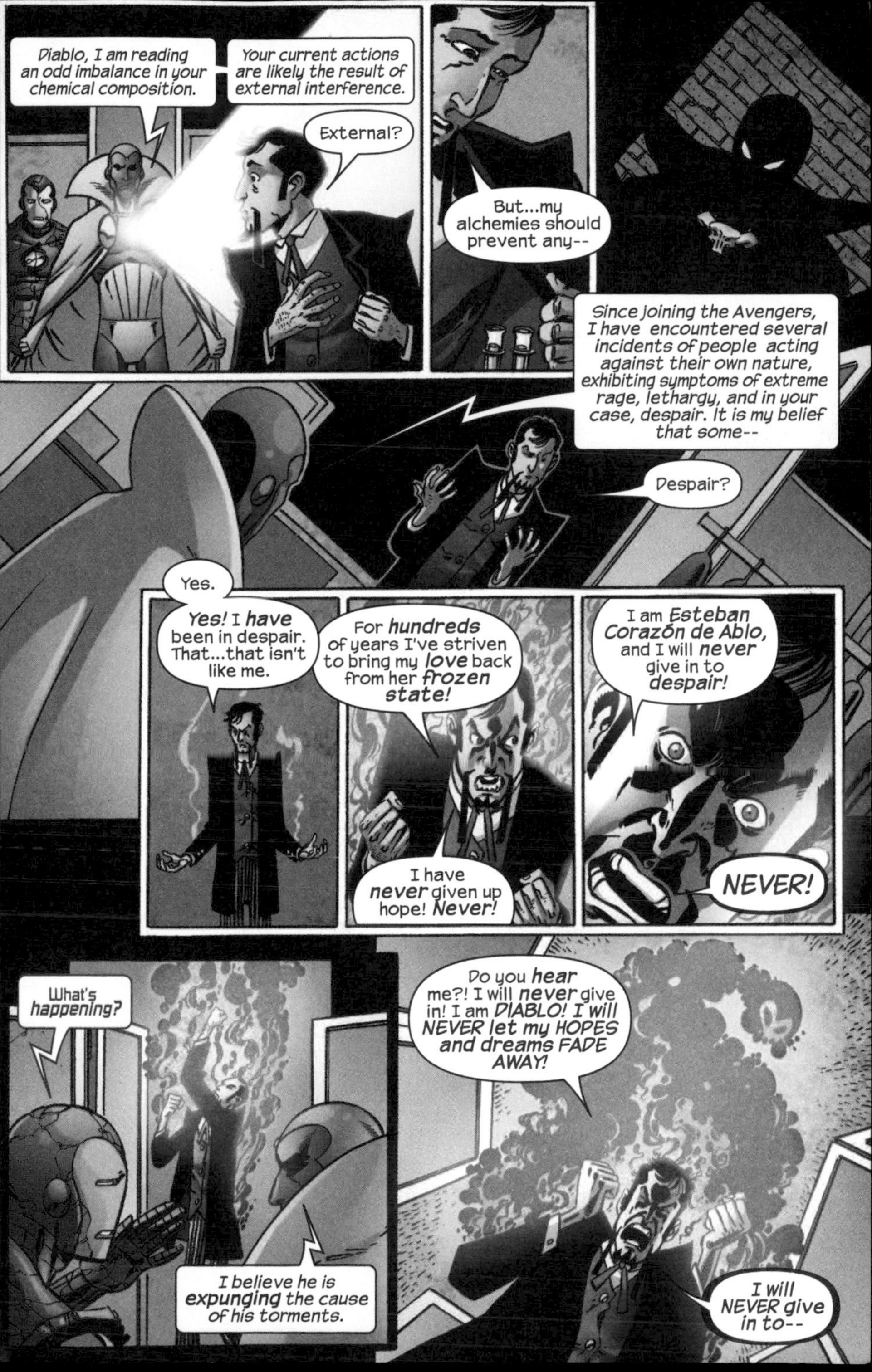
Diablo, I am reading an odd imbalance in your chemical composition.
Your current actions are likely the result of external interference.
External?
But...my alchemies should prevent any--
Since joining the Avengers, I have encountered several incidents of people acting against their own nature, exhibiting symptoms of extreme rage, lethargy, and in your case, despair. It is my belief that some--
Despair?
Yes.
Yes! I have been in despair. That...that isn't like me.
For hundreds of years I've striven to bring my love back from her frozen state!
I have never given up hope! Never!
I am Esteban Corazón de Ablo, and I will never give in to despair!
NEVER!
What's happening?
I believe he is expunging the cause of his torments.
Do you hear me?! I will never give in! I am DIABLO! I will NEVER let my HOPES and dreams FADE AWAY!
I will NEVER give in to--

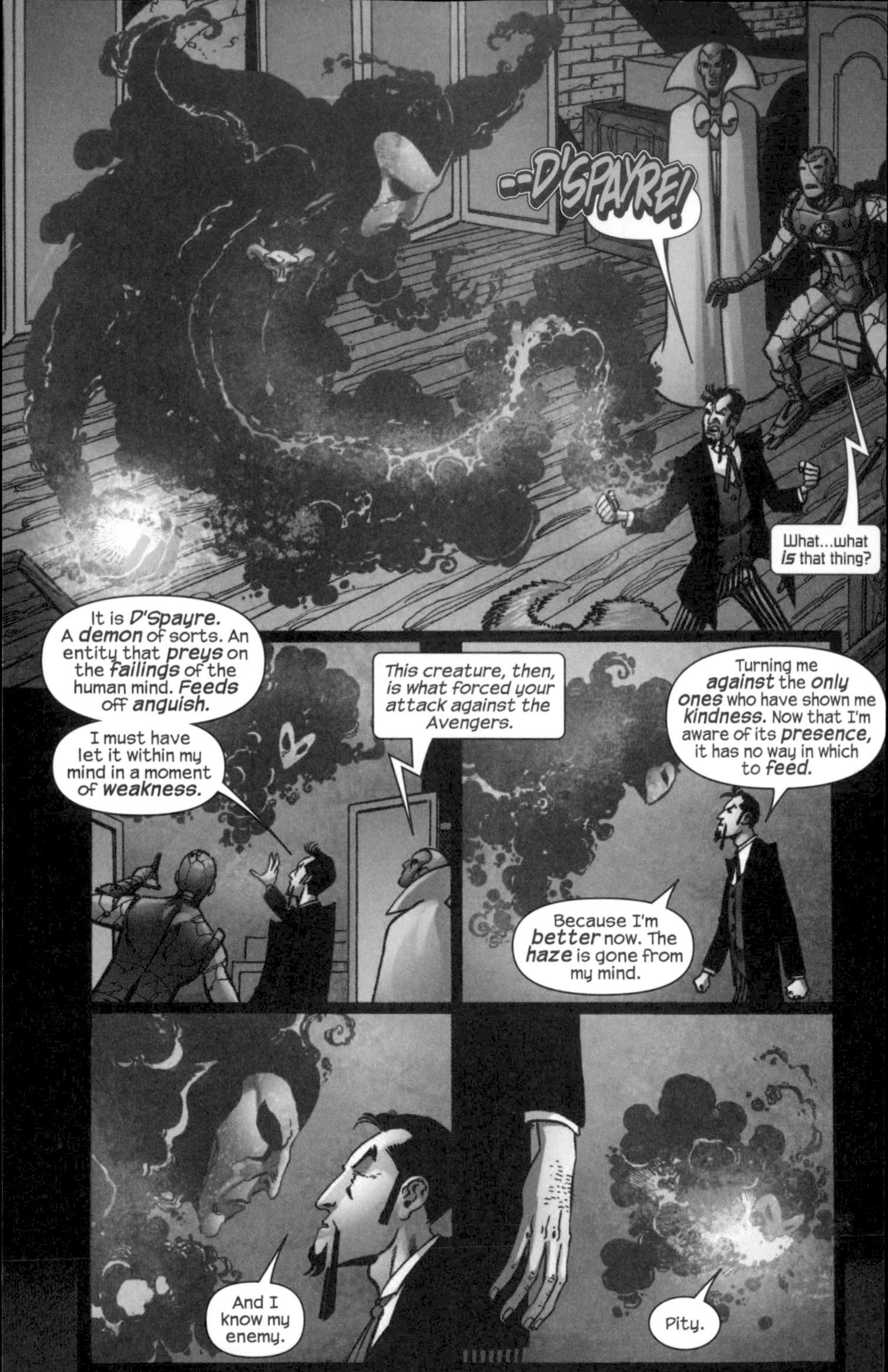
--D'SPAYRE!
What...what is that thing?
It is D'Spayre. A demon of sorts. An entity that preys on the failings of the human mind. Feeds off anguish.
I must have let it within my mind in a moment of weakness.
This creature, then, is what forced your attack against the Avengers.
Turning me against the only ones who have shown me kindness. Now that I'm aware of its presence, it has no way in which to feed.
Because I'm better now. The haze is gone from my mind.
And I know my enemy.
Pity.

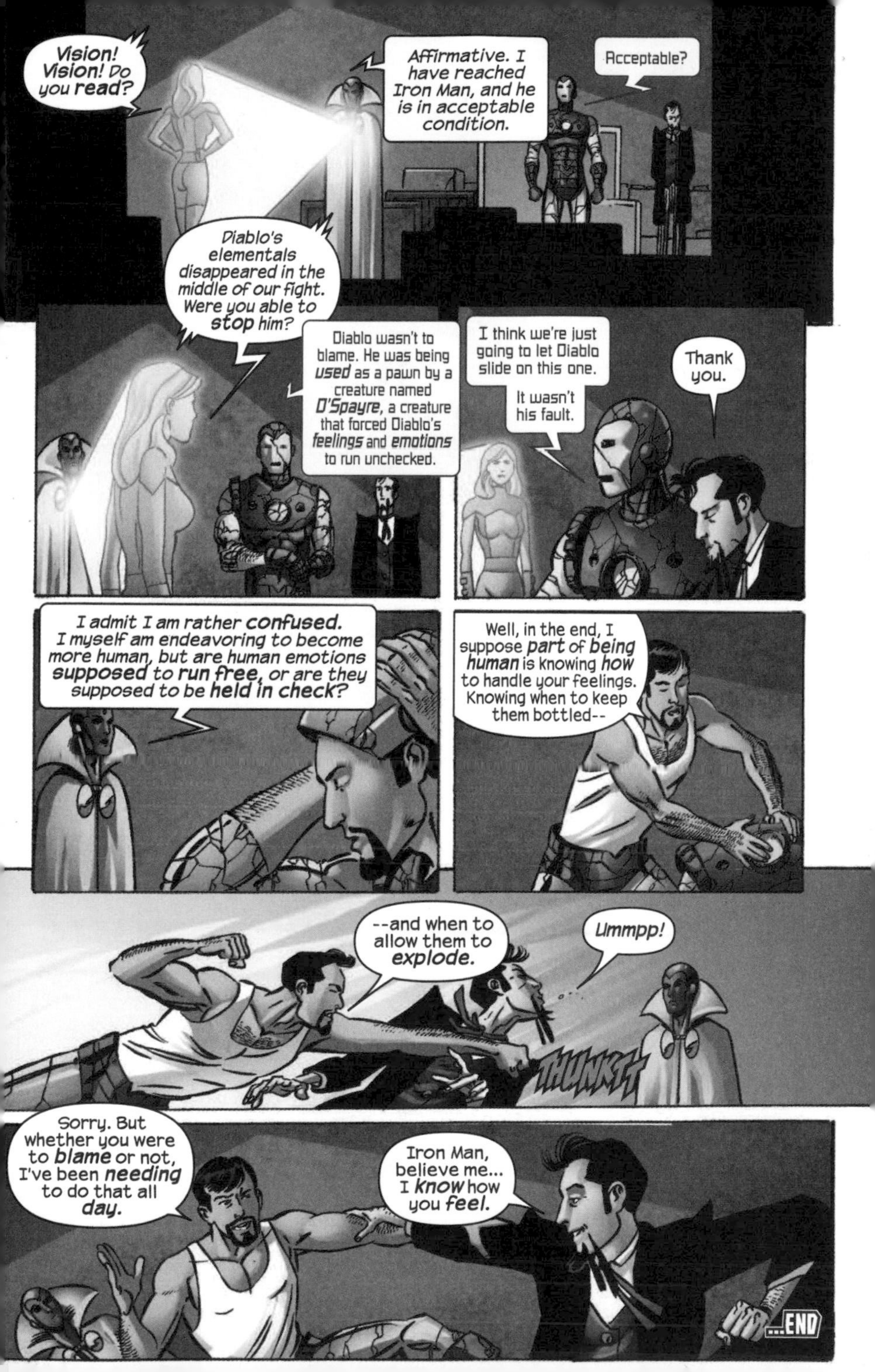
Vision! Vision! Do you read?
Affirmative. I have reached Iron Man, and he is in acceptable condition.
Acceptable?
Diablo's elementals disappeared in the middle of our fight. Were you able to stop him?
Diablo wasn't to blame. He was being used as a pawn by a creature named O'Spayre, a creature that forced Diablo's feelings and emotions to run unchecked.
I think we're just going to let Diablo slide on this one.
It wasn't his fault.
Thank you.
I admit I am rather confused. I myself am endeavoring to become more human, but are human emotions supposed to run free, or are they supposed to be held in check?
Well, in the end, I suppose part of being human is knowing how to handle your feelings. Knowing when to keep them bottled--
--and when to allow them to explode.
Ummpp!
THUNKT!
Sorry. But whether you were to blame or not, I've been needing to do that all day.
Iron Man, believe me... I know how you feel.
...END

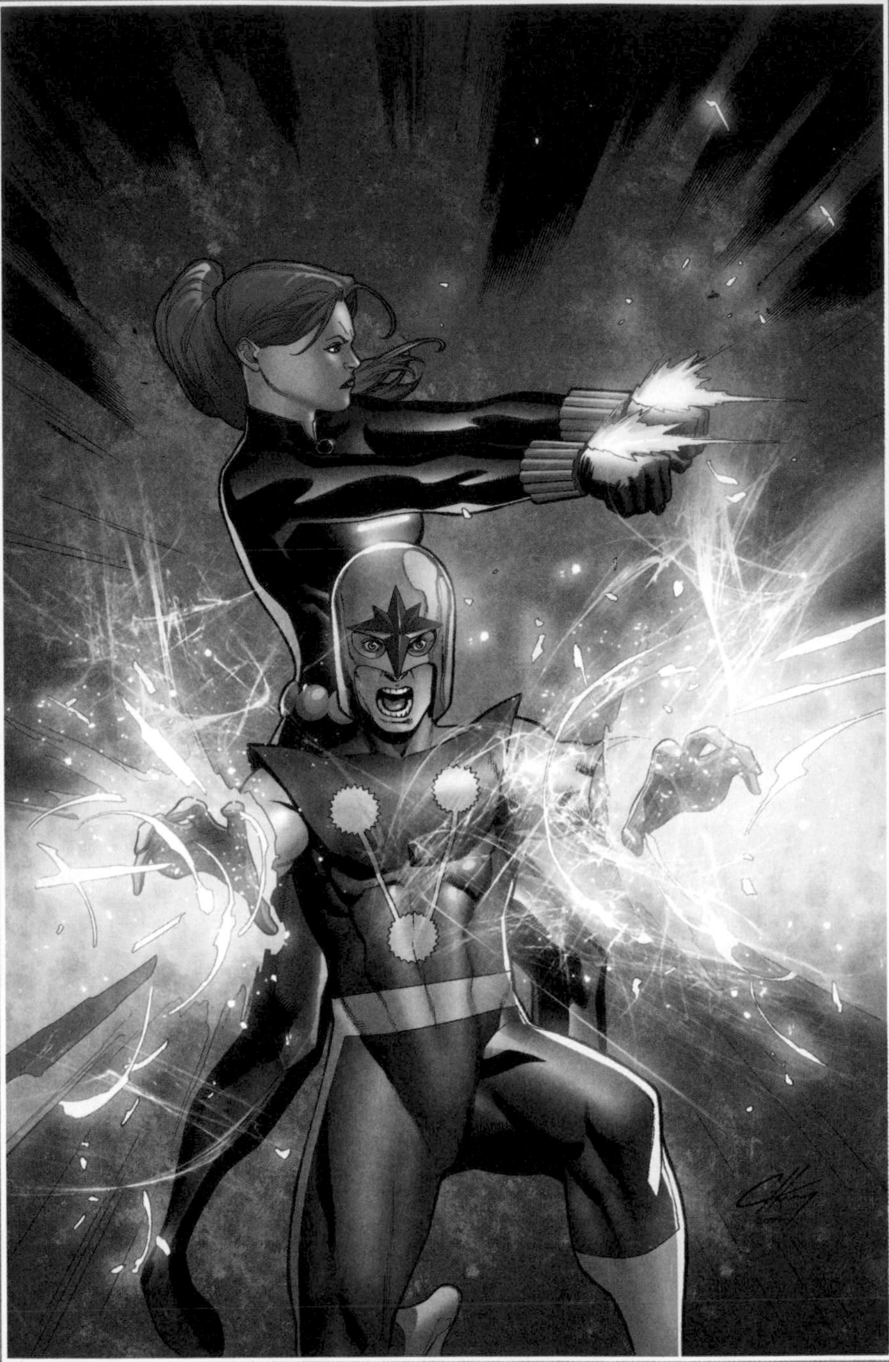

#21

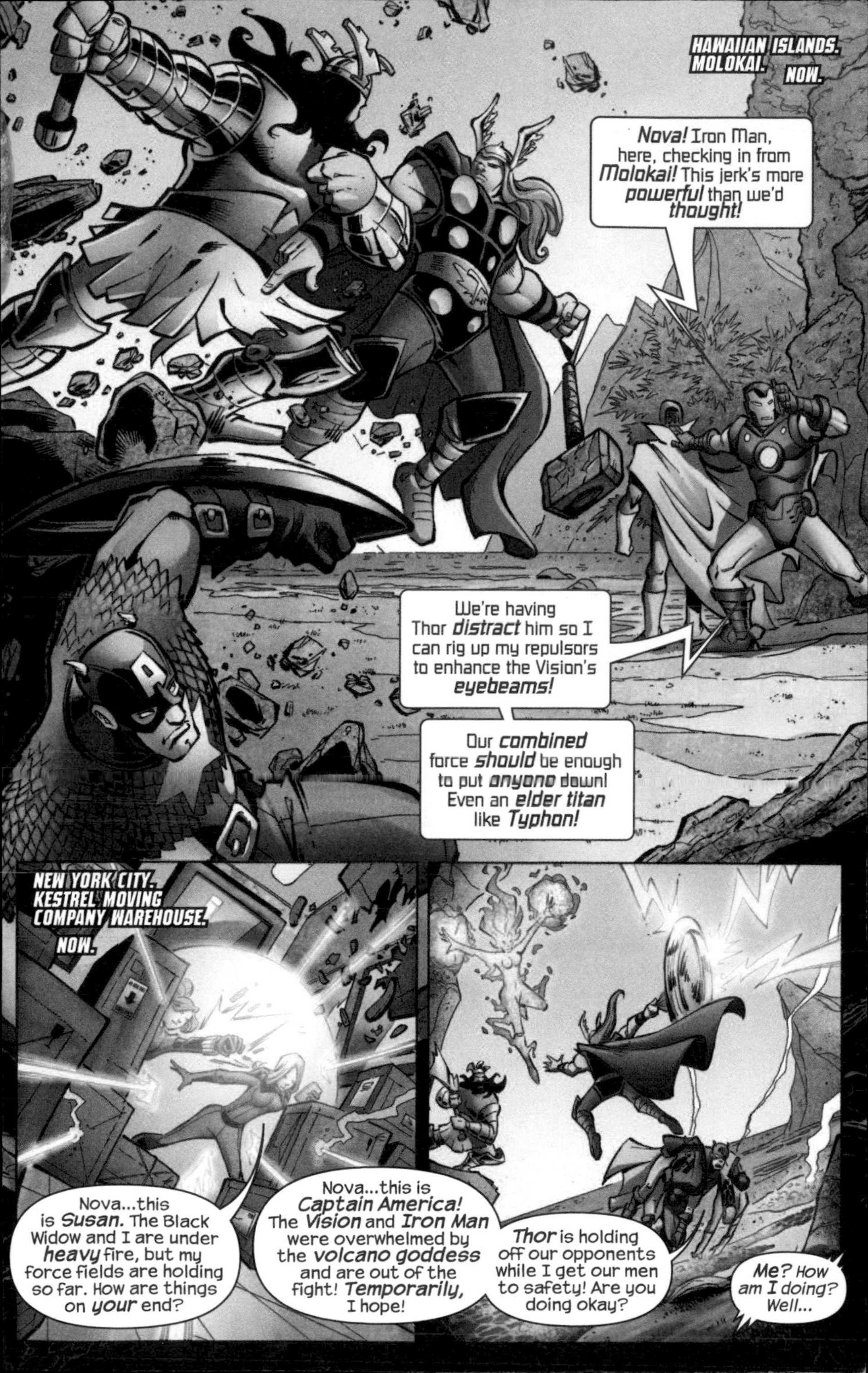
HAWAIIAN ISLANDS. MOLOKAI. NOW.
Nova! Iron Man, here, checking in from Molokai! This jerk's more powerful than we'd thought!
We're having Thor distract him so I can rig up my repulsors to enhance the Vision's eyebeams!
Our combined force should be enough to put anyone down! Even an elder titan like Typhon!
NEW YORK CITY. KESTREL MOVING COMPANY WAREHOUSE. NOW.
Nova...this is Susan. The Black Widow and I are under heavy fire, but my force fields are holding so far. How are things on your end?
Nova...this is Captain America! The Vision and Iron Man were overwhelmed by the volcano goddess and are out of the fight! Temporarily, I hope!
Thor is holding off our opponents while I get our men to safety! Are you doing okay?
Me? How am I doing? Well...

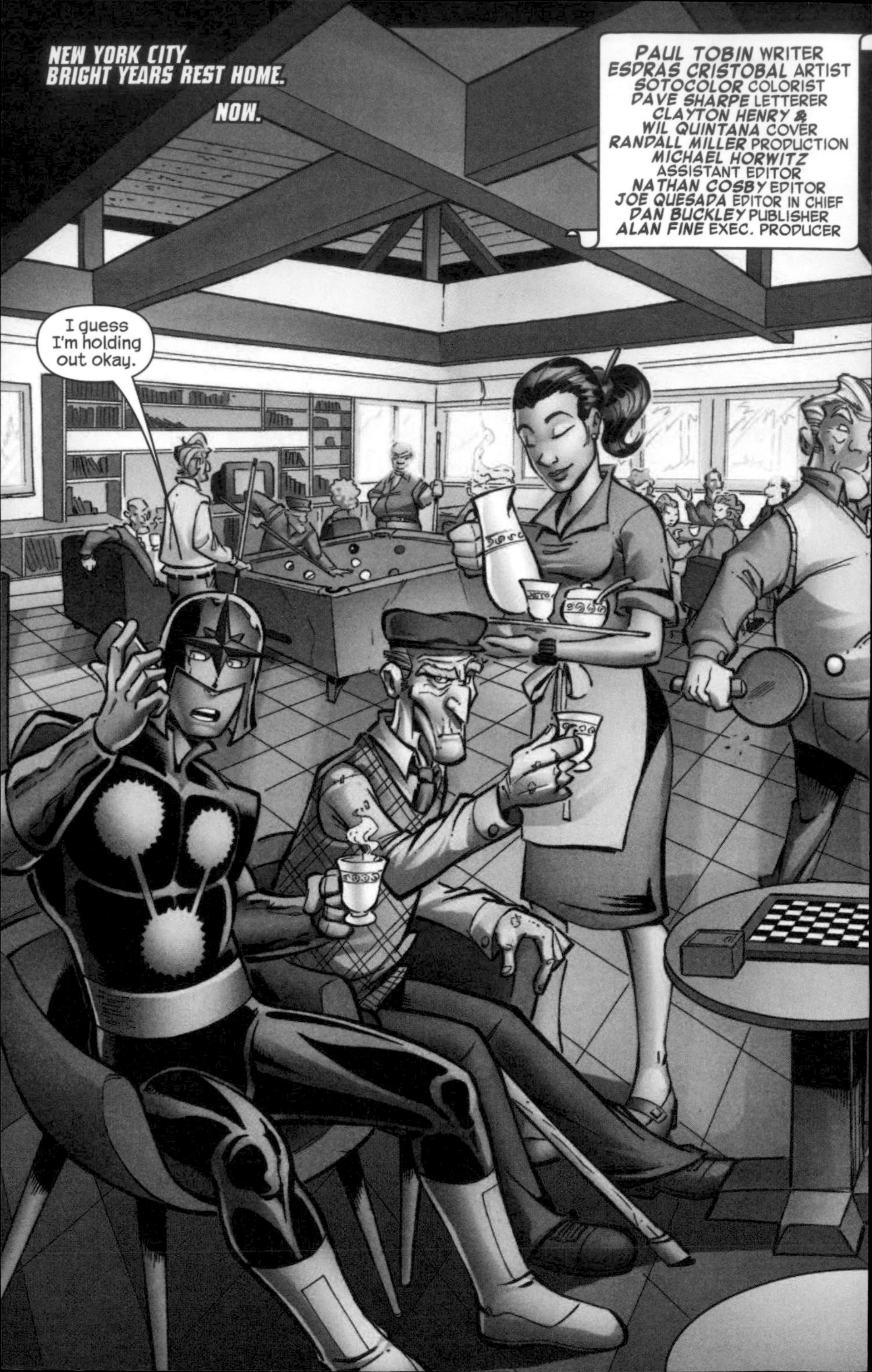
NEW YORK CITY.
BRIGHT YEARS REST HOME.
NOW.
PAUL TOBIN WRITER
ESDRAS CRISTOBAL ARTIST
SOTOCOLOR COLORIST
DAVE SHARPE LETTERER
CLAYTON HENRY & WIL QUINTANA COVER
RANDALL MILLER PRODUCTION
MICHAEL HORWITZ ASSISTANT EDITOR
NATHAN COSBY EDITOR
JOE QUESADA EDITOR IN CHIEF
DAN BUCKLEY PUBLISHER
ALAN FINE EXEC. PRODUCER
I guess I'm holding out okay.

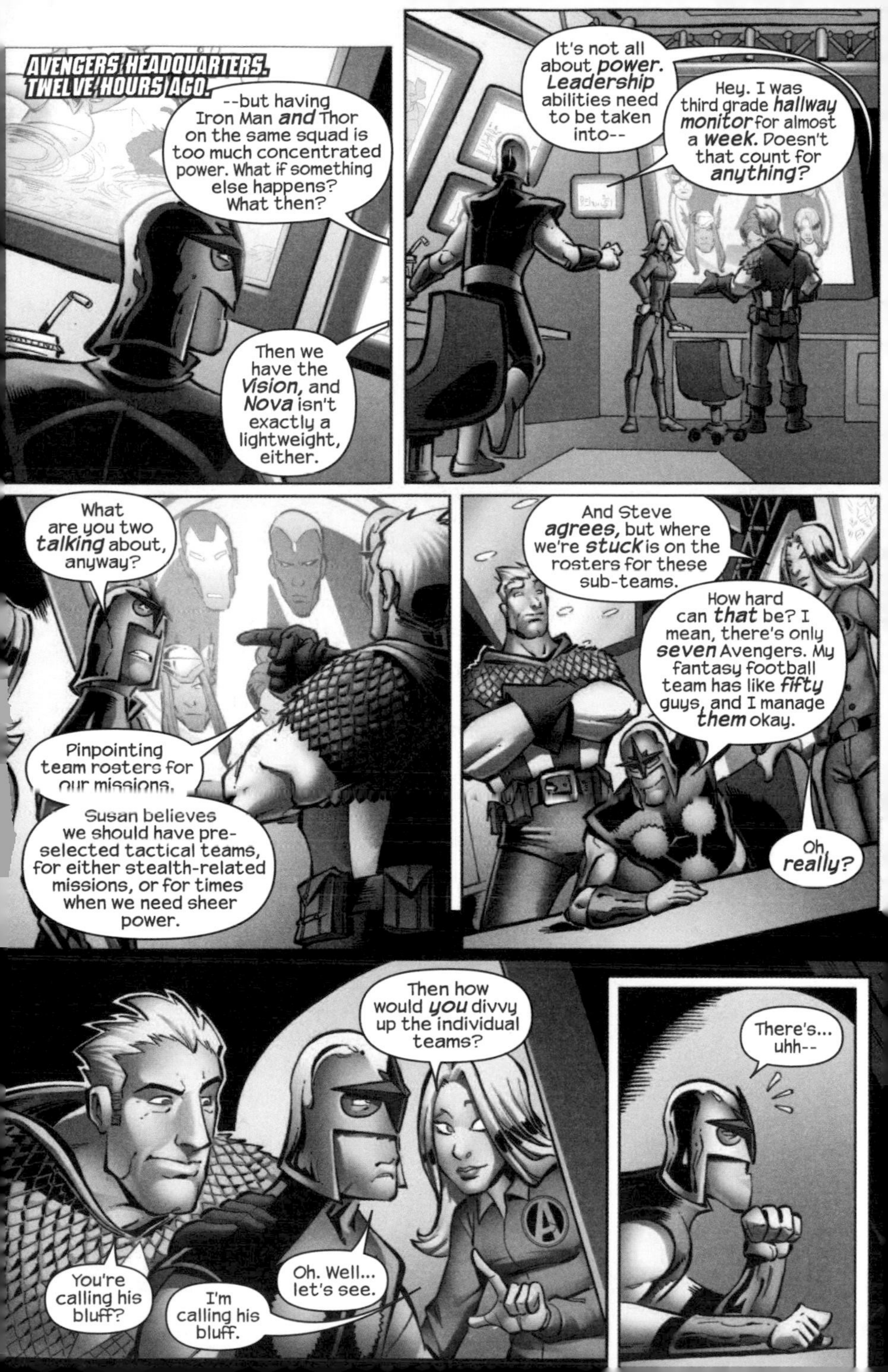
AVENGERS HEADQUARTERS. TWELVE HOURS AGO.
--but having Iron Man and Thor on the same squad is too much concentrated power. What if something else happens? What then?
Then we have the Vision, and Nova isn't exactly a lightweight, either.
It's not all about power. Leadership abilities need to be taken into--
Hey. I was third grade hallway monitor for almost a week. Doesn't that count for anything?
What are you two talking about, anyway?
Pinpointing team rosters for our missions.
Susan believes we should have pre-selected tactical teams, for either stealth-related missions, or for times when we need sheer power.
And Steve agrees, but where we're stuck is on the rosters for these sub-teams.
How hard can that be? I mean, there's only seven Avengers. My fantasy football team has like fifty guys, and I manage them okay.
Oh really?
Then how would you divvy up the individual teams?
Oh. Well... let's see.
You're calling his bluff?
I'm calling his bluff.
There's... uhh--

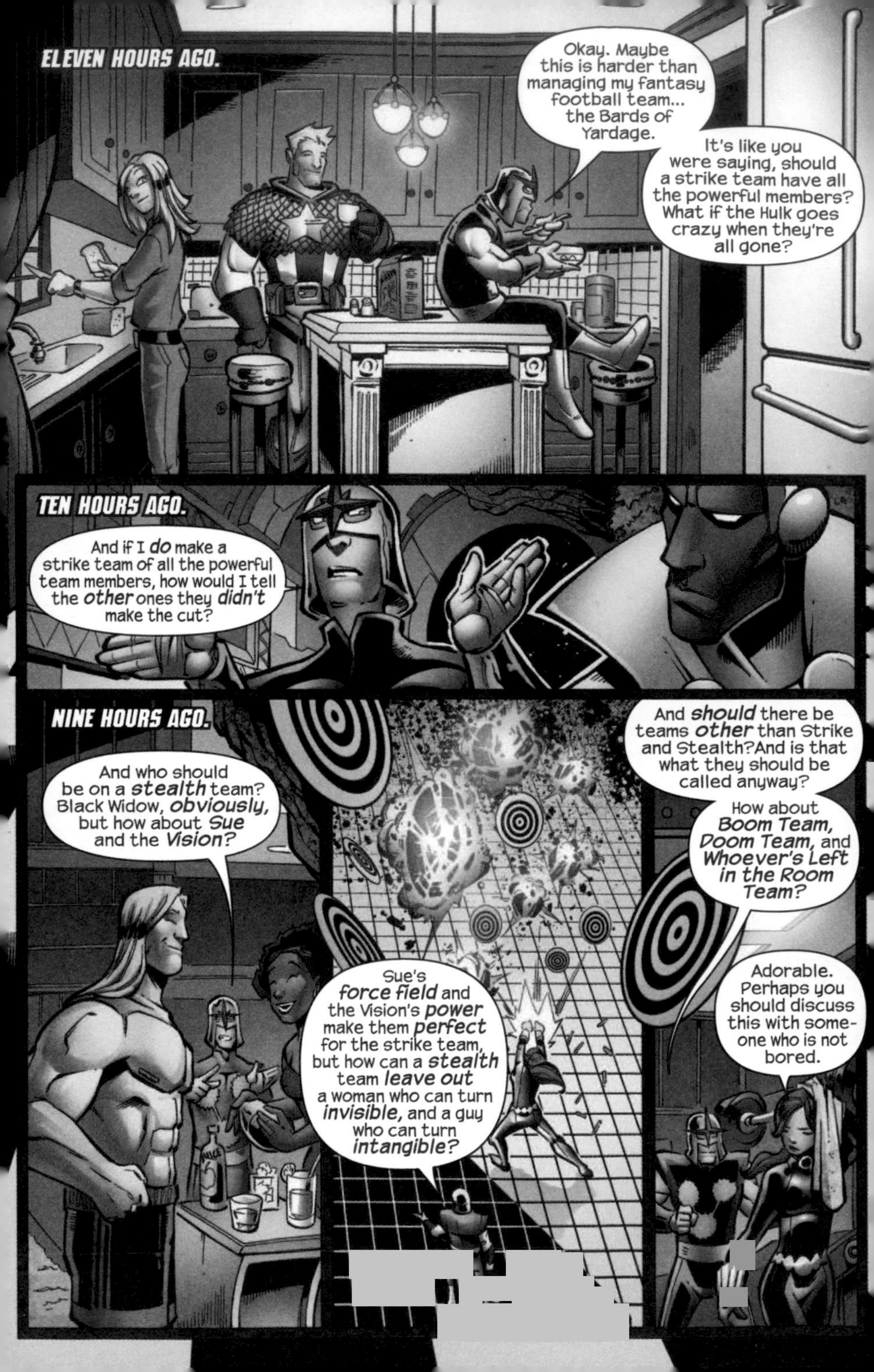
ELEVEN HOURS AGO.
Okay. Maybe this is harder than managing my fantasy football team... the Bards of Yardage.
It's like you were saying, should a strike team have all the powerful members? What if the Hulk goes crazy when they're all gone?
TEN HOURS AGO.
And if I do make a strike team of all the powerful team members, how would I tell the other ones they didn't make the cut?
NINE HOURS AGO.
And who should be on a stealth team? Black Widow, obviously, but how about Sue and the Vision?
Sue's force field and the Vision's power make them perfect for the strike team, but how can a stealth team leave out a woman who can turn invisible, and a guy who can turn intangible?
And should there be teams other than Strike and Stealth? And is that what they should be called anyway?
How about Boom Team, Doom Team, and Whoever's Left in the Room Team?
Adorable. Perhaps you should discuss this with someone who is not bored.

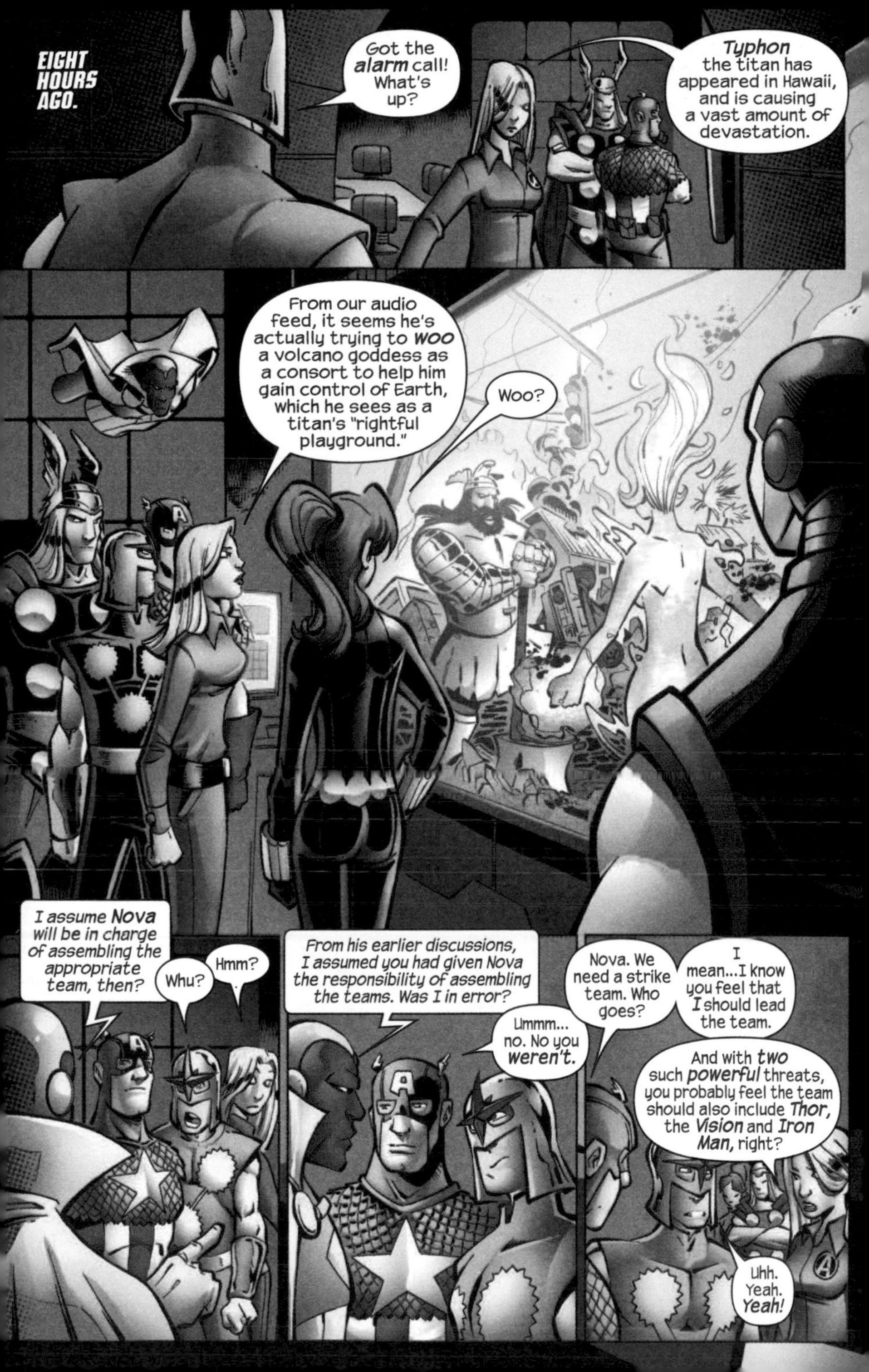
EIGHT HOURS AGO.
Got the alarm call! What's up?
Typhon the titan has appeared in Hawaii, and is causing a vast amount of devastation.
From our audio feed, it seems he's actually trying to WOO a volcano goddess as a consort to help him gain control of Earth, which he sees as a titan's "rightful playground."
Woo?
I assume Nova will be in charge of assembling the appropriate team, then?
Whu?
Hmm?
From his earlier discussions, I assumed you had given Nova the responsibility of assembling the teams. Was I in error?
Ummm... no. No you weren't.
Nova. We need a strike team. Who goes?
I mean...I know you feel that I should lead the team.
And with two such powerful threats, you probably feel the team should also include Thor, the Vision and Iron Man, right?
Uhh. Yeah. Yeah!

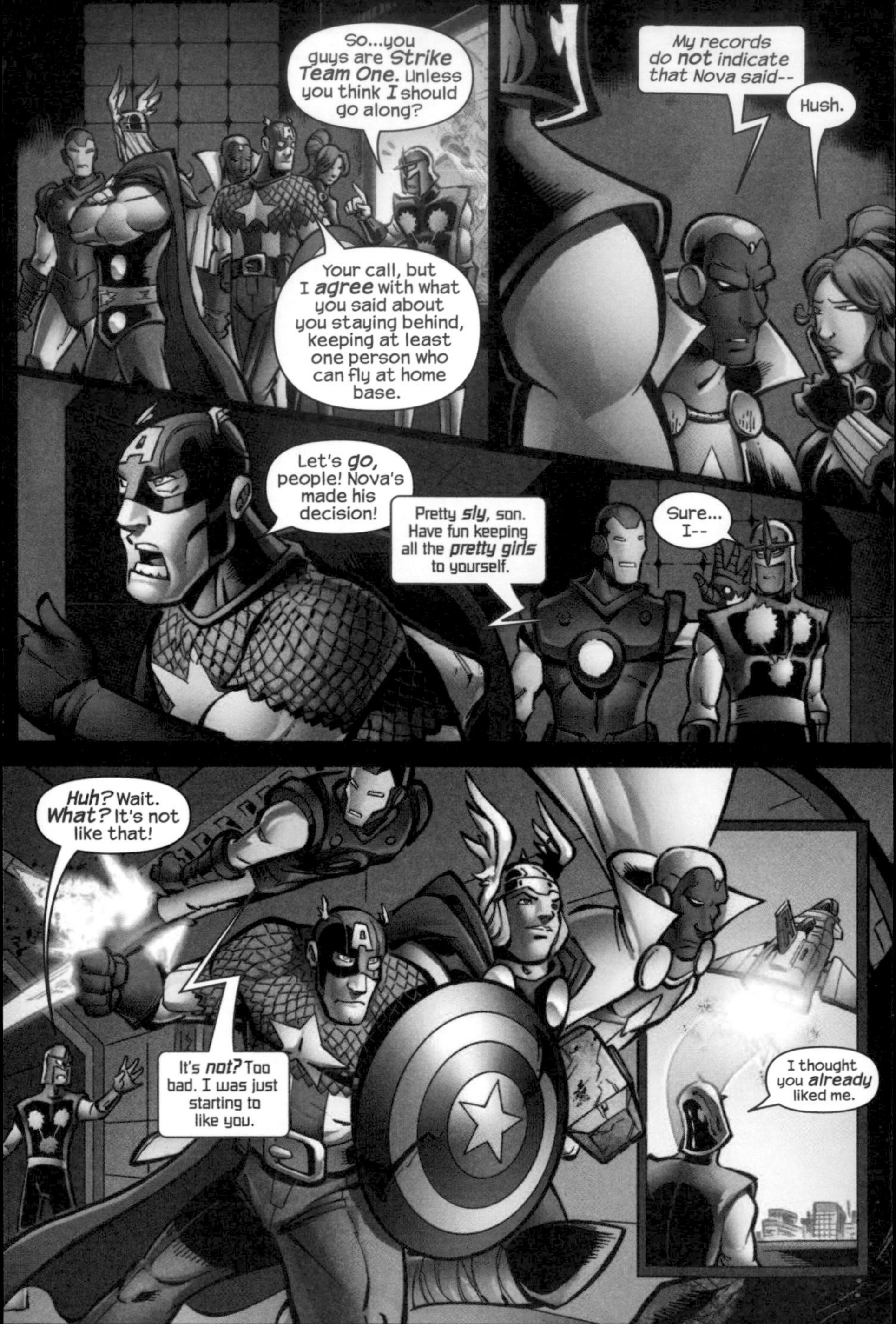

So...you guys are Strike Team One. Unless you think I should go along?
Your call, but I agree with what you said about you staying behind, keeping at least one person who can fly at home base.
My records do not indicate that Nova said--
Hush.
Let's go, people! Nova's made his decision!
Pretty sly, son. Have fun keeping all the pretty girls to yourself.
Sure... I--
Huh? Wait. What? It's not like that!
It's not? Too bad. I was just starting to like you.
I thought you already liked me.

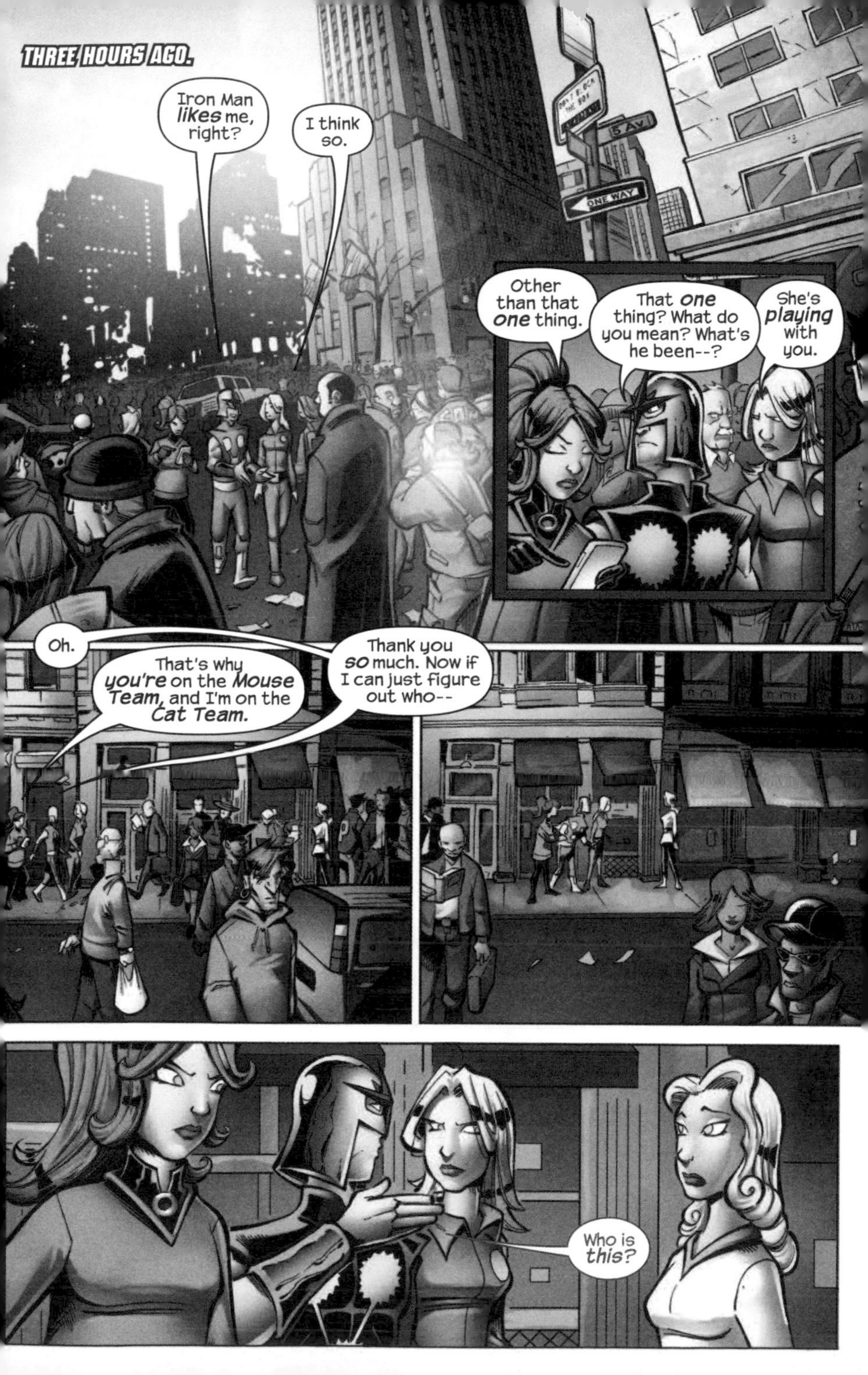
THREE HOURS AGO.
Iron Man likes me, right?
I think so.
ONE WAY
5 Av
Other than that one thing.
That one thing? What do you mean? What's he been--?
She's playing with you.
Oh.
That's why you're on the Mouse Team, and I'm on the Cat Team.
Thank you so much. Now if I can just figure out who--
Who is this?

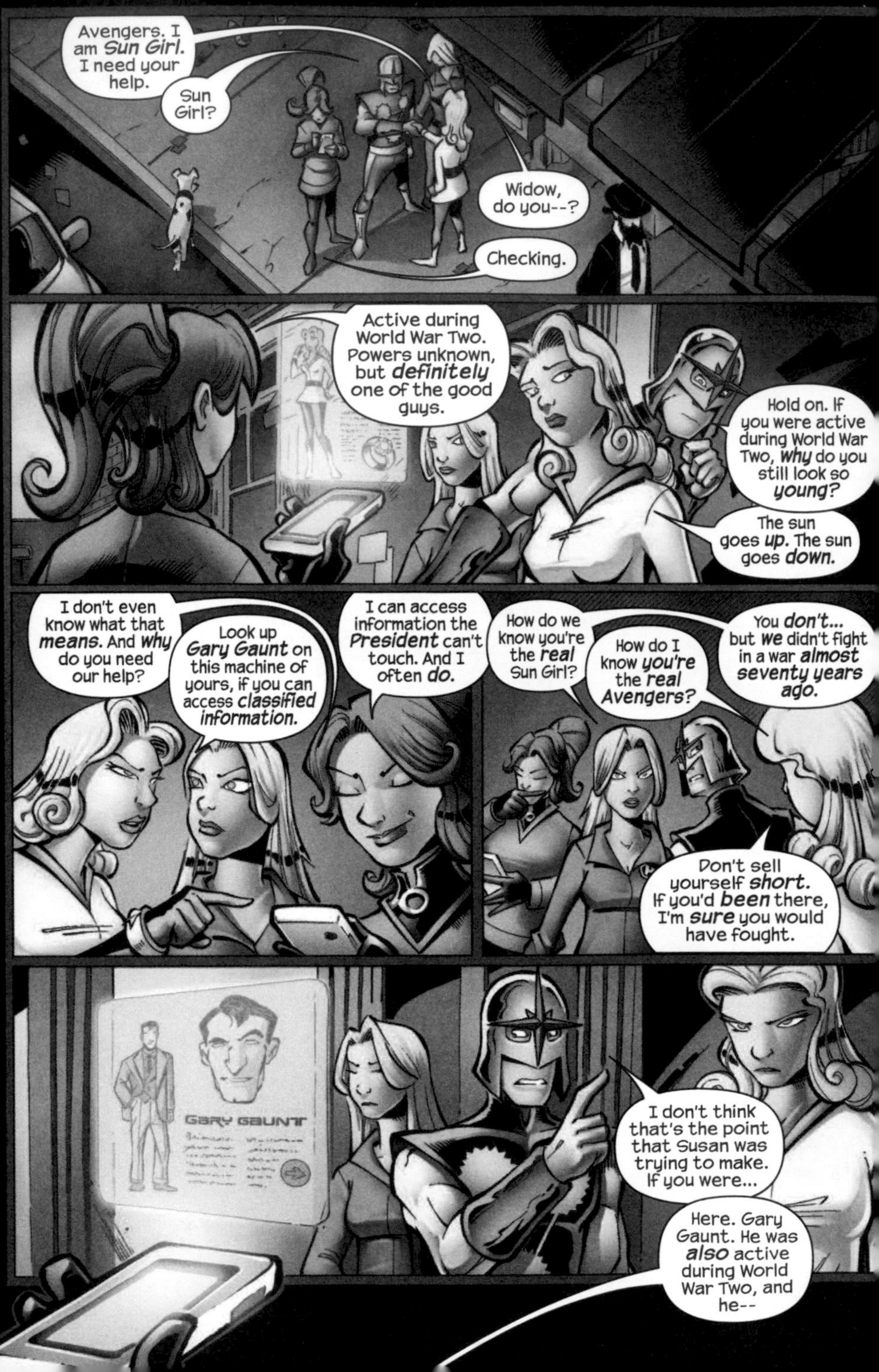
Avengers. I am Sun Girl. I need your help.
Sun Girl?
Widow, do you--?
Checking.
Active during World War Two. Powers unknown, but definitely one of the good guys.
Hold on. If you were active during World War Two, why do you still look so young?
The sun goes up. The sun goes down.
I don't even know what that means. And why do you need our help?
Look up Gary Gaunt on this machine of yours, if you can access classified information.
I can access information the President can't touch. And I often do.
How do we know you're the real Sun Girl?
How do I know you're the real Avengers?
You don't... but we didn't fight in a war almost seventy years ago.
Don't sell yourself short. If you'd been there, I'm sure you would have fought.
GARY GAUNT
I don't think that's the point that Susan was trying to make. If you were...
Here. Gary Gaunt. He was also active during World War Two, and he--

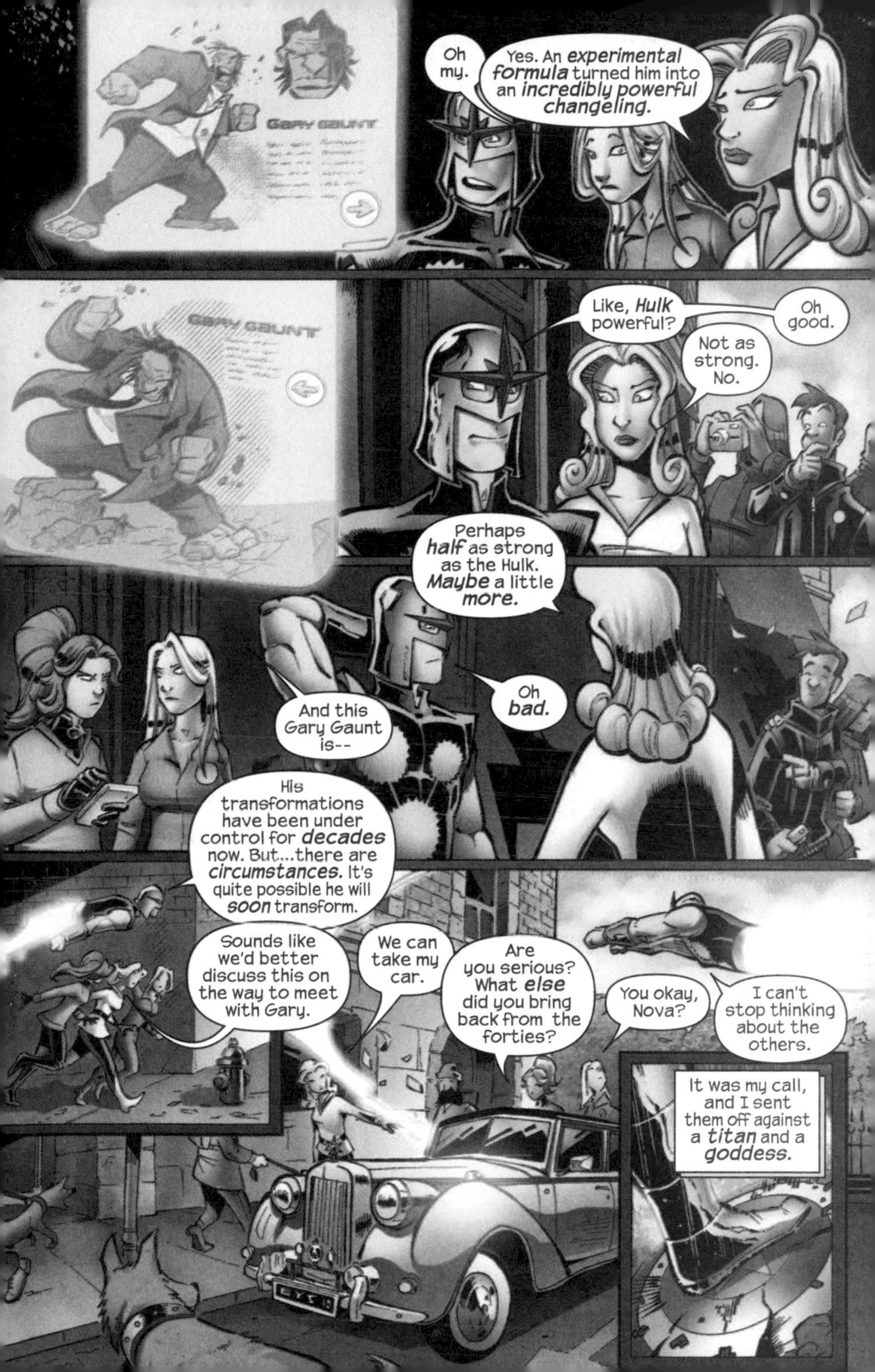

GARY GAUNT
Oh my.
Yes. An experimental formula turned him into an incredibly powerful changeling.
GARY GAUNT
Like, Hulk powerful?
Oh good.
Not as strong. No.
Perhaps half as strong as the Hulk. Maybe a little more.
Oh bad.
And this Gary Gaunt is--
His transformations have been under control for decades now. But...there are circumstances. It's quite possible he will soon transform.
Sounds like we'd better discuss this on the way to meet with Gary.
We can take my car.
Are you serious? What else did you bring back from the forties?
You okay, Nova?
I can't stop thinking about the others.
It was my call, and I sent them off against a titan and a goddess.

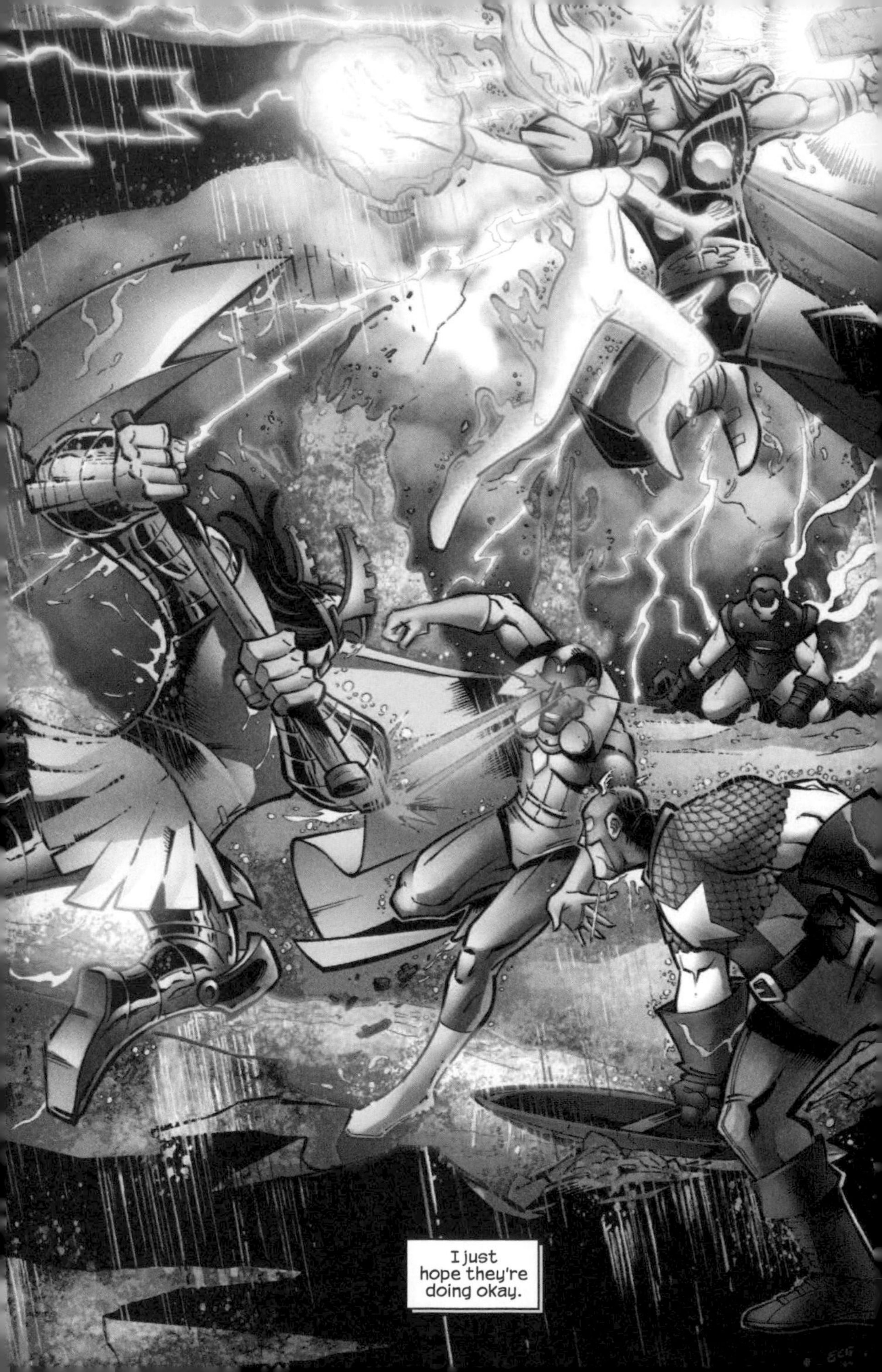
I just hope they're doing okay.

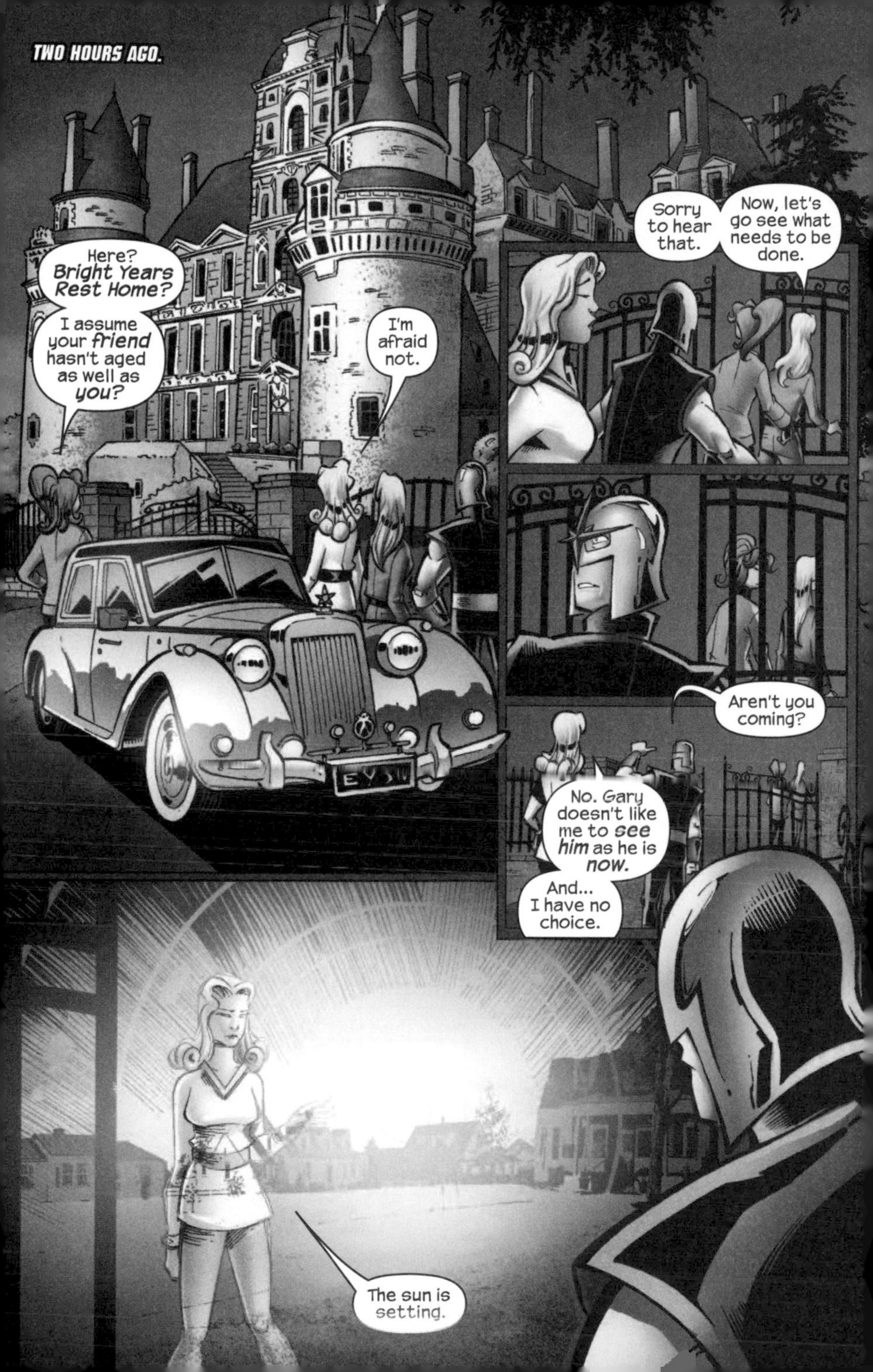
TWO HOURS AGO.
Here? Bright Years Rest Home?
I assume your friend hasn't aged as well as you?
I'm afraid not.
Sorry to hear that.
Now, let's go see what needs to be done.
Aren't you coming?
No. Gary doesn't like me to see him as he is now.
And... I have no choice.
The sun is setting.

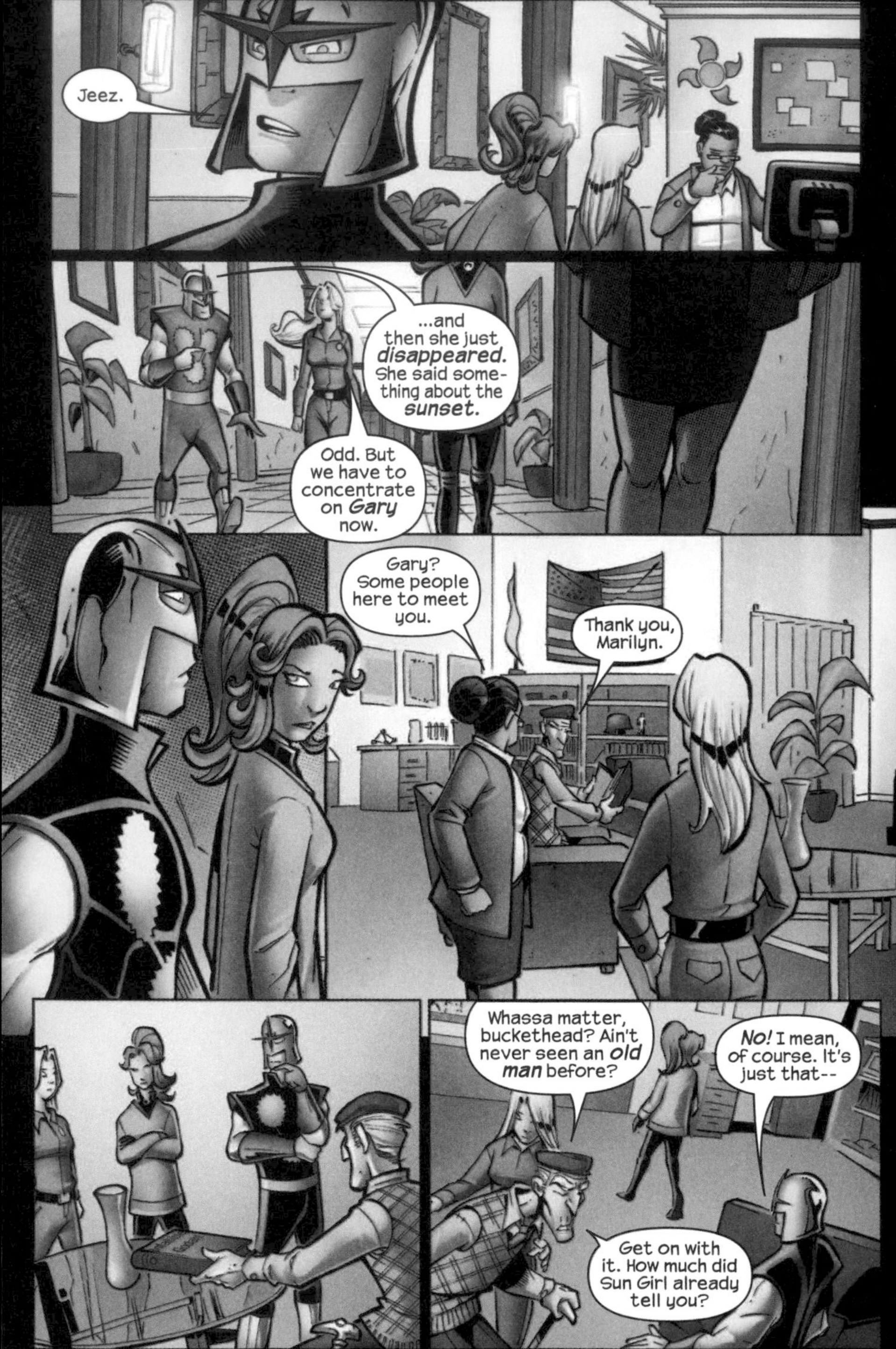
Jeez.
...and then she just disappeared. She said something about the sunset.
Odd. But we have to concentrate on Gary now.
Gary? Some people here to meet you.
Thank you, Marilyn.
Whassa matter, buckethead? Ain't never seen an old man before?
No! I mean, of course. It's just that--
Get on with it. How much did Sun Girl already tell you?

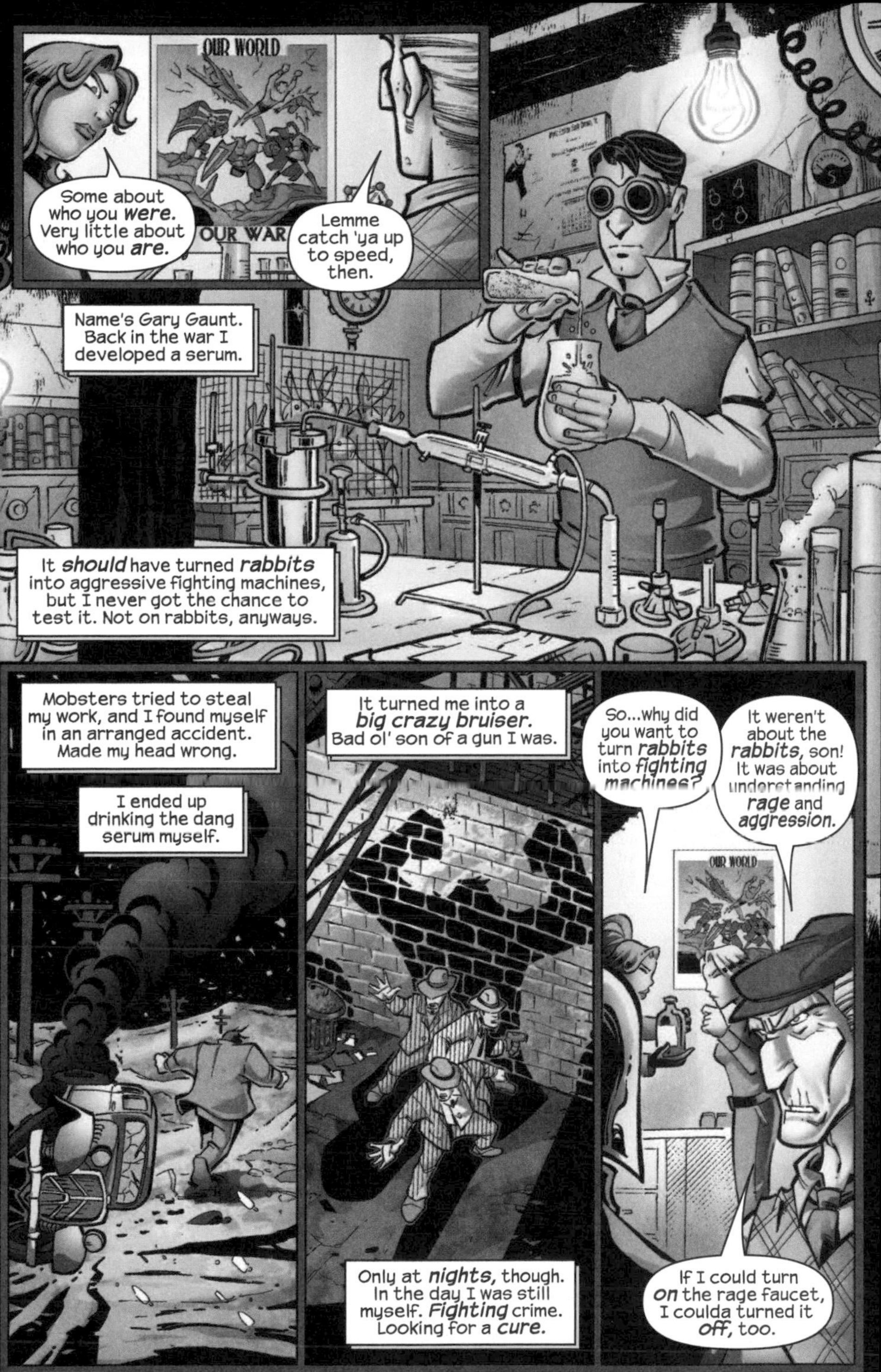
OUR WORLD
Some about who you were. Very little about who you are.
OUR WAR
Lemme catch 'ya up to speed, then.
Name's Gary Gaunt. Back in the war I developed a serum.
It should have turned rabbits into aggressive fighting machines, but I never got the chance to test it. Not on rabbits, anyways.
Mobsters tried to steal my work, and I found myself in an arranged accident. Made my head wrong.
I ended up drinking the dang serum myself.
It turned me into a big crazy bruiser. Bad ol' son of a gun I was.
Only at nights, though. In the day I was still myself. Fighting crime. Looking for a cure.
So...why did you want to turn rabbits into fighting machines?
It weren't about the rabbits, son! It was about understanding rage and aggression.
OUR WORLD
If I could turn on the rage faucet, I coulda turned it off, too.

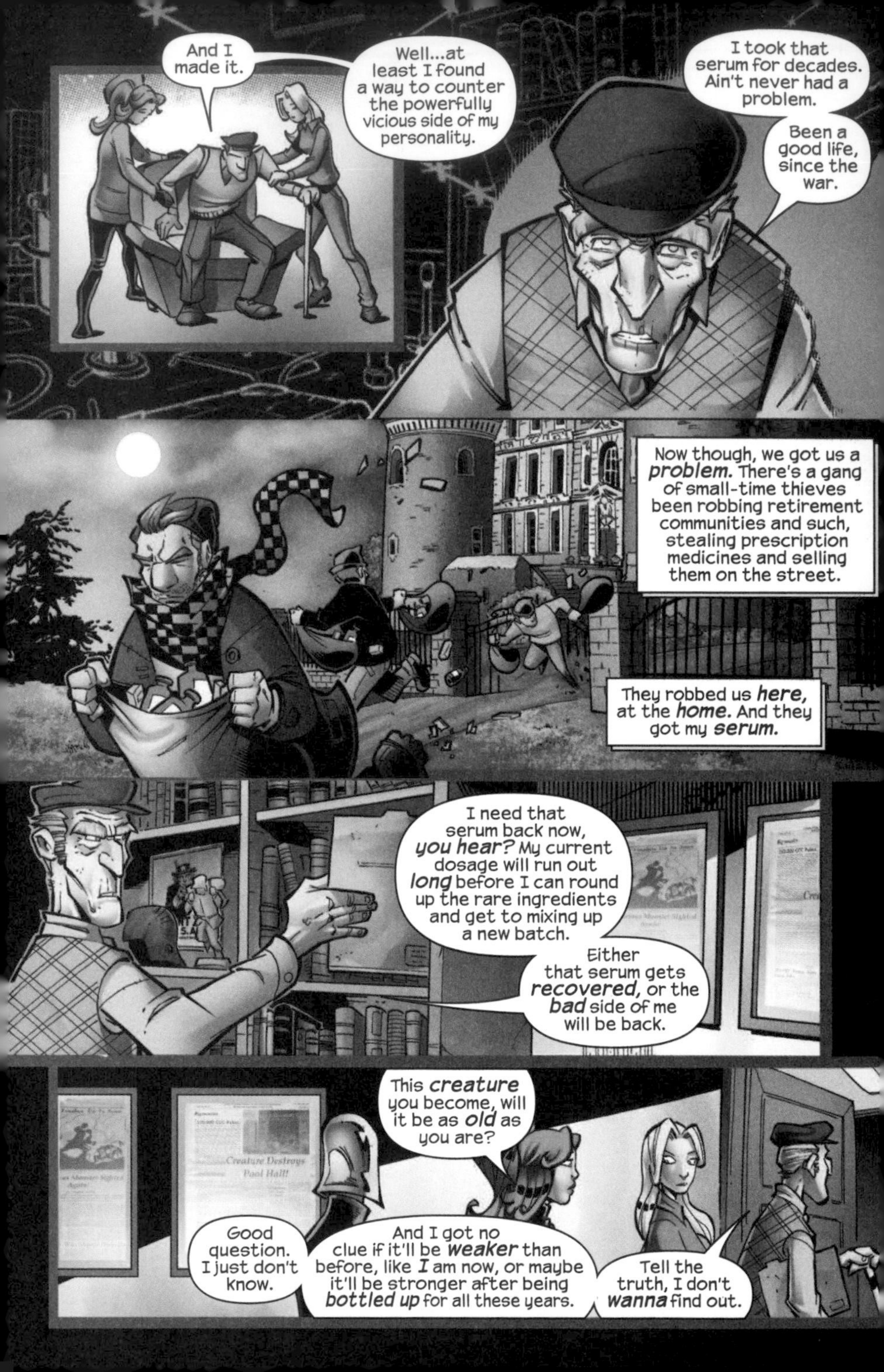

And I made it.
Well...at least I found a way to counter the powerfully vicious side of my personality.
I took that serum for decades. Ain't never had a problem.
Been a good life, since the war.
Now though, we got us a *problem.* There's a gang of small-time thieves been robbing retirement communities and such, stealing prescription medicines and selling them on the street.
They robbed us *here,* at the *home.* And they got my *serum.*
I need that serum back now, *you hear?* My current dosage will run out *long* before I can round up the rare ingredients and get to mixing up a new batch.
Either that serum gets *recovered,* or the *bad* side of me will be back.
This *creature* you become, will it be as *old* as you are?
Creature Destroys Pool Hall!
Good question. I just don't know.
And I got no clue if it'll be *weaker* than before, like *I* am now, or maybe it'll be stronger after being *bottled up* for all these years.
Tell the truth, I don't *wanna* find out.

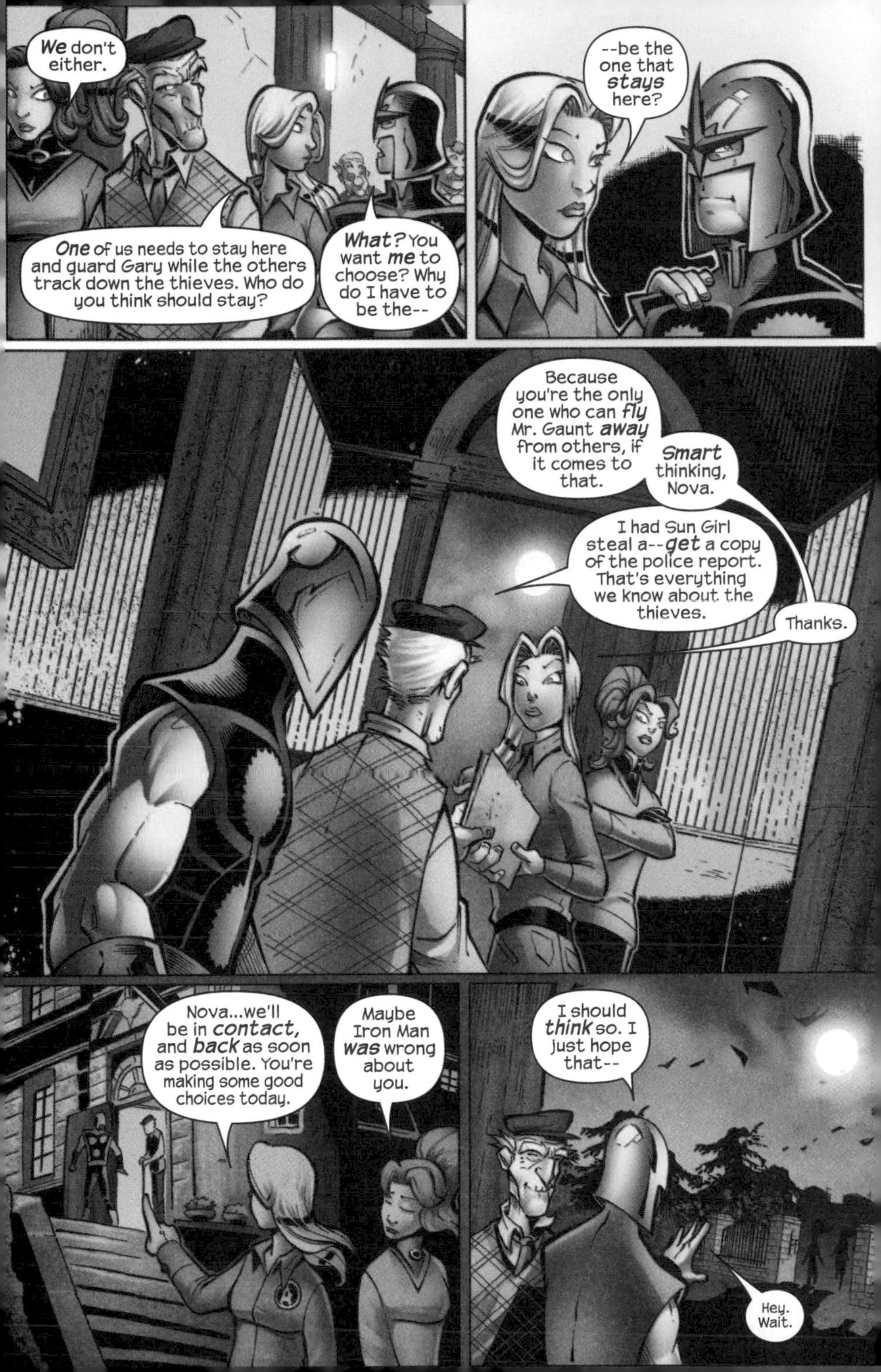
We don't either.
One of us needs to stay here and guard Gary while the others track down the thieves. Who do you think should stay?
What? You want me to choose? Why do I have to be the--
--be the one that stays here?
Because you're the only one who can fly Mr. Gaunt away from others, if it comes to that.
Smart thinking, Nova.
I had Sun Girl steal a--get a copy of the police report. That's everything we know about the thieves.
Thanks.
Nova...we'll be in contact, and back as soon as possible. You're making some good choices today.
Maybe Iron Man was wrong about you.
I should think so. I just hope that--
Hey. Wait.

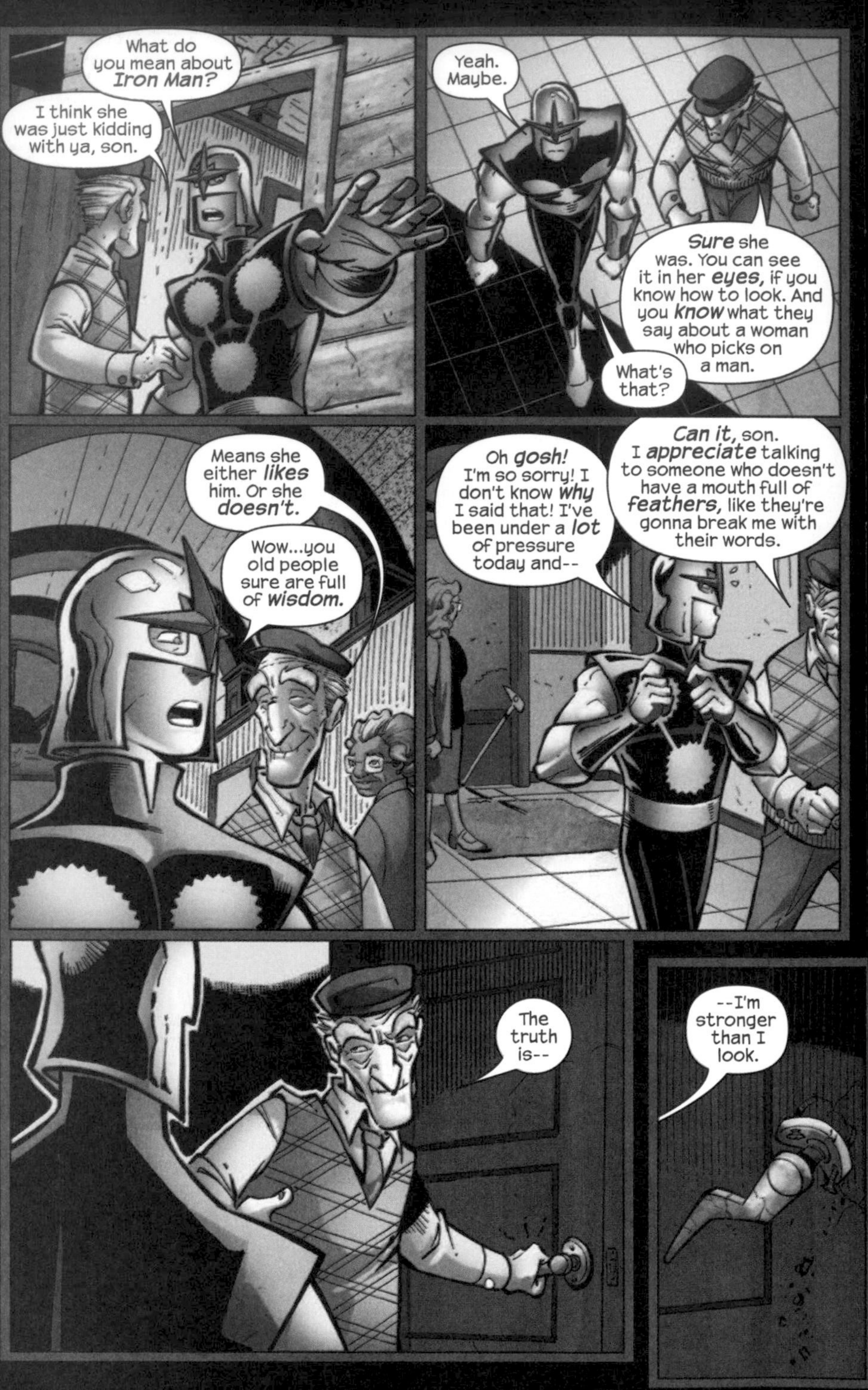
What do you mean about Iron Man?
I think she was just kidding with ya, son.
Yeah. Maybe.
Sure she was. You can see it in her eyes, if you know how to look. And you know what they say about a woman who picks on a man.
What's that?
Means she either likes him. Or she doesn't.
Wow...you old people sure are full of wisdom.
Oh gosh! I'm so sorry! I don't know why I said that! I've been under a lot of pressure today and--
Can it, son. I appreciate talking to someone who doesn't have a mouth full of feathers, like they're gonna break me with their words.
The truth is--
--I'm stronger than I look.

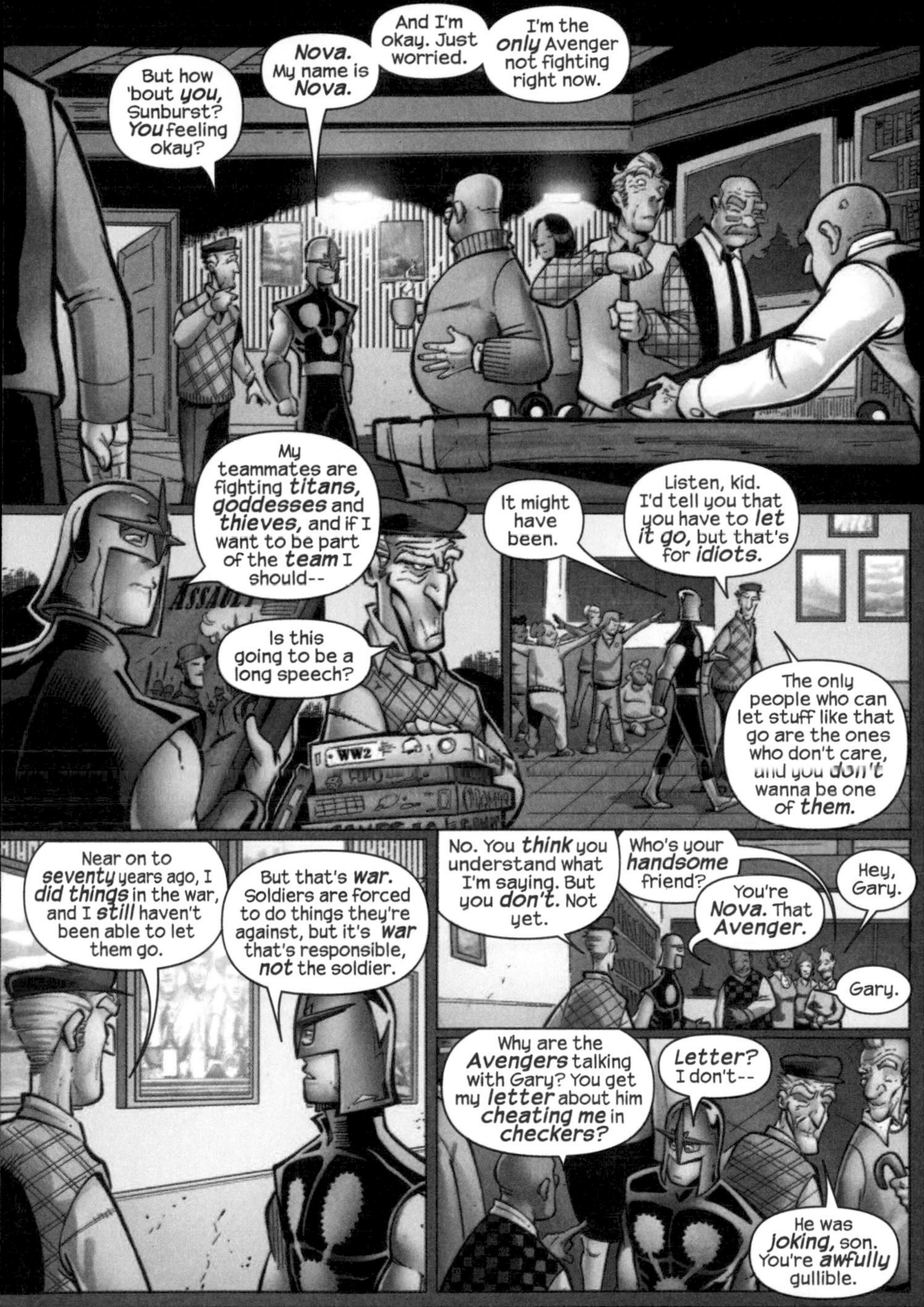

But how 'bout you, Sunburst? You feeling okay?
Nova. My name is Nova.
And I'm okay. Just worried.
I'm the only Avenger not fighting right now.
My teammates are fighting titans, goddesses and thieves, and if I want to be part of the team I should--
Is this going to be a long speech?
It might have been.
Listen, kid. I'd tell you that you have to let it go, but that's for idiots.
The only people who can let stuff like that go are the ones who don't care, and you don't wanna be one of them.
Near on to seventy years ago, I did things in the war, and I still haven't been able to let them go.
But that's war. Soldiers are forced to do things they're against, but it's war that's responsible, not the soldier.
No. You think you understand what I'm saying. But you don't. Not yet.
Who's your handsome friend?
You're Nova. That Avenger.
Hey, Gary.
Gary.
Why are the Avengers talking with Gary? You get my letter about him cheating me in checkers?
Letter? I don't--
He was joking, son. You're awfully gullible.

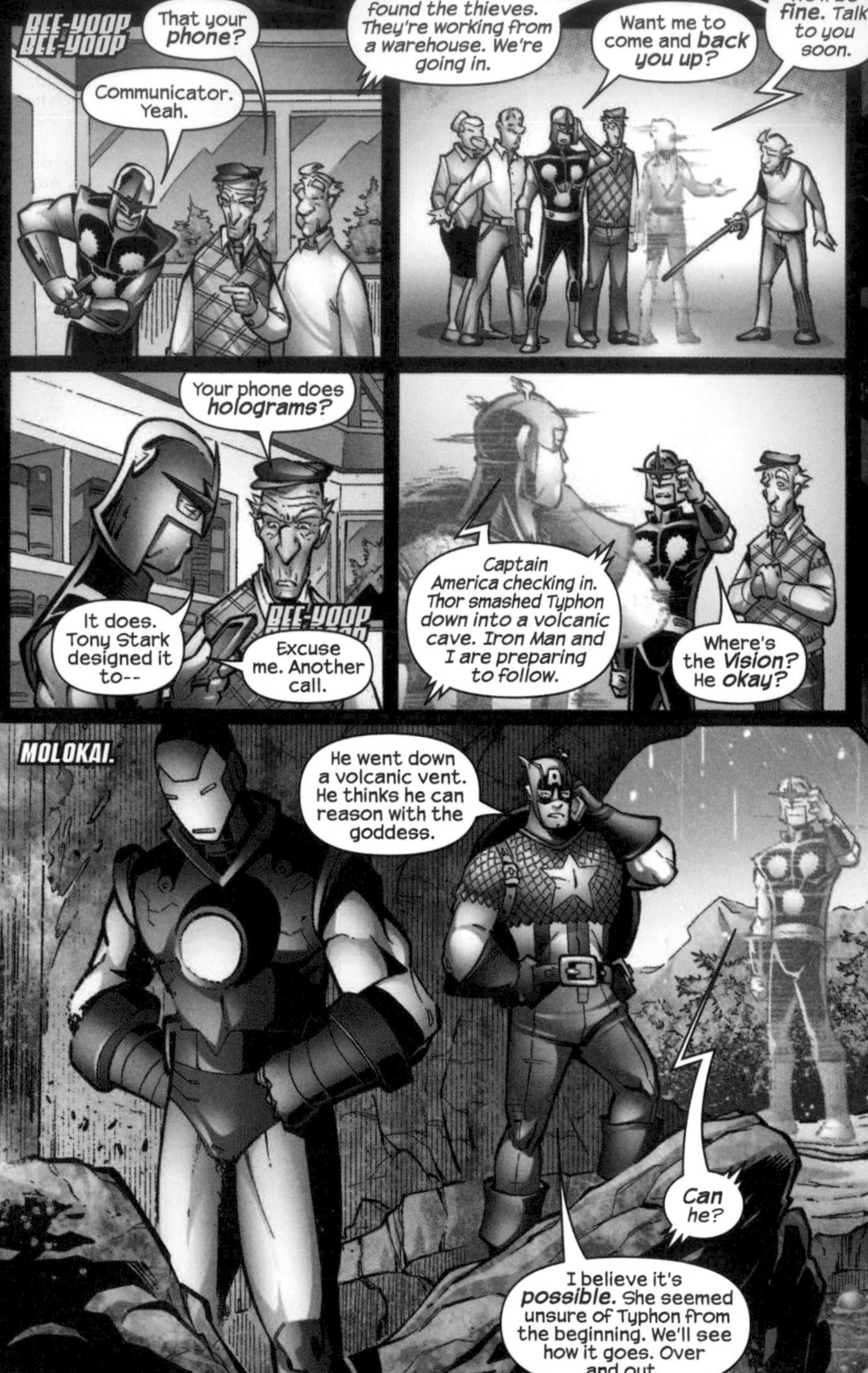
BEE-YOOP BEE-YOOP
That your phone?
Communicator. Yeah.
Nova. We've found the thieves. They're working from a warehouse. We're going in.
Want me to come and back you up?
We'll be fine. Talk to you soon.
Your phone does holograms?
It does. Tony Stark designed it to--
BEE-YOOP
Excuse me. Another call.
Captain America checking in. Thor smashed Typhon down into a volcanic cave. Iron Man and I are preparing to follow.
Where's the Vision? He okay?
MOLOKAI.
He went down a volcanic vent. He thinks he can reason with the goddess.
Can he?
I believe it's possible. She seemed unsure of Typhon from the beginning. We'll see how it goes. Over and out.

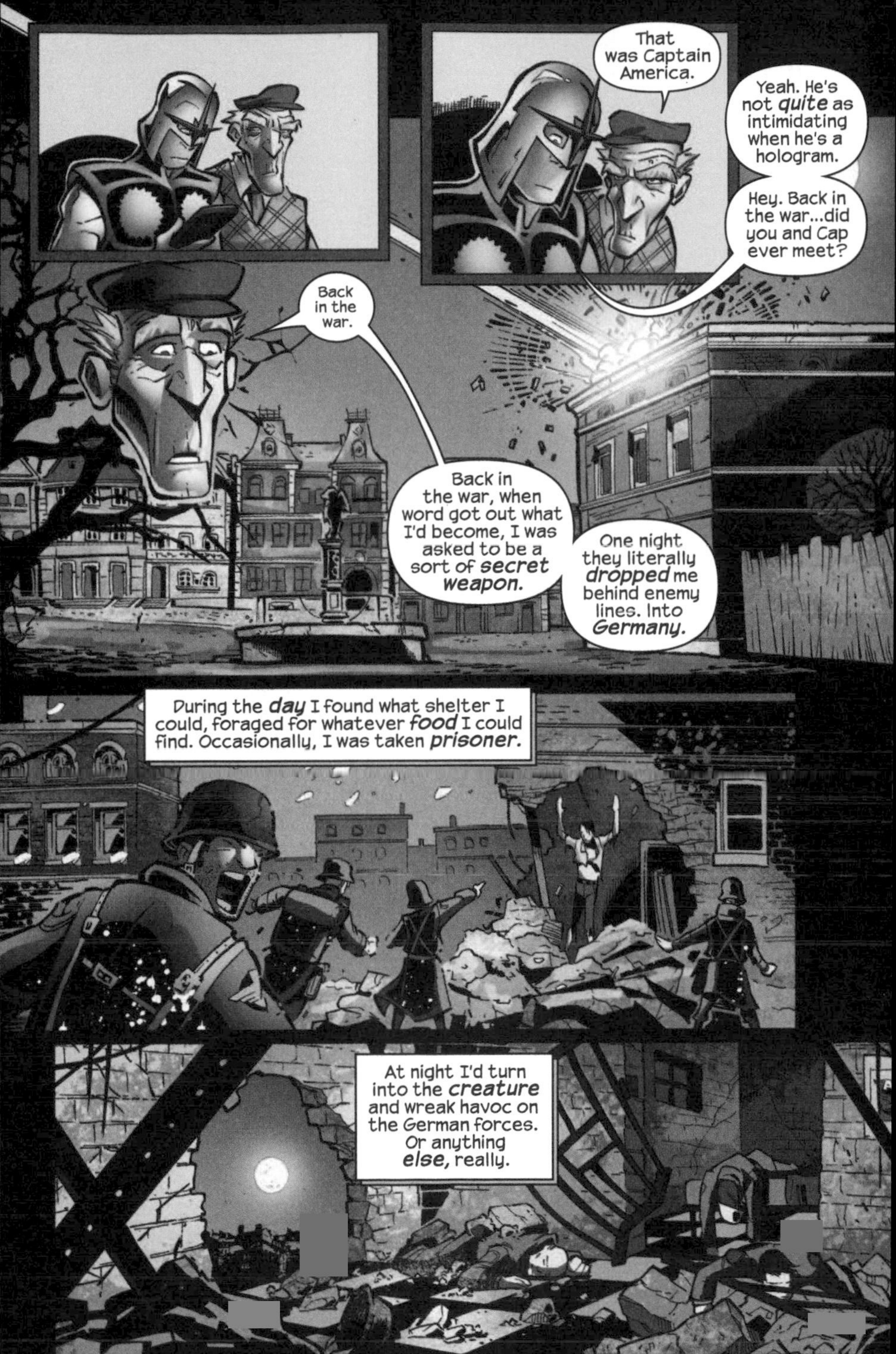
That was Captain America.
Yeah. He's not quite as intimidating when he's a hologram.
Hey. Back in the war...did you and Cap ever meet?
Back in the war.
Back in the war, when word got out what I'd become, I was asked to be a sort of secret weapon.
One night they literally dropped me behind enemy lines. Into Germany.
During the day I found what shelter I could, foraged for whatever food I could find. Occasionally, I was taken prisoner.
At night I'd turn into the creature and wreak havoc on the German forces. Or anything else, really.

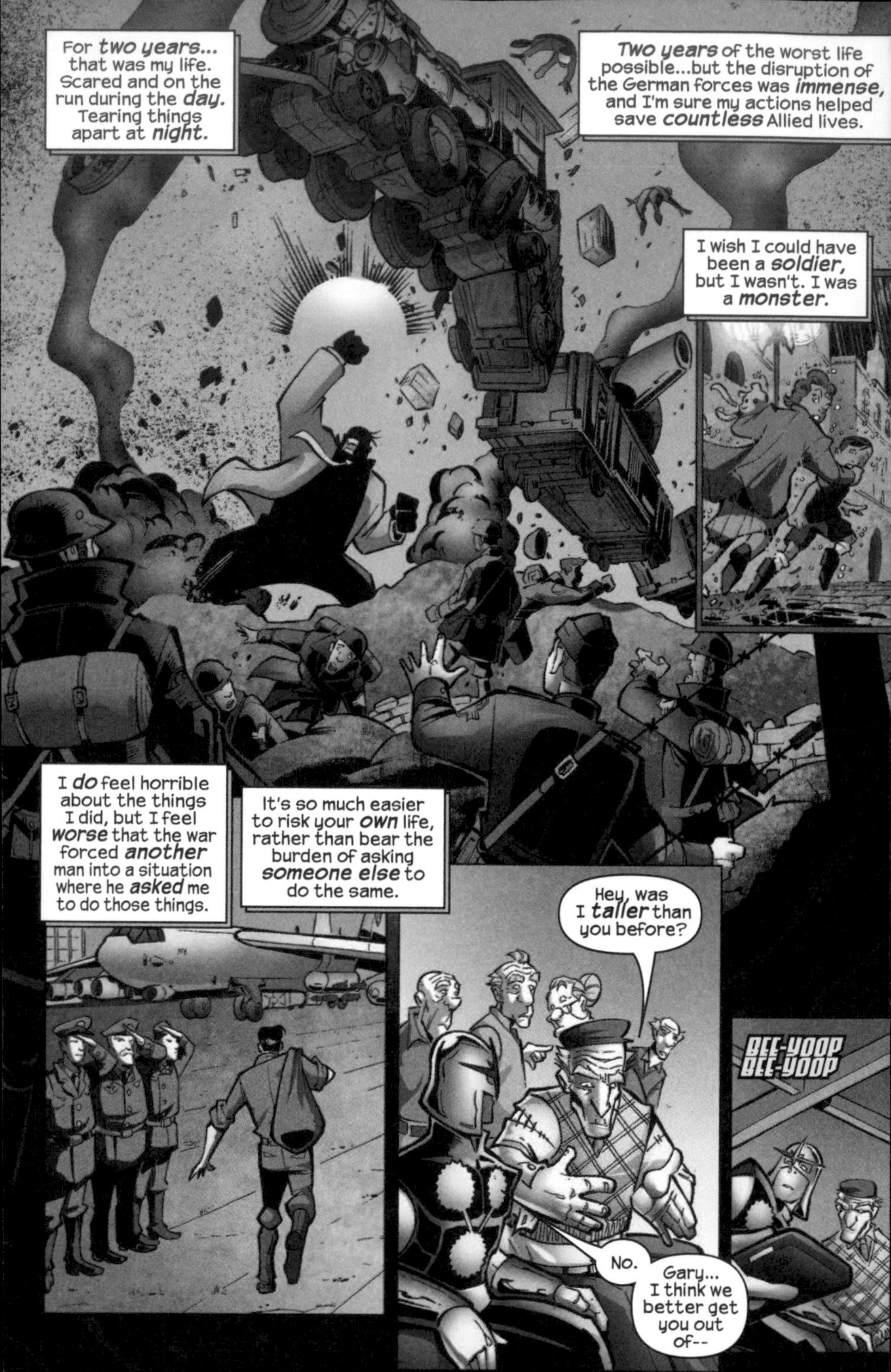
For two years... that was my life. Scared and on the run during the day. Tearing things apart at night.
Two years of the worst life possible...but the disruption of the German forces was immense, and I'm sure my actions helped save countless Allied lives.
I wish I could have been a soldier, but I wasn't. I was a monster.
I do feel horrible about the things I did, but I feel worse that the war forced another man into a situation where he asked me to do those things.
It's so much easier to risk your own life, rather than bear the burden of asking someone else to do the same.
Hey, was I taller than you before?
No.
Gary... I think we better get you out of--
BEE-YOOP BEE-YOOP

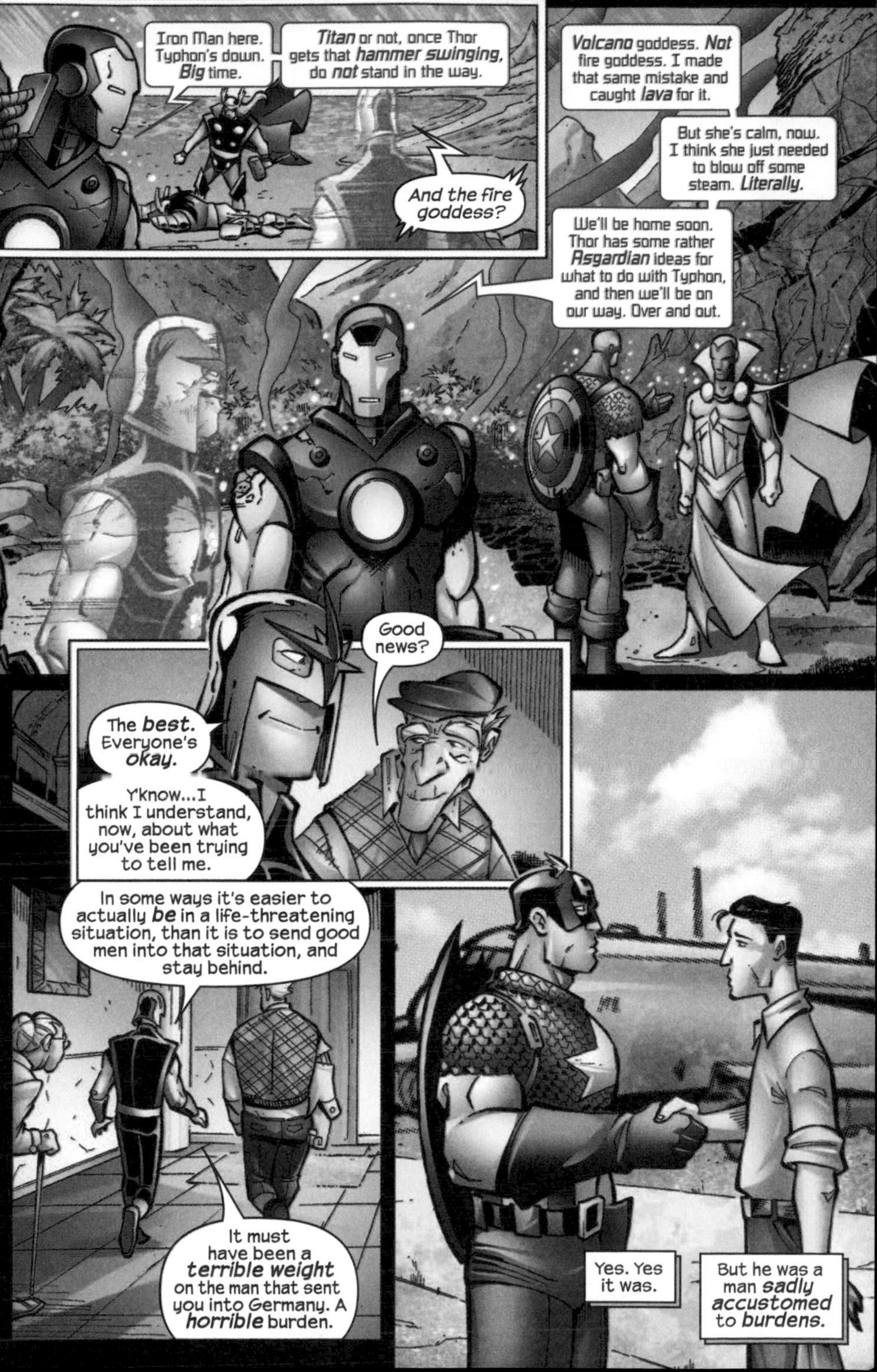

Iron Man here. Typhon's down. Big time.
Titan or not, once Thor gets that hammer swinging, do not stand in the way.
And the fire goddess?
Volcano goddess. Not fire goddess. I made that same mistake and caught lava for it.
But she's calm, now. I think she just needed to blow off some steam. Literally.
We'll be home soon. Thor has some rather Asgardian ideas for what to do with Typhon, and then we'll be on our way. Over and out.
Good news?
The best. Everyone's okay.
Y'know...I think I understand, now, about what you've been trying to tell me.
In some ways it's easier to actually be in a life-threatening situation, than it is to send good men into that situation, and stay behind.
It must have been a terrible weight on the man that sent you into Germany. A horrible burden.
Yes. Yes it was.
But he was a man sadly accustomed to burdens.

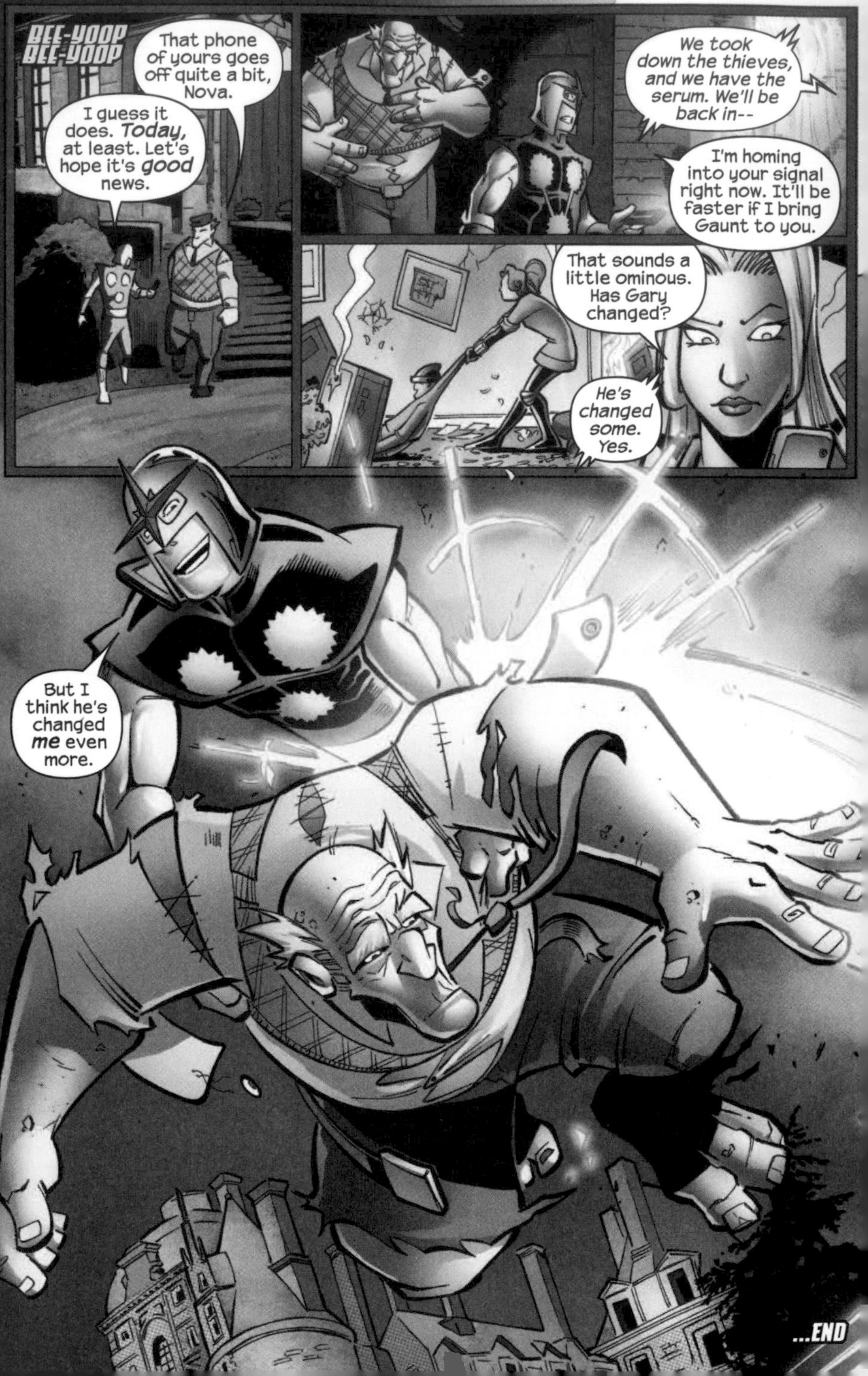
BEE-YOOP BEE-YOOP
That phone of yours goes off quite a bit, Nova.
I guess it does. *Today,* at least. Let's hope it's *good* news.
We took down the thieves, and we have the serum. We'll be back in--
I'm homing into your signal right now. It'll be faster if I bring Gaunt to you.
That sounds a little ominous. Has Gary changed?
He's changed some. Yes.
But I think he's changed *me* even more.
...END